A Knight's Temptation

CATHERINE KEAN

Medallion Press, Inc.
Printed in USA

DEDICATION:

For my father, David Lord. Thank you for sharing your love of history with me.

Published 2009 by Medallion Press, Inc.

The MEDALLION PRESS LOGO
is a registered trademark of Medallion Press, Inc.

If you purchased this book without a cover, you should be aware that this book is stolen property. It was reported as "unsold and destroyed" to the publisher, and neither the author nor the publisher has received any payment from this "stripped book."

Copyright © 2009 by Catherine Kean
Cover design by Arturo Delgado

All rights reserved. No part of this book may be reproduced or transmitted in any form or by any electronic or mechanical means, including photocopying, recording, or by any information storage and retrieval system, without written permission of the publisher, except where permitted by law.

Names, characters, places, and incidents are the products of the author's imagination or are used fictionally. Any resemblance to actual events, locales, or persons, living or dead, is entirely coincidental.

Typeset in Adobe Garamond Pro
Printed in the United States of America

ISBN:9781933836522

10 9 8 7 6 5 4 3 2 1
First Edition

ACKNOWLEDGMENTS:

Special thanks to Lisa Ault and Diane Pennea, who gave me lots of great information on allergic reactions to bee stings.

PROLOGUE

Moydenshire, England
Summer 1183

"Tie her well. She must not get free."

Eight-year-old Leona Ransley twisted her wrists, bound behind the oak tree. Turning her head against the bark, she tried to catch the attention of her eleven-year-old brother, Warden, busy securing the rope, but the broad tree trunk hid him from view. When he yanked the rope tighter, she fought not to wince.

"Hurry up, Ward."

Leona glared at the blond boy who'd called to her brother as she blew aside a strand of hair loosened from her braid. His name was Aldwin Treynarde, the son of an earl and a new friend of Ward's. Aldwin stood a few yards in front of her, brandishing a stick as though it were a knight's sword, his eyes bright with excitement. How she wished her brother had never met him!

Narrowing her eyes to what she hoped was a threatening squint, she said, "I do not want to play this game. Ward, untie me." She tugged her arms, hoping to thwart his binding.

"Nay." Aldwin's stick pressed into her shoulder. Not hard enough to hurt through the layers of her sage green silk gown and chemise, but to tell her he was in command.

Her bound hands clenched into fists. If she wasn't tied, she'd slam her fist into his jaw, a perfect punch the way Ward had taught her. Even if Aldwin was the son of a rich earl and her parents had told her to be on her best, ladylike behavior today.

"Ward," she said between her teeth. "Untie—"

"We need a maiden for our game," Aldwin cut in. "You will stay bound. And you will play your part exactly as I say." His mouth tilting in a grin, he flicked aside her loose hair with his stick. The whistling sound sent a shiver racing down her spine.

"Stop that," she bit out.

"Silence, maiden."

"I do not have to listen to you. Neither does my brother."

Aldwin laughed as though she'd said something foolish, pivoted away, and rammed his stick at an imaginary foe.

The ropes around her wrists tightened again. "Ward," she called, but at that moment, Aldwin loosed a triumphant roar, the force of his cry drowning hers. His sword listed toward the ground, suggesting his invisible opponent had collapsed, dead. Yelling again, he waved his sword in the air.

Swallowing the awful taste gathering at the back of her mouth, she realized she'd have to appeal to Ward the moment he came out from behind the tree. After all, he wasn't close friends with Aldwin. They'd only met that day, when the noble families invited to this riverside keep in Southern Moydenshire headed into the great hall for the midday feast; the castle was ruled by a friend of her father's, and the meal was to precede an important meeting of all the lords. Aldwin and Ward had sat beside each other, and the boys had giggled through the entire meal—most annoying, when, for the first time in as long as Leona could remember, her brother wouldn't tell her what was so amusing.

When the noblemen gathered at the lord's table to discuss matters of estate, and Leona's mother had gone with the other ladies to tour the rose garden, Leona had slipped outside with Aldwin and Ward to the nearby field. They'd promised she'd be part of their game.

How she'd looked forward to sword fighting with sticks, playing chase in the field near the stream, and skipping stones across the water. Head held high, she'd barely restrained an excited grin. Her whole body longed for that moment in which she jabbed Aldwin in the belly with her stick. He'd cry out in shock. His face might even go red with embarrassment, because she'd bested him. She'd prove to him that she might only be eight years old, while he was at least twelve, but she was no helpless girl.

Born a fighter, her mother always said with a tender smile. *I will never forget how you kicked, fussed, and flailed your little fists while the midwives tended you. A remarkably strong, healthy girl, they said. 'Tis why your father and I named you Leona. Your name means "lioness."*

How, then, had she become the damsel tied to the tree awaiting rescue?

A tug on Leona's long braid made her grimace. Straining to glance behind her, she scowled. "Ward!"

Her brother appeared at her side. The silk ribbon that had wrapped around the end of her braid dangled from his fingers. "A token from you, maiden," he said, holding the ribbon aloft, "for us knights to take into battle." Shoving tousled, brown hair from his eyes, he winked at her with enough charm to melt a frozen puddle. "All right, sis?"

"Nay. Did you not hear me? I do not want to play anymore."

Grass crunched as Aldwin drew near. Ward grinned at him. Gnawing the middle of the ribbon, he looked back at her. "I will not tie your legs. I think you are well enough bound."

Leona's jaw dropped on a gasp. Her brother couldn't have missed her saying she didn't want to take part any longer. A dull ache squeezed her stomach. He'd never gone against her wishes before today. Neither did he seem to notice her dismay.

"Ward." She tried not to shout.

"What?"

Why is Aldwin's game more important than I am? "Mother will not be pleased that you ruined my ribbon."

The silk began to fray. Ward ripped it in half and handed part to Aldwin. "If she asks, say you lost it. You will not tell on me, sis, will you?"

"Let me go free, and I will not tell."

Ward exchanged a glance with Aldwin, and then winked at her. A look that said, *I know you won't betray me. You owe me the favor many times over.*

"Remember what I told you about the game," Aldwin said while he began tying his ribbon scrap around his stick. "Count to ten. Then, scream as if you are being attacked by Saracens who plan to cut out your guts and eat them raw."

Grabbing his own stick from the ground, Ward swished it to and fro. "Ha! We two fearless crusaders will rush to your rescue."

"Ha!" Aldwin roared, leaping over a tree root. He lunged, slashing at another imaginary foe, then at a bee flying past. His blond hair shone in the sunlight and he moved with remarkable grace, each move elegant and precise.

Leona shook her head. "Ward, untie me. Let us go skip

rocks. Or, better yet, duel." She shot Aldwin a fierce stare. "The losers must forfeit their evening meal."

Aldwin's mouth tilted in a smug grin. He swatted at another bee buzzing around him. "Girls do not fight."

Angry heat burned her face. "I can wield a stick as well as you."

His brows raised. He clearly didn't believe her.

Oh, how she couldn't wait to trounce him! "Free me. I will gladly prove you wrong."

Aldwin snorted and looked about to roar with laughter.

"Arrogant turd," she muttered.

Ward choked. He looked unsure whether to guffaw or yell at her.

A frown darkened Aldwin's face. Pinning her with his gaze, he murmured, "What did you say?"

She smiled back, very sweetly, for her mother wasn't here to scold her for her unladylike oath, and she'd learned the word *turd* from Ward.

Her brother raised his hands, obviously eager to stop the confrontation. "Sis, please. As Aldwin said, we need a maiden for this game. Play along. When 'tis done, we will duel."

She glanced over at Aldwin. Still glowering. Good.

Raising her chin to a defiant tilt, she looked back at Ward. "Promise we will fight later?"

"Aye."

Aldwin stepped forward. *Come close enough for me to kick you*, she silently pleaded. But, alas, he didn't.

"'Tis settled," he said in that take-command voice. "One last matter, and we will start."

"What matter?" Leona's smile faded. She was securely tied,

unable to escape this wretched game even though she didn't want to play. What more could he want from her?

Aldwin looked at Ward, and they both giggled.

She swallowed a groan. When her brother's laugh tinged with mischief, that usually meant trouble. For her.

"Before the king's knights leave for crusade," Aldwin said, "they kiss their maiden."

What?! *"Nay."*

"A promise they will protect her and return for her."

"Where did you learn that? You invented it for this stupid game."

"Nay," Aldwin growled. "'Tis well known—"

"I am not kissing you! Not in this game. Not ever!" She struggled anew. "Ward!"

While she thrashed, her brother strode to her side and pressed a noisy kiss upon her cheek. "Fare thee well, fair maiden."

As Ward stepped back, Aldwin shook his head. Pulling a dangling thread from the ribbon around his stick, he said, "'Twas not a real kiss."

"She is my sister. 'Tis not natural to kiss her on the mouth."

On the mouth? Oh, nay. Nay. Nay!

"Ward," she shrieked, "when I get free—"

With a lazy swagger, Aldwin crossed to her. Before she could twist her body to kick him, his hand closed on her jaw and forced her chin up. The earthy scent of bark clung to his fingers. She shook her head from side to side, refusing to hold still and accept his kiss. Her breath hissed between her teeth. "Do not dare to kiss me!"

"Fare thee well, maiden-of-the-biting-words." Aldwin's

mouth pressed to hers.

Leona screamed, the sound trapped by his lips. Shocked fury turned her body numb.

The bold kiss took less than the space of one breath. With a lopsided grin, Aldwin stepped away, grabbed Ward's arm, and pulled him to a lope. "Come on."

She blinked. Choked. "You—!"

Laughing and shoving each other as they ran, the boys disappeared into the brush fringing the nearby trees. Startled birds winged up from the undergrowth, then swooped down into the field.

"Turd, turd, *turd!*" She kicked the dirt, sending earth spraying across the web of tree roots. She kicked a few more times, for good measure. Dropping her head back against the trunk, she groaned.

The familiar tapestry of sounds—humming insects, chirping birds, and whispering tree leaves—settled across the field.

A bee flew up beside her. She shifted her upper body, willing the insect to fly away. Another joined it, circling the tree, edging closer to her hair.

Unease crawled over her skin. She sucked in a sharp breath as one of the bees buzzed next to her ear. She jerked her head sideways. How long till the boys came to her rescue?

When another bee began to circle her, a shriek scratched her throat. She couldn't scream. If she did so before they'd run very far, Aldwin would call her a wobbly-kneed coward. *See, you are a helpless girl*, he'd taunt. *Go on. Admit you were wrong*. His mocking smile burned into her thoughts.

Blocking out the steady hum of the bees, she forced herself to count. "One," she said between her teeth. "Two . . ."

A tickling sensation began at her ankle, at the top of her leather shoe. Something was climbing up her leg, beneath her silk chemise. She shifted her weight. "Three. Four..."

A painful pinch. Another. Straining against her bonds, Leona glanced down.

Bees swarmed on the ground by her feet.

A nest.

With a frantic gasp, she dug her fingernails into the ropes. Tried to find a weak spot in the knot.

A bee landed on her skirt and crawled upward. Another landed on her arm.

Bzzz.

"Ward!" she shrieked, pulling against her bonds. "Help!"

No answer.

A sting on her elbow.

"Ow! Ward—"

"Well done, Leona!" her brother called, his voice faint. "Keep screaming."

"Help meee!" Oh, God. Bees in her hair. Scrambling. Burrowing. Their angry drone sounded louder than her own words. "I am not pretending. Help. Help!"

She yanked the ropes back and forth against the tree trunk, scraping her wrists. Again. Again. Her bonds didn't yield. Thrashing her head from side to side, she dragged in frantic breaths. "Ward!"

Try to stay calm. Ward will be here any moment.

Tears burned her eyes. Stinging heat seared her arms and legs. A bee stung below her right ear; pain shot down the side of her neck. More bees hovered before her face, a moving cloud of black dots. They looked like spots of ink spattered on the blazing glow of sunshine.

"Oh, God," she moaned.

Over the bees' furious *bzzz*, a humming noise rang in her ears. She blinked, trying to focus. The dots swirled. More stings on her legs. Her knees. Her upper arms. Soon, her whole body would be covered with stings.

"*Ward!*" She tried to twist her hands, but her arms were unbearably heavy. So were her eyelids. Impossible to keep open.

Another moan broke past her lips. What would her father say when he found her? He didn't know she'd slipped out with the boys. He expected her to be inside, with the other young ladies, entertaining themselves with a quiet game or embroidery.

A sickly heat began to spread through her body, and then numbness. Her whole body felt sluggish, a sensation akin to falling into a vat of butter and slowly submerging.

Blackness crept into her mind, smothering her consciousness. The bees sounded distant now, barely audible above the shrill humming. Mayhap they'd flown away.

Nay, Leona. You are fainting. Stay awake! Call for help. Now!

"Leona!"

Her brother's voice. It cut into the darkness. Pulled her back toward the insistent hum. And the light.

Ward sounded far away. Was he speaking to her from down by the trees? She must call to him. Tell him . . . about . . . bees.

By sheer force of will, she coaxed her chin up. Her groggy head swayed, as weighty as a boulder upon her shoulders. She tried to force her eyes open. Her lids were . . . too leaden. Why was her mind spinning, around . . . around . . . ? Must not . . . slide back . . . toward darkness.

A thudding noise.

Stones falling? Ripples of thunder?

So easy . . . to give in to . . . soothing darkness . . . To the place . . . of no pain.

Do not faint! Fight, Leona!

She struggled to drag her consciousness back. Difficult . . .

The thudding grew louder. Not stones. Not . . . thunder. Someone . . . running.

"Sis!"

"Ward," she croaked. Relief burgeoned inside her. "H-help me."

Something batted against her bodice. Hands, she realized dully, swatting at her gown. Slapping at her arms.

"There are bees all over her!" Aldwin's voice. "She stirred up a nest."

"God's bones!" *Ward.* "The welts on her arms."

Help me.

"Aldwin"—Ward sounded scared—"'tis all our fault."

"W-we must get help."

"Oh, Leona." Her brother made a sound like a sob.

She tried to move her lips, to show him she heard . . . Impossible.

The darkness . . . was growing thicker. Like a blanket wrapping itself around her. Trying to . . . suffocate her.

Help . . . me.

Hands brushed against her wrists.

Stay . . . alert. Fight.

A tug. The ropes fell away.

Free, at last. Stand . . . Show Aldwin—

Her body sagged. Her mind whirled, before she felt her shoulders connect with another body. *Ward. He'd caught her.*

Nay. Scent . . . not Ward's.

"—too many bees," her brother was saying.

"The river." Aldwin's voice resonated very near. "Drown the bees."

"But—"

"'Tis the only way. Hurry!"

Hands jostled her. *Pain!* A cry ripped from deep inside her.

"I am sorry." Her brother sounded as though he was weeping. "Leona, I am sorry..."

The shrill humming filled her ears again. Ward's voice... distorted... His words were sucked away into the darkness...

What seemed only moments later, through the fog cloaking her mind, she became aware of icy coolness. A splashing sound. A hollow sloshing.

"'Twill be all right," a young male voice murmured. His words were reassuring, but he sounded terrified. Must be Ward. His voice sounded different because he was worried.

She tried to swallow. Her mouth felt as puffy and dry as old leaves. Every bit of her body throbbed with pain.

As her senses sharpened, she realized the coldness surrounded her.

Water.

Without opening her eyes, she realized she lay with most of her body submerged. The sloshing noise was water rushing in and out of her ears.

"Ward?" she whispered past her aching throat.

"'Twill be all right," the voice said again, followed by another frigid rush of liquid over her body. She shivered, her burning skin protesting the iciness. The cold settled so deep, she could hardly breathe.

With immense effort, she forced her eyelids open. She squinted against sunlight that hurt her eyes.

Someone leaned over her, a shadow against the sun's glare. Aldwin.

Her fingers stiffened on a flare of anger. "W-Ward—"

"He has gone to get help." She heard no trace of mockery in Aldwin's tone. He held her gaze the barest moment, then looked away.

He wasn't wearing his tunic. In places, red lumps—bee stings—marked his bare chest and arms.

Her gaze crept lower, to find him kneeling in the river water. His soaked hose were coated with mud.

A grimy, green swath lapped against his knees: the skirts of her gown.

Black objects—like catkins fallen from a tree—floated in the sopping folds. Bees. *Oh, God.* She shuddered, her innards clenching so tightly, she almost vomited.

Aldwin squeezed her arm. "Most of the bees are dead."

Most? Some were still wriggling.

Leona scrambled to prop herself up on her elbows. The river blurred before her eyes. The blackness taunted, trying to smother her again.

"Lie down." Aldwin pressed upon her shoulders, urging her back.

Anguish and pain wrenched from her in a gasp. "Do not . . . touch me!"

His expression hardened. Lifting his hands from her, he said, "You should rest."

Rest? Was he mad? "B-bees—"

"They will not hurt you anymore."

Tears streamed from her eyes and seared a path down her swollen face. She must not cry. Not in front of him. But she felt so wretched. So . . . weak.

Her right arm trembled, then collapsed beneath her. With a *plop*, she fell back onto a soft, wet pillow. His boots, she realized, wrapped with his tunic, which had kept her head up out of the water.

Darkness swirled into her mind. Odd, how it sounded like the lulling lap of water. Coaxing . . . Peaceful . . .

Aldwin nudged her shoulder. "Leona. Stay awake."

She groaned. A pathetic sound. Barely a whisper.

Fight, Leona!

Even as the thought trailed through her mind, water splashed over her again.

"Listen to my voice. I promise, 'twill be all right."

All right . . .

She sighed. The darkness beckoned, more tantalizing than before.

"Do not die," he said hoarsely. "You must not die."

Die?

"Nay," Leona said, but her lips refused to move. The word echoed inside her head, a hollow, empty sound. Panic screamed in her dulling mind.

Help. Me.

Thick as swarming bees, the darkness took her.

‡ ‡ ‡

"Leona!" Aldwin cried as her head lolled. Against the muddy pillow of his tunic, her blotchy face looked too pale. His pulse kicked into a painful thunder.

"Leona." Shoving his hand under her neck, he lifted her head up out of the water. He dipped his chin, bringing his ear close to her cold lips. The barest breath warmed his hair.

Sliding his arm under his shoulders, he pulled her limp body against him and cradled her head against his chest. She'd told him not to touch her, but, unconscious now, she'd never know; he'd keep her warm and do his best to save her life.

"'Twill be all right," he whispered against her cheek. His voice caught. She *had* to be all right, for he'd brought this upon her. He'd ignored her wishes and insisted upon the game, and now . . .

Her body trembled, racked by pain, although her eyelids didn't open. He held her tighter. Water dripped from her hair, a sound akin to light rain. Helplessness ripped through him. What more should he do? How did he save her? Never, in all his life, had he felt so powerless.

In the distance, he heard hoofbeats. A group of riders approached. Thank God.

How he prayed they weren't too late.

He held her close, waiting until the pounding hoofbeats drew very near. Horses whinnied, stomped, and bridles chimed as the animals came to an abrupt halt.

Looking up, he saw men leaping down from their mounts. Leading the riders, his face a mask of fury, was his father.

Aldwin's belly lurched. Soon, he'd feel the strike of his sire's hand. He'd live with the bruises for days afterward. He'd accept every one, though—as an honorable knight would—for he deserved such punishment.

"What has happened here?" his father bellowed, striding down the muddy bank and into the water toward them, kicking up waves.

Another man—Lord Ransley, Leona's father—followed, his expression stricken with horror. "Is she alive?" he demanded, water soaking his fine silk hose and tunic.

"Aye, milord." Aldwin's teeth chattered. He hadn't felt cold until now.

More riders converged by the bank. Close behind followed a running crowd of men, women, and children, headed by Ward. Among them, he saw Leona's mother, dabbing her eyes with a handkerchief.

Swallowing down a stab of guilt, he shielded Leona against the waves rocking her body.

"Wretched boy." His sire reached down and yanked Aldwin to standing. Leona slipped from his arms and fell back toward the murky depths.

"Careful," Aldwin cried, but Leona's father caught her. Kneeling and lowering her back to the makeshift pillow, he and three other men began examining the welts on her neck and arms.

His eyes red-rimmed and accusing, Lord Ransley glared up at Aldwin. "What were you doing? Trying to kill my daughter?"

"I was drowning the bees, milord. 'Twas the best way—"

"You ordered her tied to a tree. Ward says she didn't want to play your game."

When Lord Ransley turned Leona's wrist, exposing the red rope marks, his father swore between his teeth.

Aldwin shuddered. "I never meant to hurt her. 'Twas supposed to be just a silly game. I—"

"Is this how you were taught to treat ladies?" his sire roared.

Pressing his lips together, Aldwin shook his head.

"We are a family that respects the king's laws. The great honor of knights. Chivalry."

Murmurs of agreement rippled through the gathered crowd on the bank.

Aware of water splashing behind him, Aldwin glanced back, to see Lord Ransley carrying Leona toward the shore, her loose hair dragging in the water.

"Father—" Aldwin said.

His sire turned away. He reached for an object caught in the nearby reeds—the stick, tied with the scrap of ribbon—then turned back to Aldwin.

"Lord Ransley's daughter could well die. You shame our family," his father growled. "You shame me." His fingers tightened on the branch.

"Father, 'twas an accident. Please, believe me."

"Turn around."

A sickening tremor wove through Aldwin, for he'd never seen his sire so angry. The temptation to run, as fast and far as he could, raced through him. But running would show him to be a coward. Knights didn't run from their fears. They faced them with pride and honor.

Water lapped against Aldwin's legs as he turned his back to his father. Now he faced the gathered crowd and the weight of their condemning stares.

The stick whistled through the air and smacked his bare back. Aldwin winced.

"Stop!" Ward raced toward the bank. "Milord, he tried to help Leona!"

Grabbing Ward's arm, Lord Ransley hauled him back to the horses, where Lady Ransley sobbed into her hands. Several men were preparing to get Leona onto a horse.

"Aldwin!" Ward cried, struggling.

Thwack! The stick lashed again. Claps of approval broke in the crowd.

Pain streaked across Aldwin's lower back, and he fought a groan. He must not cry out. A real knight would keep his silence.

Thwack. "Never again will you stain our family name with dishonor."

"Never!" Aldwin choked out.

"Swear it, before these witnesses." *Thwack.* "Wretched boy. *Swear it!*"

CHAPTER ONE

Moydenshire
Summer 1195

If hell were a place on earth, this might be it.

His right hand on his sword's hilt, Aldwin stood in the shadows of an oak tree outside the Raging Bull Tavern. The night breeze whispered, and, with his free hand, he yanked his cloak sleeve over his nose to quell the stench wafting from the stable a few yards away. The foul odor, combined with the smoke hissing from the wet logs on the fire outside the tavern . . . Whew.

Blinking against the smoky breeze, he focused on the laughter and voices carrying out into the night from the run-down tavern. Orange-yellow light poked out from the cracked wattle-and-daub walls, streaking into the blackness like wisps of hair, giving the place the air of a strumpet desperately past her prime who struggled to still appear comely.

A roar erupted from the drunkards by the fire, who had not yet noticed him. Smoke snaked up around the group of mostly farmers and peasants while the firelight cast their faces in grotesque orange masks. None looked likely to possess the priceless ruby pendant he sought for his lord, Geoffrey de Lanceau. Still . . .

"Oy! I asked ye ta move aside," one of the drunkards groused.

The teetering man beside him sneered. The two exchanged punches.

"Bets! Bets," another sot yelled over the fighters' pained grunts.

The others cheered.

"God's blood," Aldwin muttered. All he needed was to face a bloody brawl. *"Get the pendant and leave as quickly as possible,"* de Lanceau had instructed at Branton Keep days ago, his steel-gray gaze grim. *"The fewer who know of the missing jewel, the better."* Glancing away, his eyes shadowed with remorse. *"I cannot disappoint my lady wife, Aldwin. Not when she endured such a difficult birthing to give me a beautiful daughter. Not when for weeks I promised my love a wondrous gift."*

"I understand, milord," Aldwin said.

De Lanceau's expression didn't change. While Aldwin wondered if his lordship had heard him speak, de Lanceau's face contorted with loathing. "As you know, the man who was to deliver the jewel to me from London is missing. I have heard whispers that Baron Sedgewick of Avenley and that conniving bitch, Veronique, are in this part of England. I do no doubt they will try to undermine my rule. They will destroy me for thwarting their murderous plans to seize control of Moydenshire years ago, and do all they can to hurt my family. If they were to come into possession of the pendant . . ."

The way his lord's words trailed off to silence made cold sweat bead on Aldwin's brow. All too well he knew of the baron's evil, manipulative nature; because of the baron's lies, Aldwin had fired a crossbow bolt into de Lanceau's chest three years ago, after the battle at Wode. He'd almost killed his lordship; a mistake Aldwin sorely regretted. He struggled to tamp down intense mortification.

If he completed this mission for his lord, might he at last be awarded knighthood? How Aldwin longed to become one of de Lanceau's knights. To finally rise above the dishonor blemishing his past.

"Veronique and the baron will not get the jewel, milord," Aldwin vowed. "I will do what I must to bring it safely to you, as you ordered."

De Lanceau's harsh gaze locked with his. Nodding, he said, "Take as many men-at-arms as you wish. Horses, weapons—"

"I go alone."

"Alone?" De Lanceau frowned. "We do not know who sent word of the pendant to me here at Branton Keep."

"By going alone, I rouse fewer suspicions," Aldwin said.

"I will not have you fall prey to a trap."

The concern in de Lanceau's voice twisted Aldwin's gut. To think he had almost killed this honorable man who'd brought peace and prosperity to Moydenshire . . . "I am well capable of defending myself, milord. Moreover, if this missive is a ruse, the sender—or senders—will be expecting a convoy of armed riders. Not a lone man who will slip into their midst, seize the pendant, and vanish."

A faint smile touched de Lanceau's mouth. "Very well. If you are not back within four days, I will send my army to find you."

"I will not fail you, milord."

De Lanceau's hand tightened into a fist. "You must not. Many lives may depend on your success. Including my own."

A cry snapped Aldwin's attention back to the blazing fire. Four men were fighting now. Glancing at the two-story building, he mentally catalogued the entrances and exits, and then strode from the tree's concealing shadows.

Skirting the fighters, he headed toward the tavern door. Smoke gusted around him, stinging his eyes. His garments would reek of smoke for the rest of the eve. He reached for the crooked door handle, no more than three weathered bits of wood hammered together.

Before his fingers connected with the handle, the door flew open with the creak of rusty hinges. Light and bawdy cheers flared out into the night as a pock-faced drunkard staggered out. Aldwin slipped past him into the dimly lit interior.

The stench—bodies gone unwashed for months, rotting food scraps mashed into the dirt floor, and an ill-vented fire—made his stomach roil. Narrowing his watery eyes, he dragged a hand over his face to ward off a sneeze and sauntered forward. Somewhere in this wretched place was the person who'd hand over the pendant.

Or, as de Lanceau warned, a trap.

Aldwin scanned the room, lit by a fire in the opposite hall and candles crammed into holders. Heading toward the crowded bar, he indulged in a smile. Any man who thought to attack him would be in for hard fighting.

As he neared, several men leaned away from the wooden bar and cast bleary gazes over him. The barman, scrubbing the top with a grubby rag, glanced up. His gaze settled on Aldwin's sword and his fat mouth quivered, as though he wondered why Aldwin had set foot inside his premises.

"A drink, milord?" the bar owner said. Sweat dotted his forehead, a sign of a guilty conscience. Did he believe Aldwin had come to demand an unpaid debt? Or, mayhap the lout was in on a trap.

"In a moment." Aldwin stood at the best vantage point to assess the room and the tavern door.

"Just let me know." The man managed a nervous smile before mopping his face with his rag. "I will have yer drink right up."

Aldwin nodded his thanks. Chairs scraped across the room. Two men broke into raucous laughter, while a strumpet, squeezed into a linen gown, sidled toward a group of men motioning her over to them. She had a lovely figure; however, from the looks of her, she was old enough to be his mother.

"Hardly a wench for you, I would say," said a male close by.

Aldwin discerned amusement in the low, faintly gravelly voice. His gaze slid to the wiry man standing beside the bar, who barely reached Aldwin's shoulder. With uncombed, shoulder-length gray hair, a pointed nose, and bright blue eyes, the man resembled a creature yanked from books of lore.

A silent groan rumbled in Aldwin's throat. The last thing he wanted was to be drawn into senseless conversation. Foolish chatter could prove a deadly distraction. A knife through his back, before he even sensed an assailant.

Distracting him could be the man's purpose.

"Excuse me." Aldwin pushed away from the bar.

The old man's hand shot out. His gnarled fingers—surprisingly strong—clenched Aldwin's cloak sleeve. "The woman you desire—"

Aldwin glared at the old man.

"—has lips as red as rubies."

Aldwin tensed, then forced aside his astonishment. This old man might not know about the pendant. His words might simply be a coincidence.

"Rubies," Aldwin repeated with a faint smile. "She sounds most tempting."

An answering grin tipped the man's mouth, revealing the gap between his front teeth. He looked like a cheeky gnome. "Aye, milord, but she is." He winked. "Exquisite."

Anticipation tingled at the base of Aldwin's skull. Either the man was trying to sell him the services of a whore—for an extortionate price he'd soon reveal—or he was indicating he had information on de Lanceau's pendant. In either case, Aldwin had better not appear overly excited.

Pointedly glancing down at the wizened hand clenched into his cloak, Aldwin said, "I am intrigued, old man. I would like to see this . . . prize."

The little man beamed. Dipping his wild gray head, he said, "I hoped you would." He withdrew his hand, and then twirled it in a courteous gesture of encouragement. "Follow me."

‡ ‡ ‡

Leona stood in the tavern's shadowed back room, sipping a mug of ale. Bitter, watered-down rot, but at least it dulled her nerves.

Tipping her head back, she downed another mouthful, cringed, and then set the chipped earthenware mug on the window ledge, next to the lit candle. She pulled her waist-length braid over her shoulder and fiddled with the leather thong. She should be doing something—anything—other than pacing this grimy room that smelled of damp kegs and moldy flour sacks.

Yet, she would wait.

When the knocks came upon the door, she must be ready.

Sir Theodore Wrenleigh—Twig, she'd affectionately called him since childhood because he reminded her of a spindly tree—had slipped out some time ago, promising to report back as soon as he had any news. His fellow man-at-arms, Sir Reginald Themdale, would stand watch in the corridor outside.

"Milady, wait here. Listen for the signal." Twig had thrust

up his hand to stop her objections before she'd uttered one word. "'Tis a rough crowd in the main room. Not at all the place for you."

"Twig—"

He'd slapped his scrawny fist to the front of his cloak, his expression solemn. "Milady, these are unusual circumstances, and I am a man of my word. I made a promise before we left Pryerston Keep. I would rather cut off my own toes than see you come to harm."

Leona sighed at the memory. Dear, kindhearted Twig. Overprotective, irritating Twig. She should have brushed past him, slipped out into the corridor, and headed to a shadowed corner of the tavern, where she'd help keep watch for the man de Lanceau sent to collect the pendant. No one would recognize her as a noblewoman, hidden by the ragged cloak that covered her from head to ankle. Moreover, she was no fragile maiden who depended upon others to defend her.

She'd started to tell him so, when shouting erupted in the main tavern.

"If ill befalls you," Twig had said quietly, "who will care for Pryerston?"

Sadness deepened his voice and, in that moment, the defiance inside her had melted away. For he spoke true. Her father, drunk every day since her mother's tragic death that past spring, could barely tend to his own needs. Leona had had no choice but to take over running the keep, working alongside the servants and seeing to the necessary decisions, asking, however, that her efforts be kept a secret. As lord, her sire deserved his subjects' respect; he was still the castle's ruler.

That is, before the baron and Veronique arrived.

Thinking about them roused a surge of fury so intense, she'd clenched her teeth. "Very well. I will wait."

Twig had smiled in that gallant way of his. "Thank you." And then he and Sir Reginald had left, shutting the door behind them.

Turning around, she paced back across the floor, past empty ale barrels and a wooden crate stacked with candles. While run down, the tavern—located roughly halfway between Branton and Pryerston keeps—was the perfect site to trade the stolen pendant for the reward de Lanceau offered. Paying a traveling musician to deliver the missive she'd written about the exchange was Twig's idea, and a good one, for the man had no connection to Pryerston.

She'd never met de Lanceau, but from all she'd heard, he was no fool. If she'd sent one of the keep's servants, he or she would have been promptly arrested, questioned, and forced to reveal how the jewel came to be at Pryerston. As much as Leona wanted to be rid of the pendant, she wouldn't risk implicating her father as a traitor.

Moreover, she reminded herself, the offered reward money was desperately needed to replenish Pryerston's coffers so overdue repairs could begin about the keep. And, at last, there'd be coin for Leona to buy Adeline, the young daughter of Pryerston's cook, specially made shoes to help straighten her legs bowed from her difficult birth. In time, Adeline would walk without hobbling, and would run as fast and well as other girls her age.

Some of Leona's happiest memories were of racing Ward through the meadows near Pryerston. What child—peasant or noble born—wouldn't want that freedom?

Crash. Leona jumped at the sound, which came from the main part of the tavern. She swiveled on the heel of her worn leather boots and retraced her steps, hoping Twig wouldn't be too much longer.

Oh, Father. No matter what you have done, I still love you.

Two knocks rattled the chamber door.

The signal.

Leona's hand instinctively flew to her bosom. Her fingers brushed the oval-shaped ruby, about the size of a robin's egg and set in a delicate gold framework, hidden beneath her garments. The jewel hung on a gold chain and rested just above her cleavage, under her linen chemise. Safe against her bare skin. The pendant couldn't be snatched without her knowledge.

Or consent.

Two more knocks, slightly louder.

De Lanceau's man was approaching.

Her pulse became a drumming thunder. She longed to draw the dagger from her right boot, for an extra measure of security, but de Lanceau's man might interpret that as a threat. She didn't want any misunderstandings to delay the exchange.

With trembling fingers, she checked the hood of her cloak, drawing it as far down as possible to fully conceal her face. Perspiration moistened her palms. Her legs shook, as they had that summer day when she stood on the forest pool's rocky edge, trying to ignore her brother's teasing while she prepared to jump into the deep water, even though she wasn't sure she could swim to shore.

Footsteps sounded outside the door. Fabric brushed against the rough-hewn panel.

Leona drew a steadying breath.

I do this for you, Father. Because I love you, and will not let you destroy your life.

The door creaked inward. Hazy light spilled across the dirt floor.

Straggly-haired Twig stood in the doorway. Behind him, his hand poised to draw his sword, Sir Reginald stared at someone just out of her view.

Twig set his hand to his brow—he obviously tried to make her out in the dim room—before he bowed and strode in. "This way," he said, motioning for the person following him to enter.

Leona buried her unsteady hands in the folds of her cloak as bold footfalls sounded behind Twig. A tall man dominated the space outside the door, his right boot a hair's breadth from the threshold. One hand on his sheathed sword, he glanced inside, then scrutinized Sir Reginald, before looking back into the shadowed room.

Misgiving tingled through her. He was familiar, somehow. She couldn't quite say why.

His gaze shifted, like a hawk assessing the landscape before him. Fie, but he was an imposing man. His cloak's hood covered the crown of his head, yet his blond hair grew long enough to slip from the gaps where his hood met his shoulder. No doubt he preferred a full, unhindered view of his surroundings, for his face wasn't concealed.

He took another step forward, causing light to fall upon his features.

What a face . . .

Austere. Beautiful. A visage so handsome, she'd remember it for the rest of her days. Angular cheekbones and a strong jaw were offset by his slender, noble nose. His eyes were blue. Not the warm blue of a young, inexperienced fighter eager to please his lord, but the frosty blue of a winter sky. A warrior's gaze hardened by cunning and resolve.

When his head tilted, and his attention slid to the far corner of the room, she recognized traces of someone she knew.

When they were children.

Her breath caught, as if his cold stare pierced her. God above. Could she be mistaken? Could this man be someone other than Aldwin?

She hadn't seen him since the accident years ago. Hadn't wanted to see him ever again. Heard of him, aye. Who didn't know the popular *chanson de geste* telling of the great battle in which he shot Lord Geoffrey de Lanceau with a crossbow bolt from many yards away? The almost impossible shot was recounted with awe and horror. Most men would have died from such a wound, but 'twas said de Lanceau's true love for Lady Elizabeth Brackendale gave him the strength of spirit to overcome his grave wound and live.

The *chanson* was all she'd known of Aldwin through the years.

Until today, when their lives had touched again.

Her mind reeled, resurrecting hurt and anger from years ago. Being bound to the tree. The bee stings. The river.

As though sensing the shock welling inside her, the man's gaze settled upon her. Standing at the back of the room, with the candle's light behind her—deliberately so—and the hood covering her features, Leona doubted he could make out her face.

Still, she couldn't stop her stomach's awful fluttering. She *had* to know if this man was Aldwin. For if he was, and he recognized her, all would be lost; she wouldn't have to say one word to cast suspicion upon her sire.

Yet, would Aldwin remember her features, swollen by bee stings the last time he saw her? She looked naught like the eight-year-old girl she once was.

He stood utterly still, as though assessing the level of threat.

She, too, waited. Sweat pooled inside her boots. She mustn't give herself away. How, though, did she get this exchange over with as quickly as possible? The sooner she and Aldwin went separate ways, the better.

Twig huffed a nervous breath. "Please, come in."

The man's mouth tilted in the barest smile. "In good time."

"What you desire is in here."

"So you say." He glanced back at Sir Reginald. "However, I will not be bashed about the head and rendered senseless. Or stabbed by an unseen assailant."

As clever as the Aldwin you met before, Leona's conscience said. *Beware*.

"We will do you no harm. Come."

The man's intent gaze returned to her. "You, sirrah, can see me. You remain in shadow. An unfair advantage. I will see the knave in whom I am placing my trust." He gestured to the threshold. "Step forward."

Twig's eyebrows twitched. "Milord—"

"Step. Forward."

At his growled command, concern shot through Leona. Then, indignation. Aldwin had talked to her in that authoritative way years ago, and she'd hated it then. This man would treat her with respect now.

"Heed my man," she said with icy calm, "or walk away."

Surprise flitted across the blond man's features, and she smothered a flare of triumph. He hadn't anticipated dealing with a woman.

"Who are you?" he muttered.

"A question I ask of you." If he identified himself as Aldwin, she'd know for certain.

Suspicion darkened his expression. "You are not Veronique. Her voice is quite different. So, I imagine"—his gaze flicked over Leona's worn cloak—"is her figure."

Leona bit down on her lip. What did he mean? Had he managed to assess her through the layers of her cloak, gown, and chemise? She'd thought the cloak too loose and plain to reveal much about her, but mayhap she'd underestimated him.

She'd only met Veronique twice, both times at Pryerston Keep. Veronique seemed very much aware of her voluptuous body and its effect upon men. She hadn't hesitated to bend over to display her breasts almost bursting out of her bodice, or walk with an inviting sway, or bestow her crimson-painted smile upon every male around, even with a bawling child in her arms.

This man obviously was familiar with Veronique's charms, a fact that irritated Leona in a most peculiar manner.

"Veronique may have sent you, though," he said, "to do her bidding—"

"What is your name?" Leona cut in, more sharply than she intended.

In a voice akin to stone grating against steel, he said, "I am Aldwin Treynarde, loyal servant of Geoffrey de Lanceau, lord of Branton Keep and all of Moydenshire."

His last words became a muzzy blur. *Aldwin.*

Her gut instincts were right.

To be facing him again . . . Her throat tightened on a painful swallow.

"I have given you the courtesy of my name." His mouth eased into a thin smile. "I ask again. Who are you?"

A woman who wishes she'd never met you, for she loathes your very name.

When she didn't immediately answer, but let the silence drag, Aldwin's stare sharpened with determination. Twig also glanced at her, his gaze mirroring the knowledge of what had happened in her childhood, when he helped her father carry her out of the river.

"If you are the Aldwin of the *chanson*," Twig said, a clear attempt to divert Aldwin's attention, "you are very skilled with a crossbow."

"True." Aldwin's stare didn't shift from Leona.

"Thus, you should be well able to defend yourself, if you are under threat. Which you are not."

"If I am to believe what you say."

Leona tried to restrain a shudder. He was trying to manipulate the situation to his control.

In that instant, she knew she couldn't simply hand over the pendant, take the reward, and send him on his way with a pleasant "good day."

He wouldn't let her go that easily.

Chilling panic flooded through her. She should have drawn the dagger from her boot, after all.

You always warned me, Mother, that my headstrong nature would get me into monumental trouble.

Trying to quell her rising worry, she nodded to Twig. "This man is not interested in what we have to offer." She glanced back at Aldwin. "Good day to you." With a wave of her hand, she ordered Sir Reginald to escort Aldwin away. To remove the menace on the threshold who unnerved her in more ways than she dared acknowledge.

Before she could put more distance between them, she caught the creak of leather. A male scent, tinged with a trace of mint, wafted to her.

Aldwin had stepped inside.

"You will not shut me out." A mocking lilt softened his voice. "Not when I do not even know your name. And when I have not yet taken what I desire."

CHAPTER TWO

As Aldwin's gaze adjusted to the shadows in the back room, he clenched his jaw. This woman before him—a throaty-voiced temptress who taunted him with retreat before their negotiations had even begun—wouldn't be rid of him that quickly. Not when he'd traveled with little sleep to find this tavern.

Not when he'd given his solemn vow to de Lanceau to get the pendant and bring it safely to Branton Keep.

Stepping closer brought the wench a little better into view, but not much. The room was poorly lit, no doubt to hide her features. Still, despite her broad, drooping hood, he'd glimpsed the lower third of her face when she'd turned and gestured to her men: a firm jaw; a generous mouth; and a gently curved chin. How irritating that his curious mind scrambled to fill in the rest of her features, completing her image with sultry, long-lashed eyes, a delicate nose, and fine cheekbones. Idiotic, how much he wanted to see what she really looked like.

He would.

Soon.

If she'd meant to remain anonymous, well, she'd challenged the wrong man. By the end of their meeting, he'd wrench that hood from her face and see exactly who dared to speak to him with such defiance—and who dared to deceive a man as powerful as de Lanceau.

She shifted under his stare. A smile pulled at his lips and he decided to let her squirm a bit longer.

Not caring to temper his scrutiny, he glanced her over. Despite her worn cloak, there was no disguising her slender figure or the delicate poise of her hands, clasped in front of her. She wore no rings or any other kind of identifying ornamentation. Her posture appeared almost regal, as if she were more than common born.

Her manner of speech, too, suggested she wasn't a commoner. However, he'd met a few courtesans—including Veronique, a poor farmer's daughter—who imagined themselves beyond their humble births and entitled to the silk finery, perfumes, and privileges of the noblility.

No titled lady would step inside this grimy hell pit of a tavern. If, for some reason, she had matters to attend here, she'd send a servant in her place.

This woman before him was a well-paid courtesan who'd somehow got hold of the pendant—stolen it from a client after a passionate tryst, mayhap—and intended to claim the reward for herself.

Before he was done with her, he'd find out exactly where she got the jewel.

Just as the thought skittered into his mind, her other guard stepped in behind him. Aldwin almost laughed. The man was no threat. Two good punches and Aldwin could fell the lout, who looked old enough to be his grandfather.

With a squealed groan, the door swung closed. The panel clicked into place, muting the roars and drunken cries carrying from the main room. The room plunged into near darkness, illuminated by the one candle's spindly flame.

He remembered seeing more candles on a crate by her. She could have provided more light, if she wished. But she'd wanted to remain hidden.

Not that it mattered. He stood between her and the door now. She couldn't dash past him. Whatever she thought, her two aging accomplices were a poor defense against him. Moreover, the one candle—held up to her face—would give enough light to see her features.

As the silence dragged, she made a small sound that reminded him of a cat's growl.

"Still I am waiting," he said, "for you to tell me who you are."

Again, she didn't respond. He tried to stifle his rising annoyance.

"I am a lady," she said at last. "'Tis all you need to know."

He snorted. "Lady."

Her head raised a notch, as if she resented his scorn. Behind him, the old man exhaled a sharp breath.

"I expect you are as eager as I," she said, "to be done with our negotiations—"

"Not at all." He waved a careless hand. "I have traveled many leagues to get here. A few moments more do not matter to me." Raising his eyebrows, he added, "How can I trust any of our dealings, if I do not know your name?"

Her head turned slightly as she glanced at the wiry gnome who'd brought Aldwin to this room. "My name is . . . Lady L."

"Ah. The name of an expensive strumpet."

The little man's shoulders jerked back.

The woman gasped.

"A *lady* of the seedy tavern underworld," Aldwin continued, bolstered by their shock. If he insulted them enough, they might accidentally reveal important information. Dropping into a bow, he threw his arms wide in deliberate mockery. "What a pleasure to meet you."

The man choked. "How dare you insult mi—"

"Shh!" the woman snapped to her associate. Then, her cloaked head turning in Aldwin's direction, she said, "Beware, or you shall leave without your prize."

"Oh, I do not think so."

Her breath rushed out on a hiss.

"Lady L, do you have the ruby pendant?"

"A-aye."

"Draw over the candle, and let me see it." *Bring the light to your features, so I can see your face.*

She shook her head, stirring the drape of her hood. "First, I will know you have the reward. The missive tacked up in the main room promised forty silver coins."

Aldwin ground his teeth. He patted the side of his cloak. Money jingled.

Her shoulders lowered on a sigh. "Good."

Stretching out his hand, Aldwin said, "Give me the jewel. When I am satisfied 'tis genuine, and the pendant I seek, you will have your reward."

She muttered words he couldn't hear. He didn't mistake her mutinous tone, though, or the angry stiffening of her posture.

He'd come too far to be denied by this wench.

Before the biting words to coerce her heated his mouth, her fingers moved to her cloak. She began to draw it aside at the neck.

A rustling, then a chime—the *clink* of metal—sounded before her hand lifted from her garments to reveal a slender chain. Even in the dim light, the chain's gold links glimmered. The gleaming ruby hung just below just below her fingertips.

Fierce satisfaction rushed through him, at the same moment his mind calculated the length of the necklace and where it had nestled beneath her garments: in the slope between her breasts.

Mayhap even against her skin. Warmed by her flesh . . .

His jaw clenched tighter. Holding out his hand, he said, "Take off the necklace. Give it to me."

She snapped her hand back, as if she expected him to grab the pendant. "I am no fool."

Aye, Lady L, you most certainly are.

"The pendant. Then you will receive your money."

"Put the bag of coins on the floor and step back."

God's bones, she was an obstinate wench. In a tone reserved for the most dim-witted fool, he said, "My instructions were quite clear—"

A low, angry growl rumbled from her. The sound scratched across his nerves.

Her hands moved to tuck the pendant back inside her garments.

Impatience surged, as hot as fire in his blood. Before he could caution the rash impulse, he grabbed for her, intending to catch her wrist and stay her. To prove to her she'd do as he commanded.

"Milady!" the wiry gnome yelled.

Aldwin's hand locked around her wrist. Slim. Delicate—

Milady?

A solid weight slammed into the back of his head.

Lights swirled behind his eyelids.

Blackness.

‡ ‡ ‡

"Did you kill him?" Staring at Aldwin's slumped body, held upright by Twig and Sir Reginald, Leona pressed her hands to her mouth.

Never had she intended Aldwin harm. True, in the preceding moments, she'd longed to scratch his arrogant eyes out. She'd wanted so very badly to kick him where it hurt the most, then scream at him with the anger and pain she'd held inside her since she was eight years old. Still, 'twas a far cry from murder.

Sir Reginald tipped his head toward the wood he'd used to wallop Aldwin. "I thought he was going to hurt you, milady."

Leona groaned.

His mouth opening and shutting like a stranded fish, Sir Reginald added, "I did not hit him hard. Truly, I did not."

Always the cheery one, Twig said, "Fear not, milady. He is merely knocked senseless."

The faintest waver in his voice fueled her doubts. "Are you certain? What if he is alive now, but succumbs to the blow? What if you cracked his skull?"

With loud huffs and grunts, the two men carefully lowered Aldwin to the dirt floor. He collapsed on his right side, his long hair tangled into his cloak's hood.

Her whole body shaking, Leona hurried to the windowsill, snatched up the candle, and rushed back. The flame dimmed on a draft, threatening to go out, and she curled her hand close to the light to protect it.

Glancing down at Aldwin's motionless form, she fought a wave of guilt. His lips were parted, as though the force of the blow had knocked the breath out of him. More of his golden hair spilled across the dirt beneath him.

Stop knotting yourself into a panic, Leona. Trust Twig.

Having fought alongside her father's men-at-arms for many years, he knew far more about subduing opponents than she—and, whether or not a man was dead.

Taking a steadying breath, she knelt on the grimy floor, trying very hard not to notice the fetid odors wafting up from it, and set the candle down with a gritty *thud*. The broad hood of her cloak brushed against her cheek; the scratchy wool hindered her vision. She yanked the hood back. Then, with gentle fingers, she brushed aside the hair at the back of Aldwin's head.

No blood. But a nasty bump was already forming.

Easing back on her heels, she glanced at his face, relaxed in oblivion. The candlelight illuminated his stunning profile. Bold, uncompromising cheekbones. A masterful mouth. Long lashes and a dusting of stubble on his jawline. So very handsome.

And dangerous.

Her fingertips tingled. She didn't want to touch him again. The silky brush of his hair against her fingers had sent curious sensations skittering through her. In the nearly forgotten reaches of her mind, dreamlike thoughts stirred of him holding her body tight against him and whispering against her cheek.

Her face burned. Why would she think such? The last thing she wanted was to be in his embrace. Even crouched beside him was far too close for her liking. Still, she must be certain he was breathing. Edging her hand forward, she placed it close to his lips. His breath warmed her skin.

She blew out a grateful sigh.

"Is he all right, as I told you?" Twig peered down at Aldwin.

"He is."

Twig straightened, his chest puffed out, and he looked immensely proud of himself. "'Tis far easier to deal with him now, if I do say so myself."

Leona frowned, for her plans for the meeting, relayed earlier to Twig and Sir Reginald, had not involved bashing de Lanceau's man about the head.

"Reach inside his cloak and take the coin, milady. Then, tuck the pendant in his pocket. We can leave him here, to rouse when he wishes, while we ride away." He smacked his hands together. "Perfect!"

Leona's mouth fell open. Twisting on her knees, she gaped at the nodding and grinning men-at-arms. "You mean to leave him here? Unconscious?"

The two men exchanged glances. "Well—"

"Did you not see the murderous-looking oafs in the bar?" Leona struggled to keep her voice down. "If those cutthroats found him lying here, they would rob him. Mayhap even beat and kill him."

Twig threw out his hands. "Oh, nay, milady. They would not."

She scowled at him, and he quickly averted his gaze. He appeared to be blushing. And, most telling of all, his mouth twitched like a rabbit munching on a tough carrot.

"I will not be responsible for this man's death." While she recalled only snatches of what happened after being stung, Ward had told her how Aldwin tried to save her by drowning the bees in the river. Leaving Aldwin here injured and defenseless was simply . . . wrong.

"Milady, he is not going to die."

"We cannot leave him this way. No matter how urgent 'tis that we return home."

Images of what might be transpiring filled Leona's mind: her sire slumped over the lord's table in the great hall, surrounded by ale mugs and snoring in a drunken stupor; Veronique ordering the servants about as though she were lady of the keep, while she and the baron gratified their whims—even though they'd already squandered more than the castle could afford to waste; Veronique and the baron stealing Pryerston's valuables to sell and pocket the money. Her father would not be able to stop them.

Anger boiled inside Leona and she shook her head, willing herself to focus on the dilemma at hand: Aldwin. She reached inside her cloak and drew out two silver coins. More than she should dare spend, but she mustn't dwell on the expense. Holding them out to Twig, she said, "Go fetch a strong drink."

"A drink, milady?"

"Ask for the tavern keeper's strongest liquor."

Twig took the coins and blinked in obvious disbelief. "You believe I would benefit from such a drink?"

She bit back an oath. "Twig!"

"Of course. 'Tis for you, milady. To settle your . . . er . . . ladylike constitution."

Ladylike constitution?! Her patience came very close to snapping. "The drink is for Aldwin. To revive him."

Twig's eyes bulged. Now he resembled a rabbit choking on his carrot. "You are going to waste liquor on—I mean, you expect him to drink it? How?"

"We will find a way. Two of us can hold him upright, and the third can coax the liquor down his throat."

"Without killing him?"

"Aye."

Twig closed his eyes and pressed a gnarled hand to his forehead.

"Twig, go. Now."

"But—"

"The longer you delay, the longer we stay in this vile tavern. We both know how important 'tis that we return to the keep."

"Aye, milady." He spun on his heel, his frizzy hair wisping out behind him, and reached for the door's handle. "I will return shortly."

"Be sure you do. You must not be distracted, no matter how enticing the strumpets are."

Twig, too, must have recalled the big-breasted, red-haired wench who'd pinched his skinny arse and cooed at him when they first arrived at the tavern. The little man's shoulders shoved back. "I know my duty, milady. Not one distraction will waylay me. I will go straight to the bar and come straight back."

The door creaked open, letting in muted light along with cheers and boisterous singing. Leona glanced back at Aldwin. Despite the cacophony, he lay motionless. If he slept through such a racket, he wasn't likely to wake on his own unless provoked.

"Stay close to her, Sir Reginald," Twig said from the doorway, "in case Aldwin should wake."

Sir Reginald moved nearer to her, his hand on his sword.

"Hurry," Leona said over her shoulder.

The door closed. Musty darkness settled in around her, and she sighed. Dropping her chin, letting her braid ripple down over her shoulder, she massaged the back of her neck, cramped from looking up at an odd angle at her men.

In the tense quiet, the anxiety of the past few days weighed heavily upon her, more pressing even than the pendant between her breasts. She tried to force the anguish away. Once she, Twig, and Sir Reginald were safely away from here, journeying back to

Pryerston, she could indulge her tattered emotions. Now, she had a knave to revive, a pendant to relinquish, and a reward to claim—far more important than her grief.

She looked again at Aldwin's prone body. Pressing her lips together, she forced her gaze down his cloak's bunched folds to where his muscled leg, bent at the knee, escaped from the heavy wool. His booted lower leg was clearly visible. However, the upper portion remained hidden by his cloak.

Racked by a peculiar shudder, she studied the fabric gathered over his stomach and thigh. Aldwin had jingled the coins earlier, in a bag at his hip. Right side, or left? She couldn't remember, but she must be sure. When he started to wake, they'd have precious few moments to snatch the coins, drop the pendant, and run.

To peek under his cloak was . . . an unnerving prospect.

Yet, she must.

Snatch the coins. Drop the pendant. Run, she silently repeated. *For you, Father. Because I love you.*

Drying her sweaty palms on her cloak, Leona leaned forward on her knees. Her braid slithered. With a faint rasp, the ends brushed the dirt.

"Milady?" Sir Reginald whispered. "Did he stir?"

"Nay." *Snatch the coins. Drop the pendant. Run.*

She reached for his cloak's edge.

And heard the faintest noise.

Leona froze, her fingers splayed in midair. She held her breath.

What, exactly, had she heard? Not a rustle. Not a whisper. But—

Sweat dampened her brow. Her gaze slid to Aldwin's face.

His mouth was closed.

Not parted, as moments before.

In that same, agonizing moment, she sensed he was fully cognizant. Aware of his surroundings. Of her.

Gasping, she scooted backward. "Sir Reg—"

An astonished grunt. Sir Reginald's feet flew out from under him. *Thud.* He crashed into the keg behind him.

She grabbed for her knife.

Aldwin's hand clamped around her wrist.

Chapter Three

Veronique Desjardin pushed aside the linen sheets of the wide rope bed in Pryerston Keep's solar. Restlessness plagued her, keeping her from falling asleep, but she didn't resent the excitement bubbling inside her like a simmering cauldron. In truth, she welcomed it. For soon, the elements of her careful scheme would blend together in wondrous vengeance upon the man who'd spurned her years ago: Moydenshire's lord, Geoffrey de Lanceau.

As she left the warm bedding, causing the straw mattress to yield with a faint *creak*, the cool night air kissed her nakedness. She crossed the plank floor to the solar window and drew open the shutters. Night air swirled in, along with watery moonlight. Standing in its glow, she pushed her long hair back over her shoulders, then smoothed her hands over her chilled skin. In a slow, sensual caress, she ran her palms across her flat stomach, up over her ribs, and then to her breasts and taut nipples.

A groan rumbled in her throat.

Lord Ransley was a kind host, indeed, for giving up his bed to sleep with the servants.

Laughter welled inside her. Ransley, kind? Nay, a drunken fool.

From the first night she and Baron Sedgewick arrived at the keep, uninvited guests, they'd slept in the solar, while he drank himself to sleep in the great hall.

"She was so beautiful, my wife," he'd blubbered yestereve while seated at the lord's table, his eyes streaming tears. "A lady of such grace. Why, when she stepped into this hall"—he waved an unsteady hand—"all inside fell to a hush, without her saying one word."

"Imagine." Veronique had patted his arm, taking care not to reveal her disgust over his filthy tunic. How simple it had been, while seated on an oak chair beside him, to lean sideways on the table. To cause their arms to brush. To bestow upon him a perfect view of her cleavage, straining against her scarlet-colored bodice.

His gaze had riveted to her bosom—as she'd intended.

His bushy eyebrows had snapped up before confusion and longing widened his gaze.

Trailing her fingers down his sleeve in a lazy caress, she'd said, "Please. Go on."

"I . . . Um . . ." He'd shaken his mass of unruly gray hair and looked down at his wine goblet. "Ah . . ."

Raising her hand from his sleeve, she'd picked up the ale jug, filled his goblet, and said in the gentlest tone, "I would like to hear more. 'Tis clear you miss your wife very much."

His hand shook as he lifted the wine to his lips and swallowed with noisy gulps. Setting the vessel down with an awkward *clunk*, he nodded. "I still cannot believe she is dead. Taken from me in a terrible accident I had never expected. I am lost without her." He drew in a ragged breath. "I do not wish to bore you. A lovely woman like you"—his gaze fell again to her breasts—"must desire much more interesting pursuits."

Veronique laughed and poured yet more wine. "Not at all." She squeezed his arm, lingering in the caress. "I am honored, milord, that you share your memories with me."

Ransley blinked, his lashes spiked with tears. Then anger glinted in his gaze before he shoved his goblet away, sloshing wine onto the stained tablecloth. "You mock me. You think I am a stupid old fool."

Caution had shrieked inside her. She'd sensed the distrustful stares of the servants nearby. If she wasn't careful, her patiently woven snare would disintegrate in her hands. As much as she loathed Ransley's pathetic display of grief, she needed his cooperation. For a while longer, at least.

She held Ransley's bloodshot stare. "I do not think you are foolish."

"Nay?" he grumbled, rubbing at the wine spreading across the tablecloth. "My daughter does."

"Daughter?" Veronique recalled the young woman who'd drawn Ransley aside and spoken with him in hushed tones the day she and Sedgewick had arrived at the castle gates. The woman hadn't worn a lady's garments; she appeared to have been toiling in the dirt. But at the time, Veronique had noted a strong physical resemblance between the woman and Ransley.

"Leona," Ransley said.

Leona. Veronique had committed the name to memory and resolved to keep watch on Ransley's daughter. And while Veronique had his lordship's attention, she'd very make certain he confided in *her* when needed. No one else.

Squeezing forward a little more—her breasts on the verge of popping from her gown—Veronique retrieved his goblet and slid it back before him. Trailing one slender finger down the vessel's stem, she'd smiled at him. "If I may be so bold, milord," she'd murmured, "your daughter is the foolish one. How can she be so insensitive to your torment? She should be more thoughtful toward her own father."

His brow had wrinkled with a frown. "In her heart, I know she means well. 'Twas a shock for her, when she lost her mother so suddenly."

Veronique had slid her hand toward him, then gently linked her fingers through his. A brazen move. To touch a lord of his status without invitation was a tremendous risk—but she'd invited the attentions of other lonely noblemen in the past, with success. In her and the baron's years evading de Lanceau's influence, they'd done whatever was necessary to keep themselves in a manner enjoyed by the noble elite. She'd become good at quiet murders, theft, and betrayal, among other talents.

Too much lay at risk now for Ransley to elude her manipulations.

He looked down at their joined hands. His mouth flattened.

Veronique braced herself for his bellowed command to withdraw her hand, while she tried to think of a clever way to keep him in her emotional trap.

But he didn't push her away.

Good.

"Tell me about your wife," she'd whispered, forcing tenderness into her voice.

And he had. Until, eyes rolling back into his head, he'd collapsed face first onto the table.

For all she knew—and cared—he still lay there.

Thinking of the way he'd rambled on and on caused the muscles between Veronique's shoulder blades to tighten. Reaching back, she rubbed at the tension and expelled a breath through her teeth.

A sound came from the bed behind her.

A muffled snort.

Turning on her heel, she strolled past the moonlit bed, her gaze sliding up the rumpled sheets to the bloated swell of Baron Sedgewick's belly, barely covered by the bedding. He lay with one arm over his flabby torso, the other flung out by his side. His mouth drooped in sleep. Saliva, running from the corner of his lip, glistened on his chin.

His skin was almost the same pasty color as the sheets. Only linen didn't grow wiry hairs that looked ridiculously out of place on his torso. So unlike the beautiful, muscular body of Geoffrey de Lanceau, whose chest hair had rendered him even more masculine and appealing. Long ago, when she'd curled her fingers through his hair, felt his muscles flex beneath her fingertips . . .

How despicable, that the memory of him—after all he'd done to her—should elicit a shiver of desire. Quickening her strides, she walked to the trestle table pushed against the wall and picked up her polished steel mirror before returning to the moonlight by the window. Her reflection stared back, naked, but not so unattractive.

Tilting the mirror, she inspected her body, almost as slim as years ago. The herbal tonics, creams, and foul-smelling potions crafted by toothless crones had helped her become slender and supple again. Staying beautiful was worth any price. Certainly worth every bit of silver she'd stolen or coaxed out of her victims.

Geoffrey de Lanceau, Lord of Moydenshire and one of the

most respected men in all of England, had desired her. For two years—before he cast her aside for a lady who became his wife—she'd shared his bed.

Never would he forget it.

A shrill giggle rose inside Veronique. Holding the mirror up to her face, she smoothed chestnut curls away from her face. Never, until the day he died, would she allow him to forget.

"Every day, you become more exquisite," a nasal voice said behind her. Bedding rustled.

Revulsion clenched her stomach. As she had every day since she and the baron escaped together from the king's dungeons, where Geoffrey had sent them to await trial and punishment, she forced a sultry smile and turned to the bed.

The baron lay with his head propped up on one arm, studying her with his small, bright eyes. The sheet had slipped farther down his belly. Scandalously low. Springy dark hair peeked above the bunched linen at his groin. Why, if the bedding moved a fraction more, she'd see his—

He growled. "My thoughts exactly."

Arching one eyebrow, she said, "And what was I thinking?"

Lust glinted in his eyes. "You were wondering if I wanted to fornicate, as we did earlier tonight." His tongue flickered out over his bottom lip. "'Twas a lusty tryst. Satisfying, I vow, for both of us."

He'd squealed like a pig with a trapped hoof. Veronique smothered the urge to laugh. God's blood, but he was revolting.

He raised a fat hand, beckoning her to join him in the bed, while his gaze gorged upon her nakedness. "Did I tell you how magnificent you were last eve?" He smiled, revealing his chipped and stained teeth. "The way you manipulated Ransley . . . He was like a witless ass."

Of course he was; she'd made certain of it. "We need him," she said with a lazy shrug. "At least, until the mercenaries arrive."

Sedgewick nodded. "Clif will keep his word. Within the next day, they will be here."

Clif. Veronique well remembered the rough-looking poacher with a scar cutting close to his mouth from their meetings weeks ago, when she and Sedgewick began their plot to take control of Pryerston. 'Twould be the first of many keeps they'd seize in Moydenshire. With the help of mercenaries paid with coin raised by selling de Lanceau's pendant, they'd take castle by castle. While Geoffrey struggled to manage his cloth empire and lead his armies, they'd wrest the entire county from his control.

Clif knew many folk in Moydenshire. A smile touched her lips, for he was a forceful man, not only in his negotiations, but as a lover, as she'd discovered in their impassioned coupling in the stable while Sedgewick arranged a night's lodgings.

"Our plan is going well, then," she said, holding the baron's gaze.

He grinned. "Sometimes, Veronique, you are so devious, you terrify me."

She smiled back, but inside, she relished a smug cackle. He should be frightened. But for now, he had no reason to worry.

A soft rustle, and the bedding shifted. He followed her gaze to his swollen loins. A flush stained his face, glistening with sweat. "Just the thought of you last night—"

Another spasm rippled through her. "So I see." His skills could never come close to the exciting lovemaking she enjoyed with Geoffrey, but Sedgewick never left her unsatisfied. Why waste the desire prowling inside her, even if 'twas not for him?

With loose, enticing strides, she moved toward the bed.

A child's wail carried from somewhere outside the solar door. Veronique glanced toward the wooden panel, bolted shut. With an irritated sigh, she dragged her gaze away, smiled, and again glided toward the bed.

"Veronique," the baron whined, pushing up to sitting. His body quivered, like a naughty boy awaiting a wicked reward.

The distant crying grew louder. Now, the child was howling.

The baron's lips pursed. "Surely not—"

A knock sounded on the door.

Veronique threw up her hands.

With a frustrated grunt, the baron collapsed back against his pillow. Snatching at the sheets, he yanked them over his lower body.

Another knock. "Lady Desjardin," a woman said, her voice muffled through the door. The bawling child was gulping breaths.

Veronique scowled at the panel. She knew that sound well.

Her bare feet thumping on the planks, she crossed to the door.

"Should you not cover yourself?" the baron called after her. "There is a blanket—"

"I will not be long."

Veronique flipped the bolt and wrenched the door open, bringing in a fresh draft of cold air.

A pretty, blond maidservant stood outside in the torch-lit passage, holding a little boy clad in a grubby tunic and hose. Her eyes flew wide, before she lowered her gaze and stumbled back a step. The child immediately silenced, startled by his sudden jostling, then started crying again. Squeezing his hand into a fist, he pounded it against the woman's neck.

Blushing, the young woman said, "I . . . am sorry to disturb ye—"

Veronique set her hand on her hip. "Really." Her gaze slid

to the sobbing boy looking at her with huge, watery eyes. A tiny part of her heart softened.

"I cannot seem ta make 'im 'appy." The woman trembled. "'E asked for ye."

The little boy shuddered a breath. "Ma."

The loving little sound poked at the tender part of Veronique. The part reminding her that he'd grown inside her for long months, before he burst forth from her womb.

A tentative smile touched the child's pudgy mouth. "Ma?"

Veronique sighed, but the sound had far less fury than she'd hoped. "Tye." She reached out and took him from the woman's arms. He curled his arms around her neck.

"I will bring him back to you shortly," Veronique said.

"Aye, milady." The woman curtsied, spun on her heel, and hurried away.

Shifting Tye to her right hip, Veronique pushed the door closed with one hand.

"Not happy," Tye grumbled, his mouth pinched into a scowl.

Lying on his side in bed, the baron scowled. "Neither am I."

"Wanted Ma."

"Of course you did," Veronique cooed, nuzzling her son's flushed cheek. She inhaled the sweetish scent of her child and struggled against another bloom of maternal instinct.

She smiled down into her little boy's face. He grinned back, his golden-brown hair an uncombed mess, his eyes bright as berries.

A handsome child, just like his father.

Veronique's smile hardened. Aye, indeed.

Just like his father.

‡ ‡ ‡

Aldwin chuckled as the tavern wench cried out in dismay. *Got you, Lady L.*

"Sir Reginald," she cried.

Holding tight to her arm, ignoring her desperate struggling, Aldwin pushed himself up to sitting, wincing at the ache at the back of his head. He blinked to clear dizziness from his vision. How long he'd been awake he couldn't say. Discomfort had roused him from unconsciousness, along with the mutterings of two men and a husky-voiced woman: the temptress, Lady L.

He blinked again, while the blur of darkness and faint light around him gradually sharpened. Upon waking moments earlier, he'd wanted to lunge to his feet and pummel the louts who'd hit him. Aldwin had sensed them standing close, looking down at him lying on the floor that reeked of God knows what.

His wits had sharpened enough for him to realize he was at a disadvantage rising groggily from the ground. He could easily defeat the two old men. But he'd be wiser to wait for a better opportunity to fight them. So he'd pretended to still be unconscious.

What sweet reward that he'd opted for restraint. He'd only had to subdue one of her guards, who now sprawled on his back, motionless, his sword only partway drawn.

"Sir Reginald," Lady L said hoarsely. "Can you hear me?"

Sitting upright now, Aldwin settled his gaze upon her. While his vision hadn't completely cleared, he realized she was on her knees before him and furious at being captured.

She twisted. Squirmed. Arched her body back, as far away from him as she could go—like a cat with its paw trapped.

Surprising, how strong she was, for a woman. He tightened

his grip, aware of her wrist bones jumping against his palm. A memory stirred in his mind, of a creature Ward had described to him one night, shortly before he died. Ward had called the large, catlike beast, caged by its captors and on display in an Eastern bazaar, a lion.

Aldwin focused upon the blur of Lady L's face. Her features became more distinct, and anticipation coiled up inside him. At last, he'd look her straight in the eyes.

"Oh, God," she gasped, tugging hard on her wrist and seizing advantage of his moment of gloating. He pitched forward, almost careening headfirst into her chest. Slamming his free hand against the filthy floor, he caught his balance. Scowling, he yanked her back.

With a startled squawk and a *thump*, she bumped against him. Her wool-clad shoulder hit his before she wrenched away.

A soft breath escaped him, knocked from him by their colliding bodies, but also by the stunning impact of their touch: her warm breath against his face; her sweet, honeysuckle scent; and her hair brushing his cheek. For a moment, the assault upon his senses rendered him immobile.

He shook his head, forcing the sensations away. However enticing the contact, this wench was no lady innocent. She wore de Lanceau's stolen pendant. Moreover, she might know the whereabouts of the baron and Veronique. If Aldwin brought about their capture, he'd be knighted for certain.

Aldwin pulled Lady L firmly back toward him.

Her breath rushed between her teeth. Her head wrenched sideways and she glanced once more at her unconscious comrade, while digging her fingernails—rather grubby ones, Aldwin noticed—into his hand. He ignored the pain. He wouldn't let go even if she drew blood.

Slowly, he pulled her forward, until her face, still turned to him in profile and wisped with streaks of hair, was a mere breath away.

She swallowed, as though she finally accepted she was caught.

Then she turned to look at him.

The weak candlelight provided less than satisfying light. What he saw, though, snatched the air from his lungs.

Lady L was exquisite. More so than he'd ever imagined.

Her honey-brown hair, once plaited into a braid, snarled out around her to frame her face like a mane. Her wide, almond-shaped eyes, golden as a feline's, sharpened in a glare that promised him all kinds of torments once she escaped. When she blinked, sparing him her outrage for the barest moment, her dark golden eyelashes swept against skin dotted with freckles.

That defiant stare . . . His memories shot back to a distant summer and the girl he'd ordered tied to a tree. She'd looked at him with such spirit. Yet this woman couldn't possibly be Leona Ransley; she'd died from bee stings years ago.

Refusing to heed the wench's threatening stare, Aldwin skimmed his gaze down the delicate line of her nose, also dusted with freckles, further proof she wasn't of the noble class; almost all ladies of his acquaintance—with the exception of Lady Elizabeth—avoided the sun to keep their pale, unblemished complexions.

Despite her freckles, this wench had a fetching nose, surprisingly slender and aristocratic. Was there noble blood in her, after all? She might be the illegitimate daughter of a lord who'd pleasured himself with one of the local strumpets and refused to acknowledge the resultant child as his. Aldwin had heard of such before. The likely explanation played into her amusing title, Lady L.

Resisting a smile, he glanced lower. His gaze settled on her mouth's rosy fullness. Her teeth were still clenched, and her breaths rasped between her slightly parted lips. A shiver of desire ran through him, for she had the fullest, most intriguing mouth he'd ever seen on a woman. Her bottom lip was plumper than the top one. It gave her a sensual pout that promised all manner of pleasurable sins.

His groin warmed. Being a courtesan, she'd know how to deliver those sins well.

Tossing her head back, she pulled hard on her arm.

"Stop," he said, surprised by the huskiness in his voice. "You will hurt yourself."

She stilled, but her gaze spat pure fury. "I will not be hurt if you let me go."

Her commanding voice made him want to shiver again. "That I cannot do," he said, tamping down his inconvenient desire.

"You could if you wanted."

He indulged in a lopsided grin. No way in hellfire was he obliging.

A frustrated growl rumbled in her throat, barely visible above the neckline of her cloak, which looked dusty and worn. "Release me," she said, biting out each word, "and I will hand over the pendant."

"A tempting offer."

She arched a slender eyebrow. "A wise one. I will not abide you groping around in my garments."

Groping around in her garments? A tantalizing mental image. He dragged his gaze down the front of her cloak and stared long enough at the swell of her breasts that she couldn't possibly misinterpret his meaning. "Pity. A strumpet like you must enjoy a good grope."

He caught the whisper-rustle of her garments, sensed her fist flying toward his face, and ducked. Not fast enough. Her knuckles slammed into his jaw. The deft wallop cracked his teeth together. Certainly not a punch he expected from a woman.

Where had she learned to hit like a man? Were there moments, in her service for less than favorable clients, when she had to defend herself with her fists? Had she needed to fight for her life when her two ancient bodyguards weren't around to protect her?

With a pained grimace, Aldwin rubbed his face. At the same moment, she twisted her restrained arm and broke free, almost tripping over Sir Reginald, still unconscious.

Aldwin grabbed for her, but she scrambled backward, stumbling on her cloak's hem. Sparing Sir Reginald a worried glance, she straightened and pushed to standing. When she rose, she reached into her boot, and he spied the glint of a knife in her right hand. Her hair snaked down her back like a silken rope as she spun and hurried toward the door.

Aldwin stood, taking the candle with him. The bitter taste of defeat tainted his mouth. Pushing the candleholder onto a nearby shelf, he fought the near blinding urge to chase her. If he pursued, she'd bolt out into the tavern crowd. For all he knew, she had many loyal friends in this tavern who'd beat him senseless before they let him capture her.

If she escaped him, he forfeited his promise to de Lanceau, as well as his chance for knighthood. Not only would Aldwin return to Branton Keep a disappointment to his lord and himself, but such failure promised dire consequences—especially if Veronique and the baron got hold of the pendant. If they sold it and used the funds to hire themselves an army of thugs, de Lanceau—indeed, all of Moydenshire—would be in terrible danger.

Stop her, his conscience screamed.

"Wait!" he called.

She held the knife in her left hand now. Her right hand on the door handle, she looked back at him. Her face tautened with defiance.

He forced himself to stand very still. If he made even the slightest threatening gesture, she'd be out the door. "We have not yet made our exchange," he said.

Her slender fingers tightened on the handle. With a faint *click*, she drew the door open a fraction, letting in light and noise. She hesitated, long enough he sensed he might still be able to barter with her. To coax her back into his arena of control. That is, if he treated her with the respectful care one gave an untamed lioness.

"I traveled a long way for that pendant." Aldwin reached inside his cloak and withdrew the bag of coins. He shook it, causing the silver to *clink*. "I cannot leave without the jewel."

"Pity. A knave like you must hate to fail."

Insolent wench! He bit his tongue and tried to ignore the sting of her words. "Indeed," he agreed, "I would."

Her hand flexed again on the handle, as though to draw the door farther open. Such elegant fingers, for a woman of harsh circumstances. For one bizarre moment, he wondered how those fingers would feel running over his bare skin.

"You still want the pendant, then?" Lady L murmured.

"I do."

She waved the knife, indicating the floor between them. "Drop the bag of coins."

He frowned.

"Drop it," she repeated, "where I can reach it."

Anger hummed inside him. If she thought to grab the reward

and run, she was in for a nasty surprise. "Agreed," he said softly. "Then you will hand me the pendant."

"Fine."

For all her determination to flee, she sounded as eager to be rid of the jewel as he was to get it. How intriguing. If she'd wanted to forfeit the responsibility of such a treasure, she could have sold it during the days it took him to reach the tavern. She could have found a less-than-reputable merchant who would have bought it at a fraction of its real value. Less risk for her, and she still would have walked away with a payment.

Which led to yet another question. Why had she contacted de Lanceau to arrange the meeting at this tavern? Why was it important to her that the pendant be returned to his lordship?

Questions de Lanceau had every right to ask her himself.

And he would.

Aldwin tried not to smile as a new plan played out in his mind. He stepped forward, the bag in his outstretched hand. *Beware*, his mind whispered. *Don't let her guess what you intend.*

Halfway between them, he opened his fingers. The bag plummeted to the floor with a musical *thud*. Spreading both arms wide in a gesture of surrender, he stepped back.

Her gaze dropped to the coin. An odd expression flitted over her face, a poignant mix of relief and regret. Then, releasing her white-knuckled hold on the door, she edged toward him. Her wary gaze still upon him, she stooped to pick up the bag.

The moment her focus left him, Aldwin lunged. He kicked the knife from her hand, sending it flying across the room, at the same moment her fingers closed on the coin. He followed, his hand crushing down upon hers.

"What—?" she cried.

"Pity," he said, "that I had to deceive you."

She sprang back, grabbing for the door. Her fingers touched the panel, but he wrenched her away. With a sharp tug, he drew her into his embrace. Her honeysuckle scent hit him a moment before her body slammed against him. Chest to chest.

His arm clamped around her waist, smaller beneath the cloak than he'd suspected.

Her breath rushed out on a huff. "Why, you—!"

With his free hand, he snatched the bag of coins. "I will take that." He shoved the sack inside his cloak.

She writhed in his hold. "Sir Reginald!"

"Still unconscious," Aldwin said.

"Twig!" she shrieked.

"Cannot hear you."

Her gaze became a frigid gleam, an instant before her knee jerked upward. He twisted to the side, avoiding a blow to his groin that would have left him crumpled in agony on the floor near Sir Reginald. Instead her knee bumped against his inner thigh, protected by his cloak.

Aldwin crushed her tighter against him. "Tsk-tsk. How unladylike of you."

A wicked glint lit her eyes.

He smiled. "Pity, that you underestimate me."

Her body tautened in his grasp. Before she carried out whatever assault she was contemplating, he dropped to a crouch, slid his arm down behind her legs, and tossed her over his left shoulder. She landed with a gasp.

Grunting at her weight, he stood.

"Put. Me. Down," she cried, trying to rise up on his shoulder.

"I would gladly do so." He tightened his hold on her

thrashing legs. "You weigh far more than any lady I know."

"Oh!" Her elbow jabbed into his ear.

He almost laughed. While her bulky cloak concealed the contours of her body well enough, he'd already determined her enticing proportions. Full breasts. A rounded bottom. Long legs. He resisted a groan. For what he had in mind, he'd have preferred her old, ugly, and completely undesirable.

Her toes whacked into his gut, knocking the breath from him on a grunt.

He bounced her, once, on his shoulder.

"God's teeth," she spluttered.

Squaring his shoulders, Aldwin turned to the open doorway.

Her hands pounded his buttocks. He felt little more than dull punches through his wool cloak. "I warn you," she said, her words muffled against the fabric. "Put. Me—"

"Down?" Aldwin laughed. "Nay, Lady L. You are coming with me."

CHAPTER FOUR

The swell of noise from the main tavern room mirrored the roar of blood rushing into Leona's head. Being thrown over an arrogant knave's shoulder like a sack of beans and dangling upside down was most disorienting. Not to mention mortifying.

When Aldwin moved toward the door, causing her to bounce against his back, she fisted her hands into his cloak. Oh, God. The laughter, singing, and a chorus of cheers seemed to focus right in her throbbing brow.

Nevertheless, she was not going to allow this arrogant oaf to carry her away as if he were an ogre from one of her childhood nightmares. She squirmed with all her might. The scratchy wool of his cloak abraded her cheek, as did the rope of her braid she'd looped around her neck, her only means of keeping it from dragging on the ground.

He swatted her legs. "Stop struggling."

She tilted her face away from his cloak. "I warn you," she yelled. "Put—"

The door creaked farther open, spilling light over Sir Reginald's prone form.

Hammering her fists against Aldwin's arse again, she yelled, "Sir Reginald!" Why did he not wake? And where was Twig with that accursed drink?

Aldwin strode into the corridor. His boots raised a cloud of dust . . . or whatever lay on the floor in a fine coating. He paused, clearly deciding whether to proceed through the crowded main room or find another way out.

A draft edged up under the hem of her gown, as if a ghostly sot tried to peep at her undergarments. Kicking her legs, she glared at Aldwin's back. How galling for the tavern's patrons to see her bottom up.

His arms tightened around her thighs, restricting her struggles. She punched him again and raised her head. "Twig!"

Hearty laughter swarmed from the bar, followed by a chorus of "Down in one! Down in one!" A drinking contest. No wonder Twig hadn't returned with the liquor.

"*Twig!*" she screamed again, hoping he heard her over the din.

Aldwin pivoted, and she guessed he now faced the rear door, the source of the draft. Turning her face, she caught a glimpse of the main room. Past the tables where two men were arguing over a whore, she spied Twig. Clutching an earthenware mug in one scrawny hand, holding it high above the crowd so it wouldn't spill, he elbowed his way through the throng. Intent on dodging the drunkards, he hadn't seen her.

"Tw—!" she began with all the breath in her lungs, but before the screech broke full force, Aldwin jostled her again. "—ig!" she groaned.

With brisk strides, Aldwin headed down the corridor toward the back door.

Thrashing her legs, Leona inhaled another breath. "Tw—!" Aldwin shifted her weight on his shoulder. She started sliding toward the ground. Headfirst. Her scream died on a frightened squawk.

She fell the space of one gasp before Aldwin grabbed secure hold of her again. Not that she would have hit the floor. Her hands firmly gripped his cloak.

He laughed softly, and her gaze clouded with fury. He'd almost dropped her on purpose. To let her know she was wholly in his control.

The cool air in the corridor intensified. He approached the area where the tavern keeper received deliveries of ale and other goods. Barrels, topped by folded cloth sacks, were propped against the wall.

Leona gnawed her lip, for she would *not* be hauled outside into the darkness with Aldwin. They might have met when they were children, but she didn't know this warrior Aldwin at all. Who knew what he intended for her in the grimy yard, beyond the watchful eyes of the revelers and her father's men?

Mayhap he planned to carry her behind the stable, slit her throat, and take the pendant. He might return to the tavern and kill Twig and Sir Reginald, too, leaving no witnesses to their earlier meeting.

If she didn't escape, she risked Twig and Sir Reginald's lives. They'd already hazarded a great deal to help her.

She thought of the dagger Aldwin had kicked from her hand. If only she had some way to defend herself . . .

Few warriors traveled without knives. She'd take Aldwin's.

She carefully loosened one hand and, stretching sideways, reached around for the cloak's front opening. She found the edge of the fabric, then the softer wool of his tunic.

Then the leather belt at his waist.

"Beware, Lady L," he muttered. "You might find more than you expected."

Bold knave! Her fingertips bumped the hilt of a dagger. Aha! He'd treat her differently when she turned his own weapon upon him—

"I think not." Aldwin shrugged his shoulder.

Tightening her grip on his cloak, she grabbed again for the dagger.

He growled, before the broad muscles supporting her shifted. She careened sideways. As she cursed and struggled, fighting to reclaim her position, iron hinges creaked, and then cool summer air swept over her, enveloping her like a monster's mouth.

Glancing sideways, she spied the battered door. She grabbed hold of it, clinging to it like a limpet to a sea stone.

"I will not let go," she yelled. Wood bit into her palms.

"Really?" Aldwin kept on walking. With an eerie groan, the door closed, pulled by her hands. If she didn't relinquish her grip, her fingers would be caught between the embrasure and the door. A painful prospect. She needed her fingers intact.

Spitting a curse, she drew her hands in. The door clicked into place.

Darkness, the smell of wood smoke, and a foul odor surrounded her. If he hadn't brought her out here to kill her, she'd die from the stench. Using part of his cloak, she covered her nose.

From somewhere nearby came coarse voices and sounds of vicious fist fighting. Not at all promising for a rescue.

Aldwin's boots crunched on the dirt as he walked. When her eyes began to adjust to the blackness, she made out the stable's rough-hewn wall. Trying to focus her thoughts, she recalled the tavern's surroundings: the open area outside the building; the sagging-roofed stable; the old trees lining the short drive into the tavern; and the road leading into the forest beyond.

His strides didn't slow as he neared the stable, which meant he hadn't tethered a mount there and wasn't taking her away on horseback. Fear crawled up her skull, for that suggested he wasn't carrying her far.

Dropping the fabric shielding her face, she shrieked, "Help!"

"Quiet," Aldwin snapped over his shoulder. "You will draw the attention of the tavern thugs."

"Exactly!"

"Trust me. 'Tis not wise."

"Why not?" She spat the words at his back. Raising her head again, she screeched, "Help!"

"Those men are a violent lot. You are more likely to be raped than be rescued."

"How gallant of you to worry about my welfare," she shot back. "Should I thank you for tossing me over your shoulder? For knocking the breath out of me several times?"

A snarl rumbled from him.

"I vow the danger is from you, not the thugs. I will not make your efforts easy. In fact, I swear upon my brother's grave that I will fight you and get away."

"You can try."

Aldwin's arrogant tone brought a hot flush to her face. How she'd enjoy slamming her fist into his jaw again—this time hard enough to knock him senseless.

The stable ended. The battered side wall, patched by warped boards, blended into the darkness as Aldwin strode on. The wood smoke smell intensified, bolstered by the roaring crackle of a bonfire.

Fear ran through her in an icy tremor as, twisting sideways, she glanced at the blaze and the rough-looking men gathered there. Some sported bloody noses and ripped clothes. Others were delivering punches and kicks in the ongoing brawl. Surrounded by smoke, the thugs looked almost demonic. Yet she was running out of chances to escape.

Aldwin's footsteps quickened. No doubt he hoped to be away from the fighting as soon as possible. She had to act *now*.

"Help!" Leona cried again. With shaking hands, she grabbed handfuls of Aldwin's cloak, scrambling to find his belt again. He wore his dagger on his right side. Which meant the sack of coins was on his left.

Aldwin grunted in warning, but she clawed her hands into his tunic. "Help me! Please."

"Oy!" a thug called. "You there. What ye doin' ta that wensssch?"

With shivers of relief and panic, she realized the man was addressing Aldwin.

"Help me!" she cried. "He plans to kill me."

"Indeed," Aldwin muttered in a voice only she could hear, "I am sorely tempted to strangle you."

"Put 'er down," another man shouted, while the sounds of fist fighting quieted.

Aldwin halted. He must have felt her hand skating across his belt, but he ignored her. Turning to face the men—which meant she couldn't see them anymore—he said, "Put her down?" He laughed. "I paid good money for a tumble with this strumpet."

Several thugs muttered.

"What?" Leona spluttered.

"Ish that ssshhho?" another man shouted.

"She is a feisty one," Aldwin said. "Enjoys a bit of drama, I am told. Likes to pretend she is a lady carried off by her lusty lover."

More raucous laughter.

Leona kicked her legs, heedless of the draft wafting up her skirt. "He is lying! Please! Help me." Her fingers bumped the coin bag. She tugged it from Aldwin's belt. "He has silver! Help me, and the money is yours."

Strong fingers snatched the bag from her hand. Before she could say one word, she heard the silver jingle, then the *clink-clink-clink* of coins landing on the dirt.

"Drinks for all of you," Aldwin yelled. Over hearty roars, she heard the men scrambling for the coins. No doubt Aldwin had tossed enough for drinks to render them all daft, so they'd be of no help to Twig and Sir Reginald when they searched for her.

"My friends," Aldwin said, "the lady and I do not wish to be disturbed."

"We will not interrupt ye," one drunkard said with a rude cackle.

"Not unlesshhh we can 'ave a go with 'er," another yelled.

"Nay," Leona choked.

"This one is all mine." Aldwin's tone held menace. "Remember, if anyone asks, you did not see us."

"Ssshee who?" another man said, to bawdy laughter.

Leona groaned.

Spinning around again, Aldwin continued toward the forest. Again, she fought him, trying to wriggle free of his grasp, but he didn't lessen his grip the slightest bit.

The smoke and firelight thinned, giving way to darkness lit by a weak moon. Unable to change her position, exhausted from her struggles, Leona stared down at the rocky dirt passing beneath Aldwin's boots. Somehow, she had to find a way to let Twig and Sir Reginald know where to search for her. Taking hold of the end of her braid, she untied the bit of leather and dropped it to the ground.

Dirt gave way to a verge of grass and weeds, and then ferns growing alongside trees and brush. The scents of mold and rotting leaves rose up from the damp earth. A night creature rustled in the undergrowth, an unseen hunter stalking prey.

Leona yanked on the cloak. "Where are you taking me?"

Fallen branches snapped beneath Aldwin's boots. He didn't answer, but kept walking.

"What are you going to do?" She whacked him with her fist. "Are you listening? If you do not answer me—"

A breathy snort sounded, followed by the metallic *tinkle* of a bridle. His horse, tethered in the forest shadows.

Aldwin's strides slowed. Oh, God. Did he mean to throw her to the ground, kill her, take the pendant, and ride away? Or—an even more unsettling thought—did he mean to shove her up onto his horse and gallop away with her, to murder with her elsewhere?

Whatever he intended, she'd not be a coward; she'd give him a fight he'd never forget. Through countless scuffles when they were children, Ward—peace upon his departed soul—had made certain she knew how to defend herself.

Aldwin shifted her upon his shoulder and then his hold on her legs eased. Freeing her hands from his cloak, she curled them into fists, preparing to strike out at him. Faster than she believed possible, he bent, set her feet on the ground, and stepped back.

Finally upright again, she fingered hair out of her eyes. The forest spun around her, and it took a moment before it settled into focus. Her numb legs wobbled.

Before her legs folded beneath her, Aldwin caught her wrist, his hold firm but, at the same time, reassuring.

She scowled and tried to pull away.

"Can you stand?"

"Aye."

"Your legs are no longer numb?"

Not as much as before, but they still feel as if insects are crawling up them.

She began to shake, struggling against the memories of bees on her skin. Why did he care about the condition of her legs? Lifting her chin, she glared at him.

"Good." He grinned as if she'd bestowed upon him her most affectionate smile.

He didn't let go of her arm.

Before she could tell him to unhand her, he hauled her toward a tree. Stumbling and skidding across the moldering leaves, she was forced to follow. A saddled destrier stood tethered to the tree. The magnificent animal seemed to recognize Aldwin, for it shook its mane and then nuzzled his shoulder.

"Hello, Romulus." He patted the horse's glossy neck and then reached for the leather bag tied to the saddle. Or was he reaching for the crossbow, slung beside the bag? Fired at this close range, she'd be dead before she could draw in a breath. A quick, efficient murder.

"Nay!" she gasped and yanked back on her arm. His fingers tightened on her wrist until she gasped again. He flipped open the saddlebag, plunged his hand inside, and drew out a length of thin, leather rope. It uncoiled, whispering toward the ground like a snake.

He meant to bind her before he shot her. Revulsion turned her mouth dry. As though she were a young girl again, she remembered being tied to the tree, unable to move, the ropes digging into her skin.

Aldwin's head tilted. Silvery moonlight touched the hard gleam of his eyes and uncompromising set of his mouth. "Give me your other wrist, Lady L."

CHAPTER FIVE

When Lady L's face tautened with fear and rebellion, Aldwin bit back an oath. She seemed determined to battle him at every opportunity. When would she accept 'twould be far more pleasant for both of them if she did as he asked?

He drew more of the rope between his fingers. She was no titled lady, worthy of delicate handling. Still, he'd rather not force her to his demands.

But he would.

Her men would soon be searching for her outside, and he intended to be gone from this forest by then.

"Lady L." He gestured to her free wrist, while keeping an iron grip on the other.

Her gaze narrowed, and then she glanced at the trees behind him, no doubt searching for a way of escape. Uncertainty glimmered in her eyes, and a peculiar tension squeezed his innards. An inconvenient sense of chivalry. From his youngest days, he'd aspired to live by the knight's code of honor, to respect those of noble birth, to fight for his king and lord, and to champion those less fortunate or in peril. Binding a woman's hands and whisking her off into the night, against her will, seemed a contradiction of those morals.

At least some of them. His duty to de Lanceau, however, took priority over her needs. If her testimony could save Moydenshire from the baron and Veronique's evil, then he must take her to Branton Keep. As quickly as possible.

"I will ask but one more time," he said quietly.

Lady L's focus snapped back to him. Her eyes looked huge against her ashen skin, her face taut with resolve. Her unraveling braid, rippling down the front of her cloak, was a snarled mess. No longer was she the poised temptress, but a wild woman ruled by instinct.

Her body tensed. She clearly prepared to bolt.

"Do as I ask. I will not hurt you."

A brittle laugh broke from her. "You want to tie my hands."

"Only so you do not injure me. Or yourself."

Her wrist tendons tightened in his grasp, and he felt a shudder jar through her, as if she feared for her life. Did she think he was lying to her? That he intended to restrain her before hurting her?

Aye, he'd given her ample reason to distrust him. But why would she believe he meant her grave harm?

She began to fight anew. Leaves rustled as she kicked at his shins while wrenching her arm. "I will not let you tie me. I know what you intend to do."

God's teeth! She was going to damage her shoulder with her struggles.

"Calm yourself." He turned the rope in his fingers, waiting for the right moment to snatch her other hand. The faster he tied her, the better.

"Tie me to a tree, shoot me dead, take the pendant, and gallop away. 'Tis what you plan." Her voice turned shrill. "I will not let you!"

He might have laughed at her ridiculous assertion, except at that moment, she glanced at Rom. Her mouth flattened. A warning buzz in Aldwin's mind reminded him of his crossbow tied there, even as her gaze lit with determination.

She lunged toward the destrier.

Hauling her back, spinning her toward him, he grabbed her other wrist.

"Nay!" she shrieked.

The terror in her voice struck him deep, but he ignored his inner voice that told him to treat her more kindly. She spat, kicked, and fought like a cornered cat. Holding her firm, he looped the rope around and between her wrists and made a knot. He cinched the bonds tight.

His hands fell away. Dismay crumpled Lady L's features as she stared down at her tied wrists. She tried to twist her hands, but he'd made sure she couldn't.

"Not . . . again," she whispered.

Not again? What did she mean? Had someone tied her hands before? Mayhap one of her less reputable clients? He shouldn't care, but the blend of horror and anger on her face chilled him. "Lady L?"

Blinking hard, she stumbled backward, her steps as awkward as a drunkard's. Any moment, she'd trip on a branch and fall on her bottom.

Matching her strides, he caught her shoulders. The wool of her cloak grazed his palms. "Listen to me. I am not going to hurt you."

"Liar!"

He shook her, thwarting her attempts to swat him with her bound hands. "I am not going to tie you to a tree. I do not intend to shoot you."

Her gaze locked with his. "Why not?"

Because you are incredibly beautiful, and, God help me, I desire you. "Because you have important information."

"W-what information?"

He held her stare before glancing down at the faint bump beneath her cloak where the ruby lay. "My lord will be very interested to know how you got hold of that pendant, which belongs to him."

A soft oath parted her lips. She glanced at the horse again. "You mean—"

"I am taking you to Geoffrey de Lanceau."

She shook her head, her eyes enormous now.

Grabbing her tied hands, he drew her toward Rom.

Dragging her feet, twisting her body, she said, "I cannot go with you."

"You already are."

"Take the pendant. Keep the reward money." Her voice wobbled. "I do not want it anymore."

"You will wear the pendant for safekeeping." Aldwin's tone darkened. "Do not try to take it off. I will be watching you."

"Please. Just let me go."

Aldwin stopped beside Rom and refused to acknowledge her desperate gaze. Her body trembled in his grasp. How clever of her to try to manipulate his emotions with those impassioned words, which had faded into a breathless little moan.

He scowled and began to untether Rom. Three years ago, he'd been less careful and had allowed his loyalties and emotions to be manipulated. By distorting the truth, Baron Sedgewick had convinced Aldwin that de Lanceau had raped Lady Elizabeth while she was held hostage at Branton Keep—before the two were married, and during the time when de Lanceau sought vengeance for his father's death and his blood right to be lord of Moydenshire. So loathsome was the thought of Lady Elizabeth being defiled, Aldwin had sworn to kill de Lanceau.

To avenge her tainted honor, Aldwin shot de Lanceau in the chest with a crossbow bolt. Later, Aldwin learned his lordship was innocent of the baron's accusations; he'd wanted de Lanceau dead so he could wed Lady Elizabeth himself, and he and Veronique could fulfill their murderous ambitions to rule Moydenshire.

Knowing he'd been a naïve puppet haunted Aldwin to this day. Never again would his loyalties be manipulated.

"Do not ignore me," Lady L cried.

"You are coming with me." The reins slipped free from the tree branch. "'Tis not a matter for negotiation."

She scratched at him with her bound hands. "Others depend upon me."

He faced her then, steeling himself against the watery fire of her gaze. "As others, including my lord, depend on me." Aldwin gestured to the saddle. "Up."

Fury flashed in her eyes.

Men's voices carried from the tavern's yard. "Milady! Milady, where are you?"

Her head swiveled. Hope brightened her features before she sucked in a breath to scream.

Grabbing her around the waist, Aldwin threw her onto his

horse's back. She landed flat on her belly on the saddle. She gasped and floundered, trying to scramble upright. Rom sidestepped, flailing his head.

"Steady, Rom," Aldwin muttered. Dodging Lady L's flailing feet, he looped the reins over the front of the saddle, shoved his boot into the stirrup, and swung up behind her.

Her hair lashing him, she righted herself. "Tw—!"

He clamped a hand over her mouth, trapping her cry.

"Mmmfff!" she screeched, tossing her head from side to side.

"Silence," he growled.

"*Mmmfff?*" Her breath gusted against his fingers. Without doubt, her reply meant "Roast in hellfire."

Her companions' calls were growing louder. Aldwin pinned her head back against his shoulder and drew his knife. Her eyes flared, but, ignoring her racing breathing, he reached around her, found the hem of her gown, sliced off a strip, and sheathed his dagger.

"Mmm!" she choked.

"Sorry." Before she guessed his intentions, he lifted his hand, rammed the cloth into her mouth, and knotted the ends behind her head.

She jerked away from him, her hands flying up to the gag. Reaching around her once more, he snatched up the reins and spurred Rom through the trees, toward the road.

Lady L slammed back against Aldwin, hard enough to knock the wind from his lungs. He reeled backward, wincing from where her head smacked into his chin.

"*Mmmfff!*" she screeched, clawing at the gag.

"Quiet"—he reached for his crossbow—"or I will kill your men."

She stilled, her shoulders rising and falling with her frantic breaths.

"Even from a moving horse, and yards away, I am an excellent shot."

"Milady!" Sir Reginald's cry echoed, fainter this time. "Milady!"

Aldwin clamped his rein-holding arm around her waist, aware of the shivers jarring through her. He urged Rom through a gap in the trees. As the brush thinned, giving way to the moonlit dirt road, he spurred the destrier to a canter.

‡ ‡ ‡

Her back as rigid as a wooden plank, Leona stared ahead into the darkness, the *thud-thud-thud* of Rom's hoofbeats pounding in her ears. The gag pinched the corners of her mouth and tasted vile. But, as hard as she'd tried, she couldn't shift it. When she'd turned her head and raised her bound fingers to the knot, Aldwin had shoved her hands away. "Try that again," he'd snarled against her hair, "and I will render you unconscious."

His hot breath close to her ear had elicited a flurry of tremors within her, and she'd jerked forward, all too aware of the tension radiating from Aldwin's muscled body behind her. Blinking against the night breeze, she'd decided to cooperate—until she could make her escape.

Sitting still, though, was its own kind of torment. Rom's powerful strides caused her bottom to bump against Aldwin's spread thighs. The heat of his body permeated the thickness of her cloak, offering to warm her against the night's chill. Clinging to Rom's mane, she tilted her body forward and pressed against Aldwin's confining arm at her waist. A small gesture of defiance. But she wouldn't have him believe she liked the intimate brush of their bodies.

The road, hardly visible and streaked with silver-gray, flew beneath Rom's hooves. Moonlight swept the horse's neck and highlighted the muscles rippling beneath his coat. Rom seemed sure-footed even in the darkness. As Aldwin, no doubt, knew.

Rom's hooves rang on stones buried in the dirt and she swallowed down unease. How far did Aldwin intend to travel tonight? Riding in the dark was not only dangerous for horse and rider, but made them easy prey for night thieves and cutthroats.

She'd demand to know his plans, if she could talk.

She sighed through her nostrils, hating Aldwin more with each passing moment. Hating being as helpless as a dull-witted damsel. Hating that her careful strategy had all gone wrong, and that because of her, Twig and Sir Reginald were now on their own at the tavern and Pryerston Keep was falling further into the grip of the baron and Veronique.

Father, I am sorry that I failed you.

Leona blinked hard, fighting her misery. She was *not* going to shed tears before Aldwin. After enduring the news of her brother's death on crusade, her mother's accident a few months ago, and her father's decline into drunken despair, she'd learned how to hide her despondency. And, by God, she would.

Aldwin shifted behind her, causing his broad thighs to nudge against her. A peculiar ache dragged through her, a sensation she'd not felt before. Somehow, it seemed to make her even more aware of his bold, masculine presence behind her. He was so impossibly . . . warm.

Scowling, she leaned farther forward.

Aldwin chuckled.

She held her head higher. Discomfort shot through her neck

muscles, and she winced, glad he couldn't see.

"Lady L, you are going to strain your back." He tried to draw in his arm at her waist, to pull her against him, but she held firm.

"You cannot be comfortable sitting that way."

"Mmm. *Mmm.*"

"Really?" A laugh rumbled in his chest, and she welcomed a surge of rage. She'd answered as best she could with the gag. How dare he mock her?

The reins shifted in Aldwin's hands, and then Rom's strides slowed to a trot, then a walk.

Aldwin's fingers brushed the back of her head.

"Mmm—!"

"Hold still, and I will untie the knot."

She obeyed, waiting for that wondrous moment when she'd get the taste of wet wool from her mouth and inhale fresh air.

The cloth fell away. She drew a breath and rubbed her mouth.

"Try to scream for help," he warned, "and I will gag you again. Understand?"

She nodded.

"Are you comfortable now?"

"Perfectly." If she said "nay," would he untie her hands? Let her go? Not likely.

Another laugh, this one tinged with disbelief. "Are you afraid of our bodies touching?"

She snorted. "Afraid?"

"I vow you are." He paused, long enough for her to sense his keen appraisal of her. "I find such modesty curious, especially for a . . . *lady* of your profession."

Leona bit the inside of her mouth. He was enjoying taunting her. Rage and frustration boiled up inside her. Yet she mustn't let her emotions overrule her common sense. A rational mind and sheer cunning were the only ways to escape a man like Aldwin.

"I do not want our bodies to touch," she said over her shoulder, "because I despise you."

Their gazes met in the darkness. He shrugged and then grinned, his teeth a white slash. "Very well."

Facing the road again, she saw trees now surrounded both sides. If she guessed his route correctly, he was taking her into an old forest rumored to be haunted by spirits of the dead. More than one peasant had seen Roman soldiers marching through the trees on the way to an ancient battle.

"A-are we riding through the woods?" she asked.

"'Tis the fastest route to Branton Keep."

A shudder crawled down her spine. "You cannot mean to travel through the forest at night."

A low chuckle brushed across her hair. "Lady L, your concern is most touching."

"I do not care what happens to you," she said, "but I would hate to fall prey to ruffians, or see such a fine horse injured because of your recklessness."

Aldwin's breath expelled on an oath. Her words must have wounded him, for he fell silent.

The forest's earthy scent carried on the breeze as they headed farther into the trees. Moonlight shivered down through the branches overhead and grazed the bushes growing close to the road, rendering the darkness even more eerie.

She half-expected a ghostly apparition to leap out from the undergrowth, poised to attack.

"Not much farther," Aldwin said.

"W-we are stopping?"

"Aye. We will make camp by the river and stay there until dawn."

Along with the undead Romans.

Leona's gaze traveled over the silent trees, and she fought a fresh surge of anxiety. Whatever the locals said about these woods, she must use this stop to her advantage. She had to convince him to let her go. If that failed, she must find a way to escape.

His arm at her waist moved again, a lazy, purposeful shift upward that brought it immodestly close to her bosom. She might have commented upon such barbarity, but at that moment, Aldwin hauled her back against him, with such ease, she realized he could have done so, whenever he wished, during their journey.

"Stopping does not mean you will have a chance to escape," he said against her cheek. "If that is what you intend, you will find these woods very dangerous indeed."

CHAPTER SIX

Aldwin studied the forest ahead, so silent, they might be riding in a tomb. Lady L shivered in his hold, and, with a silent groan, he resisted the urge to tighten his arm in a reassuring squeeze. While his conscience told him to be chivalrous and offer her comfort, he mustn't. Stopping in the woods for the night was a risk. She must perceive him as a threat; otherwise, she'd try to get away. With all the fallen trees, half-buried Roman ruins, and unstable ground in this area, she'd more likely kill herself than escape.

Studying the road ahead, he looked for the marker that would guide him onto the deer path toward the river. If only Lady L's hair didn't smell so deliciously sweet. If only her body didn't fit so neatly against his. If only the feel of her in his arms didn't make his body buzz with awareness.

What he felt for Lady L was . . . intriguing. He knew how to pleasure women, and how to entice them to satisfy him, but few had left a lasting impression on him. Only one woman had rendered him so besotted, he would have plunged a sword through his own heart had she asked—and they hadn't so much as kissed.

To this day, he knew no woman quite like her: Lady Elizabeth.

Geoffrey de Lanceau's wife.

The mother of his children.

Years ago, when Aldwin had been as a squire in her father Lord Arthur Brackendale's household, she'd entranced him with her love of his tales of gallant knights. Before she was abducted by de Lanceau and fell in love with him, Aldwin had hoped to offer for her hand in marriage.

Still, he couldn't hold back a stab of jealousy whenever he envisioned her stunning beauty. Intelligent, loving, and loyal, she championed all the ideal qualities of a noblewoman. All he desired in a lady wife.

But she loved de Lanceau. With a passionate sincerity that ate at Aldwin's soul every time he saw them exchange a glance or a kiss, or stroll hand in hand to their private solar.

He'd never let his feelings be known, though. As penance for shooting de Lanceau years ago, Aldwin had sworn lifelong allegiance to him, and would never dishonor that vow by betraying his lord in any way—especially by admitting his desire for Lady Elizabeth.

Someday, mayhap, Aldwin would find another lady to equal her. But that woman wasn't Lady L, no matter how much she fascinated him.

To the left, he spied the tree with the crooked trunk. He guided Rom off the road and onto the path weaving into the forest.

Lady L batted away a grasping branch and muttered under her breath.

Resisting another nudge of his conscience to comfort her, he guided Rom around a broken stump. Light glistened on the river beyond the trees. As they neared the water, the forest thinned, giving way to broken stone walls thrusting up from the ground, the ruins of a long-abandoned Roman fortification. Rocks scattered across the grassy dirt—enough to serve as weapons if by chance they were attacked.

The night breeze whispered the length of the stone walls while he drew Rom to a halt in the shelter of the ruins. 'Twas cool this eve for summer, but the walls would take the brunt of the wind.

Lady L huddled into her cloak. "You cannot mean to stop here."

"I do."

Her head swiveled, and he blinked against the stinging whip of her hair. "But—"

"The walls will protect us from the breeze, and there is plenty of firewood about." Even as he spoke, he mentally scorned his explanation. He didn't have to defend his actions to her.

The knowledge that he'd done so, as if she were his equal or more, rather than a common wench, roused stinging irritation. "If still find yourself cold"—he raised his eyebrows—"I am sure we can find ways to stay warm."

Before she could bite out a retort, he drew his arms from around her and slid from Rom's back, keeping a firm hold on his crossbow. He raised his hand to help her dismount.

She glared down at him, her hair tangled from their journey. All she needed was an ancient helm, spear, and shield, and she'd look just like the image of Britannia he'd seen on an old Roman coin.

"Come down, Lady L."

A grim smile touched her lips before she looked straight ahead, no doubt choosing her route before spurring his destrier into motion.

"Rom is no help to you. He is trained to obey my commands."

Aldwin forced a careless shrug. "Of course, I would shoot you before you got five paces."

"I would not be able to give you much information then, would I?"

Her defiant beauty pulled at him, condemning him for his reckless threat. "As I said before, I do not want to hurt you. But I will stop you escaping. A bolt through your arm would bring you down off my horse. You would also spill a great deal of blood, suffer pain for the rest of our travels, and mayhap lose the use of your arm."

Her face tautened with revulsion.

"I give you fair warning, for I know much about crossbow wounds."

"Because of what you did to de Lanceau," she said.

He nodded and offered his hand again. "I am trying to be chivalrous, Lady L. Come down. I will light a fire. I have food and drink in my saddlebag."

Her posture stiffened. She clearly interpreted his offer of food and warmth as a bribe. In truth, 'twas. A warm drink would be most welcome.

Her lips parted on a sigh that made her shoulders slump. Turning her face away—and pointedly ignoring his offer of assistance—she gripped the front of the saddle, eased her other leg over, and slid down from Rom. A flash of linen caught his gaze while she descended and he tried not to recall the tempting curves of her body pressed against him during their ride.

She stood, shaking out the folds of her cloak despite her bound hands. Brushing past her, he untied his rolled blanket and saddlebag and slung the strap over his shoulder. Taking hold of her elbow, he led her toward the ruins.

She stumbled on a partly buried stone and spat an oath fit for a foulmouthed squire.

Aldwin laughed. "You learned that at the tavern?"

"Nay, from my brother."

Aldwin remembered that earlier, she'd spoken of a sibling. Later tonight, he'd try to learn more about her upbringing and even her family.

Upon reaching the wall's shadows, Aldwin dropped the blanket on the ground and unrolled it with his boot. With the crossbow, he motioned for her to sit.

She glowered.

Fine. If she refused to sit, she'd stand.

After flipping open his saddlebag, Aldwin pulled out another length of rope. Her eyes flew wide. "What—?"

"I am making certain you cannot run off."

Her face blanched. Then an angry flush stained her face. "You are *not* going to tether me like a horse."

The way she spoke to him . . . As though she commanded this land and all who lived in it. He barely resisted the urge to bellow at her.

"You tied my hands. 'Tis enough."

He bit back a growl. "Lady L—"

"Exactly. *Lady.*" She cut him a blistering stare. "You are foul, indeed, to treat me in such a manner."

Jerking her wrists forward, he loomed over her. Her luscious scent teased, as aggravating as her words. "We have discussed this before. You are not a noble lady, but a *courtesan.*"

"*You* told me I was a courtesan. I never made such a ridiculous claim."

He raised his brows. "Aye, well—"

Her eyes blazed. "I am, indeed, of noble blood. If you believe you will go unpunished for kidnapping, mistreating, and binding me, you are mad. I will have your wretched arse."

She spoke with such dignified fury, he almost believed her. Shaking his head, he began to tie the rope around the knots at her wrists.

Pulling her hands away, she screeched, "Did you not hear one word?"

He drew her hands back. "I did."

"And still, you treat me like an animal?" Tears glistened at the corners of her eyes. Soon, she'd be weeping to try to sway him. But he'd be immune to that ploy.

"You are no lady."

She twisted her wrists, complicating his task. "What, pray tell, convinces you of that?"

With a firm tug, he secured the second rope. "Ladies strive for a pale and flawless complexion. You have more freckles than any lady I know."

"Because I spend some of my days in the sun."

He thrust her hands in her face. "Your hands are not soft and smooth; they are chapped from days of work."

"Because—"

"And you have dirt under your nails."

"From tending my dead mother's rose garden," she shot back, anguish, now, in her expression. "Are you so thick-skulled you cannot believe ladies put their hands in the earth now and again?"

All right. So she made a fair point. Lady Elizabeth enjoyed spending time outdoors, and on occasion, she picked flowers from the garden.

"Your clothes—"

"Old garments for traveling!" She choked out a furious sigh. "Would you wear fine silk into that tavern? I did not want to draw attention to myself."

Another good point. This wench was determined to befuddle him.

Turning his back on her, Aldwin fed the rope through two holes in the wall behind her where the mortar between the stones had crumbled. One hole was a hand's span higher than the other, but that didn't matter, as long as the rope held.

Aldwin knotted the rope, tugged on the length trailing from the wall to be sure it was secure, and then stepped away to face her again. He'd given her just enough lead to sit or lie down on the blanket when she got tired.

If Lady L could reach him, she'd gouge his eyes out. Without doubt.

"How kind of you, sir," she muttered, "for tying me to the wall."

"Now I know you will still be here when I return from watering Rom. Once I come back, I will start the fire." He spun on his heel, then glanced back at her. "No *lady* would have set one foot within that tavern. She would have sent someone else."

‡ ‡ ‡

Blinking against the breeze, Leona watched Aldwin lead Rom toward the river. They disappeared behind a screen of brush, and the footsteps and the *clop* of hooves faded into the hissing wind.

She was alone.

For now.

She would *not* stand idle and wait for Aldwin to come sauntering back, his expression one of conceited triumph when he saw her tied as he'd left her. He'd trusted his bonds to keep her captive; she'd break free and show *him* who'd been the fool.

Turning to the stone wall, she raised her hands and inspected the ropes. Shivering, she dug her fingernails into the uppermost knot and tried to loosen it.

Aldwin's words rang in her mind, as if he stood at her back watching her. *You have more freckles than any lady I know. Your hands aren't soft and smooth; they're chapped from days of work. No lady would have set one foot within that tavern.*

He'd spoken true. Every word—almost. She had good reason, though, for the flaws he'd pointed out. In her opinion, they didn't make her any less of a noblewoman. Nobility stemmed from one's bloodlines, and someday, she hoped she had the chance to shove her family's documented lineage, tracing back to an earl in King William the Conqueror's royal court, in Aldwin's face.

She frowned down at the wretched knot. It wasn't yielding.

Lifting it her mouth, she gnawed at it.

Aldwin had found fault with her freckles? As long as she could remember, she'd had them. In her childhood, they'd come from time spent outdoors with Ward, each day filled with exciting adventures. After the bee stinging accident, she was taken by cart to the castle of one of her uncles, who knew a healer—"a witch who works miracles," he'd called her—with experience in treating severe stings. The poultices, herbal infusions, and leechings had saved Leona's life, and, once recovered, she'd stayed in her uncle's household to begin her formal tutoring to become a lady. She'd spent most of her days indoors, learning but also helping her aunt care for their young daughter, crippled at birth, who later died. Leona had cared deeply for the girl, and wept for her as if she were her own child.

When Leona received a missive from her father telling of Ward's death in an Eastern battle with the Turks, she'd returned to Pryerston. In the spring, her mother had perished in the fall from her horse, and Leona's sire, still grieving over the death of his only son and heir, plunged into drunken despair. Leona quickly realized she must step in to manage the castle. Ward would've assumed the responsibility, if he were alive. But he was gone, and the duty had fallen to her.

As money for the maintaining the keep dwindled, she'd had to let some of the paid guards go. Some of the servants, uncertain about the keep's future, disappeared in the night, taking their families with them. Putting aside her silk gowns, she'd donned commoners' clothes and toiled alongside the other castle folk, airing tapestries, scrubbing linens, tending the gardens, and whatever else needed to be done. All the while, she'd tried to rouse her father from his despondency and make him want to *live* again.

Her eyes stung as she studied the rope, slightly frayed from her teeth. Still, it didn't give.

Aldwin would return soon.

Hurry, Leona.

The wind gusted, rising to a wail when it scoured the ancient stone. The sound could be a human cry, the shriek of a tormented Roman soul. She shuddered.

Hurry!

Leona felt along the wall, hoping to find a protruding edge of stone to help wear down the rope. Her gaze traveled to the ground. By the edge of the blanket, she made out the shapes of semi-buried stones. If she found a rough bit . . .

She dropped to her knees on the blanket and scraped her palms across the earth. There. A jagged edge. Her breath rushed from her lips as she tilted her wrists to the stone and began to saw back and forth.

Sweat beaded on Leona's brow. She pressed harder into the stroke and flinched as stone scraped her flesh.

Back. Forth.

Oh, God. Hurry!

Over the rasp of the rope, she strained to hear sounds of Aldwin returning. If he saw what she was doing, he'd be furious. However, she might not get another chance to escape.

She could only imagine what Veronique was asking her father to do now. A memory flashed through Leona's mind, of Veronique strolling across Pryerston's bailey when she and the baron first arrived. She'd glanced over the looming keep and its outbuildings with an almost greedy interest. When her father had greeted her, Veronique had fluttered her lashes in a coy smile and dipped into a curtsey that displayed a scandalous amount of her cleavage.

Leona's father hadn't even appeared shocked.

An angry sob burned Leona's throat. She rammed her wrists against the stone.

The rope gave.

‡ ‡ ‡

His crossbow at the ready, Aldwin waited for Rom to finish drinking. The river lay like black stone chiseled in small waves by the wind. Reeds stirred close by along the bank, the rustling sound akin to a hidden assailant creeping nearer.

Adjusting his hold on his weapon, Aldwin assessed the patch of reeds. No reason for concern. The noise was caused by the wind, not a human opponent—or a Roman ghost. Those sightings of warrior spirits were mere stories, to keep children from venturing into the dangerous forest.

Shoving a hand through his mussed hair, he thought of Lady L standing alone in the eerie ruins, awaiting the fire and fare he'd promised. He'd see to those the moment he returned. Caring for Rom had taken priority, for the horse had borne the weight of two riders over a fair distance. Rom deserved a drink and a rest, especially when they'd be traveling on the morrow.

Aldwin trailed his hand down his horse's silky neck. The destrier had cost him almost his entire savings, but he and Rom would be together for many years. Every knight had a good steed; soon, hopefully, Aldwin would also have those coveted spurs of knighthood.

He thought again of his captive and the way she'd challenged him when he told her she was a courtesan. Her eyes lit with golden fire, her expression gut-wrenchingly beautiful, she'd roused in him a wave of desire and fury he could scarcely contain. *I am, indeed, of noble blood,* she'd said in that throaty way of hers. *If you believe you will go unpunished for kidnapping, mistreating, and binding me, you are mad. I will have your wretched arse.* Astonishing, that he could remember what she'd said, for all he could think of while she railed at him was hurling aside the rope, clamping his hands on her bottom, and yanking her flush against him for a plundering kiss.

Somehow, he'd managed to rein in that rash impulse. Confronting her point by point—her freckles, work-worn hands, and the like—was his only way to focus on something other than his need to kiss her.

And, also, from admitting her replies made perfect sense.

If Lady L *was* a woman of esteemed birth, he'd treated her badly. Many would consider his actions foolish and reckless— just like his firing a crossbow bolt into de Lanceau's chest—and deserving of punishment.

Rom raised his head, his coat rippling under Aldwin's palm. As Aldwin took hold of the horse's dangling reins, he wondered if he'd had any other recourse but to seize Lady L and whisk her off into the night? Nay. His actions had kept de Lanceau's pendant safe, and if she had any information on Veronique and the baron's whereabouts, Aldwin's duty required that he deliver her to de Lanceau for questioning.

"Whoever she is, though," Aldwin murmured, "we will find out."

Rom's hooves scraped on the riverbank as Aldwin turned toward the forest. After tethering Rom in a sheltered spot, he'd start the fire and offer her the bread and cheese in his saddlebag. A rather plain meal for a lady, but 'twould do.

When they neared the dark ruins, Aldwin called out, "Lady L." Best to alert her to his approach. She'd been uneasy traveling through the woods, and he didn't want her to mistake him for an undead Roman.

No reply.

Grinning, he shook his head. She didn't answer because she was furious he'd left her tied. He imagined her standing against the wall, fuming, her chin at that fetching angle that warned him she was in a temper.

"I did not wish to startle you," he said as the area where he'd left her came into view. "I—" His voice faded to a groan.

After tethering Rom to another part of the wall, he ran to where the rope dangled to the ground. It was still tied to the bonds that had encircled her wrists.

Squatting, he examined the cut rope. Worn through. She'd rubbed it against a stone.

Or someone had cut her loose.

Aldwin shoved to standing, concern and rage boiling inside him. He shouldn't have left her alone.

She could be in mortal danger.

‡ ‡ ‡

Leona darted into the forest. Beneath the trees, little moonlight reached the ground—excellent for hiding, but not for making a quick escape. Still, she'd rather break both her legs than be tied to the wall and at Aldwin's mercy.

Wind whistled through the leaves and branches overhead. Moonlight spliced through the shadows to reveal mounds of earth with parts of stone walls thrusting through—evidence of more ancient ruins buried over the centuries by flooding. Some of the trees had fallen, creating a tangle of branches that blocked her path.

The perfect place for a bees' nest.

Fear clouded her mind. Being summer, there could be hundreds of nests in the forest. If she stumbled upon one in the dark . . .

But she wouldn't. Oh, God, she *wouldn't!*

A sickly sweat broke across Leona's skin, but she picked her way around the trees and pressed on. Flattening against a broad trunk, she snatched a breath and listened for any signs of pursuit. Was she headed toward the road? She hoped so. While she couldn't see the glimmer of the river any longer, that didn't mean she was traveling in the right direction.

A rustling noise came from a nearby patch of ferns. She froze, pressing back against a tree, while she strained to hear more. Had Aldwin come looking for her already? Had she been so preoccupied with her escape that she hadn't heard him stalking her?

She held her breath. The night itself seemed a living entity. Close by, she sensed creatures she couldn't see.

Animals. Aye. *Not* Roman ghosts.

Afraid of the night? God's teeth, Leona! Your will is as soft as pastry dough—just like all the other pale-skinned ladies who don't have freckles. No warrior worth spit is afraid of a little darkness.

Mentally squashing her unease, she looked down at the ground for some kind of weapon to defend herself. Broken stones. Sticks. Enough to fight with, if need be.

She lowered to a crouch. The rustling grew louder, followed by a scampering sound. A fawn bounded through a slant of light, toward a doe standing watch in the shadows. Leona blew out a sigh. Not Aldwin or . . . a ghostly Roman.

As she continued on, more ruins emerged from the shadows, and then she saw the deer track winding through the woods. The one they'd traveled earlier? Her body warmed with a surge of hope.

She hurried forward. Branches, hidden by layers of rotting leaves, crackled beneath her boots. She paused, her heartbeat pounding. Had Aldwin heard the noise?

Please, nay!

She waited long moments, afraid to even reach up to wipe the sweat from her face. If he'd heard, he wasn't racing toward her. Daring to continue on, she walked onto the trail.

Aldwin stood leaning against a tree, holding his crossbow. The weapon pointed toward the ground, but was nevertheless cocked.

Their gazes locked in the darkness.

The skin across her breasts tingled. The pendant's weight brushing her cleavage seemed even more noticeable, somehow, as if she'd suddenly become aware of every place it touched.

An awful sense of entrapment squeezed in upon her. Was this how a deer felt when it faced the hunter about to bring it to its knees?

Aldwin made no move, yet she sensed him preparing his trap to close in on her.

"How did you get free?" His voice sounded deceptively soft. Almost admiring.

"I rubbed the rope against a stone."

He nodded, and his eyes narrowed a fraction. Somehow, she knew he was relieved by her answer. Had he thought someone else had cut her loose?

As though following her thoughts, he said, "These are hazardous woods, Lady L. I did not mention before, but there are poachers' traps—"

"And knaves who kidnap ladies," she cut in. "Those are the most dangerous of all."

He smiled. "Come back with me now."

"Nay."

"*Nay?*" His voice reminded her of the growl of thunder. "We both know I am in command here."

Aldwin had spoken to her in the same manner years ago, while Ward was tying her to the tree. What *he'd* wanted was all that mattered. And look what had happened then.

Familiar rage and anguish whipped through Leona. She

hated for Aldwin to see her trembling—to see her weak—but she couldn't control the tremors. The thought of being tied, helpless, with him deciding what happened to her, made her want to scream. "I am not going back with you."

He eased away from the tree. "Lady L, start walking toward the river." He pointed. "That way."

Leona shook her head.

His fingers flexed on the crossbow. "Let us be sensible and make this easy on both of us."

"Easiest," she said, "for you."

"Agreed. Yet we both know you cannot escape me."

She took a step back. A deliberate taunt. "You will not shoot me."

"We discussed this earlier." His smile hardened. "I warn you. Do not tempt me."

"If you shoot me—injure me—you will have to care for my wound. The inconvenience will delay your return to Branton Keep. If the injury becomes corrupt, I might die. You will not risk it."

She took another backward step, her boots crushing dry leaves.

Aldwin matched her retreat with a forward step. "I have cared for wounds before. The inconvenience will not deter me."

Would he really shoot her? The uncompromising set of his jaw warned he would, indeed, fire the weapon.

"Do not tempt me, Lady L," he said again, very quietly. "I have given you ample warning."

He had. However, she must escape, and not only because she wanted her freedom. Aldwin had spoken before of responsibilities; the good folk of Pryerston Keep needed her help, now more than ever. Her sire couldn't rid the castle of Veronique and the baron on his own.

Leona took another step away from Aldwin, shivering inside as his mouth tightened. She'd almost reached the trees. He might be an expert shot, but if she dodged and wove, as in the game she and Ward had played in the woods, she might outwit Aldwin. At some point, he'd run out of bolts.

Aldwin edged nearer. He moved as though his body were tightly coiled, waiting for the precise moment to lunge. Just as he raised the crossbow, his right boot sank into the earth.

"What—?" he muttered.

Leona spun, her cloak whirling at her ankles, and dashed into the trees.

Aldwin roared an oath.

Her breath scorching her lungs, she darted from side to side, behind bushes, trees, and low branches. The forest became a muddied blur of light and murky shadows.

Run, Leona!

Footfalls crashed behind her. Too close behind.

The toe of her boot slammed into a buried branch, causing her to pitch forward. She gasped, regained her balance, and rushed on.

The footsteps behind her quieted.

Panic rushed through her. Pausing the barest moment, she glanced back, raising her hand to sweep hair out of her eyes.

The forest behind her was empty.

Silent.

Wrong!

Oh, God! Run!

As Leona spurred herself forward, she heard a faint *click*. The sound of a firing crossbow.

Before she could gasp, the steel-tipped bolt slammed into her.

CHAPTER SEVEN

Aldwin lowered the crossbow, loaded another bolt, and shrugged aside the tension knotting his shoulder muscles. His arms ached with the need to slam his fist into the nearest tree.

He'd warned Lady L.

Her foolish protest was finished.

Leaves smashed under his boots as he strode toward her. She stood in a stream of moonlight, tugging at the bolt buried in the oak behind her. The steel tip had pierced the lower part of her wide cloak sleeve and pinned it the tree, holding her fast.

Her breaths came in desperate gasps. Eyes luminous, she glanced at him, streaks of her hair cutting across her cheek, before she looked back at the bolt and gave it another tug.

Cloth tore.

"Please," she moaned.

In that one word, Aldwin heard a plea, a curse, and a wealth of frustration. He steeled himself against the instinctive bloom of sympathy, drawing instead upon the rage and desire humming like a dark song in his blood. He'd tried to be gallant. He'd warned her, offered her the chance to return to the ruins of her own free will, and she'd refused to cooperate.

Now she'd accept the consequences.

Lady L muttered under her breath, words he couldn't distinguish. No matter. What he'd hear, from her lips, was acknowledgment that he'd won this confrontation. She'd admit she couldn't escape him.

Five more strides and he stood close enough to catch her scent, piquant in the damp earthiness of the night forest. He breathed her in, her fragrance filling his mind until all he sensed was her. Desire tugged at his loins, coaxing him to claim that gap between them.

She must have sensed his unruly emotions, for her hand, clasped around the bolt, fell away. Caution shadowed her features as she faced him, her trapped arm spread wide, her other arm at her side.

"The chase is done, Lady L."

Defiance hardened her gaze.

"When I remove the bolt, you will come with me. No running. No fighting."

Her chin nudged up. Moonlight glistened on her full, pursed mouth. She clearly wasn't going to agree he'd bested her.

His control snapped, like a weighty branch breaking and plummeting to the ground. *Beware your recklessness, Aldwin. Remember how your impulsiveness caused you to almost murder de Lanceau.*

More powerful than his conscience, however, was the need to conquer her willfulness.

Now.

He stepped nearer, raising the crossbow. Closer again, and

the bolt's tip nudged the front of her cloak. Resting, he realized with a flare of lust, above the roundness of her right breast.

Her breath hitched. Her lips moved with a swallow.

"Tell me you concede." He hardly recognized that ragged voice as his own.

"If"—she swallowed again—"I do not?"

God's blood! It seemed she was even more impetuous than he. Forcing a wicked smile, he said, "Then you leave me no choice."

"W-what choice?" she whispered, her gaze astonishingly steady, despite the weapon against her breast.

Anger hammered against his temple. How good 'twould feel to give voice to his fury, to yell into the night and hear it echo around them. She'd take that display of emotion, though, as another victory in her fight with him.

To subdue her will, he must be controlled. Relentless.

Persuasive.

A tiny groan welled inside him as he slid the crossbow, achingly slowly, across her cloak. Apprehension flickered in her eyes, but she made no sound as the bolt whispered between her breasts. Over the raised swell of the pendant. Down the plane of her belly. At last, he ended the contact, withdrawing the crossbow to hold it pointing down against his side.

She exhaled a tense sigh.

Before the sound faded, he moved, forcing their bodies into intimate proximity. She struggled, but, raising his hand, he pressed it against the pale slope of her neck. His thumb and forefinger fitted against her throat.

So very soft, her skin. Smooth, like a lady's. Unblemished, apart from her freckles. A silent, appreciative growl rumbled inside him.

Propping his thumb under her chin, he forced her head back against the bark. She tried to twist away, but he held her firm. Her liquid glaze sparked with loathing so intense, he guessed she connected this moment with a past indignity. Again, he thought of Leona Ransley's defiance, but quickly shoved the memory aside. Whatever had happened to Lady L was hers to resolve; right now, she needed to heed him.

"I should leave you here," he muttered, "to spend the night alone, without warmth or food."

"Fine," she shot back.

"What a find for the poachers, when they come to check their traps."

Her lashes lowered a fraction.

"I wonder what they would do, when they found you?"

"They would let me go."

Aldwin laughed. "I do not think so."

She jerked at his touch. His hand splayed wider, capturing more of her. He found her pulse, thumping beneath her skin.

"Is that what you intend, then? To leave me here?"

Aldwin leaned in closer, bringing his mouth next to hers. "After your foolishness tonight, I would gladly do just that." He shut his eyes against the fury boiling within him. "A less skilled marksman might have killed you. To risk your life, in such a foolhardy manner . . ."

"I had to escape."

His opened his eyes to hold her gaze. "I will never let you go. Nor will you escape me. Your life is mine now."

She thrashed in his hold. "Never!"

"Aye."

"You—!"

He lowered his lips. Chased her breath. Pressed his mouth over hers.

She shrieked against his lips while shaking her head from side to side. Strands of her hair caught in the bark like shimmering spiderwebs.

"Mine," he growled.

Where their mouths met, warmth seeped into him, a tantalizing heat different from aught he'd ever known before. She was akin to a summer deluge—threatening to drown him with his desire, but so beautiful, he couldn't deny himself. Her lush lips and downy skin coaxed him to touch and explore her. She gasped, no doubt indignant, while he slanted his lips across hers again, taking what he craved.

Impulsive, Aldwin, his conscience yelped. *Take heed. If she is a lady . . .*

He blocked out the annoying voice, just as he ignored her muffled shrieks. How he wanted her. The force of his need sent a tremor jolting through him. His mouth continued to plunder hers, while his hand shifted, urging her head back even further. He pressed his lower body flush against her, their hips joined as closely as possible with their garments between them. A movement designed not only to intimidate her, but prevent her from kneeing him in the groin—for she seemed angry enough to try such.

She wrenched her mouth from his. Spluttered. Struggled.

He trailed his lips across the indent at the corner of her mouth, along the line of her jaw, and down her neck's creamy curve; tiny, calculated kisses that delivered a sensory attack.

The sweetness of her skin . . . Addictive.

"Stop!" she gasped, her hand swatting his arm. Not enough force, though, behind the punch to do him harm.

"Stop?" He nibbled her neck. "Why?"

"I—" She shuddered.

Aldwin nibbled again, this time drawing her skin between his teeth.

"That is not—" She shivered. "I-I mean—"

He sensed her defiance wavering.

At last.

"You tempted me tonight," he said against her mouth, "more than once. Why should I not indulge my pleasure?"

"Nay!"

"Aye, Lady L." He skimmed his thumb across her bottom lip, relishing her short, angry moan.

Her moist gaze lifted, piercing him with her anguish. "Cease"—she spoke with tremendous effort—"and I will go with you."

Triumph whooshed through him. The words he wanted to hear. Still, he couldn't stop himself from taking one last kiss. "Willingly?" he asked against her mouth.

"A-aye."

"If you try to deceive me—"

"I give you my word."

He chuckled before nuzzling the plane of her cheek. "Easier to trust a starved lion."

"What would a bastard like you know about lions?"

The resentment in her voice made him pause. He wasn't born out of wedlock. He might have enjoyed impressing that significant fact upon her, but his thoughts had already traveled back to Ward's last days. Sitting by Ward's bedside, listening to his fever-induced ramblings about the hot desert lands while the strength seeped from his dying body, had been torment. But Aldwin had owed those difficult days to Ward, because of their game gone awry many summers ago, when Ward's sister perished.

"I know more about lions, Lady L, than you can ever imagine." Aldwin stepped back, adjusted his hold on the crossbow, and tipped his head. "Move."

‡ ‡ ‡

Leona trudged through the forest, aware of Aldwin close behind her. Holding her head high, she fought the frustration gnawing at her. She *would* escape him. She *would* find a way back to Pryerston Keep. He couldn't keep watch on her with his crossbow forever.

The night wind stirred her hair, and she brushed strands from her lips, hating the way her mouth felt hot and tender from his kisses. Her neck still sensed his callused fingers pressing against her, and her innards . . .

She wouldn't think of those sensations. Ever again.

"Veer left," Aldwin said, before a splintered, moss-covered stump became visible in the darkness ahead.

Without giving any indication she'd heard his order, she changed direction. With a wry laugh, he followed.

His laughter seemed to find its way inside her, to poke at memories she'd tried to keep trapped in her consciousness. But from the instant his mouth had crushed down upon hers, the memories had floated free. Once again, she was eight years old and unable to get away, while Sir Aldwin with the make-believe sword forced her chin up. Ignoring her protests, he pressed his lips to hers.

Her first kiss. Quick. Passionless. Not at all like his kisses tonight. Somehow, though, that past moment had stuck in her mind and refused to fade. Mayhap because 'twas the one and only kiss she'd ever experienced, until moments ago.

How many nights had she lain awake in her bed at her uncle's keep, staring up at the overhead beams while thinking of that fleeting kiss? Wondering why, as part of his game, Aldwin had insisted upon it? She'd heard many knightly tales since then, and not all of the heroes kissed their ladies before heading off to combat.

Mayhap one day she'd know his reasons.

Or not.

Even if he did remember what he was thinking long ago, he wouldn't tell her. Not unless he knew who she really was. She'd rather be sucked dry by leeches than reveal her true identity and thereby implicate her sire in the stealing of the pendant.

Also, Aldwin would have to trust her to confide in her. That wasn't likely.

Easier to trust a starved lion, he'd said, suggesting he knew all about lions. How? Had he been to the East and seen them firsthand, like Ward? Not that she knew.

While she'd never seen a lion herself, she'd heard stories of the great beasts with shaggy manes, huge teeth, and roars so fearsome, they'd send children screaming. Ward's drawings and notes in his sketchbook, delivered to Pryerston after his death, had created a clear picture of such awe-inspiring animals.

For Aldwin to say he knew about lions was arrogant. And a lie.

Holding onto a tree branch for balance, she stepped over a raised, uneven section of wall obscured by fallen leaves. Hearing Aldwin come up behind her, she released the branch to snap back against him, and smiled at his irritated grunt.

"That way." He pointed his crossbow at a slight incline.

"'Tis easier to go that direction," she countered, gesturing.

"True, but I wish to get back to Rom." The crossbow bolt nudged her back. "Go."

Rebellion seethed inside her, but she started forward. Truth be told, she was exhausted. A drink, a cheery fire, and a meal would be—

Her foot slipped on uneven ground. She gasped, just as Aldwin's arm slid around her from behind, steadying her and stopping her from falling. At his touch, heat shot through her body, and she lurched away.

A fallen tree blocked her path, but she marched on, climbing up over it and down the other side. She'd ducked behind similar trees when playing chase through the woods with Ward. Once, he'd given her a clear shot while he stood looking for her. When she hit him in the arse with a slingshot-fired acorn, he'd yelped like a girl.

How she wished she had a slingshot this eve.

Not far ahead, river water glistened between the trees. The air smelled of damp loam.

Another large, fallen tree. She scrambled over it, glad to get her feet on solid ground. Yet she'd taken no more than five steps when the earth beneath her shifted and seemed about to disintegrate.

Leona hesitated, her arms splayed wide.

"Keep moving."

She glanced back at Aldwin, standing on the log behind her. "'Tis not safe. The ground—"

Her boots began to sink into the earth. Spinning her arms so she didn't fall, she scrambled back.

Aldwin climbed down from the log. "What is wrong?"

"I—Oh!"

The dirt beneath her slid away, as though being swallowed by an underground monster.

"Lady L!"

Leona shrieked.

The cry still burning her throat, she plunged into darkness.

CHAPTER EIGHT

Aldwin hurried toward the gaping hole where Lady L had disappeared. Dread mocked him for forcing her to take the route he wanted—because he could.

A *splash* echoed from belowground.

Lady L gasped, the sound clearly wrenched from her lungs. "Oh, God."

A sharp sigh left his lips. She was alive. Was she hurt?

Setting aside his crossbow, Aldwin crouched before the yawning cavity. He couldn't see her at all, only blackness. Where his hands pressed, dirt crumbled down into the hole.

"Lady L?"

More splashes. A spitting sound, then a cough, rose from below.

"Are you all right?" His voice resonated, carried back up to him by the darkness.

"I . . . think so." A shaky sigh. "The water is not too deep. W-where am I?"

"You may have fallen into a buried building." He tried to keep his tone steady and calm. "Do not worry. I will get you out."

Water sloshed. "Ow! God's teeth—"

"Hold still. I will fetch a torch."

"Something is moving down here." Lady L's voice wavered.

"Stay still. I will be right back."

"Y-you cannot leave me here!"

"I will be quick. I promise."

Her angry snort echoed. "If you *dare* leave me here . . ."

You will do what? his mind taunted. But he'd heard her anxiety. More insistent than his longing to taunt her was the need to know she was safe. He was responsible for her life and well-being.

Aldwin pushed to standing and retrieved his crossbow. With a gritty whisper, dirt fell down into the hole.

More spitting. "You did that on purpose!"

Her furious muttering chased him as he headed toward the river.

Rom stood in the shelter of the wall where Aldwin had left him. The destrier raised his head and snuffled a greeting.

After untying the rope still secured to the wall and rolling up the blanket on the ground, he shoved them into his saddlebag. He untethered Rom and led him into the woods, closer to where Lady L had fallen and where he'd be better protected from the elements. Aldwin withdrew a flint from his bag, snatched up some dry brush, and lit a small fire, then shoved a branch into the flames. Each step seemed to take an eternity.

What if Lady L had refused to stay still? What if she'd fallen in the water and knocked her head? What if the creature she'd heard moving down there was a starved predator?

He glared at the branch. *Catch fire.*

With a faint crackle, the wood finally caught. He slung his saddlebag over his shoulder, and, cupping his hand before the flame, hurried back to the cavity in the ground.

"Aldwin?" Lady L's voice rose up to him.

"Aye." He knelt and dropped his crossbow and bag on the ground, wondering if she sensed how relieved he was to hear her voice.

"T-thank God."

"Stand aside. I will lower down the torch."

"Stand aside," she repeated. "I cannot even see my fingers before my face."

Holding the branch between his knees, Aldwin knotted the rope around it, and then lowered it into the inkiness. The flame sputtered. He saw Lady L standing a fair distance below, up to her waist in water, but little else of where she'd fallen. As he'd ordered, she stepped backward, her garments dragging in the depths; she'd obviously understood he wanted to protect her from the swaying flame, and that she'd take the branch when 'twas at a level she could reach.

While he fed the rope down, he wondered if 'twas wise for him to give her a weapon. Still, if she wished him harm, there must be rocks to pick up in the water and throw. At this point, since he was her only means out of the ground, she'd be foolish to attack him. If she seemed to be contemplating an assault, he'd remind her of that fact.

Wind blew against his back and he shivered, thinking of the fire still burning. He stopped lowering the rope. "Can you take the torch now?"

"A-aye." Teeth chattering, she sloshed over to it. Stifling a pang of regret, he waited while she caught hold of branch and untied it with shaking hands.

The rope slithered loose.

With brisk tugs, he whisked back up.

"W-what—?" she choked out.

"I am not leaving you."

"Then w-what are you doing? Aldwin!"

He turned away from the cavity, strode to the fallen tree, and knotted the rope around a stout branch. After stamping out the fire, he returned to the hole where faint light now glimmered. He slipped his saddlebag and crossbow onto his shoulder, then grabbed hold of the rope. He slid into the cavity.

As he descended, he realized Lady L had fallen into an underground cavern. She no longer stood in the liquid depths, but on a mud bank strewn with rocks, fallen trees, branches, and other debris. Holding the torch high, she was taking a good look at the surroundings. From the slow but clear-flowing water, he guessed the cave had been gouged out by years of rising and diminishing floodwaters, and that the current joined the rest of the river not far away.

Still holding tight to the rope while he hovered just above the water, he shifted his weight. The rope began to swing. Not far to the large rock jutting from the water, and then, but a leap to the bank.

To *her*.

As he swung nearer the rock, Lady L turned, and their gazes locked. She looked utterly bedraggled. Her wet hair spilled down the front of her dripping cloak caked with mud. Her gaze, though, seemed strong and clear. A good sign. Hopefully she hadn't suffered any injuries in her fall.

His boots scraped the rock. He dropped onto it, and then leapt to the bank.

As Lady L wiped water from her face, Aldwin squared his

shoulders, preparing for the verbal flaying she'd no doubt unleash upon him for causing her to end up in this place.

She gestured to the ground. "Look."

He dared a glance. Half-buried in the mud by his feet lay broken columns and chunks of pottery.

"There is more beneath the water."

"Swept here by floods," he guessed aloud.

The torchlight shifted and cast long shadows. He followed her gaze upward to the haphazard ceiling of rock, decaying trees, and mud.

"The c-creature I heard before might be l-living up there." Her throat moved with a loud swallow. "W-will that ceiling c-collapse upon us?"

"We are safe enough, I vow."

Her attention snapped back to him. Her body shook as she thrust the torch up toward the hole. "Safe? As I was, w-walking over unstable g-ground?"

A flush warmed his cheekbones. "I did not expect the earth to give way."

"I t-tried to tell you, but you w-would not l-listen." Her brows drew together. "You were too busy g-gloating."

Aldwin scowled. If she weren't soaked, and if this situation weren't entirely his fault, he might have grabbed her by the front of her cloak, hauled her up onto her tiptoes, and growled in her face. He could roar loudly enough to startle the challenge from her eyes.

If she still didn't yield, he'd kiss her again.

His loins heated at the thought, and, his scowl deepening, he shoved the inconvenient desire away. Indulging his temper would solve naught. This wench might test every single one of his knightly values, but she would *not* get the better of him.

"Very well," he agreed. "I was gloating."

She rolled her eyes.

"Therefore, I accept full blame for our circumstances."

She set her hand on her hip. "Good."

"Since 'tis my fault you fell in here, I take complete responsibility for getting you out."

"Thank you." Her boots squelched as she started toward the rope. "Now, if you w-will help me—"

"Of course. As soon as 'tis light."

Her back to him, Lady L froze. He sensed her struggle to control her ire. "What did you say?"

"We will climb out in the morn. 'Twill be safer."

She turned, very slowly. Her lips, bluish purple in the dim light, flattened, and she eyed him as though he were the one who'd fallen through the ground—and cracked his skull on the way.

"You c-cannot mean to spend the n-night here."

"Why not? There is plenty of firewood." He patted his saddlebag. "I have food and drink."

Lady L shook her head. "I am *n-not*—"

"'Tis only for one night. I agree 'tis not the most comfortable place. Certainly not what a *lady* is used to, but—"

He sensed the moment her patience shattered. Her lips curled back from her teeth in a growl.

The torch hissed through the air, spitting smoke. Wielding it like a sword, she slashed at his stomach. A deft thrust. Who'd taught her to swordfight?

"Stop this foolishness, Lady L."

She slashed again. He dodged the strike. Just.

"Injure me," he warned, "and we will be here longer than

one night."

"You might be. I will climb the rope by myself." Again, she struck out, the torch slicing the air with a menacing *hiss*.

"You cannot ride Rom. Remember?"

Hiss. "Then I will go on foot."

Aldwin leapt back. His boot heels skidded on loose rocks, and he felt the heat of the torch whistle close to his body. "Who will protect you from the poachers?"

Her chin jutted up. "I can defend myself."

She tensed to strike again.

He studied. Waited.

The flame swung toward him. Lunging forward, he caught her wrist. "Who will protect you," he said, "from yourself?"

They stood together, frozen like ancient statues, while the torch crackled and spit.

As if she'd been stabbed, a moan broke from her. Her hand holding the torch opened, and the flame clattered to the ground.

He released her wrist.

"What did you say?" Her voice was barely a whisper.

Frowning, he repeated, "Who will protect you from yourself?"

A terrible sadness haunted Lady L's gaze before a violent tremor shook her. She spun, crossed to a pile of rubble, and slumped down on a large rock. She dropped her face into her hands.

Aldwin stooped and picked up the torch, which, thank God, had not gone out. What in hellfire had just happened?

He crossed to her. "Lady L?"

Her shoulders stiffened, but she didn't glance up.

"What is wrong?"

Raising her head, she looked at him, her expression stark with anguish. "Go away."

Her pain gouged deep. The chivalrous part of his nature urged him to sit beside her, slip his arm around her, and murmur soothing words. He'd do such for any woman in distress. At the very least, he'd like to understand why his words had upset her.

But caution also clamored inside him. She was a cunning wench, determined to escape. If he let down his wariness for a moment to comfort her, she might try to deceive him.

As though aware of his dilemma, she hugged herself and turned her face away. "Stand guard at that wretched r-rope, for all I care. L-leave me alone."

‡ ‡ ‡

Ignoring the freezing water trickling down into her lap, Leona willed Aldwin to walk away. She sensed his keen stare upon her until, at last, he left her side.

Good. For she was within a breath of picking up the nearest rock and hurling it at him. Thanks to Ward's tutelage, she never missed.

She blew out a weary breath and tried catch hold of her emotions unraveling inside her. *Who will protect you from yourself?* How many times had Ward said those exact words? To hear them from Aldwin had been a complete shock.

A scraping noise echoed in the cavern, and she dared a glance. Aldwin squatted some distance away, mounding branches and debris to start a fire. When he reached for another bit of wood, his hose stretched over his thighs, outlining thick-hewn muscles.

Leona looked away, forcing aside the memory of those broad thighs pinned against her in the forest. Shivering again, she hugged her arms tighter across her soggy bodice. What a peculiar predicament, for her heart to ache so fiercely, while her body turned numb.

Who will protect you from yourself? Usually Ward had said that right before she intended to take a risk.

Such as the night he'd caught her in Pryerston's armory, a few weeks before she was stung by the bees.

"What are you up to?"

Starting at the sound of her brother's voice, she spun around, almost dropping the helm in her hands. Ward stood in the armory doorway, his shoulder-length hair shining in the light cast by the wall torch.

Crossing his scrawny arms, Ward leaned against the embrasure and leveled her a stern look.

She'd never get away with her plan now.

"Leona?" He raised one eyebrow, a gesture he'd inherited from their sire. Her brother, though, was nowhere near as intimidating. More often than not, she could turn his brotherly scowl into a reluctant grin. Mayhap she could persuade him to help her?

"I needed a helm," she said, holding up the one in her hands. It looked too large for her head. However, she could stuff undergarments inside to tighten the fit and would grow into it.

"Why do you need a helm?"

The tricky question. If her palms didn't stop sweating, she'd drop the wretched headpiece on the floor. What a colossal clang *that would make. "One day, I might need one."*

His frown intensified. "You are eight years old."

"I know, but—"

"You are a lady, Leona." He sighed. "We fight with pretend swords and wrestle in the lake, but that is just play. You are not destined to fight battles."

She managed a lazy little shrug. "How do you know? What if you and Father are not able to defend the keep and it is attacked?"

Ward tsked.

"'Tis a wise question."

"Father would leave enough men-at-arms to defend Pryerston. When you are grown, your husband will deal with such matters."

Husband? Ugh. "What if he is away settling a dispute in another part of our lands?"

"He will have assigned another to handle such matters for him." Her brother shook his head. "Leona, be sensible."

"I am. I do not want to be a lady. I wish to train to be a squire, like you." Frustration thickened her voice. "I hate learning to embroider. I cannot stand those quiet games, and that boring chatter drives me mad!"

A grin tugged at her brother's lips. Oh, marvelous. Maybe she could convince him, after all.

Her silk gown rustled as she again stepped closer. "I will take this helm and leave, now. Do not tell Father, all right?"

Ward snorted.

"Why do you make that foul noise?"

"Because I know you. If trouble is to be had with that helm, you will find it."

"Not true," she grumbled. But he was probably right.

Ward eased away from the door. His gaze tender, he closed the distance between them and put his hand on her shoulder. "When will you stop trying to be a boy? You are a girl." He smiled. "The most beautiful sister in all of England."

A blush warmed her face. "You are trying to sway me. You want me to put down the helm, return to my chamber, and say no more about being a squire."

"Father does not need two sons. He loves you as his daughter."

An awful tightness filled her breast. "He wished I were a son.

We have both heard him say how he regrets his second boy was stillborn."

"Father loves you, Leona. Never forget that. And no matter what you say or do, you will always be one of the fairer sex. A lady who deserves a protector."

She squarely met Ward's gaze. "I am not some wilting damsel. I do not need you, or anyone else, to defend me. I can fire a slingshot as well as you. I can ride a horse equally well, and last time, I hit more targets with rocks."

An affectionate smile touched his mouth. "You are also stubborn of will, hot-tempered, and far too curious for your own good."

She huffed a breath. "Well—!"

He plucked the helm from her hands and set it with the others. "As much as you might deserve that helm, Leona, I cannot let you have it. For who will protect you from yourself?"

The tang of smoke wafted to Leona, drawing her from her thoughts. Daring a glance, she saw Aldwin setting more branches on the fire that had just begun to burn.

He looked up at her and shook his head, as though he didn't like what he saw. She tried to quell him with a disdainful glare— the kind that had even made Ward squirm—but her teeth were chattering so badly, 'twas impossible.

Muttering under his breath, Aldwin dropped the last of the debris on the fire and reached for his saddlebag. Pushing up the leather flap, he rummaged inside and withdrew a garment. He rose and marched toward her. His boots sounded an ominous *crunch, crunch*.

Aldwin looked angry enough to ram that clothing down her throat.

Trying to ignore her rising alarm, she shoved to her feet and walked down to the river. Her garments clung to her legs, while water ran down her ankles into her boots. She tried to imagine a scorching summer day, with a sun as golden-orange as the torchlight reflected in the river. It cast enough light to see her reflection; she also saw Aldwin change his direction and stride toward her.

"Lady L."

She stooped to pick up a broken stick. Two good, dry pieces to put on the fire.

His scuffed boots appeared in her line of vision. She was still bent over at the waist, her hand rising from the ground. He stood close enough she could touch his boots' muddy toes. To stand so near was a blatant disregard for the invisible boundaries between strangers.

Mayhap, after their kiss in the forest, he didn't consider her a stranger to him anymore?

If he thought such, he was a bold man indeed.

Aldwin didn't move or speak, but waited for her to notice him. Another attempt to intimidate her.

She reached for another stick.

"Lady L," he repeated. His tone implied if she didn't immediately rise and look at him, there would be repercussions.

Making certain their bodies didn't touch, she straightened, the sticks clenched in her hand. Her face came level with his neck. Strands of his blond hair were caught in his cloak's fastening and for one, ridiculous moment, she wanted to reach out and brush them aside.

What *was* she thinking?

"You wished to s-speak to me?" she said.

"Aye." His brows raised. "For a moment, I thought I might have to request an audience with you."

If he didn't understand she had no wish to talk to him, 'twas not her fault. Indicating the sticks, she said, "We w-will need more f-firewood."

He nodded. "We shall, for the fire to last until dawn."

"Good, then I—"

"Thank you."

"—s-shall continue."

Wait. *Thank you?*

Their gazes locked. Leona shivered, and not entirely from cold. His masculine scent taunted her, a reminder of their bodies crushed together. Her treacherous mouth heated, as though remembering how his lips had claimed hers.

Or wished they would.

God's bones! Was she becoming addled over this arrogant knave?

Anger at her own idiotic thoughts brought heat to her face. She began to turn away.

"Hold," he said and then sighed. "I mean—"

An odd note in his voice made her pause.

"I am . . . sorry for . . . upsetting you earlier. Whatever I said . . ."

Irritation glittered in his eyes, but also genuine concern. If he looked at a woman that way for long, she'd become utterly witless.

Leona looked down at the sticks. "Thank you." Why, suddenly, couldn't she put more than two words together?

He pushed the garment he was holding toward her. "Here."

Oh, nay. She was *not* going to wear his clothes. Her own might be wet, but they'd dry while she sat by the fire. To smell him against her skin all eve would be sheer torment.

Shaking her head, she said, "I am—"

"Cold. I know."

"After I have w-warmed myself by the fire, I w-will—"

"Still be cold. Your garments are soaked. Your fingernails are blue." He offered the garment again. "Wear my tunic. 'Tis not a woman's garb, but 'tis dry and warm. You might fall ill if you sleep in those sodden clothes and boots."

She certainly didn't want to succumb to sickness. Not when she needed to escape and find her way back to Pryerston. Still . . .

Before she could say another word, Aldwin raised his hand. "I can guess your reasons for wanting to refuse, and I respect your stubborn pride. However, you know 'tis the wisest decision."

He spoke as though 'twere the *only* decision. She frowned.

As Leona sucked in a breath to reply, he draped the tunic over her arm. "'Tis only a temporary inconvenience." He gestured to the fire, now a sizeable blaze. "We will lay your clothes and boots out to dry. With luck, they will be all right to wear in the morn. My tunic will go back in my saddlebag and no one will ever know."

"Except us."

He nodded, once, before he shrugged. "I will not tell. Will you?"

"Of course not." Leona cringed, for her shrill tone made her sound uneasy. Weak.

After shoving the sticks into his hand, she snatched up the tunic. "Let us get on with it, then."

For the briefest moment, Aldwin looked stunned. He'd obviously expected her to put up more of a protest.

"Are you surprised I agree with you? 'Tis only for one night." She arched an eyebrow. "As you said, staying in wet garments might make me ill. I couldn't escape then, could I?"

His face darkened with a scowl.

A giggle welled inside Leona while she spun and took three steps toward the fire—before coming to an abrupt halt. She tried not to shudder, but between the frigid cling of her garments and the unsettling realization . . . "Um . . . One more thought."

His lazy footfalls came up behind her. "Mmm?"

She faced him. Judging by his grin, he'd guessed her dilemma.

"I will not peek," he said.

"You certainly will not! Neither will you watch my reflection in the water."

He glanced at the river. "I had not thought of such. That is, until you so kindly pointed it out."

Leona growled a sigh. "I will find a spot where you cannot see." Whirling around again, she stomped past the fire, looking left and right. Despite its brilliant gleam, the light didn't reach all of the cavern's shadows.

"Over there." Aldwin waved at a boulder barely visible along the wall. "I will give you the torch." Crossing to the flaming branch, he pulled it from between two tightly wedged rocks and handed it to her. "Do not be long."

"Might there be a way out, behind the boulder, I wonder?" She raised the torch so its light played over the cavern wall.

"I cannot say." Aldwin smiled, stooped near the fire, and withdrew a small pot from his saddlebag. "You will not have a chance to find out. If you are not back by the time I have heated some water, I will come and get you—whether or not you are dressed."

CHAPTER NINE

Lady L hurried toward the boulder, and Aldwin smothered a chuckle. 'Twas not fair of him to taunt her. Somehow, though, he couldn't help himself. Every sharpening of her gaze and willful tensing of her body sparked a fiery glow within him. She amused him, as well as being quite a handful.

A determined handful, he reminded himself, while he lowered the water-filled pot onto the iron trivet he'd set in the fire, near the edge where the flames didn't burn as high. He dare not trust Lady L, or he'd find himself returning to de Lanceau without the ruby pendant or a captive. Aldwin's wishes for knighthood would disappear like the powdery ash of a cold fire.

Lady L is quite a handful in other ways, too, his conscience added. As if he needed reminding. Aldwin yanked at a branch pinned beneath a column lying on its side like a storm-tossed log, while fighting the memory of her standing disheveled but still beautiful before him. How he'd yearned to reach out and run his fingers down her cheek. That hand would have slid down to cup her breast, the beginning of a coaxed seduction that would have left them both naked, gasping, and undeniably warm.

Lust seared through him. Exhaling a harsh breath, he willed away his wanton musings. She'd sooner skewer him with a stick than warm her body with him.

But the way she'd looked at him, once, when she didn't guard her expression . . .

He tugged again at the branch. With a gritty *rasp*, it pulled loose.

The torchlight, reflected like a fluid dot in the river, wavered, then dimmed. He glanced over his shoulder. Lady L had gone behind the rock.

Next, she'd be unfastening her wet cloak, before drawing it off to reveal her damp gown molded to every swell of her body—

Stop.

He whacked the branch against a rock, breaking the wood into several pieces, then rose and tossed the sections into the fire. After striding a few paces down the bank, he snatched up more branches while nudging aside stones and rubble. At least the noise he made hid any sounds coming from behind the rock.

He adjusted his armload of wood. By now, her garments would be lying rumpled on the ground. She'd be slipping his tunic over her head and down over those firm, round breasts . . .

He kicked a buried column, welcoming the pain radiating through his toes. Far better to focus on something other than her donning his favorite, spare tunic. Five winters old, and it grew more comfortable with each washing. Every time she moved, she'd feel it against her bare skin . . .

Scowling, he returned to the fire, where he stacked his supply of wood. Steam swirled up from the pot as he brushed off his hands.

Lady L should have returned by now.

He'd best check on her. A matter of honor. He'd told her he'd fetch her if she didn't return when he expected.

Just as he turned toward the boulder, he heard the clatter of stones. Wearing his tunic, Lady L walked toward him, carrying her clothes and the torch.

The pendant's gold chain glinted at her neckline. The tunic, large on her slender figure, hung to her knees. His gaze snapped to the flash of skin at the garment's hem, where her bare legs disappeared into her boots. His mouth suddenly seemed dry.

When she neared, he reached for her clothes. "Give me your boots, as well. I will set them out to dry."

She pulled back, thwarting his courtesy.

"You will need your boots and clothes to be dry on the morrow."

Her mouth—slightly less blue than before—curved in a saucy smile. "I know I will."

She spoke as if she'd discovered a way out of the cavern. Aldwin resisted glancing at the boulder, for it didn't matter if she had. He wouldn't give her the chance to get away.

"Give me your things, then."

Her gaze shadowed with a hint of modesty. Was she embarrassed by the thought of him handling her garments?

"I will care for my clothes." She brushed past him, dropped her belongings with a watery *plop*, and began to drape them across the fallen column.

When she bent forward, her hair slipped in glossy ribbons against the darker colored tunic. The garment clung to her bottom. The hem edged a fraction higher, not enough to be deliberately provocative, but still . . . More luscious skin.

Whew.

Grabbing a branch from the stacked pile, Aldwin sat and poked at the flames. A useless task, but 'twas better than ogling.

Wood popped, and sparks soared in a crimson cloud. Blinking against the ensuing smoke, he stole another glance at what he could see of her legs. Firm. Well-muscled. Not fleshy like some ladies'.

He couldn't remember seeing more enticing legs—not even among the pretty maidservants at Branton Keep.

Lady L straightened and glanced over her spread-out cloak, gown, and chemise. After removing her boots, she propped them upside down against a rock, and then smoothed her hands over her tunic—*his* tunic—so it again covered the top of her knees.

Jabbing the fire once more, Aldwin watched her hands. They were finely boned; his earlier suspicion she might have noble blood in her could well be right. Tonight, he'd learn the truth about this wench who in so many ways was still a mystery to him.

"You are staring." Lady L didn't even look at him when she spoke.

He forced his attention back to the fire. "I was seeing if you needed help."

Setting her hands on her hips, she faced him.

"You seemed to have the task well in hand," he added.

"You were staring. Do not pretend otherwise. An honorable man would never lie to a lady."

He almost laughed, and not because she was throwing chivalry in his face. She looked so fetching in all her tousled fury. "Very well," he said. "I was staring."

"Just like a man," she muttered, so softly, he almost didn't hear.

"What do you mean?" That sad note had colored her voice again, suggesting when she spoke, her thoughts pertained to one man in particular.

A client? Friend?

Lover?

He suddenly wondered how many men had been part of her life. Most of all, how many she'd taken to her bed.

She looked tired as she made her way to the fire. He rose, offering his hand to assist her, but she waved him away. Reaching a flattish rock, she sat and stretched her bare feet toward the fire.

Her shoulders lowered on a sigh.

Aldwin dropped down on a nearby rock, close enough to catch her if she ran, but far enough to give her a little freedom. Firelight flickered over her features, tinting her hair with gold and softening the taut press of her mouth. Crossing her arms, she leaned forward, clearly anxious to soak up every bit of warmth.

Aldwin smothered a low groan. After all the trouble she'd given him, he shouldn't feel sorry for her. But he did.

And he couldn't look at those lovely legs all night.

He drew over his saddlebag, reached inside, and handed her the blanket.

"I will be all right in a moment," she said.

"You can give it back to me then."

He thought she'd refuse, but, with a nod, she took the blanket. Another sigh broke from her as she wrapped it around her body.

"Thank you."

He shrugged. However, those two words, kindly spoken, warmed him.

Aldwin, do not become addled by this wench.

He dug in his bag again and drew out a small wooden bowl, along with a cloth-wrapped parcel of bread and cheese. After ladling some hot water into the bowl, he handed it to her, then passed her the food. "Dip the bread to soften it. 'Tis not much, but 'twill help to warm you."

After breaking off some bread and cheese, she handed the parcel back. Then she dipped a chunk of the coarse brown bread into the water and ventured a nibble. Lady L had remarkably even, white teeth. Most of the common folk he knew had rotten teeth or none at all.

She paused mid-chew, as though assessing the watery bread's flavor, and then swallowed. At least she hadn't cringed or spat it out.

Dragging his gaze away, Aldwin nudged the pot off the trivet and onto a flat bit of wood. He took a portion of the fare, then slid a bit of bread through the water and ate it. Rather bland, but at least he and Lady L wouldn't go to sleep tonight with empty bellies.

She still seemed to be shivering, though. He needed to get her warm quickly, as well as get her talking. And he knew just how to accomplish both.

From the side pocket of his saddlebag, he withdrew a leather flask. He uncorked it and inhaled the ambrosial scent of the liquor inside.

After wiping the top of the flask with his sleeve, he offered her the drink. "Cherry brandy."

She shook her head.

"'Tis an excellent one, made by monks in a monastery near Branton Keep." Aldwin grinned. "Strong enough to warm you in an instant."

"Aye." She smiled back. "And to render me senseless."

"Why would I do that?"

"So I cannot escape during the night."

A very good point.

He thumbed a scratch on the leather flask's side. "I have no wish to get you drunk, only to ease your discomfort. 'Tis up to you, after all, how much you drink."

Downing another mouthful of bread and water, she looked at him. "True. You cannot force me to swallow that liquor."

He almost grinned. She might regret that challenge, if he weren't so concerned with prying useful information from her. Taking care not to drop his bread and cheese, he held the flask out again. "The choice, then, is entirely yours." Still, he couldn't resist a little taunt. "Unless, of course, you cannot tolerate strong drink?"

Her mouth pinched.

God's blood, but she was beautiful when riled.

Her fingers brushed against his as she took the flask. Pressing it to her lips, she tipped her head back.

"Careful!"

She blinked several times. Tears streamed from her eyes. Then she swallowed. Gasped. Coughed as though she'd chewed a mouthful of peppercorns. "Oh!"

He chuckled. "Your face has color again."

She dragged her hand over her reddened lips. "The liquor"—she wheezed a breath—"is burning all the way down to my stomach. 'Tis like swallowing fire."

"Do you feel warmer?"

"I"—she blinked again—"I do."

"Good."

She wiped the flask on the blanket and handed it back to him.

He drank. As the potent liquor flowed down inside him, he resisted a grin. "Well," he said, "since we have a long night ahead, mayhap we should make the most of it."

Her shoulders stiffened. Pushing more bread into her bowl, she said, "In what way?"

"Lady L, I do not even know your real name."

Wariness crept into her gaze. She looked back at the fire. "I have told you more than once that I am a noblewoman. 'Tis enough."

"Not to me. You know who I am."

A wry smile touched her lips. "As does most of Moydenshire. Your name is well-known, because of that famous *chanson*."

Heat crept up Aldwin's neck. He took a large mouthful of brandy, savoring the fiery burn, and then set the flask on a stone beside him. "The incident retold in those songs happened three years ago."

"De Lanceau is one of the richest, most prominent lords in all of England," she said, clearly fascinated. "I am surprised he did not kill you for almost murdering him with that crossbow bolt. Surely he saw it as treachery?"

Aldwin gritted his teeth. "'Tis a long and complicated tale," he said, hoping—but doubting—that explanation would be enough for her. "If I had known, at the time, that de Lanceau was an honorable knight and deserved to be lord of Moydenshire, I would never have shot him."

He pushed the rest of his meal away, curling his hands against cresting rage and shame. How easily the baron and Veronique had manipulated his passionate ideals to their own selfish desire to see de Lanceau dead.

"Why *did* you shoot de Lanceau?" Curiosity softened Lady L's voice. She was looking at his fisted hands.

He hated that his heart pinched, encouraging him to yield to her request. "You claim to have heard the *chanson*," he growled. "Did you miss the part where they say I desired his future wife, Lady Elizabeth Brackendale? That, fearing de Lanceau had won her love, I shot him out of jealousy?"

"I heard such." She nibbled a morsel of cheese. "I always wondered if 'twas the truth, or told that way to be more entertaining."

Aldwin choked down an astonished laugh. Few people wanted to know his version of the events, preferring the popular song's violent drama.

He picked up a stick and poked at the blaze. There was some truth to the *chanson*. He had, indeed, desired the beautiful Lady Elizabeth, in the most idealistic and chivalrous of ways. There was more to the shooting, though, than an emotional impulse to pull the crossbow's trigger.

Why did Lady L care to know his version of what happened? He didn't have to tell her. Yet if he confided in her, and thereby won from her a margin of trust, she might willingly share what she knew with him. For the first time in months, he actually felt compelled to talk about the agony that seethed inside him day after day, and night after night.

"I was deceived," he finally said while he watched sparks swirl up from the fire. "De Lanceau had kidnapped Lady Elizabeth and was holding her for ransom at Branton Keep. 'Twas part of his plan to exact vengeance for his father's mortal wounding in a long-ago siege ordered by the king, who believed the older de Lanceau to be a traitor."

"God's teeth," Elizabeth murmured.

"A claim later proven to be false. At the time of Lady Elizabeth's abduction, however, de Lanceau believed his sire was run through by her father. Not long after the ransom demand was delivered, I was told de Lanceau had mistreated Lady Elizabeth."

"Oh, nay!"

"I could not bear to hear that my dear friend, a lady of exquisite virtue and beauty, had been brutally raped."

Lady L gasped. "Raped? By de Lanceau?"

Aldwin shook his head. "He never violated her. None of the men at Branton Keep did. I did not realize what I heard was a lie and part of a calculated plot to make me commit a most foul deed."

The blanket whispered as Lady L drew it closer about her. "Who told you such a lie?"

"A man I wish to die a painful death." Aldwin stabbed at the fire. "A man I would gladly kill myself, given the chance."

She raised her eyebrows, even as her face whitened. "What man?"

"Baron Sedgewick of Avenley."

Her eyes lit with acknowledgment. She seemed to know the baron more than by name. Did she know the bastard's whereabouts? He wanted to ask her outright, but he must ensure she knew the truth about them.

"Sedgewick was sent to the king's dungeon for plotting to kill de Lanceau and Lady Elizabeth's sire, as well as his cruel deceptions that led to the death of de Lanceau's father eighteen years prior. The baron's conspirator, de Lanceau's former courtesan by the name of Veronique Desjardin, was also imprisoned for trying to poison and stab de Lanceau. Somehow, they escaped. They were never recaptured. De Lanceau once heard they had fled England for Normandy, but this was never proven. For years, there was no word of them."

Again, affirmation shone in Lady L's gaze.

"'Tis rumored the baron and Veronique have returned to Moydenshire," Aldwin said, choosing his words carefully, "and they are once again plotting against de Lanceau."

Lady L's head turned a fraction. Firelight etched her profile. "Where, in Moydenshire, might they be?"

"We do not know. De Lanceau has spies throughout his

lands, but Moydenshire is a large county. The reports so far have yielded naught."

A peculiar expression swept her features: curiosity, concern, and indecision. He sensed the armor of secrecy around her yielding a notch. Now he just had to find a way to slip past those weak links, to strip that armor from her bit by bit, until he revealed the truth.

"You seem familiar with the names Baron Sedgewick and Veronique," he said, keeping his tone casual.

The blanket slipped from her shoulder as she shifted on the rock. Pulling the fabric back into place, she said, "Not as familiar as you, I vow."

She'd evaded the intent behind his words. Well, he had all night to draw what she knew out of her.

After poking the fire one last time, Aldwin set aside the stick, then picked up the flask. He handed it to her. When she took it, their fingers touched for half of a breath. Her lashes flickered and she bit her bottom lip, implying that contact evoked a sensual reaction within her.

A greedy coil of desire rose inside him. If she didn't talk, he'd have to resort to more physical means of persuasion. To begin, a kiss, right where she'd bitten.

"If you have heard of the baron and Veronique—even in passing conversation—I would like to know." He paused, mulling how best to present his arguments. "Whatever evil they are plotting will cause great harm not only to de Lanceau and his family, but the good folk of Moydenshire. The baron and Veronique are manipulative, ruthless killers. Those two conspirators will not hesitate to murder any man, woman, or child who gets in the way of their ambitions."

She tugged again at the blanket. From her shuddered sigh, he sensed his harsh words had made an impact upon her.

"De Lanceau brought peace to these lands for King Richard and means to keep that peace. If lives can be spared, de Lanceau will do all within his power to save them. Yet, he depends upon his loyal subjects—like you—to alert him of a threat," Aldwin said.

She met his stare. Her wary gaze hinted at dangerous secrets.

At last, would she confide in him?

Silence.

"Are you loyal to de Lanceau, Lady L?"

"What?" She blinked. "Of course."

"Then I remind you, 'tis your duty to reveal to me what you know."

Her fingertips edged from beneath the blanket to touch the pendant's gold chain. It emitted a soft *chime,* while anguish moistened her eyes. Then, as though annoyed with herself for letting him see her inner turmoil, she looked away across the water.

His hand crushed to the flask. What could be more important than loyalty to her lord? Why would she risk her own honor? Did she fear betraying someone she loved?

"You are foolish to keep your silence. Do you want to be named a traitor?"

"Never."

"Whether you are a courtesan or in fact a lady, de Lanceau is a just lord. If you have become caught up in a . . . predicament, he will help you." Aldwin paused. "And those you care about."

"My situation is not so simple," she said quietly. "And no matter how important a knight you are in his household, you cannot speak for de Lanceau."

Aldwin struggled not to correct her assumption he was a

knight as well as challenge her insult. Anger now would only bolster her resolve not to trust him. "You are right. I cannot speak for my lord," he said, proud he didn't snarl the words. "However, I have served him for many years, and that is why I am sure he will assist you."

"I am not as certain." Her words ended on a sad laugh.

Aldwin frowned. What reason did she have to believe de Lanceau wouldn't help her, especially if her dilemma involved the baron and Veronique? Mayhap she feared that by having the pendant she was considered a conspirator, and, no matter what she said or did, she'd be spending the rest of her days in a dungeon cell?

"Whatever you can tell me, I would be grateful. I will be sure to tell de Lanceau how you cooperated," Aldwin coaxed. How sincerely he meant those words; she must sense that.

She stared at him a long, thoughtful moment. Then she grabbed the flask, wiped the top, and downed a gigantic mouthful. She squeezed her eyes shut and shuddered several times.

"The burn is not so bad now, is it, Lady L?"

Gasping, she blinked at him. "'Tis still like ingesting fire. And my name is not Lady L. 'Tis . . . Leona. Lady Leona Ransley."

CHAPTER TEN

Whatever Leona had expected from Aldwin, 'twas not the ruthless fury clenching his features. His brows drew together in a scowl so ominous, she struggled to breathe.

With almost painful slowness, his hands flattened against his thighs. Not in a relaxed manner, but one that implied he might lunge and seize her by the throat.

"What did you say?"

His brittle tone sent chills racing through her as she carefully set down the flask. No matter how menacing he looked, she wouldn't turn into a cowering damsel. She held his glower, drawing upon the rage that had lived with her since that childhood day she'd been a victim of his whims.

Think of the bee stings. Think of his arrogance that afternoon and today. Think of how he hauled you from the tavern, forced you to ride to this forest, and the indignity of his kiss.

"My name," she said, "is Leona Ransley."

"Is that so?"

He practically growled the words. She didn't discern the

slightest regret. Neither did she hear any hint of an apology.

Fury rose to a hum inside her. He couldn't have forgotten what happened that summer afternoon. Did he not consider himself responsible? Did he see himself as blameless? A man with a clean-as-freshly-fallen-snow conscience?

Arrogant, pigheaded turd!

"You are a bold woman," he bit out, "to speak that name to me."

She heaved a breath. "Are you—?"

"Furious? Aye." His scowl blackened. "To attempt such a deceitful ruse—"

She threw up her hands. "'Tis my given name!"

"Impossible!" His lips curled as he leaned forward, into the too small space separating them. "Leona Ransley died years ago."

"*What?*" Shock threatened to knock her sideways. Lowering one hand, she clung to the stone beneath her to keep herself upright.

"You were one of the onlookers on the riverbank." His furious gaze pierced her. "A child huddled against her mother's skirts."

Rage boiled so hot inside her, she could hardly speak. He'd thought she'd died? Why? Had someone told him such?

"You witnessed what transpired that day," he went on, wrenching her from her thoughts. "Now, attempting to cast doubt in my mind and win my sympathy, you pretend to be Lady Ransley."

She glared back. "I do not speak false. I am Leona. And I will never forget what you did to me."

Anguish touched his eyes before his mouth curved into a hard smile. "What, exactly, did I do to you?"

"Convinced my brother to tie me to a tree. Forced me to be part of your game even when I asked more than once to be set free. And . . ." *Kissed me on the lips. A kiss I have not forgotten to this day.* Nay. She was not going to remind him of that embarrassment.

"And?" he growled.

"Ignored my cries for help when the bees started attacking me."

He raised his brows. "Those facts are well known. Not only by those who rushed to the river that day."

"Meaning?" She raised her brows back at him.

"You have proved naught."

"If you choose not to believe me, 'tis your own wretched fault."

Aldwin snorted and picked up the flask.

"What proof do you need? *Why* do you not believe me?"

"Why?" His voice dropped to a gritty rasp. "I saw the stings covering her. There were too many. No one could have survived."

"I did," she said, huddling inside the blanket. "For reasons I have yet to understand."

As he exhaled another sharp breath, the torment of that period in her life rushed into her thoughts. "The healers said I would never recover. I remember that much—snatches of them talking to my parents. I do not recall much else. The pain from the bee stings was terrible. My mind faded in and out. My mother was weeping. My father, raging"—she swallowed hard—"as the old women tended me. They said if I survived, 'twould be a divine miracle."

Quickly! Fetch the leeches! Salves. Poultices. Even those may not be enough.

Aldwin's eyes narrowed. "I rode to Pryerston Keep the following morning. The guards at the gatehouse refused to let me in."

"My father was angry with you. He ordered them not to let you in."

"That, I understand. But the men said Leona Ransley no longer lived there."

Which was true. "So you assumed I had died?"

He shrugged. "Not at first. I rode home and asked to speak with my father, to find out what had become of you. The day before, he had beaten me. That afternoon, he let me ask my question. Then, without giving me a definite answer, he hit me, told me I had ruined his chances for a profitable alliance with your sire, and ordered me to never again speak of the incident. My mother, also, was furious at the embarrassment I had caused. The following dawn, men-at-arms escorted me to a keep many leagues from home, where I began my training to become a page and then a squire." A rough laugh broke from him. "Since that day, my relationship with my parents was . . . difficult. I preferred to stay away rather than visit. When they learned I had shot de Lanceau—the greatest dishonor in my respected family's history—they told me never to return home."

Leona shouldn't feel the slightest remorse. Still, what parents could be so heartless to their own son? While she and her sire had disagreed on many occasions, she didn't doubt he loved her.

"In the months after the accident with the bees," Aldwin went on, "I heard naught of a Lady Leona Ransley at Pryerston Keep. I even asked peddlers, mummers, and musicians who'd journeyed through that part of Moydenshire. They had no word of her."

"Because I did not go home. The same day I was injured, I was taken in the back of a wagon to my uncle's castle some distance from Pryerston. My father paid the healers to go with me. Ward went, as well."

"If what you say is true, 'tis no wonder Ward did not answer my letter."

Aldwin had written to her brother, asking about her? "When the letter arrived at Pryerston," she said, thinking the likely events through aloud, "my father must have destroyed it. He was furious enough, then, to have done so."

"Mayhap. Still, I am not convinced by your tale," Aldwin said. "If you were gravely hurt, why did your sire send you so far from home?"

"My uncle knew of a local healer who had treated a man who fell into a large hive while harvesting honey. He survived. For weeks, that same woman watched over me."

"Weeks?" Suspicion still darkened Aldwin voice. Finally, though, she sensed he might be starting to believe her.

"It took much longer for me to fully recover. But the healer was patient. My uncle was kind. My parents visited often, and Ward was at my bedside night and day." She managed a smile. "He encouraged me to take the horrid potions the woman made me. And he told me stories, usually about what he had written or drawn in his sketchbook that day."

Aldwin looked down at the fire. "If that is true, when did you return to Pryerston? Once you were healed?"

"I did not go back until this past spring. You see, once better, I was of an age to begin my tutelage to become a lady."

He muttered under his breath.

Choosing to ignore him, she said, "There were two other girls, besides myself, who were tutored at my uncle's keep. After Ward left for another lord's household, to begin his training to be a squire, I could not imagine going back to Pryerston without him. As part of my duties, I cared for my uncle and aunt's youngest daughter, who was crippled, until she died. My aunt also came to suffer pains in her joints and needed help with her daily duties. She and I became fast friends and I . . . I could not leave her. When my mother died—she was killed in a fall from her horse—I finally returned home. I have lived at Pryerston ever since." *Because my father and his servants need me.*

"I see." Aldwin's stare bored into her.

Leona moistened her dry mouth. "Now do you believe me? I swear to you, I *am* Lady Leona Ransley."

‡ ‡ ‡

Without answering, Aldwin stood and walked down toward the river. Setting his hands on his hips, he looked out across the silent water.

Could Leona Ransley be alive? God's holy blood.

His head throbbed. His hands, coated in sweat, shook, and he curled them tighter into the folds of his cloak. How many nights after the accident had he lain awake on his pallet amongst the other sleeping pages and squires, fighting overwhelming dread that his actions had caused her death? Tears had stung his eyes and gouged his conscience, but he'd dared not share his anguish with his friends. A true knight would accept his blame. He'd find strength in his pain, learn from his failings, and use that knowledge to excel in his duties for his lord.

As grueling days of training dragged into months, and still he'd heard no news of Leona, he'd come to accept his worst thoughts must be true. Years passed, and he became a loyal squire to Lord Arthur Brackendale and, after the shooting, to de Lanceau.

During an errand for de Lanceau in northern Moydenshire,

when by astonishing chance fate reunited him and Ward again but for a few brief days, Aldwin had intended to ask about Leona. But as Ward lay in the inn's upstairs room, the fever held him in a merciless grip; it dragged his mind through years of his life, forcing his private thoughts—including his love for his sister—from him in disjointed memories. In Ward's rare, lucid moments, Aldwin hadn't managed to mention Leona, in part, because he hadn't wanted to cause Ward any more anguish. Moreover, he'd had to constantly assure Ward he wouldn't summon Lord Ransley, that Ward's return from the East and the reasons why would stay secret until after his passing.

When Ward died, Aldwin had wept for his friend. Knowing he'd never be welcome at Pryerston, Aldwin wrote down the details of Ward's death and sent the letter by messenger; Aldwin included Ward's sketchbook. He'd urged Lord Ransley to contact him at Branton Keep if he wanted to know more of Ward's death—but, no reply came.

That part of Aldwin's life had ended.

Or so he'd thought.

A muffled sigh reminded him of the woman sitting by the fire who might be Leona, if her story was true. By her fighting spirit alone, he might believe she was.

Yet he still had doubts. She'd not given him definite proof, only a convincing sequence of events. When she'd listed what he did to her the day of the accident, she hadn't mentioned his kiss. A telling omission, for with Ward dead, only Aldwin and Leona Ransley were aware that kiss had happened.

What he did know, without the slightest trace of doubt, was she made his body hunger. He craved her with each breath, each look, each word. He ached with that craving, which seemed to nurture the lonely desires within him and make him want them all the more.

How could she—one fiery-spirited woman—undermine him so, when he'd worked hard to subdue his impulsive nature with discipline and loyalty?

He sensed her gaze traveling over him, even as he listened for any attempted escape. She'd looked too exhausted to bolt for the dangling rope, but he'd not risk her getting away.

Not when there was too much he didn't know, such as how she got hold of the pendant. Why she'd been so determined to get the ransom. And why, if she really was Lady Leona Ransley, she didn't tell him so at the tavern?

That, above all, rekindled his anger.

He shoved his hand into his right cloak pocket and withdrew a round piece of amber. His fingers had long ago memorized each of the resin's bumps and dips. Even without enough light to fully see the memento, he saw the frozen struggle of the bee entombed within. Wings extended, it flew forever in the hard, golden sky.

He rubbed his thumb over the amber before dropping it back into his pocket. As he braced himself to head back to the fire, he thought he knew how to get the truth from her.

‡ ‡ ‡

Leona settled back against a rock, bent her blanket-covered legs, and looped her arms around her knees. The cavern's silence seemed more smothering and eerie, somehow, since Aldwin strode off toward the water, leaving her alone.

The damp cold seeped into her bare feet and bottom, adding to the chill that seemed to have settled within her, despite her swallows of brandy. She'd told Aldwin her real name. He hadn't believed her, even though he'd said that if she spoke the truth, he'd help her and those she loved. Even now, as he stood by the water, he looked unapproachable.

With a groan, she dropped her forehead against her arms, her shoulders stiff with fatigue. Her head swam from the liquor, and she shut her eyes. How she wished she hadn't drunk quite so much. However, she couldn't take those swallows back now.

Her closed eyes ached. She'd done what she believed was right by stealing the pendant from the baron and Veronique, and would do the same again if given the same choices, for she'd wanted the jewel returned to its rightful owner. When she reached Branton Keep, de Lanceau would hear that from her own lips.

Aldwin, too, must hear truth, no matter what burdensome memories lay between them. She wanted him to know her reasons, and that she was proud of her work-worn hands, tired garments, and freckles, because they proved she hadn't given up.

Not on herself.

Not on her father.

She yawned and nestled her cheek against the blanket that smelled faintly of horse. *Stay awake. When Aldwin falls asleep, you can escape.*

Aye, she would keep alert, but she'd use this chance for a quick rest . . .

"Leona."

Through a sleepy fog, she became aware of a man addressing her. Her awakening senses alerted her to the wool tickling her cheek, the numbness of her arm upon which her head rested, and the smell of burning wood.

Her heavy eyelids flickered.

A gentle nudge on her shoulder. "Leona, wake up."

Ugh. She knew that voice.

Lifting her groggy head—and wincing at the cramp in her neck—she saw Aldwin squatting nearby. How had she not heard him return to the fire?

"Go away," she groused, rubbing the back of her neck.

"You cried out."

"I did?"

He nodded. "Are you all right?"

"I must have been dreaming. About you." How delicious that lie sounded.

He didn't scowl, as she'd expected, but shook his head. Laughter rumbled from him. "Dreaming about me? I had not expected such."

She hadn't meant her words to amuse him. "Not a pleasant dream. A nightmare."

His gaze darkened, and then turned thoughtful. "Pity, that you were not dreaming about my kiss."

He emphasized "kiss," as though 'twere important. She scrambled to sharpen her fuzzy mind still cobwebbed by sleep. Had Aldwin guessed that in her naïve youth, she *had* dreamed of his kiss? Or was he hoping to hear her speak highly of his kissing technique?

Ha! He'd wait a long time for her flattery.

His glinting stare challenged her to answer. He clearly expected some kind of reaction from her. She swallowed, trying to think of a cutting reply. None materialized. To her horror—and surely because of the strong brandy—a blush warmed her face.

"God's teeth!" Leona grumbled. She managed to turn partway from him before he grabbed her blanket-covered arm.

Glancing back, she snapped, "Will you leave me alone?"

"Leona—"

"What more can you possibly want from me tonight?"

Even as she spoke the unfortunate words, a shudder snaked through her. His fingers flexed, indicating he'd felt her tremble. If he'd brought up kissing because he intended to force himself upon her—

Regret shadowed his expression. His lips flattened, as though he held back what he'd wanted to say. "All right. I realize you are tired. We will speak more in the morning."

About kissing? Not likely.

A rasping noise snapped her gaze to the rope trailing on the stone beside him.

"Nay!" she choked.

Before she could bolt, he reached into the blanket and caught her wrist.

If he bound her, how would she flee in the night? She *had* to persuade him not to tie her.

She struggled, fighting the rope coiling around her flesh. "How will I sleep?"

He cinched a knot. "You will. I will only tie this hand. We both know if I do not bind you, you will try to climb up that rope."

How wretched that he knew her so well! Hoping to divert his suspicions, she rolled her eyes. "Who would be foolish enough to attempt such in the dark?"

Aldwin paused in the midst of securing a second knot. His gaze flicked up to meet hers.

He smiled.

Chapter Eleven

With the rustle of silk, Veronique turned away from Pryerston Keep's solar window. "Is it done?"

She looked across the chamber drenched in early morning light to Sedgewick hunched over the trestle table; the quill in his hand scratched over a parchment stretched flat between pots of facial cream and candleholders. He grunted in answer to her question, and as she walked near, she saw lines of concentration at his mouth.

Why did writing a letter take so long? Her fingers curled into her gown's skirt. She hoped he was scribing exactly what she'd told him; he could be writing nonsense, for all she knew, since as a lowborn peasant, she hadn't learned to read or write—a fact he well knew. Sedgewick seemed too enamored with her, though, to think of betrayal.

She'd best make certain.

Strolling up behind him, she pressed against him and curved her arms around his bulging stomach. With a petulant sigh, she dropped her chin to his shoulder. "You are ignoring me."

The quill hit the parchment with a loud *tap*. "There." He dropped the writing instrument to wipe ink from his fingers. "Just as you told me."

"Exactly?" She nibbled his earlobe, which reeked of sweat.

He giggled. "Exactly. How I would love to see de Lanceau's face when he reads this letter."

A wicked laugh broke from her. "As would I."

Sedgewick's mouth quivered as he turned to face her. His greedy gaze slid to the unmade bed. "The reward you promised me for writing the letter . . ."

What she'd offered made Veronique want to retch; however, the missive had to be written, and Ransley was still slumbering. He mightn't have agreed, either. "You shall have it," she purred while stroking the baron's sweat-dampened face. "First, though, we must send this missive."

While Sedgewick rolled the parchment, she fetched a lit candle from beside the bed. "Whose seal will we use?" he asked. "Or will we forego the seal?"

She smiled. "We will use Ransley's. That is certain to get Geoffrey's attention."

The baron looked puzzled. "Is that wise?"

"Geoffrey's spies will soon warn him we have taken control of this keep. By then, there will be plenty of mercenaries here to defend us from an attack."

"How will you convince Ransley to let us use his seal?"

"Convince?" She swirled away and headed for the solar door. "Bring the parchment and follow me."

Their footfalls carried in the dank passageway as she headed toward the great hall. When she stepped into the stone stairwell leading down, voices drifted up to her. Two men were climbing the stairs up to the hall while conversing in angry, secretive tones. She paused, holding up a cautioning hand for Sedgewick to stop and listen, too.

"Do ye not see what is happenin'?" a man said, obviously trying to keep his voice hushed.

"Aye," another said, sounding nervous, "but what can we do? We are only servants."

"We must be rid of that baron and false lady. Did ye know they 'ave taken over Lord Ransley's solar?"

"So I 'eard."

"A short while ago, some mercenaries arrived at the gates. More I vow are on the way. Next, the keep's foin silver will start disappearin'. I tell ye, they are a wicked pair who'll bring dishonor upon this keep. After all that Lady Leona's done fer us—"

"Tell me what ta do," the second man said, "and I will tell the others—"

Like hellfire he would.

Veronique exchanged a glance with Sedgewick, who smirked and nodded. One benefit of their years together: he knew what needed to be done, without her having to say a word.

With brisk strides, she descended the stairwell and swept into the great hall, where servants set wooden boards of bread and ale jugs on the trestle tables for the first meal of the day. Several rough-looking men—mercenaries, who must have recently arrived—stood at the far end of the hall, talking. Still slumped at the lord's table, Ransley slept on.

Her gaze settled on two men repairing a broken table leg. They rose to greet her.

"Milady," the taller man with graying hair said before dropping into a half bow. Ah. The most vocal of the two dissenters.

"Good day." She forced a smile. "Do not let me interrupt your work."

After glancing at each other, the men again crouched by the table.

Veronique reached the dais and waved the baron over. Snatching a candle from a nearby table, she said, "Hold the parchment at both ends. I will do the seal." As Sedgewick held the rolled missive, she tilted the taper, causing wax to drop onto the document's rough edge. Then, she picked up Ransley's hand, turned it to reveal his gold seal ring, and shoved the ring into the wax.

"What are ye doin', milady?"

She looked up to see the two men approaching. "It does not concern you."

The wax had set. Veronique tossed aside Ransley's hand and nodded to the baron. He tucked the parchment into his belt, next to his dagger.

"Why are ye placin' Lord Ransley's seal on that parchment? 'E is asleep." The man's frown deepened. "Does 'e know what it says?"

The younger man—little more than one score years old—stepped forward. "Why are ye bringin' mercenaries into this keep, milady? We do not want 'em 'ere."

She smiled at the two men and motioned them closer. How fortuitous the other servants were watching and listening, as were the mercenaries.

"You are good men to speak your concerns," she said, aware of Sedgewick nearing them. "Are there others, here, who are concerned about what is happening at Pryerston?"

Several of the maidservants blushed and looked down at the rushes, but said naught.

"Take note," Veronique said, "for we appreciate your honesty."

The baron now stood by the men. His gaze met hers, and, with a thin smile, she nodded.

He drew his dagger. As a stunned cry broke from the taller man, the baron plunged the knife into his stomach.

The younger man shrieked, as did the maidservants.

When the taller man gurgled and slumped toward the rushes, the baron yanked his knife free. Blood dripped from the blade while he stalked the younger man.

"Wait!" he pleaded, scrambling backward while the maidservants screamed. "I—"

With a sneered grunt, the baron slammed the knife into the young man's chest. He gasped. Clutched at the knife. Fell to his knees. One of the maidservants raced to his side, weeping. "Nay!" she sobbed. "Nay!"

Sedgewick yanked his dagger free. As the body landed on the floor with a grisly *thud*, the baron bellowed, "Anyone else?"

Silence stretched across the hall.

Veronique crossed her arms and stared at each of the remaining servants. Some were wiping tears from their faces. Others stared in mute horror at the corpses. "Go back to your duties," she snapped.

They turned back to their work, while Sedgewick summoned over the mercenaries. "Get rid of them," he said, gesturing to the bodies.

Veronique strolled to his side. "Well done."

"I am glad I . . . pleased you." Sedgewick's lips formed a lecherous grin. "Have I earned another reward?"

"Indeed, you have." She tipped her head toward the mercenaries. "Tell me, which one shall I send to deliver the letter?"

Sedgewick motioned over a stocky, red-haired man.

The mercenary drew near, his hand on the hilt of his sword. "Milord?"

Veronique led him out of earshot of his colleagues. "I have an important task for you. One that will earn you twenty pieces of silver."

"A tidy sum, milady." The man's eyes glinted with interest. "What will ye 'ave me do?"

"You are to take this missive to Lord de Lanceau at Branton Keep."

Wariness narrowed the lout's gaze. "De Lanceau?"

She didn't like seeing doubt in the man's eyes; he obviously knew Geoffrey hated mercenaries. She must know this idiot would follow through with the task. He might already be thinking about tossing the parchment into a lake and claiming he'd delivered it.

If he couldn't be trusted, she'd have to kill him and find another more easily turned to her will.

"Only de Lanceau is to receive it." She tapped the parchment's end against the mercenary's tunic, while bestowing upon him a flirtatious smile. "Are you a man who can do as I ask?"

"Aye." He smiled back.

"No others. Only de Lanceau." The parchment rasped as, with a deliberate stroke, she slid it down the front of his garment to his belly. "If his men-at-arms refuse to let you speak with him? If they try to turn you away?"

His gaze slid up from the parchment in a blatant perusal of her body. "I will force the guards to let me in, even if I must kill them. They will take me to de Lanceau."

They would. Geoffrey's men were sickeningly loyal. Once they'd subdued this fool, they'd haul him before de Lanceau on his knees. It didn't matter how Geoffrey ended up with the message—as long as he did.

"Your answers please me." Her gaze wandered over his torso in an inspection he'd no doubt interpret as womanly interest. He might be ruggedly handsome, but he wasn't half as intriguing as that bastard Geoffrey.

She smothered her anguish, only to realize the mercenary was grinning. His very direct stare told her he'd noticed, and appreciated, her glance over.

Sedgewick shifted beside her. Judging by his scowl, he didn't like her playing coy with this man. Unfortunate, but she'd do what she must to get that letter delivered.

She raised the parchment and held it out to the mercenary.

His fingers closed on it. Brushed against hers.

Now, to offer one last enticement, before she let him go.

Leaning forward to reveal more of her bosom, she trailed her fingers over his hand curled around the parchment. "When you return," she murmured, "you will have the silver I promised. And, if you desire . . ." *Me.*

His lust-darkened gaze clung to her mouth. "Ten pieces now. The rest when I return."

She laughed.

"Ye know 'tis fair, milady."

With a seductive swivel of her hips, she turned away. "You will receive naught until you return. Not till I know you did as I asked."

"How will I prove such to you?"

She cast him a brazen wink. "I will know."

‡ ‡ ‡

A faint sound roused Leona from slumber. Eyes still closed, she focused her hazy mind to concentrate on the noise. Again, she heard the barely audible *whoosh*.

She opened one eye. Her blurry gaze focused on a smooth rock close to her face. She remembered Aldwin binding her hand before she fell asleep in the musty darkness, but, somehow, she'd ended up lying on her right side, facing the stone-ringed fire, the blanket still wrapped around her.

A slight headache reminded her of the liquor she'd downed yestereve. Raising her head a fraction, and trying not to wince, she glanced about.

The *whoosh* came again, followed by a soft trickling. The sound of someone . . . swimming.

Tilting her head, she glanced at her right arm, which had served as a makeshift pillow. She followed the rope snaking across the ground. Last eve, Aldwin had tied the other end to his wrist; now that section of rope was secured to the fallen column nearby.

Caution tightened every muscle in Leona's body. He might not be sitting by her, but he'd be keeping watch on her while he swam. He'd be looking for a sign that she was waking.

Could she fool him long enough to untie herself and run for the rope to freedom?

Just when she slipped her other hand up to the knot at her wrist, movement in the water snared her gaze. Aldwin surfaced on a near silent gasp, and then stood, his body rising from the water with almost no sound.

The broad muscles of his chest expanded and released as he drew a deep breath. Plowing both hands into his dripping hair, he tipped his head back to look up at the cavern ceiling. Sunlight caught the water sliding from his muscled shoulder; the droplets winked as they ran like tiny, liquid caresses down his rib cage to his taut abdomen, and lower still, to where his loins disappeared into the water.

Her breath caught. God's holy teeth. He appeared to be . . . naked.

Most warriors she knew bathed nude. They saw no sense in getting clothes wet, if it could be avoided. She shouldn't be shocked.

But shock didn't quite describe the wanton sparks racing through her to settle in her most intimate of places.

If he was naked, she *did not* care. Nor would she indulge her nagging curiosity and look at his privates. She'd seen a man's parts before. Why that odd-looking, dangling appendage was mentioned in countless jests, she'd never understand.

His head started to turn her way, and she quickly shut her eyes, willing herself to remain still. Did he sense she was awake? She didn't dare breathe.

Water sloshed, and she cracked open her eyes again.

Bending forward slightly—and revealing his buttock's enticing curve—Aldwin reached to a floating scrap of bark holding a white object: soap. His hand moved over his chest in broad circles, leaving behind a pale froth. He must have brought the soap in his saddlebag. When he dipped the bar into the river once more and began lathering his shoulders, a minty scent drifted to her.

He scrubbed the back of his neck and sighed.

The primitive sound of pleasure made her shiver. She frowned and, hauling her thoughts back to escape, began to work on the knot restraining her wrist. She didn't care that he enjoyed his bathing—although 'twould be lovely to wash away the grime on her skin and feel refreshed.

Lying as motionless as possible, she dug her nails into the rope. Aldwin continued to scrub, bending forward again to do his back. Wet hair slid forward, masking part of his face, but she sensed he was still mindful of his surroundings.

But unaware, so far, that she'd awakened.

He dropped down into the water, rinsed off, and then rose again.

The knot loosened. He clearly hadn't tied her as securely as before. Leona dug her nails in farther and managed to wiggle a fingertip into the knot. She smothered an elated gasp.

Pushing his wet locks back behind his shoulders, Aldwin began to scrub them with the soap. Froth soon enveloped his hair. His fingers made no more than a foamy whisper.

The knot loosened further.

He set down the soap. His chest expanded on an indrawn breath.

A slight brush against her skin, and the rope dropped away. *Free, at last.*

Aldwin's eyes closed, and he submerged. He spun underwater and streaked through the sparkling depths.

Leona scrambled to her knees. Boots. If she didn't put them on, she'd slice the soles of her feet on the rocks.

She grabbed her boots, shoved her feet in, and dashed across the bank.

Behind her, Aldwin broke through the water with a fierce splash. *"Leona!"*

His roar reverberated in the cavern. Panic shot through her, making her misstep, but she focused on the way to freedom. She'd got this far. She wouldn't give up.

Water thrashed behind her. Glancing back, she saw Aldwin plowing toward her, waves churning at his waist. He looked angry enough to kill her.

She reached the bank's edge and leapt onto the rock. Drying her sweaty palms on Aldwin's tunic covering her, she gauged the distance to the rope.

"Stop! I warn you—"

She launched forward. Her hands closed on the rough twine as the rope swung with her weight.

Splashed water hit her ankles.

Just when she tightened her grip to start climbing, Aldwin's hard, wet body crashed into her. His arms clamped around her waist, jerking her back and down against him with such force, she lost hold of the rope.

She shrieked. Kicked up water. Dug her fingernails into his arms restraining her.

His hold shifted—her only warning—before he slammed her face first into the river.

She submerged, her scream swallowed by the cold water. It flooded her nostrils and filled her ears with a heavy dullness. Her hands flailed. Trying frantically not to cough underwater, she fell deeper, the sunlit remains of a column looming on the river bottom before her.

She thrashed to break her fall. Twisted sideways. Kicked out. Her foot hit Aldwin's thigh. Despite being submerged, she heard him growl. When she tried to surface, his hand plunged into the water and grabbed for her. His fingers narrowly missed her arm.

She darted backward, water rushing against her shoulders. Lungs burning, spluttering, she broke through to air.

He was there. Waiting for her.

She lunged back once more, but he'd clearly expected such a tactic. Water swirling between them, he grabbed her elbow. Ignoring her coughing, he hauled her forward, against the slick planes of his body, to pin her arm between them. Forced to stand flush against him, she gasped for breath. Her entire being seemed to feel his borrowed tunic scratching against her thighs. His body warmth seeping through the thin cloth separating them. His maleness, pressed against her.

She twisted her trapped wrist. He held it such a way that she couldn't curl her fingers to scratch his chest.

Or push aside the hair dripping in her eyes.

She pulled back on her arm.

Aldwin drew her even closer, his hold like a manacle. When she continued to struggle, he pulled her elbow up, so she had to rise on tiptoes. "Stop fighting," he said between his teeth. "I will not warn you again."

Her free hand flew toward him. He ducked, trying to dodge the blow, but she caught him across the ear. His head jerked with the impact, sending water droplets flying.

His eyes cinched into slits, and then he yanked her sideways. With an angry yelp, she lost her footing. She careened toward the water, while fighting to regain her balance.

He tugged her again.

She was falling!

Suddenly, she was hurtling backward through the depths, like a fallen tree caught on a rushing current and propelled by a more powerful force.

Her back hit firm ground.

With a watery *crunch*, her head smacked down on a mat of

leaves and branches. The muted golds, grays, and browns of the cavern swirled overhead. She blinked, her dazed mind struggling to focus, as water lapped against her legs.

A heavy weight came down upon her.

Aldwin.

Her hands flew up to fight him, but he grabbed one of her arms, and then the other. She bucked beneath him, but he wrenched her arms above her head and held them to the ground.

Sucking in furious breaths, she glared up at him. Leaning on his left forearm, his lower body pressed upon her in a most indecent way, he looked down at her.

"Get . . . off . . . me!" she ground out, trying again—in vain—to dislodge him.

He said nothing, merely raised one eyebrow. Water slid down his face to drip onto her cheek. The droplet's soft *tap* sent a shiver trailing through her.

Why did he simply stare? At least when they were fighting, she knew what to expect from him. "Are your ears full of water? I said—"

"I heard you."

Each word broke from his lips like chipped stone. She shivered. Not because she was afraid—of course not!—but her soaked tunic seemed to magnify the chill seeping up from the ground.

When another shiver ran through her, his hands pinning her wrists shifted their grip. His head tilted, enabling his gaze to travel down her face and throat. The muscles in her neck pinched, stopping her from lifting her head to follow his stare, but she felt his heated gaze linger upon her breasts.

And then, with a little growl, his focus shifted. She sensed him studying her belly, and then the tunic bunched around her thighs. *Oh, God.* The fabric hadn't ridden high enough for him to see her womanhood, but still . . .

"Stop," she choked out.

His attention slowly returned to her face. She almost gasped, for his smoldering stare burned into her. "Stop what, Leona?"

"Staring."

"There is no harm in a look. You do not seem to be hurt, only cold."

"Then—"

"Quiet," he growled. "God help me, I am angry enough to . . ." His voice trailed off.

To do what? her conscience shrilled.

His gaze fixed upon her lips, causing a sudden yearning to tighten her innards. Her mouth warmed, recalling his kiss. *Look away*, a voice inside her cried. *Don't taunt him. If he kisses you, you will forfeit this battle.* Trying to stop the unwelcome tingling, she squeezed her lips together.

The faintest chuckle rumbled in his chest, and then he shifted above her.

"What—?"

His thighs nudged hers farther apart, allowing him to lie more fully upon her.

She gasped. Writhed. "Hold! You cannot—"

His hips flexed, and she gasped again. A hard, warm weight nudged her thigh.

Her eyes widened.

"Aye," he rasped.

Leona swallowed, not daring to acknowledge the quivering in her womb. Anger. Wariness. She mentally grabbed for them, as a drowning woman would reach for branches bobbing on the water's surface. "Aye, what?" she demanded.

"Despite my anger, despite all I know of a knight's honor . . . you tempt me."

"*Tempt* you?"

"Aye, Lioness. You make me *want*."

A dangerous shudder seared through her. *Want.* How well she understood that word. She bit back the moan tickling her throat.

Aldwin had almost caused her death years ago. He'd taken her captive and kept her from aiding her father. He'd thwarted her escape attempt. To feel aught but loathing for him was . . . madness.

Yet of all indignities, the heat simmering within her wasn't hatred.

His lower body shifted. His manhood pressed against her again.

She glared at him. "Do that again, and—"

"You will wallop my other ear?" His gaze shifted to her pinned wrists. "Not likely." He grinned. "But I know you are pondering it."

Pondering that and far more. "I cannot *wait* to knock you senseless."

"Mmm." Something flickered in his gaze. "Curious, that. Most young women cannot wait to be lying beneath me."

Leona snorted. Next, he'd be lauding his sexual prowess, and she'd have no choice but to listen.

"Only one woman, in all my years, has despised me."

Disquiet whispered in the back of her mind. "Imagine."

"This woman—but a girl when I met her—believed herself as much of a boy as her older brother. She even wanted to duel with sticks."

Long-ago memories swarmed into Leona's mind. She

struggled to fortify her emotional barriers and maintain her fury. "Why are you telling me this?"

"Because she was like no girl I had ever met. She did not swoon, giggle, or blush when I spoke to her. I liked that. She made me . . . *feel*."

"Feel?"

"Infuriated. Intrigued." He paused. "Alive."

She'd intrigued him? Was that why he'd insisted on that ridiculous kiss?

"You claim to be that girl, Lady Leona Ransley."

"I am."

His eyelids lowered a fraction. "I am not convinced."

She hissed a breath. "Why not? What proof—?"

"Exactly. Proof." His bold blue gaze pierced her. "Tell me what only you and I would know." His attention slid again to her mouth. "For example, the first time we kissed."

He wanted her to admit to that mortifying moment? Why? So he could remind her how she was at his mercy then—as she was now?

She must have uttered a sound, because Aldwin leaned closer. "What did you say?"

"Naught." Turning her head to the side, she stared at a mottled stone.

His sigh swept across her cheek. For one, idiotic moment, she wondered how it would feel if he brushed his lips across her skin. Would his mouth be warm and gentle, or icy and possessive? Would she feel those same, wondrous sensations in her belly?

Oh, God. She shouldn't have such thoughts.

"Well?" he demanded.

That one word fired the dread—and the fury—within her.

She scowled, refusing to look at him. She wasn't his to command. Last eve, she'd told him the truth about who she was; her account held more than enough proof. If he didn't believe her, well—

Aldwin's right hand suddenly slid up to take hold of her wrists. His left hand brushed the side of her neck. Before she guessed his intentions, the matted leaves beneath her cheek shifted. He'd pushed his hand between them and her face.

She thrashed beneath him. "You—"

His thumb and fingers closed on her chin. With gentle but unrelenting pressure, he forced her to look at him. His eyes blazed beneath the tangled fall of his hair.

"Arrogant turd?" he finished for her. His mouth, dangerously near hers, crooked up at the corner.

Leona inhaled on a startled rush. He even remembered her cursing him?

Her head spun, a sensation akin to falling out of a tree and landing in the grass. She fought to reclaim her anger, to raise that fury like a shield and deflect his unexpected parry.

But as the air left her lungs, her fury melded into anguish. In his gaze, she saw the hint of him as a boy, leaning over her, sluicing water over her swollen body to drown the bees. *'Twill be all right*, he'd said, his voice shaking. *'Twill be all right*.

Fight, Leona. But she couldn't stop the deluge of emotions. Memories of horrible sensations—helplessness, fear, and pain—hovered, threatening to drown her. Tears stung her eyes.

Leona! Don't cry before him!

Even as she rallied a retort, he muttered an oath. Still holding her jaw, he dipped his head. His lips touched the bridge of her nose, and then the side of her cheek, in the gentlest of kisses.

A choked breath wrenched from her. Before she could think

to stop him, his mouth was moving again, kissing a path down to her chin.

To her mouth.

Her pulse jolted. Aldwin had *no* right to kiss her. Did he really think she'd let him? That soon, she'd lie willingly beneath him like the other women he'd mentioned?

She fought to turn her head. "N-Nay! Do . . . *not*—"

His mouth brushed hers, catching her refusal, breaking each word into nonsensical sounds that melted on her lips. *Why* did he kiss her? Hatred, she welcomed. But this . . .

His kiss deepened, and she groaned. *Warm and tender*, she acknowledged, while her stomach seemed to dive right down to her toes. *And he tastes glorious.*

‡ ‡ ‡

Capturing Leona's provocative groan with his lips, Aldwin couldn't hold back a shudder. The desire within him roared, glorying in the passion of their kiss. He slid his tongue between her lips, and her sigh mingled with his.

She tasted as he remembered, a blend of spice and sweetness. Through the long night, he'd thought about all she'd told him, what he'd noticed about her when he took her captive, and the ways she tormented him. Sleep? Impossible. While he sat watching the fire burn down, his exhausted mind had turned to her kiss. How their animosity could create a kiss that good was yet another question that needed answering.

Watching over her while she slept, he'd craved her. As he wanted her now.

Her eyes closed, and, sensing her rallying another fight, he moved his mouth in a lazy dance over hers. He'd make her completely and utterly aware of him.

As he'd been aware of her when he roused in the dawn light, stripped off his clothes, and slipped into the river, hoping the water would cool his desire.

And then, she'd taunted him with escape.

He caught her full bottom lip and grazed it with his teeth. Her breathing hitched, and heat shot to his loins. Never had he felt such astonishing sensations from just a kiss. Need so intense, it overruled his anger.

Kiss her again, his mind taunted. *Make her need as much as you.*

Don't, his conscience shrilled. *If she is Lady Ransley, you shouldn't treat her so.*

True. But she'd provoked his anger. And he was powerless to draw away. Her scent, warmth, and the desire humming within him all refused to let him go.

He swept his tongue into her mouth. How his body *ached*. He nibbled, sucked, drew upon her lips as though to sap every drop of mutiny from her.

"Stop"—she moaned—"kissing me."

"Nay."

Before his reply had left his lips, she matched his tongue's thrust. Met each nibble with fierce bites of her own. Desire licked like fire over his skin.

God's bones! He wanted to run his hands all over her, to *feel* every warm bit of her, but if he released his grip on her wrists . . .

A muffled sound stole into his thoughts.

A distant shout.

Aldwin stilled, his lips still pressed to hers.

She bit his upper lip, even as he raised his head to listen.

"—by the water," a man said. He sounded furious. Snapping branches marked his footsteps close to the fallen trees above.

Another man answered, his words indistinct.

Aldwin looked down, to see Leona's eyes open. She'd heard the voices.

Before she could scream, he clamped his free hand over her mouth.

Her eyes sparked with fury.

"Hush," he whispered, his lips close to hers.

"Mffgghh!"

"You think those are your men, looking for you?" He held her gaze. "They are more likely to be poachers."

Scowling, she tried to dislodge his hand.

Maintaining his hold, he strained to hear more from aboveground.

"—clean cut. Someone used a knife. When I find the bastard—"

A horse whinnied. The *thud* of hoofbeats carried.

"Get that horse!"

"Rom," Aldwin whispered. If the poachers had found Rom, they knew whoever had destroyed their traps—Aldwin had while pursuing Leona last night—was still in the forest. Moreover, Rom wasn't a scruffy work animal, but a destrier. The criminals would realize the man who owned him was of the nobility, loyal to his lord and king; he'd be honor bound not only to protect the king's deer from poachers, but see the criminals punished.

An excellent reason for the poachers not to leave witnesses.

Aldwin looked down at Leona, concern drumming in his veins. "If the poachers find us, they will murder us."

Her eyes bright with defiance, she returned his stare.

"I must protect Rom and you. Now, I am going to remove my hand. When I do, you will not try to scream."

Her throat moved with a swallow.

"If we die here, years may pass before anyone finds our bodies. *If* they find us," he said quietly. "Be forewarned, Leona. If I have the slightest doubt you will stay silent, I will knock you senseless. I do not want to hit you, but I will. Understand?"

‡ ‡ ‡

Staring up at Aldwin's determined face, Leona nodded. She didn't want to be hit about the head, especially if their lives were in jeopardy.

Aldwin's expression softened with relief before he released her wrists. While she lowered her arms to cover her breasts, he rose to standing with effortless grace, a powerful display of flesh, bone, and muscle. He strode toward his garments.

Her face warmed while she recalled exactly what she'd seen while he stood: bronzed legs dusted with hair; muscled thighs; and . . .

A splendid physique. *Everywhere.* That glimpse of his nakedness had a strength all its own, grabbing her concentration and holding it hostage.

More shouts carried from above, a stark reminder she hadn't moved from the water's edge. Leona pushed herself up on her right elbow, while the rasp of Aldwin pulling on his boots came from near the fire pit. She shouldn't look his way. But when she rose, water running down her legs, she couldn't resist a glance.

He'd already donned his hose and boots. With a swift tug, he yanked his tunic over his head, smoothed it over his torso, and then flicked aside his hair. His expression stern, he reached for his crossbow and bolts.

A shiver wove through her. Only moments ago, she'd lain beneath him. Kissed him. Been drawn into a sensual bliss unlike any she'd experienced. And now, he was preparing to battle the men in the forest above, one warrior against how many?

She suddenly realized Aldwin was looking right at her. While he fastened his leather knife belt at his waist, he pointed to her gown and chemise. He obviously wanted her to get dressed.

Leona nodded.

Another whinny, shriller than before, sounded in the forest above. Aldwin frowned and loped toward the dangling rope. He leapt to it, and, while swinging with its arc, swiftly climbed up and disappeared. A moment later, the rope slid up, preventing her from escaping.

Or so he thought.

Once dressed, she'd explore the cavern for another way out.

Leona crossed to her where garments lay. Her hands shaking with cold, she caught hold of the wet tunic covering her and, in several tugs, drew it up over her head. As she moved, the pendant's weight slid against her bosom.

Water dripped onto her head and ran down her bare shoulder, and she resisted cursing aloud. She didn't want the poachers finding her, especially while undressed.

More voices reached her. One sounded like Aldwin's. Was he negotiating with the poachers?

Leona dropped the tunic onto the column and snatched up her still-damp chemise. She struggled to put it on, for it clung to her skin. With stiff fingers, she worked the fabric down below her knees.

A shadow fell across the cavity opening.

Shouts rang out, followed by the *thud* of arrows plowing into wood.

A man screamed.

A keen ache pressed upon her. Fighting alone, Aldwin was likely to be hurt. Or killed.

She shrugged off her unease. With his crossbow skills, he'd be a formidable opponent. Worrying about him was pointless, for he meant naught to her.

Even if he'd helped her after the bee stings years ago.

Even if he'd kissed her, years ago, and but moments ago.

A bubble of protest popped inside her, and, frowning, she brushed aside the awful feeling that she was lying to herself.

More cries and sounds of battle filtered down from above.

Leona picked up her gown and began to pull it on. She mustn't let Aldwin's kisses sway her common sense. Once he'd finished with the poachers, he still intended to take her as his prisoner to Branton Keep and hand her over to his lord. While he'd said de Lanceau would help her, Aldwin couldn't know that for certain and it could be days before de Lanceau sent men to her father's keep. She couldn't wait that long.

Every day that passed, Veronique and the baron mired her sire deeper in their plots. In his dismal state, they'd easily manipulate him—until he wasn't useful to them anymore. What might happen to him then?

Leona tugged her gown into place and tried not to mull the frightening possibilities. After donning her cloak, she glanced along the cavern wall to where it curved into the river. There, she'd look for a way out.

But first . . .

She crouched beside Aldwin's saddlebag, left behind in his rush to reach the surface. Stifling a twinge of guilt, she looked inside for a weapon.

The light coming in through the hole shifted again. Dirt crumbled down into the water, followed by the *splash* of clumped earth.

Someone was standing by the opening. A poacher? Any sound might betray her.

She stayed very still.

More earth fell, followed by a startled curse.

A sickly chill crawled across her scalp. Glancing up, she met the wide-eyed stare of a bearded man who'd stuck his head down into the hole. His gaze ran over her, then riveted to where the gold chain trailed along her neck.

He grinned. "Wot 'ave we got 'ere?"

CHAPTER TWELVE

Aldwin gathered up the rope as he crept across the dew-laden ground, the bolts in his quiver making a faint rattle. If the poachers discovered the rope disappearing into the ground—he hoped they hadn't already—Leona could be in grave danger.

He'd do all he could to protect her.

Judging by their voices, the poachers were on the other side of the nearby fallen tree. Aldwin forced his mind to concentrate on the challenge ahead, and not upon Leona as he'd seen her before he'd turned away. Her unruly hair, kiss-reddened lips, and glazed eyes had coaxed him to continue seducing her.

He might have done so, if the poachers hadn't distracted him. A pinch of his conscience made him scowl, for where had his gallantry gone? How could his knightly morals vanish when tempted by Leona's kisses and scented skin?

He tightened his grip on his crossbow and vowed to work harder to keep his impulsive nature tightly reined.

Thudded footfalls came from the tree's opposite side. He reached the moss-covered trunk, where the rope's other end was secured. Untying the knot would take time. Hoping the rope wasn't noticeable, he shoved the coiled section under the tree and then slowly rose.

"They're 'ere somewhere," said a man with graying brown hair that swept his cloak's shoulder. "I can sense 'em."

He stood with his back to Aldwin, his hands on his hips and a pair of slain rabbits slung over his right shoulder. A young, dead stag lay on the ground. When the poacher limped several paces, studying the earth, the rabbits' heads bounced.

Warning chilled Aldwin's skin, for the poacher had found the footprints from last eve. Aldwin glanced back at the cavity, only to see more prints. Not just his and Leona's.

"Clif, those tracks could 'ave been from days ago," said a younger man also garbed in a green wool cloak. "Romans, even."

"Romans." Clif snorted. "Sometimes, Emmet, I cannot believe ye are a grown man."

Emmet flushed. "I searched the woods around 'ere, as ye told me. I did not find anyone. If the others 'ad, they would 'ave brought 'em ta ye."

"They're 'ere," Clif repeated. "No knight would leave 'is fine 'orse. And, as I told ye, there are two people." His shoulders rose and fell on a sigh. "Where are the others? Must I go catch that 'orse meself?"

As Clif spoke, he turned to scan the woods. Sunlight grazed his face, as brown as a hazelnut and hardened by years spent outdoors. A scar cut across his jaw to the edge of his mouth. An injury from poaching or a fight? A face Aldwin would remember, for when he reported these poachers to de Lanceau.

"At least we got one deer. We will get the baron's payment."

Aldwin's gaze sharpened. Baron? Did he mean Sedgewick?

Hoofbeats carried from the forest.

"Get it!" a male voice shouted. Running men became visible in the woods. Reins dangling, Rom cantered through the forest, moving at an angle to the fallen tree.

Clif growled. "If we cannot catch it, we will kill it."

Not likely.

Aldwin aimed his crossbow.

Drawing a knife, Clif started toward Rom.

With a *click*, Aldwin's crossbow trigger released. The deadly bolt whistled past Clif's head to slam into a tree.

Emmet spun. Clif stumbled back a step and turned to look at Aldwin.

"Stay away from my horse." Aldwin stepped onto the fallen tree and quickly fitted another bolt into his weapon.

Grabbing hold of the rabbits sliding toward the ground, Clif scowled. Eyes wide, Emmet gaped. His fingers twitched. He clearly couldn't decide whether to reach for the sheathed knife strapped to his waist, or remain still.

Raising his hand, Clif signaled his other men. They slowed their pursuit of Rom and came toward the nearby trees.

"Who are ye?" Cliff demanded.

"Aldwin Treynarde. Loyal servant of Geoffrey de Lanceau."

The poacher's brows raised. "*The* Aldwin Treynarde? From the *chanson?*"

"The same."

"A pleasure ta meet ye." His gaze slid behind Aldwin. "Where is yer friend?"

"I am alone."

"Really?" Clif glanced at Emmet and grinned.

Aldwin managed a noncommittal smile. He'd never give

away Leona's hiding place. At least she was staying silent. Thank God.

The other poachers slunk closer, using trees to shield them. They'd let Rom go—the horse had vanished into the forest—but were well armed with bows and arrows. Aldwin would have to work fast to keep them from overpowering him.

As though guessing his thoughts, Clif laughed. "Ye're outnumbered, Aldwin Treynarde. Some o' us are mercenaries who know 'ow ta fight men like ye."

Five louts ahead of him, Aldwin noted, and at least one creeping up on his back. He didn't mistake the *crunch* of a rotten branch close behind him.

The thrill of impending battle tightened his body as he offered one last, chivalrous appeal. "You and your men will put down your weapons. Set them on the ground, and step away."

Clif shook his head. "Put down yer crossbow. We might be merciful and let ye die quickly."

"I meant to say the same to you."

Clif guffawed.

Emmet chuckled. So did the other poachers.

Footsteps rushed up behind Aldwin, as Clif muttered, "Fool."

‡ ‡ ‡

A scream scratched Leona's mouth as the man's grin broadened.

Her eyes smarting, she forced the cry into submission. If she screamed, she might distract Aldwin at a critical moment. Then, there'd be no hope for either of them.

The man disappeared. A moment later, the rope rippled

down into the cavern. Scuffed boots came into view.

He was coming down the rope.

Leona refused to acknowledge her dread. If he thought to steal the necklace and kill her, he'd be in for one spectacular fight.

Glancing away for a moment, she raked through Aldwin's bag. He hadn't left her one item that could be used to defend herself. Grabbing a handful of stones, she rose and faced the man swinging over the water.

His boots hit the large stone. Beneath his cloak, he had shoulders as large across as a blacksmith's. The oaf's greedy gaze slid over her before he released the rope and jumped to shore.

Leona stepped backward, putting distance between them.

"'Allo, love." The man smiled, revealing gaps in his teeth.

"Stay away."

He chuckled and crooked a finger. "C'mere, love. Come ta Peyton."

"I said, stay away."

Peyton's smile faded. "Ye're not listenin'." He pushed aside the opening of his cloak to reveal the hunting dagger in his belt.

Oh, God.

She retreated again, wondering how many more steps she had left before reaching the river's edge.

The knife made a metallic *hiss* as he drew it from its scabbard. His hungry stare flicked to her breasts outlined by her damp cloak. "'Tis yer lover up there?"

Her face warmed. "Nay."

"Good. Then ye will not miss 'im."

"Miss—?"

"'E's dead."

Her breath became a brutal pain in her chest. Aldwin had

been killed? The cavern spun before her.

"'E was tryin' ta protect ye, but 'e cannot save ye now." Peyton motioned to her again. "Come ta me, love. Or I will 'ave ta come get ye."

Blinking hard, she shifted the stones in her fingers. *Aldwin was dead.* A confusing rush of anguish crashed through her. Nay. She wouldn't believe it. Not until she saw his body. This thug would tell her anything to get her to cooperate.

Impatience, now, defined Peyton's mouth. "Come show me what ye 'ave under yer cloak. That necklace"—his attention slid down to her thighs—"ta start."

She took another step backward.

He rushed at her.

Drawing back her arm, she flung a stone. It whacked into the side of Peyton's bearded jaw, and then clattered on the ground. He jerked back, scowling, and touched the bleeding cut with his fingers.

"Ye shouldn't 'ave done that."

She glanced at the rope. Could she run to it? She had to try.

Peyton's lips twisted. When he started toward her, she raced to the water, but he caught her left arm in a bone-crushing grip.

She gasped

"Aye," he said, wrenching her to him. The stench of unwashed skin and dirty clothes assaulted her senses, almost causing her to choke. "If ye'd come as I told ye, I wouldn't 'ave ta hurt ye." He looked down at her neckline. "Ta think I 'ave not even begun."

Bastard. "Let go of my arm."

"Ye 'ave a bit o' fight in ye? Ye won't when I am done."

How her fingers begged to claw into his leering face. Trembling with fury and fear, she forced herself to remain still. If she wanted to escape this predicament unharmed, she must use her wits.

Taunting Peyton would only provoke his cruelty. Therefore, she must react as he expected. Like a . . . damsel.

Ugh.

Lowering her head, she let her shoulders slump. She forced a sniffle.

"That's better." His fingers shifted on her arm. "Now—"

Leona brought her leg up in a swift jerk. Her knee slammed into his groin.

He howled.

The knife flashed toward her. She jumped back and snatched up a branch from the ground.

One hand cupped over his privates, his eyes wet with pain, Peyton glowered at her. He raised the knife again, his hand trembling. "Ye will *beg* me ta—"

"I will not." Holding the branch with both hands, she swung it hard. Peyton staggered backward, but his boot heel hit a stone. He wavered, and she swung again. With a grisly *clunk*, the wood smacked into the side of his head. His body stiffened. He teetered sideways, and then fell to the ground, the knife still clenched in his fingers.

The force of the blow burned in Leona's arms. Raising the stick to strike again if necessary, she edged toward Peyton. He didn't move.

Had she killed him? The thought sparked a horrible twinge inside her. He might be vile, but to have taken his life . . .

He still breathed. Relief rushed out of her on a sigh. However, when Peyton woke, he'd be angry enough to kill her. She had to escape *now*.

Throwing aside the branch, she spun toward the rope.

Aldwin stood on the rock, holding his crossbow.

Leona froze. Her body flooded with warmth. Joy? Relief? Mayhap a deluge of both.

"Well done," he murmured.

She nodded and dried her sweaty hands on her cloak. Pride and an unnerving awkwardness welled up inside her. *Remember, Leona, he's not your lover, but your captor.*

He stepped off the rock onto the shore.

"I was told you died." She hated the way her voice caught.

"Not this day. Two of the poachers, however, are dead." Aldwin shifted his near empty quiver. Blood spattered across the front of his tunic, and his left sleeve was torn near his wrist.

His gaze shifted past her to the unconscious poacher. "Did you kill him?"

"Nay, only knocked him senseless."

His crossbow aimed at Peyton, Aldwin strode to him, squatted, and searched his cloak. Clearly finding naught of importance, he pried the knife from Peyton's fingers. "He will wake soon. We must leave."

When Aldwin rose, he grimaced. She noticed a blood-stained slash in the side of his tunic she hadn't noticed before. "You are wounded!"

"A scratch."

"More than a scratch."

"I will be fine." He walked back to her. "And you?"

"Fine."

"Good." He paused in front of her and his gaze softened. Was he glad she was unharmed because he cared about her? Or was he relieved she wouldn't be a burden for the rest of their travels?

Likely the latter. Still, heat lingered in his eyes. She felt that poignant glimmer deep inside her—the same sensation she'd experienced when he kissed her.

His gaze fell to her lips. His mouth opened, and he looked about to say something important.

Then he blinked and turned away. "We must leave, as soon as possible. The poachers who survived ran off. They will be back, though, to collect their friends' bodies and help this man. They may come with reinforcements."

He spoke as if each word was a struggle. He seemed to be resisting what he really wished to tell her.

Had he meant to say he cared about her? Nay. More likely, events had occurred aboveground that he regretted.

He hadn't mentioned his horse.

As Aldwin tossed Peyton's knife into the river, she said, "What about Rom?"

"He ran into the woods. We will find him."

Without the horse, they'd have to make their way on foot. They'd be easy prey for the returning poachers. Even more vulnerable than if they stayed in this cavern. "What if we don't find Rom? What then?"

Aldwin crossed to his saddlebag. After removing his quiver, he retrieved his cloak and put it on. She thought he wasn't going to answer, but as he shoved his saddlebag and quiver back onto his shoulder, he said, "We will worry about that situation if and when we need to. Now this is what we will do. I will—"

He spoke just like Ward when he'd asserted his "older and wiser than you" authority. How tired she was of Aldwin's orders. Tired of being cold, damp, and trapped when the situation at Pryerston might be dire.

Brushing past him, she started toward the rope.

"Leona."

"You said we should leave here as soon as possible."

His strides carried behind her, followed by the *thwap* of his wet tunic being snatched from the column. "I did say such, but I will climb up first."

She reached the water's edge and leapt to the rock.

His footfalls quickened, and then he landed behind her. He stood indecently close, consuming the miniscule space separating their bodies. "I will go first," he repeated, his breath stirring her hair.

Wicked heat spiraled through her, while her patience fought his demand to lead. He didn't want her going first because she might pull up the rope before he'd climbed it, leaving him down here with Peyton.

"'Tis best if I go first," Aldwin said. "I will make sure the poachers are not waiting for us."

"How noble of you." His reasoning, though, made sense. He was better prepared to defend both of them if the ruffians lay in wait. Indeed, 'twas noble of him to put himself in jeopardy.

Annoying, though, that his actions seemed gallant.

Aldwin must have sensed her irritation, because he chuckled. "Protecting you *is* my responsibility." He stepped past her to better approach the rope.

"Protecting me while holding me hostage and hauling me halfway across Moydenshire," she grumbled.

"Mmm."

He leapt for the rope. When his hands clenched around it, his face contorted with pain.

Just as she planned to ask if he was all right to climb, he started up. His cloak parted at the waist, revealing his strong legs flexing with each movement. His boots whispered against the rope, marking his upward progression. He moved as if 'twere no effort at all.

She glanced back at Peyton who hadn't yet stirred, glad of something to look at other than Aldwin's physique. "In truth, I am relieved you are going first. I did not want you looking up my gown."

Aldwin's indignant laugh carried down to her.

She squinted up at him. Now he'd say he was too much of a knight to do such a thing? Ha.

A groan carried from across the cavern.

She glanced back at Peyton. Still lying on the ground, he reached up to touch his forehead.

"He is waking," she called to Aldwin, who neared the sunlight above.

Aldwin grunted, a sound of annoyance and pain. Dirt showered down on the water, and then he was through the opening.

He leaned down into the hole. "Jump to the rope. I will pull you up."

"What about your wound?"

Scowling, he said, "Do not argue. Just—"

Another groan from Peyton. She glanced over her shoulder, to see him rise up to sitting, his enraged gaze on her.

Leona threw herself to the rope. Its roughness scratched her palms and the insides of her wrists, but, looking to Aldwin above, she started to climb.

The rope jerked as he pulled her higher.

Rocks clattered behind her. "Bitch," Peyton yelled. "Ye will not get away."

A fist-sized stone soared past her right elbow and slammed into the cavern ceiling. Dirt rained on her head.

She grabbed higher up the rope, while at the same time,

Aldwin hauled her upward. Just a little farther and she'd be in sunlight.

Another rock flew, barely missing her torso. Aldwin tugged again on the rope. Her head cleared the hole, and then her shoulders. Clawing her hands into the ground, she pulled herself out.

Scrambling to her knees, she spun and reached for the rope, relishing the moment she yanked it out of Peyton's reach. However, the rope's end was already in Aldwin's grasp.

He grinned at her, while a roar echoed up from the cavern.

She brushed off her hands, even as he tossed aside the rope. His crossbow at the ready, he darted toward the fallen tree. Crouched behind it, he studied the surroundings.

Leona crept up behind him.

"Do not look beyond the log."

"Why not?"

"'Tis not a pleasant sight."

Indeed? Did he think she was weak of stomach?

Raising his weapon, he edged forward, as though to better see into the woods. Curiosity gnawed at her and she glanced beyond the log. Several yards from a fallen stag, two young men lay dead. The closest one sprawled on his back, a crossbow bolt buried in his chest. The other, his face twisted in agony, curled on his side, his hand clutching the bolt piercing his gut; another bolt jutted from his hip. Blood darkened the ground around them.

Leona tore her gaze away. She'd seen death before. Only months ago, she'd helped bathe her mother's body and ready her for burial. Still—

"I told you not to look," Aldwin said, his expression grim.

"Aye."

"I did not want to kill those men, but I had no choice. They refused to put down their weapons. They would have killed me—*us*—if I had not killed them. Remember that." He rose, swung his legs over the tree, and started down toward the woods.

Aldwin hadn't grabbed her hand, tied her, or ordered her to stay by him. But, Leona realized, he didn't have to. She'd rather be his hostage than be at the poachers' mercy. After clambering over the tree, she started after him. He didn't say a word or glance at her, yet she sensed he knew she followed.

His crossbow poised in case of an attack, he called, "Rom."

Silence stretched through the forest. A bird rustled in a nearby tree before swooping down to land on a low branch.

"Rom," Aldwin shouted again.

A rustling came from the bushes a short distance away. Rom appeared out of the forest's shadows and trotted toward Aldwin. After halting before his master, the horse whinnied, and then exhaled a breathy snort.

Leaves dangled from Rom's mane. "'Tis all right," Aldwin murmured, running his palm over the destrier's neck.

Leona swallowed. He'd spoken to her like that long ago, when he knelt beside her in the river and splashed water over her burning skin.

"'Tis all right," Aldwin said again, while his splayed hand moved over the destrier's coat. He must be looking for injuries.

Flexing her hands on her stick, she scanned the forest. His attention might be focused elsewhere, but she'd not let the poachers surprise them. Neither would she work herself into a breathless swoon while watching his caresses. With fierce concentration, she scrutinized the bushes and fallen logs.

Still, she couldn't ignore the imagined feel of his hands roving over her, skimming down her face to her neck, and then to the neckline of her gown . . .

"Stop, Leona," she muttered aloud, swishing her stick. "Stop—"

Aldwin appeared at her side, aiming his crossbow at the woods. "You saw someone?"

Argh! "Nay."

"What did you say, then?"

"I was reminding myself of . . . an important matter."

He raised an eyebrow and looked about to laugh.

Annoyance crackled inside her like fat spitting in a pan. Waving her stick at the forest, she said, "At least I am keeping watch."

"As am I. I wanted to be sure Rom wasn't hurt before we traveled on. He, too, is my responsibility."

Touching words, spoken by a warrior. 'Twas admirable he cared so much for his horse.

After returning to Rom, Aldwin took the reins and led the animal forward. "I will lead him to the tree stump over there. 'Twill be easier for you to climb onto his back."

Leona waited for Aldwin to summon her to follow.

He strode on. Sunshine played over his broad back. He looked as strong as his horse. And he was strong, she recalled with a shiver. And warm. And clever. He didn't have to tell her to follow him, because he knew he'd catch her if she ran—just as he knew she didn't want to be stranded in the woods when the poachers returned.

A silent groan broke inside her. He had all the advantage. And he knew it.

Aldwin halted Rom beside the stump. Bowing at the waist in a most elegant way, Aldwin motioned to the saddle.

She rolled her eyes.

"Come, milady. You would not be so foolish as to refuse."

Leona frowned.

"All right. You might, indeed, be so foolish as to refuse. However, you also know that if you disobey, I will come after you and force you onto Rom against your wishes. Therefore, you realize you are wiser *not* to refuse. You will come as I ask."

God above. Her head hurt trying to keep track of his arguments.

"I will come." She strolled to him. "Not because you wish it, but because I am eager to leave these woods."

As she walked, the breeze stirred her damp garments and she silently acknowledged the other reasons why she'd agreed: cold and fatigue. While her body ached with exhaustion, she had little hope of outwitting him.

She drew near, and Aldwin dipped his head. "Thank you."

She smothered an astonished gasp. Why did he bother to be chivalrous? They both knew 'twas irrelevant. "I make no promises for the rest of our travels." She stepped up onto the weathered stump, fingered her hair back over her shoulder, and smiled down at him.

Aldwin's glinting gaze locked with hers. "Do not tempt me, Leona."

He'd bitten out the word *tempt*. The sound held a savage quality that suggested his rational thoughts were losing their fight with his emotions.

"I did not know you were so easily tempted."

As the words left her lips, she realized how coy they sounded. *Ugh!*

She clambered onto Rom's back, smoothed her clothing, and dared to glance down at Aldwin adjusting Rom's bridle. His jaw looked hard enough to snap.

He hadn't answered her. Why not?

Sweat dampened her palms. Before she could dry them, he drew Rom to a walk.

‡ ‡ ‡

Sedgewick yanked open the solar door and shoved Veronique inside. His sweaty hands squeezed her breasts while he breathed in feverish pants. "Now," he said, "my reward."

"And you shall have it," she purred, her tongue clashing with his in a hot, slippery kiss. "But first, I want to see the necklace."

Sedgewick whined. "Later." He nuzzled her while edging her toward the bed.

Setting her palm against his chest, she kissed him while easing away. "I want to wear it. Once we sell it, 'twill be gone." She bit his lip on a wild little moan. "I want to feel that ruby rubbing against my skin, while you—"

"While I what?" he urged.

Veronique laughed. "Whatever you desire."

His eyes dropped on a lusty shudder, and she took the opportunity to step toward the small, rectangular chest on the table. Ransley had put the pendant inside during their meeting, promising no one would touch it since this was his private chamber.

She tried to lift the lid, but the box seemed to be locked.

"Where is the key?" she muttered.

Sedgewick sighed. "I do not know." His hands slid up her waist from behind to fondle her breasts. "Forget the pendant."

Foreboding gnawed at her, a gut instinct she couldn't ignore. She had no reason to distrust Ransley. Did she?

"I want to see the jewel." Veronique pulled out of Sedgewick's grasp.

"If the box is locked—"

She grabbed it from the table and hurled it against the stone wall. One of the sides splintered, but the wood held together.

Rage flared as she snatched the box from the floor. With an angry shriek, she threw it again. The box collapsed. Bits of wood and items from inside landed on the planks.

She bent and examined the rubble. Gold rings that had likely belonged to Ransley's wife; a delicate circlet; a heavy silver pin wrapped in cloth; and—

Sedgewick swore, even as shock crashed through her. No ruby pendant.

After pocketing the rings and pin, Veronique stood. Fury blazed inside her. "Where. Is. It?" She whirled on the baron. "Did you take it?"

"Of course not! I saw Ransley lock it away." Sedgewick scowled. "Which means someone else who knew of the chest came into the solar and took it."

"More likely Ransley," Veronique said. "He means to deceive us. Betray us to Geoffrey."

"He hates de Lanceau."

"Does he? Or was that all an act?"

The baron's face paled. "God's blood!"

Veronique strode to the door, drawing her knife from her sleeve's hem, aware of Sedgewick's jostled strides behind her. Without slowing her pace, she hurried down to the great hall, where Ransley was standing beside the lord's table, one unsteady hand gripping the oak to hold him upright while he raked his other hand through his hair.

He motioned to a maidservant. "Where is Leona?"

Leona. Veronique ground her teeth. She hadn't been

included in the meeting, but mayhap she'd found out about the pendant. Would Ransley's daughter have decided to take her father's loyalties into her own hands?

The girl curtsied. "I have not seen Lady Ransley today, milord."

"I wish to speak with her." He rubbed his brow as though battling a brutal headache. "Tell her I . . . 'twould please me very much."

The girl's gaze slid to Veronique and widened with fright before she said, "Aye, milord," and hurried away.

Ransley's bloodshot gaze met Veronique's as she approached. "Have you seen my daughter?"

"I have not," Veronique said, careful to steel the anger from her voice. "How odd, but I do not remember seeing her since we arrived."

"Nor do I," Sedgewick muttered.

Ransley's frown deepened. "'Tis not like her. She must be busy about the keep."

"Or she has run off."

"What?" Ransley roared, and then grimaced. "What do you—?" His gaze dropped to the dagger in her hand. "Put that knife away."

"Where is the pendant?"

Ransley's mouth tightened. "I ordered you to put the knife away."

Veronique's fingers flexed on the handle. "I asked you about the pendant."

Ransley's unshaven face reddened as he thrust a finger at her. "You are a guest of my household. When I order you to—"

"Shut up!" She raised the dagger, aiming it at his chest.

"Where is the pendant?"

"Why, you impertinent—Guards!" Ransley bellowed. "Arrest this woman!"

Wretched, naïve fool! A harsh laugh grated from Veronique's lips, an unearthly sound that echoed in the quiet hall.

"Guards!" Ransley bellowed again.

"Summon them all you like," Sedgewick sneered. "Your men will not help you."

Ransley motioned to the men-at-arms standing near the wall. They dropped their gazes. He started toward them. "Look at me! I am the lord of this keep. I order you—"

"I order *you*," Veronique said coldly. "The pendant. Where is it? I will not ask again."

Ransley spun, his eyes hard as stone. "Do you *dare* to threaten me?"

She raised her eyebrows. Oh, she dared. Tipping her head, she motioned to the mercenaries lingering near the entrance to the stairwell. "Tie him to his chair."

Ransley reached for his sword. The scabbard was empty.

"I took your blade last night," she said, gloating, as the mercenaries grabbed Ransley's arms and hauled him backward to the dais. He fought, but was no match for the four large men, who bound him hand and foot to the oak chair.

"I demand that you untie me," Ransley yelled.

"The baron and I make the demands now." Veronique stepped up on the dais and, pressing her palms flat on the stained tablecloth, leaned over him. "Now, you will tell me about the pendant, or—"

The chair rocked as he struggled. "'Tis safe in the box where I left it. You saw."

She shook her head. "'Tis gone."

He stilled. Shock widened his gaze. "Where is it, then?"

"You tell me."

"I do not—"

Despite the odor of his filthy garments, she leaned even closer, fixing him with a frosty glare. "You might not have taken it, but you could have told Leona where 'twas hidden."

"Leona?" Worry darkened his eyes. "I told her naught."

Veronique raised the knife, holding it so light glinted off its surface. Glancing up at the nearest mercenary, she said, "Search the keep. Find Leona Ransley. Bring her to me."

CHAPTER THIRTEEN

Refusing to look back at Leona, even though he sensed her questioning stare, Aldwin led Rom back to the fallen tree where he'd fought the poachers.

I did not know you were so easily tempted.

Her words repeated in Aldwin's mind. She'd spoken with such guilelessness. But those words were another reminder he couldn't trust her. After their tousle in the cavern, she knew the physical effect she had upon him.

He *was* easily tempted. By her. That knowledge both infuriated and fascinated him, for if she decided to pursue that temptation, he knew, without doubt, he'd lose to his rash nature. God only knew what might happen then.

He halted Rom by the fallen poachers. Leaving them to their comrades, he clenched his teeth against the pain in his side and hoisted the stag up behind her. Then he headed to the river and tossed the carcass into the water. When the poachers returned, they wouldn't find their illegal spoils still waiting for them.

He washed his hands in the water. Then, drawing in a

fortifying breath, he swung up into the saddle behind Leona.

I did not know you were so easily tempted.

Her words teased again as he settled against her, trying to ignore his hose dragging against her gown, her hair brushing his arm, and her scent. His loins stirred.

He spurred Rom into the forest, even as he heard once more: *I did not know you were so easily tempted.* This time, her voice sounded husky with desire—the way she'd speak when she meant to seduce him. Aching heat stretched his groin, not helped by the jostling together of their bodies as Rom traveled uneven ground.

His side ached, too, but in a very different way. Once he got Leona to safety, he must see to his wound.

Leona shifted forward, putting distance between them, as she had the other eve when they rode to the forest. Not enough distance that he could forget her sitting between his thighs, but he'd endure. She looked uncomfortable, though, with her back as straight as a roofing truss. If a leaf dropped on her shoulder, she'd likely shriek and jump in the air.

He glowered at her lustrous hair, close enough to seize in his fist. How his fingers itched to pluck a leaf from a branch and toss it at her, to see her flinch. To torment her, as she tormented him.

Such unchivalrous thoughts. He should not indulge such folly.

Aldwin forced his attention to the forest. No sign yet of the poachers' return. He steered Rom toward the road.

Leona's head turned. Sunlight softened the curve of her cheek as she asked, "Where are we headed?"

"A village where we will spend the night."

Did her posture stiffen even more? He hadn't thought it possible.

"Where, exactly?"

"Does it matter? You will go where Rom and I take you."

Her eyes hardened beneath the sweep of her lashes. "I am, indeed, going where you say. Thus, because my question is of little consequence, you have no reason to deny me an answer."

She'd mimicked his exact tone when he challenged her refusal to obey him a short while ago. Laughter rumbled in his chest. "Very well, then. We are headed to a village north of this forest, a day's journey from Branton Keep."

"Oh, that one."

He grinned.

The trees ahead thinned. Moments later, Rom's hooves clopped on the hard-packed dirt road.

"Hold onto Rom's mane," Aldwin said.

"Did you see poachers?"

"Nay, and I do not wish to." Aldwin kicked Rom to a gallop.

Even when they'd cleared the forest, he kept Rom at a brisk pace. Twice, he stopped to water Rom at the river and give Leona a moment to stretch her legs; while she attended to her private needs, he washed his wound. In a small town where boats bobbed at a dock, he halted only long enough to lean down from Rom's back and buy two pork pies from a street vendor before nudging the destrier onward.

When the afternoon sun slid toward the hill ahead, he knew they neared their destination. Good. From the pain in his side, he knew he'd be wise not to travel much farther this day.

"We are almost at the village," he said, breaking the silence between him and Leona that had persisted most of the day. He'd tried to initiate conversation, without much success. No matter. Once they were settled for the eve, he'd ask her how she got the pendant, as well as the other questions he'd thought of during the ride.

Leona's head turned. "This landscape seems familiar." Her gaze fixed on the church steeple rising from behind slate-roofed buildings. "Is this Anwenbury?"

"Aye." Hellfire. If she knew her surroundings, she might well know the roads away from here.

"My parents brought me and Ward to a fair here when we were children," she said over her shoulder. "My father pointed out the church because of the stone carvings above the door. My mother found silk for a special gown for me. I wore it when . . ." She shrugged. "Never mind."

"When you were stung," he finished for her.

She nodded. He sensed her retreating into her thoughts again.

"This eve, we will eat well and rest," he said. "'Tis safest for both of us if you do as I ask tonight. All right?"

"I will not pose as your wife and share your bed. If you even *think* to ask that of me—"

Aldwin laughed.

"'Tis not amusing." She rammed her elbow back, knocking his arm against his side.

He groaned.

She twisted to look back at him. "Oh! I am sorry."

He exhaled a shuddered gasp and willed the agony to diminish.

"I did not mean to . . . I am sorry," she repeated, her expression one of genuine regret.

"I am all right," he ground out. How he wished for a strong pint of ale. That would dim the pain as well as quench his thirst.

He turned Rom off the main road and down a narrower one dotted with wattle-and-daub cottages. Squinting against the dust, he looked for the sign: a carved wooden chicken hanging from a post by the road. There. Two cottages down.

He guided Rom into the dirt yard. Hens scratched in the earth beside the low-roofed barn while a black and white dog darted to and fro, keeping them herded together. Neat rows of vegetables grew in a fenced area beyond the home. When they drew near, the dog rushed forward, barking.

The cottage door flew open, and a man with dark brown hair trudged out. When his gaze lit upon Rom, his eyes widened.

"Are you Neale Vale?" Aldwin called.

"I am." As the dog raced around Rom's legs, Neale hurried forward. "Soot, come 'ere." He grabbed the leather strip around the dog's neck and pulled her back. "Hush."

Tongue lolling, Soot barked once more and reluctantly sat, while casting a baleful glance at the chickens straying from their neat grouping.

"My name is Aldwin Treynarde. My lord, Geoffrey de Lanceau, said I could call upon you if needed."

Neale bowed.

Aldwin flicked aside part of Leona's skirt to reach into the saddlebag and draw out a sealed parchment. "He said to give this to you." Leaning down—and wincing at the pain—he offered the document to Neale, who took and unfurled it. A moment later, his gaze rose.

Aldwin waited for the exchange that must come next. If one word was incorrect, he must turn Rom and gallop away.

"I 'ave 'eard tales of a mighty boar in this county," Neale said with care.

"A demented boar," Aldwin added, "who fell in love with a black-haired beauty."

He sensed Leona shifting in the saddle. "Aldwin, what—?"

He raised a hand to stay her.

"A knight's quest fer vengeance," Neale said.

"In love, they found truth and honor."

Neale grinned and nodded.

"Demented boar?" Leona said. "Quests?"

"Part of a secret code," Aldwin murmured against her hair, "made up of four unique sentences. Only de Lanceau's most trusted men know them."

"I am 'onored, Aldwin, ta welcome ye to me 'ome." Neale said, releasing Soot to return to herding the hens. "Whatever ye need—"

"Neale!" The shout came from inside the cottage, before a chicken, flapping and squawking, scrambled through the open doorway into the yard. "Fool 'usband! 'Ow many times must I ask ye ta close the door? Where 'ave ye got to—?"

A plump, graying-haired woman with a baby on her hip appeared on the doorstep. The instant she saw the horse, she fell silent.

"Wot is it, Mama?" A dark-haired girl who looked about twelve years old and strongly resembled Neale appeared at the wife's side, followed by two younger boys.

"Stay inside." The mother shooed them away. Casting her husband a worried glance, she shut the door.

"Me family." Neale's wry smile intensified the wrinkles around his eyes. "Please fergive me wife's manner, milord. There 'ave been too many riders on the road lately."

Aldwin sensed an underlying message in Neale's words. "You must tell me about these riders."

"Of course." Neale's gaze slipped to Leona. "What else, milord, might ye need of me?"

"Food and lodging. Can you offer such?"

"Aye. Our 'ome is small, but—" Neale clapped his hands. "Wait. Me wife's sister and 'er family are away. Ye can use their cottage."

"Thank you."

Neale bowed again, and his scuffed boots scraped on the dirt as he turned to the cottage. "I will fetch the key and me children ta assist ye. 'Tis the fourth cottage down with the wood piled near the barn. I will meet ye there."

‡ ‡ ‡

"We would've been 'ere earlier," a man was saying to Sedgewick, "but we ran into a bit o' a fight."

Veronique drew her gaze from the unconscious Ransley, whom Sedgewick had walloped a short while ago for trying to bribe a mercenary to untie him, and fought a flare of lust. She knew that gravelly voice. Glancing across the hall, she spied a broad-shouldered man with shaggy, graying brown hair flanked by several younger men. *Clif.*

As he drew a tied pair of dead rabbits from his shoulder, he winced, drawing her focus to his facial scar. Not a repulsive disfigurement, but one that somehow made him all the more interesting to her.

Her hips gliding in lazy steps, she approached the men. The baron smiled at her, while Clif bowed. "Milady."

His voice held the hint of a caress, a reminder of their tryst. Her womb throbbed.

"How good to see you again." She shifted her stance to accentuate her body's feminine sway, while holding Clif's stare. Was he enough of a man to accept such a subtle challenge, especially in front of Sedgewick?

Interest sparkled in Clif's eyes. He held up the rabbits. "For ye, milady. I meant ta bring ye venison, as ye asked, but—"

The baron frowned. "You said you had a fight?"

A scowl darkened Clif's face. "One o' de Lanceau's men destroyed some o' me traps. 'E was in the woods when we went this morn. A man named Treynarde."

Sedgewick's gaze flew to Veronique. "*Aldwin* Treynarde?"

"The same," Clif said. "'E killed me nephew Emmet, and another of me men. Some o' the others"—he indicated the poachers behind him—"especially me men outside, need a 'ealer."

The baron wiped sweat from his upper lip. "Did Aldwin follow you here? If you brought de Lanceau's man—"

"'E did not follow. I do not know where 'e is now. 'E's travelin' with a woman. One of me men saw 'er."

"A woman?" Suspicion quickened Veronique's pulse. "What did she look like?"

"Peyton." Clif motioned for a poacher standing a few steps behind to answer.

"Tall. Long 'air. A spirited wench. Was wearin' a gold chain around 'er neck," Peyton said, while rubbing at a sore on his face.

A dull pounding filled Veronique's ears. She looked at the baron, who looked equally stunned. "Peyton, did you see the necklace?"

The man shook his head. "'Twas beneath her clothes. The chain was gold, though."

Clif's lip curled. "I will find that Treynarde and run 'im through fer killin' Emmet—"

"Did you catch the woman's name?" Veronique cut in.

Peyton nodded. "Leona."

Ignoring Clif's grumbling, Veronique tightened her hands into fists. No wonder Ransley's daughter wasn't found at the keep. Somehow, she'd met up with Aldwin. Was the necklace she wore the ruby pendant? A vital question that must be answered.

Veronique looked at Sedgewick, to find him grinning. "Aldwin is one of de Lanceau's trusted men. His life would be worth a great deal to his lordship."

A smug cackle broke from her. "True. Moreover, you deserve your chance to make him suffer for betraying you to Geoffrey's allies after the crossbow shooting. Aldwin's account helped send you to the king's dungeons, did it not?"

"Aye."

She turned to Clif, who appeared disgruntled. With a coaxing smile, she said, "Thank you for the rabbits and the good information you have given us."

His head dipped in a stiff nod.

"We have asked much of you and your men, but there is one more task we require. Bring Aldwin, Leona, and that pendant she is wearing to us"—Veronique trailed her fingers down his cloak—"and you will be very well rewarded."

Clif licked his bottom lip. "How well?"

"You and your men will be rich enough to live as lords."

Pleased murmurs rippled through the poachers behind him.

"Lords," Clif said with a rough growl, "who deserve ladies."

Veronique smothered a sharp flutter of desire. "Do you agree?"

"An enticing offer." Cliff's mouth eased into a brazen grin. "I do agree, milady, fer I live ta please ye."

‡ ‡ ‡

Leona stepped inside the one-room, dirt-floored cottage and rubbed her arms with her hands. This was obviously home to a family. A length of twine stretched below the beams running between opposite walls, providing a clothesline where assorted garments hung in an orderly row. A clean but scratched oak table and benches provided an eating area near the small kitchen. Against the far wall were two cupboards, three pallets covered with patched blankets, a wooden stool, and a cot.

Aldwin and Neale's voices carried from outside the doorway, close enough she knew she couldn't flee. Not that she meant to run right now. Her dry throat begged for a drink and her legs ached from the day's ride. They hadn't hurt this much even when she'd beaten her brother home from their summer swim in the river and won their bet. She'd almost fainted from gasping for breath. For losing the bet, Ward had to wear one of her gowns to the evening meal, but somehow, he'd turned the embarrassing event into a jest that had the entire hall laughing.

Ward, how I miss you. Especially now.

She turned at footfalls behind her. The light in the doorway shifted as Aldwin strode through.

"This should serve us well," he said.

"Remember, I am not posing as your wife."

His attention settled on her. "I remember."

"How, exactly, did you explain us traveling together?"

"I told Neale that you are a runaway wife. De Lanceau sent me to find you."

"*What—?*"

"I am to return you to your lord husband, who is a good

friend of de Lanceau's."

Relief warred with her annoyance. Aldwin had kept his promise and not claimed she was his wife. His lie, however, left him fully in control in their dealings with Neale's family. Describing her as a runaway eliminated any chance for her to secretly ask for help; none of them would risk offending de Lanceau, or her supposed lord husband, by helping her to escape Aldwin.

How clever of him.

Was that triumph glittering in his eyes?

"I did not forget what you asked of me," Aldwin said quietly. "Now I ask you to respect my wishes and accept the hospitality these good folk are providing us."

More footsteps carried from beyond, and then Neale walked in with his daughter, who carried an armload of firewood. The girl hurried to the stone fire pit in the middle of the cottage and began building a fire.

"I spoke with me wife," Neale said to Aldwin. "Me sons will be along soon with food and wine. Me oldest is carin' fer yer 'orse now."

Aldwin smiled. "Please thank him for me."

Neale waved a hand. "We are glad ta 'elp. Oh, and me wife is readyin' water. I will fetch the bathing tub from the barn fer ye."

Leona blinked. Bathing tub?

She looked at Aldwin. He winked.

Shimmering warmth slipped through her. Before she could say a word, the girl hurried past and out the door. Neale raised his brows and looked at Aldwin. A silent question.

"We will speak in here," Aldwin said.

Neale's cautious gaze shifted to Leona, but then, with a nod, he pulled the door closed.

"What you hear cannot be repeated, Leona," Aldwin said. "Do you understand?"

"All right."

Turning to Neale, Aldwin said, "You mentioned travelers earlier."

"Aye. As ye may or may not know, I sell eggs and vegetables at the town market. I deliver two dozen eggs to the baker each morn. Me brother also owns the local tavern. O'er the past days, we 'ave seen many strangers ta this village. Too many fer this time o' year and this quiet village."

"Go on."

"The travelers," Neale said, "are mercenaries."

"Mercenaries!" Aldwin scowled. "Are you certain?"

"Aye. They're 'eaded to Pryerston Keep."

"*Pryerston?*" Leona choked out. Her father didn't trust mercenaries. He thought them a ruthless, greedy, unreliable lot. "You are mistaken."

Aldwin touched her arm. "Leona—"

She shrugged off his hold. "You have confused the keep's name."

Neale's eyes narrowed. "I am certain 'twas Pryerston."

Denial burned inside her. "Who told you? Your brother? He must have got it wrong."

Neale's expression hardened before he looked at Aldwin. "A couple o' days ago, me brother noticed three mercenaries come into 'is tavern. 'E sent word ta me, and I rode to the tavern and pretended ta drink. Not long after, the men stepped outside. I followed and peeked through a split panel in the stable's wall. They met with a fellow with a scarred face and limp—"

"Clif," Aldwin murmured.

"—'E told them they'd get silver if they went ta Pryerston and did as instructed."

Aldwin's scowl deepened. "Did this man say what they must do?"

Neale shook his head. "Someone came ta the stable. I didn't want ta be caught so I went back inside the tavern. When I went back out a short while later, the men 'ad gone."

"Did you inform de Lanceau of this meeting?" Aldwin asked.

"Aye."

Leona forced down a painful swallow. When de Lanceau got Neale's message, he'd send men to Pryerston to investigate.

"An honorable man, Lord Ransley, 'afore 'is wife died." Regret softened Neale's voice.

"*Still* an honorable man," Leona said, holding his gaze.

If her suspicions were correct, Veronique and the baron had summoned the mercenaries. Why? How did Pryerston Keep fit into their wretched plots?

Even more daunting . . . If the baron and Veronique wielded such authority, what had happened to her father?

Chapter Fourteen

When Neale and his two sons left the cottage with empty buckets, Aldwin gestured to the large, round wooden bathing tub by the fireside. "For you, Leona."

The steaming water glinted. Neale and his sons had toiled for some time to fill the tub, while the daughter brought towels, soap, and fresh garments.

Gnawing a fingernail, Leona nodded in thanks. Her thoughts, though, were still heavy with what she'd heard about Pryerston. Misery and worry ate at her. How could she indulge in a cleansing soak when she had far more urgent concerns?

As if reading her thoughts, Aldwin said, "Whatever you are thinking, it can wait until after you have bathed. Aye?"

He was right. Moreover, a bath might help refresh her tired mind. As soon as Leona acknowledged such, she barely resisted the urge to tear off her grimy clothes. Yet as much as she appreciated the bath, she wasn't going to let him stand guard over her while she undressed and scrubbed her body.

A frown touched Aldwin's brow. "Do you not wish to bathe?"

"I do. But—"

"I will wait outside."

Good.

Especially good, she realized with a burst of hope. His chivalrous gesture might work to her advantage. The cottage had two shuttered windows; she'd be out one before he guessed she'd got away.

Her gaze slid longingly to the bath, which looked high enough to reach her hips; Neale had drawn over the wooden stool in case she wished to set it in the tub to help her bathe. He'd also left an extra bucket of water for rinsing her hair. Her exhausted body ached to slip into the warm, soothing depths. A shame, not to be able to indulge, but cleanliness took second place to her escape.

Stifling a surge of excitement, she nodded. "Thank you."

Aldwin smiled. That deliberate tilt of his mouth sent unease rippling through her.

"I am sure you will not cause Gillian any worry," he said. "But, in case you were going to try to escape, I should warn you, you will only be wasting your efforts."

Really? He was one man. He couldn't possibly guard both windows and the door.

She tried very hard not to smile back. "How courteous of you to warn me."

He didn't appear courteous. He looked as though his emotions seethed.

What could be running through his mind? Was he mulling what Neale had told him about Pryerston? Or was Aldwin displeased at having to spend coin on a bath for her? Did he resent her bathing first, when he was tired and wounded? Or mayhap the thought of her removing her garments unsettled him.

Their gazes clashed, and a glimmering heat washed over her, roused by the intensity of his stare. For a moment, she felt again his body's bold weight against hers, their breaths blending, and the silky glide of his lips.

He stood very still, watching her. Was he reminding her that he controlled all elements of their relationship, akin to long-ago Romans and their slaves?

He might think such. However, she was no man's lady.

A dangerous shudder rippled through Leona. She slid her hand up between her breasts to the neckline of her gown in a slow, purposeful glide. Beneath her palm, the cloth whispered, the sound of a sigh. Fingering the fabric aside, she bared her shoulder.

"What a tempting bath."

Aldwin's lips parted on a harsh breath. A flush darkened his cheekbones before he spun, strode to the door, and pulled it open. A twilight breeze gusted inside, making the fire flicker.

The door slammed.

Lowering her hand, Leona turned to Gillian. The girl immediately curtsied. "What is your wish, mil—?"

"Gillian, you must help me."

The girl rose, her expression earnest. She clutched a bar of soap. "Of course, milady."

Touching the girl's shoulder, Leona whispered, "I must escape."

Worry shadowed Gillian's eyes. "Oh, nay—"

"You must pretend to be helping me with my bath. Splash the water. Talk, as though chatting with me. While you do such, I will slip out the window."

Gillian shook her head. "I am sorry, but I cannot."

Frustration bubbled inside Leona, threatening to boil over in a scream. "You can. Please."

"He warned me you might say such," the girl said, biting her lip. Her nails traced faint lines into the soap. "He said you—"

The shutter at the far window jarred, bumped from the outside. Leona frowned. "What—?"

Thud, thud, thud. The hammering stopped, then resumed.

Marching across the dirt floor, Leona drew open the shutters. A thick wooden board stretched diagonally across the opening. Holding up another piece of wood, obviously planning to nail it across the other to block the opening, Aldwin smiled at her. "Leona."

She stifled a groan. "Did you pay Neale for the privilege of blocking the windows?"

"I did."

God's teeth, but Aldwin was impossible! Shooting him a lethal glare, she slammed the shutters.

Thud, thud, thud.

She hurried the other window and opened the shutters. Neale stood outside, lining up a plank. He bowed. Scowling, she closed the shutters and walked back to the bath.

Gillian offered a tremulous smile. "Will you bathe now, milady? The water will get cold."

Leona's focus slid to the door. Could she make a run for it? Get out and away before Aldwin realized what she'd done? Not likely. He'd probably anticipated such an attempt.

Thud, thud, came again from outside.

She clenched her teeth. When he least suspected her to escape, she would.

As she crossed to the bath, her gaze fell upon the door panel. A tantalizing idea came to mind. Aldwin might stop her from leaving the cottage, but she'd keep him from coming in. Above all, while she was bathing.

"Milady?"

"One moment." Leona crossed to the door. Grabbing hold of the central door bolt, she slid it into place.

"'Tis not right," Gillian muttered. "I must tell Aldwin."

"Nay! Do not say a word. I do not want Aldwin to come in while I am naked, you see. The door will stay bolted until I am done. 'Tis all."

Gillian frowned. "But—"

"I would like to have my bath now."

Gillian sucked in her bottom lip, her gaze uncertain. But she came to Leona's side and began to help with her garments.

As the dirty gown and chemise pulled away from Leona's body, she sighed. How blissful 'twould be to wash.

Male voices carried from outside. Her arms instinctively crossed over her breasts, causing the pendant's chain to chime. Anxiety ran through her, but also a bubble of glee. She shouldn't fret. Aldwin wouldn't be coming back inside until she permitted it.

She removed her still damp boots, then drew the fine chain over her head and set the pendant atop her discarded clothes, where it would stay dry and safe. Holding onto the edge of the tub, she climbed into the water. The scent of wet oak surrounded her while she sank farther into the depths.

Gillian stood by the tub. She offered the soap, a coarse lye blend likely made by a local villager. For that cleansing soap, though, Leona would have traded a handful of costly spices.

Just as she dipped the soap beneath the water, a knock sounded on the door.

"Leona."

Aldwin. She paused. "Aye?"

"Are you bathing?"

Why don't you try to come in and see?

"Why must you ask?"

He cursed, the sound muted by the panel. More briskly, he said, "Are you being fair to Gillian? If not—"

"I am being fair. We are getting along well."

"Is that so, Gillian?" Aldwin asked.

"A-aye."

"Good." He didn't sound convinced.

Leona choked down a mischievous giggle. "Come in and see for yourself, if you do not believe me."

A long silence. Was he pondering that highly improper suggestion? She smothered a laugh and waited for him to try the door.

Gillian exhaled a worried-sounding sigh.

From outside, she heard another muttered oath, followed by a *smack*—the sound of a fist hitting the door. He obviously didn't like her taunting him.

This little victory was too wonderful to let slip away. "You are not coming in, then?"

"Nay, Leona," he said tightly. "I am not. And you know very well why not."

The crunch of footfalls. He'd walked away.

Smiling, she dipped her hand into the water and began scrubbing her arm. The whispered lather drew her thoughts back to that morning when she'd seen Aldwin washing in the river. As the froth slipped over her arm, she remembered the soapy swell of his shoulder and glistening skin.

So beautiful. Dangerous, but magnificent.

She plunged her hand beneath the water and then, drawing her hair aside, began washing her shoulder and neck. Her skin tingled. He'd touched her here as he turned her face to meet his gaze. When the soap skidded over her flesh, she again felt his fingertips against her jaw, and the heat that had glowed inside her.

A growl rumbled from her.

"You are displeased, milady?"

"Not with the bath."

"Is there aught else you wish? Shall I wash your hair? I will be sure to rinse it with fresh water. Aldwin said I was to help you just as a lady's maid would."

"Really?"

The girl nodded and beamed. "He said if I do well this eve, he will write a letter and tell Lord de Lanceau how skilled I am. 'Twill help me find employment at his castle."

How clever of Aldwin.

Leona leaned forward to reach the back of her neck, but the muscles in her back pinched. She winced.

"Let me help you," Gillian said, and then a gentle cloth smoothed over Leona's shoulders. Leona sighed. With so much to complete each day at Pryerston and so little money to make do, she'd given up luxurious baths months ago. Would it be so wrong to enjoy this one? Closing her eyes, she gave in to Gillian's ministrations.

Some moments later, scrubbed from scalp to toes, Leona stood and took the towel Gillian offered. Leona wrapped it around her dripping body. Holding the edges in one fist, she stepped from the tub, her teeth chattering when the cooler air brushed her damp skin and hair.

Before Leona could say a word, Gillian knelt and began to rub her legs.

Leona stepped back. "Thank you, but I can manage."

Doubt clouded Gillian's gaze. "Am I not tending you correctly?"

Leona groaned inwardly. How could she explain she'd prefer to tend to her own needs? That she'd become so used to doing such that 'twas difficult to accept help—especially when her captor had arranged it?

The girl stared down at her work-reddened hands. "I tended Mama when her belly was swollen with child. Mama grew so large, she couldn't wash her feet or dry her toes. But together, we managed."

Leona fought a pang of guilt. She hated to see Gillian disappointed. As she slipped the pendant's chain back around her neck, she asked, "Would you be able to help me with my clothes?"

Beaming, Gillian scrambled to her feet. "Aye, milady." She hurried to the table and snatched up a folded, brown linen gown and white chemise. "I'm afraid they are not silk, milady. They are clothes that no longer fit Mama and may be too large for you. But they are clean. Far fresher than the garments you . . ." She blushed. "I . . . I will wash and dry your other garments. I promise to do my best work."

Leona smiled and crossed to the table. "Thank you."

Gillian shook out the chemise, and then handed it to Leona. Setting aside her towel, Leona pulled on the worn garment. Loose and comfortable, it smelled of the sunny outdoors.

When Gillian handed over the gown, a knock rattled the door.

"Leona," Aldwin called.

The young girl squawked. Together, they pulled the gown over Leona's wet head.

"Aye?" Leona called, as her face broke free of the bunched fabric and Gillian smoothed it down into place.

"Are you finished bathing?"

Leona straightened the fabric across her bosom and eyed the

door. "I am. The bath is yours."

He cleared his throat. "Are you . . . dressed?"

Nay, I am naked and longing for your lusty kisses. She glared at the door. "Would you go away, if I said 'nay'?"

He laughed. "I am coming in now."

I think not.

Leona watched the door, anticipation swirling inside her.

Gillian tugged on her sleeve. "Milady, you haven't drawn the bolt."

The iron door handle creaked. The panel didn't budge.

A wry chuckle came from outside. "Leona."

She smothered a laugh.

"Open the door."

Not a question, not a plea, but an order. How she loathed him telling her what to do. Setting her hands on her hips, she said, "I think not."

"God's blood—"

"Since you are determined to keep me inside this cottage, I vow you would prefer to sleep outside. If you lie by the door, you will ensure I cannot escape."

"*Leona!*"

"And," she added with a sly grin, "we both know 'tis the most honorable arrangement."

She sensed his fury seeping under the panel like water. She held her breath, waited for his angry retort. To her astonishment, he chuckled.

His footfalls retreated.

Would he sleep outside? He was, after all, a warrior. He'd likely slept on the ground before, although, she realized with a twinge of remorse, that wouldn't be wise with his injury.

Men's voices reached her, indistinct over the snapping fire. Then, from the closest window, came a loud *creak* and *snap*: the sound of the boards being removed.

Gillian wailed and bit her knuckles.

"Do not worry," Leona said.

The shutters opened. Aldwin climbed over the windowsill. When his booted feet landed on the floor, pain flickered across his features, but he shoved his shoulders back and brushed off his hands. A smirk tugged at the corner of his mouth as his gaze fixed upon Leona.

She crossed her arms, determined not to appear unsettled.

Aldwin looked at Gillian and gestured to the window. "Thank you for your help. You may leave now."

"Aye, milord." Gillian gathered up Leona's garments she'd promised to wash.

After snatching up the wooden stool, Aldwin followed her to the window. She flushed as he slid his hand into hers, helped her onto the stool, and then through the window to Neale waiting beyond. Leona gnawed the inside of her lip, for Aldwin smiled at Gillian as if she were the loveliest damsel in all of England.

The shutters banged closed.

Aldwin pivoted to face her.

His smile hardened.

Refusing to look away, Leona stared him down across the space separating them. Warmth and a raw, desperate need began to build within her.

Need to escape.

Need to save her father.

Need to . . . what?

Loud thudding—Neale hammering the boards back into

place—made her jump.

Aldwin walked toward her, his strides loose and unhurried. If she'd ever imagined him an imposing man, he seemed frighteningly so now.

He stopped in front of her. Her folded arms pressed against his tunic. The wool of his cloak scratched the backs of her hands.

Be strong, Leona. Don't let him conquer your will. Don't let him sense your weakness.

His scent—a blend of horse, night air, and minty soap—teased her senses and seduced her to breathe in more deeply. The warmth inside her sharpened, and become a sensation close to anguish.

Slowly, very slowly, he lifted his hand. His fingertips trailed down her cheek. Her lashes fluttered as her mind registered the slight roughness of his skin. Warmth. Yearning.

Need.

She jerked her head to the side, breaking the contact, even as a wild heat skittered across her skin. That touch... She shouldn't crave it.

"Why do you tempt me, Leona?"

"Tempt you? I—"

"Did you bolt the door to annoy me?"

"As I said—"

"So I would come after you?"

Her breath jammed in her lungs, captured by his words. She tried to step away, but he caught her upper arms and slid his hands down, forcing her to uncross her arms.

Before she could wrench away, his fingers linked through hers in a gentle, but restraining, grasp.

Where their skin brushed, a fevered burning began. It licked up her palm, over her fingers, up her wrist until it seemed as though her flesh was afire. The gown that once had seemed comfortable and loose now seemed to chafe.

How mortifying—and frightening—that he could control her body so.

His sinful mouth eased into a half grin before he lifted their joined right hands. She tightened every muscle in her arm and struggled, but he outmaneuvered her, until their raised fingers were before his lips.

Was he going to kiss her hand, like a valiant knight would kiss his lady's?

A fiery spasm ran through her.

"When I touch you, Leona," he murmured against her knuckles, "do I slip past that stubborn armor of yours?"

Armor? Oh, God, the puff of his breath against her skin . . . She blinked and tried to stay focused.

"Do I make you *want*—"

"Hush!"

"—what you have never desired before?"

Drawing in an unsteady breath, she glared at him. "You make no sense."

"I do. You know I do." A brazen smile tilted his mouth. Pursing his lips, he blew across her fingers.

Astonishing sensations leapt through her. Heat. Cold. Longing.

Need.

She shuddered, unable to stop her body from trembling. "Stop."

He blew again. His soft exhalation swept her skin like the brush of the sheerest silk. "Do I tempt you—"

"Stop!"

"—to be—"

"Stop!"

"—a woman?" He kissed her fingers.

Her lips parted on a gasp, and her knees wobbled. That kiss... She felt it down in her womb.

As he raised his chin, she yanked hard on her hand. She expected him to keep her trapped, but abruptly, he released her.

She stumbled back, scrambling for balance.

He turned away. "Tempt me once more this eve, Leona, and I will do far more than kiss you."

CHAPTER FIFTEEN

Refusing to look back at Leona—although he'd love to see her expression after his threat—Aldwin headed to the tub. He *had* to walk away from her. Standing close to her, touching her, made his thoughts shift to the many pleasurable ways to spend a night in a cottage with a woman.

He clenched his hands, welcoming the discomfort. By God, he wouldn't lose his grip on the knightly morals he valued so highly. Not when by tomorrow night, they'd reach Branton Keep. Indeed, his warning he'd do more than kiss Leona was as much to caution himself as her.

When he neared the tub, he tried not to let his strides slow or let his shoulders slump. Yet his pain had worsened to a point he could barely tolerate. He longed to grab his flask and finish off the brandy; he dared not indulge. One careless mistake on his part and Leona would be gone, along with the pendant.

He dipped his fingers into the water, slightly cloudy from the soap Leona had used. The bath wasn't as warm as he'd hoped to cleanse his injury and ease his fatigue, but 'twould do. Neale and his family had done so much; Aldwin wouldn't ask for more hot water. And, after the day's ride, he longed for some quiet.

Leona, thankfully, hadn't said a word since his threat. That could well mean, however, she was up to mischief.

He glanced over his shoulder to find her standing by the pallets, running her fingers through her tresses to smooth the strands. She should be staying warm by the fire while her hair dried, but doubtless she wanted to be as far from him as possible.

Her back faced him but, clearly sensing his stare, she spun around. Suspicion sharpened her gaze and her lips pressed together. Did she think he'd changed his mind about kissing her if she tempted him again? That he wanted to kiss her now?

He did. Despite the tortuous past between them. Despite her aggravating willfulness. Despite the tired gown that swamped her body with all the allure of a turnip sack. Desire for her pulled at him, coaxing him to walk back to her and take what he wanted.

Aldwin forced himself to look at the bath. If their lips met, he wouldn't be satisfied with a kiss. Her hair, tangling in a shiny mane about her shoulders, invited his hands to plunge into it and feel its softness. Her skin, glowing from a healthy scrubbing, begged to be touched. And the gown hiding her lithe beauty . . . His fingers itched to rip off her garments and explore her nakedness.

A muffled sound—an oath?—made him look her way. She'd turned her back to him again.

"Pardon?" he said.

Leona shook her head. With jerky movements, she pulled more hair between her fingers.

"You are not tempting me, are you?"

"Nay!" Leona gaped at him. "Why would you think that?"

He shrugged, then flinched at the pain in his side. "While

I am bathing, do not think about running for the door. I can be out of this tub faster than you imagine. Neale is also keeping watch."

Aldwin caught the hem of his tunic and began drawing it up over his stomach.

"What are you doing?"

"Undressing." When the garment pulled past his rib cage, he groaned. The pain made his stomach churn.

"'Tis . . . 'Tis not—"

"Proper? You do not have to look." Resisting the temptation to remind her in the cavern she'd seen all of him anyway, Aldwin yanked the tunic over his head and dropped it on the floor. He released his breath on a gust.

More muttering. He caught the words *hellfire* and *wretched*.

He fought a grin. "You must have seen your brother undress."

"Aye, years ago." A pause. "He was my *brother*."

Her wobbled voice made him grin. He shouldn't tease her, but she'd enjoyed tormenting him earlier, when she'd slid her fingers over her fetching bosom and then bared her shoulder.

Trying to shake off that enticing memory, he said, "Surely you have seen men-at-arms disrobe. Most warriors do after an afternoon practicing their fighting skills."

"I have," she agreed, "but—"

He flexed his shoulder muscles and rubbed at the tension knotted there.

She made a breathy sound.

A noise a woman made while experiencing bliss.

Desire grabbed at his loins like a whore's hands. God's blood! What she did to him was unprecedented. And she must never know, or she could use that against him. Here. Tonight.

The faster he got in the bath, the better.

His hands dropped to the overtight fastenings of his hose. "As I said, you do not have to watch."

He expected to hear frantic cursing while she turned away in maidenly outrage. Instead, he caught a soft whisper. She'd moved from beside the pallets. Toward him.

Surprise—and anticipation—slammed through him.

She stood only a few steps away, staring at his torso. Not at the bulked swell of his chest, but the slash below his rib cage. The coolness on his skin wasn't a draft, he realized, but blood.

Her gaze lifted to meet his. "'Twill need stitching."

What was she about? Didn't she realize how perilous 'twas for her, when desire raged in his veins?

"I will manage."

She shook her head. "Leave that wound, and 'twill become corrupted."

He was already corrupted, in more ways than he dared admit. Yet in terms of his wound, she spoke true.

"There is a skilled healer at Branton Keep. She will tend my injury when we arrive there."

Leona frowned. "'Twill need care before then."

"I will cleanse it well"—he unfastened one point of his hose—"while in the bath."

Leona's gaze dropped to his fingers, then his swollen loins. Her eyes widened and she stepped back.

Good. She was fleeing.

Squaring her shoulders, she held his stare. "You warriors are all alike. Proud and stubborn. Just like my brother."

"Neither of us as stubborn as you."

Leona smiled. Why did she have to look so beautiful?

Aldwin yanked another point on his hose. It hissed free of its fastening and this time, she whirled away.

"Once you have washed that wound, I will stitch it."

She spoke as a warrior queen would address a lowly foot soldier. "Will you?" he growled, willing her to look at him, but she didn't glance back as she headed for the cupboards.

Before he could protest further, she said, "Unless you close that wound, you will fall ill. Feverish, weak, you will be of little use to Lord de Lanceau."

Damnation, but—

"You got the wound while saving me from cutthroat poachers. Since I do not wish to be blamed for causing the death of the legendary crossbowman Aldwin Treynarde"—she arched an eyebrow at him—"I will stitch your wound."

Facing the cupboard, she pulled open the top drawer.

He rubbed his brow. Somehow, she'd justified her meddling by taking full responsibility for his injury.

The drawer slid shut. She pulled open another.

"Bathe," she said, "and I will find a needle and thread. There must be some about. You can give another coin to Neale to pay for it."

Leona was *not* touching his body tonight. "I will stitch the wound myself."

"Impossible. You cannot reach properly."

"How do I know you will not stab me in the eye? Or sew my skin to my—"

She sighed as though he was speaking nonsense. "I might be tempted"—she waited, clearly toying with him—"but I would not. No matter how much I hated you."

She'd bent down to rummage in a drawer. As she reached forward, her hair slipped past her shoulder in a shiny swath. The gown pulled tighter over her breasts.

Ah, God.

Aldwin tugged down his hose, stepped into the tub, and sank into the water.

Tipping his head back against the wooden side, he groaned.

He'd forgotten the soap.

‡ ‡ ‡

Leona continued to search the kitchen cupboards, trying to ignore the slosh of water. Not an easy task, when the aftereffects of Aldwin's request to bring him the soap still sparked inside her.

"Leona," he'd said in a voice so tight, she thought he'd break his teeth speaking her name. "I need the soap."

"Mmm." She'd kept searching through the clothing in the drawer. If he wanted the soap, he could fetch it himself.

"Bring it to me."

Her head snapped up. Glaring at him, she said, "'Tis on the table. Get it yourself."

His gaze lit with anger, as well as frustration. Water clinging to the ends of his hair, he looked at the table and sighed. "I thought, because of my wound—"

Ward used to speak to her in that same self-pitying way, hoping she'd tackle a task for him. Of course, his wounds had been less serious than Aldwin's.

Gripping the tub's rim, Aldwin started to rise. To know he'd soon be walking across the room behind her, naked—

"Wait!" She straightened so fast, her spine popped. "Do

not stand up."

He paused. Muscles bunched in his arms. "How else will I get the soap?"

Was he *grinning?*

"I will fetch it for you." Skewering him with another glare, she added, "For all I know, you might fall getting out of the tub."

"Imagine what I might injure then."

To her embarrassment, she could, indeed, imagine. Heat swept her face. Waving her hand, she said, "Sit down and . . . wait."

To her relief, he sat.

"You are most kind for helping me," he said, an unnerving lightness to his tone.

Kind? I didn't want to see your gorgeous, naked arse. She strode to the table and snatched up the bar. "The longer you soak your injury to cleanse it, the better."

Stay in there all night, why don't you? She almost smiled.

Until he crooked his finger. "As you ordered, I am waiting."

He watched her through the wet tangle of his hair. How wicked he looked. And heart-wrenchingly handsome. And . . .

Don't be a fool!

Leona marched to the tub.

Aldwin's eyes widened with the faintest alarm. "Thank—"

She tossed the soap into the water. It landed with a *plop* near his belly. At least, where she'd guessed his stomach to be, beneath the filmy water.

"—you."

"My pleasure," she'd gritted. Spinning on her heel, she'd gone straight to the kitchen and pulled open the closest drawer, trying not to heed her shaking hands.

As her frazzled mind focused on the items now before her,

she catalogued assorted spoons, a stone mortar and pestle, and other implements. How interesting. No knives. At some point Neale must have removed all that could be used as a weapon.

She pushed the drawer shut and opened another to find several small earthenware pots. After removing the stopper from the largest one, she inhaled the brisk herbal aroma. Ointment. Folded cloths and bandages were pushed to one corner and beside them lay a small drawstring bag. Inside it, she found a small pair of scissors, several needles, and thread.

She snatched up some cloths and the salve. With a triumphant *bang*, she shoved the drawer closed.

When she turned to announce her find, she sensed Aldwin close by. Her gaze flew to the tub. He stood between it and the table, the towel wrapped around his lean hips.

He glanced at the bag in her hand, as though to gauge any potential threat to his well-being. "Did you find a needle and thread?"

She dangled the bag between her fingers.

He didn't look relieved, but worried.

She held up the salve. "Ointment, as well."

He nodded.

Leona frowned. He looked paler than moments ago. Did he fear the pain of the stitches? Or was he concerned she'd do a rotten job?

"What is wrong?" She tried to sound sympathetic.

"Naught."

"Does your wound hurt? Do you feel faint?"

He scowled. A reddish hue tinged his cheekbones. He looked almost . . . embarrassed.

Whatever his quandary was, they'd discuss it later. She put the cloths, bag, and ointment on the table, and then returned to the kitchen for a small pot, which she filled with fresh water. She set the vessel in the fire.

"'Twill be easiest if you stand by the table," Leona said.

"All right."

She drew out a needle, dropped it into the pot, and waited for the water to heat.

As she drained the hot water into the bath to retrieve the needle, footfalls scraped behind her. Aldwin had crossed to the table.

Eyes narrowed, he watched her draw near. The flush still stained his face, and when he exhaled, he emitted a small, distressed groan.

Part of her softened. She genuinely wanted to help him. Yet he was a proud man; she mustn't let him know she'd guessed his fear.

After drawing closer the items she needed, she inspected his wound. How warm and supple his skin felt against her fingertips.

His chest rose and fell on a sharp breath.

"I have sewn stitches before," she said, withdrawing thread from the bag and sitting on the bench beside him. "Ward always came to me when he needed care."

Aldwin stared at the opposite wall, as if he'd discovered a fascinating distraction.

"I will sew first, and then rub in some ointment." She fingered her drying hair back over her shoulder, and then pressed together the edges of his wound.

He flinched.

She clucked her tongue. "I have not started yet."

His hands flexed and unflexed. "Tell me . . . Talk to me . . . about Ward."

A plea, to have a focus other than her stitching.

She might have gloated over his terror. However, she'd vowed to help him; taunting him would only hinder her efforts. Nodding to acknowledge his request, she said, "Ward was always getting into mischief"—she eased the needle into Aldwin's flesh—"right until the day he left Pryerston to begin his adventures in the East."

Aldwin winced.

"I remember him stumbling into the great hall one spring afternoon. I must have been about seven years old." With a soft rasp, she pulled the thread taut. "He clutched his left arm against his chest. My mother was telling me about a lord and his family who'd soon visit the keep. When Ward saw Mother . . ."

Leona pushed in the needle again. Using a cloth, she wiped blood from Aldwin's skin.

He grimaced. "Aye?"

"Ward croaked like a drunken frog." She laughed. "His eyes almost popped out of his head. He looked so comical, I chuckled. So did my mother."

"Then what?"

"He asked me to come outside. Mother, busy with preparations, waved me away. Ward hurried me into the stable, whereupon he pulled up his left sleeve."

Three stitches done. A few more to go.

Sensing Aldwin's stare, Leona looked up at him. He appeared less pale now. A promising sign.

"And?" he pressed.

She smiled, glad her story intrigued him. "He had fallen from a tree. His friends had dared him to climb up and snatch a starling's nest. But before he reached the fourth limb up, his foot slipped. He fell, scraping his arm on a lower branch." She shook her head. "I could have kicked him."

Aldwin chuckled. "Why?"

His easy laughter sent a strange giddiness rushing through her. "We had climbed that same tree many times. I taught him the best way up."

"*You?*"

His shock made her grin.

"My parents never knew. My father would have bellowed until he turned hoarse. Mother would have forbidden me to go outside again. Ward and I swore to keep our tree climbing to ourselves." After dabbing away more blood, she gently pulled the thread to secure another stitch. "I expect Ward ignored my advice about the tree because his friends were goading him on. Because of his carelessness, he tore one of his best tunics and needed five stitches."

Another successful stitch. The wound was coming together nicely.

"While I sewed him up, I scolded him," she went on. "I reminded him that because of his foolishness, I had to look after him."

"What did he say?"

"He reminded me I had been foolish more than once myself."

Aldwin laughed. "You, foolish?"

She frowned up at him.

Aldwin raised an apologetic hand. "I could not resist. You realize, of course, Ward did not have to ask you for help. He could have asked the castle healer or a friend."

"I know. He asked me because I would not give away his secret."

"That he fell from the tree."

"Aye." Leona took another stitch. "Also, that he was terrified of needles."

Aldwin was silent a long moment. "Ah."

"Ah," she repeated, tempted to raise a knowing eyebrow at him. But she didn't.

Their gazes met. Aldwin's brow creased. She wondered if he was angry with her for noticing his fear. But before she could venture another word, he asked, "What terrifies you?"

Her heart squeezed. "Why do you ask?"

"I am curious."

She thought of making up an answer. In this rare moment of understanding between them, though, she didn't want to lie. "Failure," she said softly.

"To escape me?"

"Aye. And to save my father's keep."

Aldwin's rib cage expanded on a breath. "As lord, your sire is responsible for his holdings."

She pulled on the thread and tried to stop her hands from trembling.

When she didn't say more, Aldwin's hand edged under her chin. Tilting her head up, he forced her to meet his stare. "Since we will reach Branton Keep tomorrow, 'tis best I *do* understand. Above all, how you came to have de Lanceau's pendant."

Her palms moistened. She didn't want to reveal her sire's moral weakness. To speak of it was akin to betrayal.

"I vowed to help you, Leona," Aldwin said. "I sense you are caught up in a situation greater than you anticipated. Yet I cannot speak to de Lanceau for you unless I know the truth."

"About the pendant," she murmured.

"To begin. How did you come to have it?"

She rubbed her lips together. "I . . . stole it."

"From the man paid to deliver the jewel to de Lanceau?"

"From the baron and Veronique. I do not know how they got it."

Aldwin's gaze brightened with interest.

She pulled from his hold, relieved he didn't try to keep her captive. As she knotted the thread, she recalled hurrying up the secret passageway that led to the locked door behind a tapestry in her father's solar; she'd huddled against the door, her ear pressed to a crack. "Days ago, they arrived at Pryerston's gates and asked to speak in private with my father. They claimed to have new details of my mother's death. I reminded him 'twas an accident and that no good could come of revisiting her demise, but my sire welcomed them in."

"Did he not know they were criminals? That de Lanceau had been searching for them for years?"

Leona shook her head. "I did not realize who they were, either. I sensed, though, when they arrived at Pryerston, that their intentions were not honorable. That is why I listened in on their meeting."

"Ah."

"My father took them to his solar. There, they presented the pendant and asked him to keep it for them for a while. He agreed."

Aldwin whistled. "He was not suspicious?"

"At first, he was." She blinked away the sting of tears. "He would have refused, I am sure, but Veronique was . . . persuasive. She preyed upon his grief. In return for his help, she promised to see my mother's death avenged."

"I thought 'twas an accident."

His harsh tone made the hair at Leona's nape prickle. "I am certain 'twas. However, Veronique insisted de Lanceau neglected his duty to repair the road my mother traveled the day she died. A terrible storm overtook her and her armed escort on their return from shopping at a nearby market, and the road turned into a sheet of mud; when her horse fell, she was crushed beneath it and died."

Aldwin rubbed Leona's shoulder. Somehow, that made the anguish inside her worse.

"My sire, at one point, believed de Lanceau responsible, too," she went on, focusing on cutting the thread. "My father was devastated by Mother's death. He drank too much and wrote a bitter letter to de Lanceau—"

"I remember it."

She didn't doubt de Lanceau had discussed her sire's fiery words with his trusted men. In his curt reply, de Lanceau had expressed his condolences and promised to have the road inspected and repaired, but hadn't accepted blame. "I urged Father to burn that letter rather than send it, but he wouldn't listen. When he agreed to aid Veronique and the baron, I refused to let him become further enmeshed in that mistake. I took the pendant from its safe box without their knowing, arranged the meeting at the tavern, and—"

"Became my captive."

"Aye."

"What of the ransom? You were determined to have it."

She sighed. "To replenish Pryerston's coffers. That coin is much needed for food, repairs, and"—*shoes to mend little Adeline's legs*—"other necessities."

Aldwin raised his brows. "The revenue from your sire's

estates, wisely spent, should pay for what you mentioned."

"It should, aye." She looked away, hating the moisture blurring her vision. "My father is a strong man. He might be unwell now, but he will rise from his despair. Until then, I must do all I can to help him." Setting aside the scissors, she picked up the ointment pot and pulled off the lid. The strong scent made her eyes water even more.

As she rubbed the greenish cream on his wound, he murmured, "You have risked your life for your sire."

"And the good folk of his keep. Ward would have done so. Since he is dead, the responsibility is mine."

"A noble—but foolish—sentiment."

She paused, and her gaze flicked up to him. His expression held no mockery, only determination.

"You and I both have strong loyalties," she said while applying more ointment.

"On that matter, we agree." A wry smile touched Aldwin's mouth.

She managed a smile back. "How do you feel?"

Dread clouded his gaze. Did he worry he'd need more stitches tonight?

"I am finished tending your wound."

"Oh." He nodded. "Good."

Shifting back on the bench, she dried her fingers on a clean cloth.

His arm muscles rippled as he slowly rolled his shoulders. The planes of his torso shifted, and she smothered an appreciative sigh. What would it feel like to run her hands over his chest? Would that skin feel as smooth as what was at his ribs?

Shaking her head, she pushed the lid back on the ointment

pot. The scissors and needle would need proper cleaning, and—

Strong fingers swept into her hair.

Leona started.

With gentle pressure, Aldwin tipped her head back, his fingers sliding against her nape. He stared down into her face. If he bent at the waist, he could kiss her. *Not* that she wanted such, for he might strain his stitches.

Her breath fluttered. The bench squeaked as she pushed up to standing.

Aldwin didn't let go of her. Neither did he step away, even though their bodies were shamefully close.

Of all wickedness, she yearned for the brush of his mouth. She remembered the delicious, demanding taste of him, and her insides seemed to melt.

He studied her lips. Was he about to say she tempted him? That he was taking the kiss he'd threatened earlier?

Oh, God, aye. Aye!

Her breath floated. Hovered, like a bird waiting to soar.

"Thank you," he murmured, "for tending me."

"Aye," she whispered back.

"I thank you, also, for telling me the truth."

She should say more—something, anything—but her mind seemed hazy. Mayhap the strong-smelling ointment had muddled her senses. Or *he* was confusing her thoughts, with his near nakedness and smile that seemed so genuine.

He is your captor, Leona. Let him into your heart, and you'll never escape.

Turning her head away, she said, "I will tidy the—"

His hand at her nape drew her back.

"Aldw—"

His lips covered hers. Not a hard, possessive kiss. Not a crushing of her will. But an honest, tender kiss that made her heart plummet to her toes.

As quickly as it began, it ended. Her breath whooshed between her lips and she blinked while the cottage gradually came into focus.

Confusion and desire rushed through her while she stared at Aldwin. She squeezed her eyes shut. She did not desire him. Nor did she wish he'd offered more than that fleeting kiss.

"I will tidy up." His footfalls echoed. "Why not eat some of the fare Neale brought, before it grows cold?"

She opened her eyes. Aldwin was pouring water into the pot she'd used to clean the needle. He glanced at her, but she saw none of the longing she'd spied when he drew away, rubbing his lips together.

"That kiss?" she asked.

He shrugged as though she'd mentioned the best way to sweep the floor.

A peculiar ache weighed upon her. "Why did you kiss me? Because, somehow, I tempted you? Because I shared memories of Ward? Because I confided in you about the pendant?"

"Because you are you, Leona. 'Tis reason enough."

‡ ‡ ‡

While Aldwin dealt with the items used to tend his wound, he discreetly watched Leona. She marched to the bathing tub and washed her hands so thoroughly, he vowed she was soaping away all memory of touching him. Then she stomped to the kitchen, fetched bowls, mugs, and spoons, and served herself some vegetable stew and wine. She sat with a huff and began to eat.

Not once did she look at him. But her face remained flushed, suggesting she was fully aware of him and that kiss he'd bestowed upon her.

Aldwin shook his head and tucked the needle, thread, and scissors back into the bag. He couldn't fault her anger. He hadn't intended to kiss her. That brush of his lips had been a whim. An impulsive need to taste her, right then.

Would he do the same again?

Aye.

Aldwin headed to the kitchen and dropped the items back in their place, groaning as he straightened and shoved the drawer shut. Every movement hurt. No doubt he'd feel better after a good meal and a sound night's sleep, as would Leona.

His gaze slid to the fireside where he'd make his bed, perfectly situated between the pallets—where Leona would sleep—and the door. He *must* sleep tonight. If he didn't rest, he'd be ill prepared to protect Leona and the pendant on the last part of their journey to Branton Keep. So close to completing his mission for de Lanceau, he wouldn't fail.

Protect Leona. The thought stirred a heady warmth within him, close to what he'd felt when he kissed her. Each kiss seemed sweeter than the last. The one moments ago, although quick, evoked such an astounding pleasure, he'd had to walk away before he decided he wanted more.

A *lot* more.

A *clank* drew his gaze to the table. Leona was serving herself more stew. Her lashes lifted a fraction and she glanced at him, and he smiled. She set her bowl before her with a *thud* and resumed eating.

The stew's fragrant aroma drew Aldwin to the table. He sat

on the opposite bench, served himself a portion, and scooped up a broth-laden spoonful of cabbage and turnips.

Leona met his gaze. "Why are you so determined to keep me captive and deliver me to de Lanceau?"

He chewed his mouthful. "He ordered me to find the pendant and bring it to him."

She leaned her spoon against the side of her bowl. "Aye, but—"

"I obey my lord's demands."

"He did not order you to take me hostage."

Aldwin shrugged. "After what you told me about the baron and Veronique's dealings at Pryerston, I am even more convinced de Lanceau must hear what you know."

She looked about to challenge his words, but pressed her lips together. A memory of her soft mouth against his flashed into his mind, and, looking down at his stew, he picked through the chunks of vegetables.

"You want to succeed in this mission because of your duty to de Lanceau," she said. "'Tis the only reason?"

Not exactly. "Do I need another?" He pushed more of the savory stew into his mouth.

She wiped her bottom lip with her thumb. "I guess not. I cannot help wondering, though, if there is more."

"I swore fealty to de Lanceau for the rest of my life. Loyalty, chivalry, and honor are very important to me."

"As to all knights. However—"

He swallowed, readying to correct her.

His expression must have alerted her, for her eyes widened. She glanced under the table at his boots. "No spurs."

"No spurs," he agreed.

"I thought—God's teeth! You are not a knight."

"Yet. I will be, soon."

Her expression turned cool. "After you deliver the lost jewel to your lord, you mean? When you return a hero, fit for a glorious *chanson* praising your victory?"

Aldwin's hand clenched so tightly on the spoon, it dug into his palm. "Aye. Then I hope to have earned knighthood."

Anger tightened her posture. "You are the most self-centered, arrogant—"

"Leona!"

"Let me go." Her voice rose. "How dare you drag me into your selfish ambitions when my sire needs my help?"

She stood, the bench moving back with a screech. Harsh gasps broke from her lips as she grabbed the pendant's chain, drew it over her head, and set the jewel on the table. "Take it. Let. Me. Go."

He set down his spoon and rose. "I cannot."

"Liar! How can you—?"

"I cannot protect you, if you are gone from my sight."

Her ranting abruptly stopped. "*Protect* me?" She threw out her hands. "I do not want your help! I can—"

"—outwit the baron and Veronique on your own? Do not be stupid. You would be dead in less than a day. So would your father." If Lord Ransley wasn't dead by their hand already. He wouldn't worry Leona, however, by voicing his suspicions.

Her eyes looked moist. "Now I am stupid? For wanting to save my sire and the keep I call home?"

Balling his hands into fists, Aldwin sighed. This discussion had no hope of being easily resolved. "I know you are upset, Leona, but you will not change my mind. I will not let you go."

Because, Lioness, the thought of losing you rips me apart inside.

He blinked, stunned by the thought. Then he gestured to the table.

"Please. Finish your stew."

"I no longer want it." Her gaze slid past him to the cottage door. Was she thinking of running away? If not now, when he was asleep?

He turned on his heel, crossed to his saddlebag, and drew out the rope.

"Nay!" She backed toward the kitchen.

Halting near the table, he extended a hand. "Give me your right wrist."

Rage glittered in her eyes. "You are *not*—"

He lunged, caught her wrist, and looped the rope around it. Leona fought him.

"I am sorry," he repeated, more gently.

She pulled hard, almost whipping the rope from his grasp. When he drew her wrist back, his stitches pinched. If he'd torn any, he'd have to fix them on his own; she wouldn't help him now.

"I sewed your side," she said in a brittle whisper. "I *cared* for you."

Cared. A word of several meanings, but he doubted she meant any that denoted tenderness. "That was kind and noble of you."

"And yet you tie me."

Aldwin tightened the knot before he raised his gaze to hers. Her anguished stare hit him like a hard slap. "I am tired, Leona." He sounded weary even to his own ears. "My side aches. I need to sleep without worrying you might slip out the door. I cannot trust you; therefore, you must be tied."

"You do not want to trust me." She glowered. "Why should you respect me in that way? I am no more to you than a means to win knighthood."

Her words cut deep. Self-loathing flared inside him. Aye, he did want de Lanceau's commendation and the honor of being dubbed a knight. He'd wanted such for years, not just to advance his military career, but to make up for the disgrace he'd brought upon his respected parents; having them accept him back into the castle where he'd grown up, with pride, was important to him.

But Leona wasn't merely a means to fulfill his ambitions.

How could she believe she meant naught to him? Had she been oblivious to his arousal and impulsive kiss? Had she not sensed, when their lips touched, what he'd revealed to her without words?

Intriguing thoughts, which made him wonder exactly how much experience she'd had with men apart from her brother.

"Leona," he said carefully, "you are not . . . I mean—"

Judging by her expression, she was too upset to listen. He'd only look a fool, stumbling over his words while he tried to convince her he cared about her safety, and that the thought of her running off into the night, alone, on the outskirts of a village harboring traitorous mercenaries, made his innards clench with dread.

He gestured to the pallets by the cupboard. "Come."

Resentment darkened her gaze. Then, as though the fight had drained out of her, she walked forward.

He led her to the pallet closest to the cupboard. "I will leave you enough rope to turn over while you sleep."

Glancing at the other pallets, she said, "Where will you sleep? Not beside me."

Stooping but keeping his body turned so as to keep watch on her, Aldwin wound the rope around the cupboard's leg several times and tied a knot. "I will take some of the blankets and lie by the fire."

He stood. She didn't slump to the bed, lower the defiant tilt of her chin, or step back to put more distance between them, although their bodies almost touched. Standing close—near enough to inhale her sweetish scent—he saw moisture along her lower lashes.

Seeing those tears . . . His gut twisted. "Leona—"

She flicked her bound wrist, making the rope snap like a whip. Then, without a word, she sat on the pallet, drew over a blanket, and lay down with her back facing him.

‡ ‡ ‡

Leona waited for Aldwin to gather his blankets and stride away, then rolled onto her other side to stare at the cupboard's turned legs. Her free hand curled under her head in a makeshift pillow. The straw-filled pallet, while lumpy, was comfortable enough.

In Aldwin's wretched opinion, he might have given her enough lead, but, if she lay on her other side, the rope snaked across her waist and belly. Enough pressure to remind her, with each breath, that she was fettered.

She scowled at the rope twisting like a dark vine around the cupboard's leg, wondering, of all things, if Aldwin's stitches were intact. She'd heard his pained gasp as he straightened away from the pallets, and his relieved grunt moments ago when he dropped the bedding. Arrogant turd. If he'd broken his stitches, he had only himself to blame. But 'twould be a shame when the wound had stitched so well.

A shame, too, that their earlier understanding had turned

to animosity. When she'd accused him of seeing her merely as a means to knighthood, he'd looked wounded. How vividly she remembered the hurt in his eyes, for it had filled her with an anguish unlike any she'd felt before.

She smothered a yawn with the edge of her blanket. How could he cause her such anxiety? What did that nagging angst inside her mean?

The scuffle of boots reached her, followed by rustling cloth. He was either organizing his bed or undressing. She bit her lip against the urge to see for herself. She did *not* care.

Reaching out a finger, Leona traced the knot. She dug in her nail, hoping to find a spot where the binding wasn't as tight. Naught.

How tempting to jump to her feet, shove against the cupboard, and send it crashing to the floor, while she yanked the rope from the leg. But she'd have to get past Aldwin. He'd easily catch her and tie her up again, which meant she'd be right back in this position.

Fatigue and despair threatened to bring her to tears. Crying would solve naught tonight. Neither would fretting about her father and the others at Pryerston Keep who meant so much to her.

Smothering another yawn, she tried not to let her thoughts return to Aldwin. She shut her eyes, tugged the blanket up around her shoulders, and listened to the crackle of the dwindling fire . . .

She stood bound to a tree, her back pressed against the bark and her hands tied behind the trunk. Aldwin stood before her. Twisting her wrists, she jerked her head to the side as he leaned down to take her mouth in a kiss.

"Nay!" She struggled, trying to evade him.

Aldwin's lips brushed hers in a coaxing kiss.

Pleasure. Oh, what pleasure.

She tore her mouth away. "Nay."

"Aye, Leona," he whispered against her cheek. "You want my kiss. Admit that you do."

"Nay," she panted, hating the tears stinging her eyes. "Untie me. Let me go."

He laughed while his hand skimmed down her cheek. She tried to fight the yearning cresting inside her, but her body arched toward his touch, needing more.

Bzzz.

"Bees," she gasped, glancing about to locate them. Her legs shook. She couldn't bear to be stung again. The agony. The horrible, painful swelling. Sickly sweat broke over her body. Fear sharpened each of her breaths.

"Bees!" she repeated.

Aldwin didn't seem to hear her. His fingers slipped down her jaw, along her throat, in tempting caresses that made her limbs weak.

Bzzz.

Leona's eyelids opened. As her sleepy mind focused, she realized the *thud-thud* in her ears was the sound of her hammering pulse.

She blinked, her muzzy gaze coming into focus. Light slipped over the dirt floor underneath the cupboard. Somehow she'd slept through the night. She'd woken from a nightmare about bees.

A shudder rippled through her and she wiped her damp brow.

Bzzz.

Panic jarred her fully awake. She pushed up to sitting, reminded, when the rope scratched her skin, that she was still tied to the cupboard. Trapped, as she'd been years ago, the day she almost died.

Fear raced through her. Had the buzzing come from inside the cottage? Or had her mind, still caught up in the nightmare, tricked her?

Sitting very still, she listened, her free hand twisting into the blankets that had tumbled to her waist. She couldn't remember covering herself with a second blanket. Aldwin must have draped it over her in the night. How thoughtful of him.

She couldn't think about that now. Her frantic gaze searched the sun-streaked cottage before falling to the blankets lying by the cold fire; the top blanket was rumpled as though cast aside when Aldwin rose.

Where was he? Somewhere in the cottage?

"Aldwin?"

As she spoke, she saw the cottage door stood slightly ajar—

Bzzz.

Oh, God. Her head swiveled. Her breath rattling in her throat, she stared at the kitchen shutters. A small, dark shape moved in the bottom corner. It ambled in a purposeful line along the window ledge.

A bee.

Oh, God, a bee!

It must have come in through the open door, which Aldwin hadn't closed behind him.

She fought a shriek burning for release. *Calm yourself, Leona. You haven't been stung since that day years ago; you won't be hurt now. 'Twill be all right.*

Aye. The width of a cottage separated her and the insect. If she sat very still, the bee would find its way out between the shutters and fly away.

'Twill be all right.

Bzzz-zzzz.

The droning grew louder. Angrier. Unable to wrench her gaze away, she watched the bee try to climb onto the right shutter. It fell back to the ledge.

Bzzz—

The bee launched itself away from the window, soaring in a wide arc toward the middle of the cottage.

Leona screamed.

CHAPTER SIXTEEN

Standing in the sun-drenched space between the cottage and the small barn, Aldwin inhaled a breath of clean morning air. Two of the three farmers Neale had hired to keep watch during the night walked away down the road, counting the silver Aldwin had just paid them. He'd sent the third man to Neale's home, as previously arranged, to tell the family Aldwin would like a meal and fresh water sent to the cottage.

Smothering a groan, he rolled his shoulders, loosening muscles in his back that ached from sleeping in an unfamiliar position to keep pressure off of his stitches. Aye, that was the reason he'd stayed on his left side, his head propped up by his saddlebag and rolled blankets—not just to watch over Leona, who looked even more beautiful as she slumbered.

"Leona," he murmured, his thoughts turning to moments ago, when he'd looked down at her curled beneath her bedding. Sound asleep, her brow had pursed with a frown. Had she been challenging him in a dream? How lovely she looked, with her features relaxed in slumber. Wisps of hair trailed over her forehead, down her smooth cheek, past her slightly parted lips. Did she have more freckles than days ago, or was he imagining such?

Simply looking at her . . . Aldwin's blood had stirred with a reckless urge to kneel beside her, press his lips to hers, and wake her with a kiss.

He'd resisted. He might have roused her, but he'd only tied one of her hands; she'd likely swat him with the other. Moreover, she'd looked exhausted yestereve. While he waited for the food to arrive, he'd let her sleep.

A good time to check his injury.

Aldwin reached for his tunic's hem, which covered the knife belted to his hip. Baring his wound to the daylight, he examined the line of stitches. No dried or fresh blood, due to Leona's fine work. This morn, he'd thank her again for her efforts. He'd have her know he respected her skill—

A scream rent the morning quiet. A sound of sheer terror.

From the cottage.

He spun, wincing at the pain in his side. He'd left the door ajar to clear the stale air; the opening didn't appear any wider. Had someone got inside, even though he stood near? Or had Leona tried to get free and hurt herself?

A more unsavory thought wove into his thoughts. Leona might be trying to trick him. She might have untied the rope and not be in peril at all, but hoping to lure him inside; then, she'd attack him and run.

His body tensed as he started toward the cottage. She might indeed try such, but he'd easily overpower her.

Yet the shrill scream hadn't sounded practiced. It rang with such horror, his skin had crawled.

A wail echoed inside the cottage. God's blood, but he

couldn't seem to move fast enough.

He reached the threshold. Shoved the door open.

With a booming *crash*, the door hit the inside wall.

Drawing his knife, he scanned the cottage interior. All appeared as he'd left it. His gaze fell upon Leona, squeezed against the cupboard's side. She sat with her back against the wall, her bent legs pressed to her chest. Her arms were crossed over her head in a protective gesture, as though to ward off an attacker. The rope still snaked from her wrist to the cupboard leg.

Or so it appeared. Had she untied the rope, but trapped the end under her palm, waiting for him to draw near? Mayhap she waited for the right moment to spring to her feet and attack? A clever ploy, if 'twas what she intended.

His fingers tightened on the dagger, wariness and suspicion clamoring inside him. He looked about the cottage again, and she sniffled and buried her fingers into her hair. And then he saw the knot securing the rope around her wrist.

She wasn't trying to trick him; she feared for her life.

There must be an intruder after all.

Dropping to a crouch, Aldwin edged toward the table.

Leona moaned. "Oh, God. Oh, God."

Pressing against the wooden bench alongside the table, Aldwin froze. Listened. He mentally catalogued all he heard: the trilling birds outside; the distant barking of a dog; and Leona's ragged breathing. None of the sounds suggested aught amiss. But she obviously had reason to be afraid.

Once more, he glanced at her. She was sobbing now, her shoulders quaking in violent shudders. Her fingers, threaded into her hair, twitched.

Why was she terrified?

Aldwin stood. "Leona."

She shuddered again.

"Are you injured? What is—?"

Bzzz. He heard the insect a moment before it flew toward him.

A bee.

Hellfire!

He tried to hold back a dizzying rush of guilt and torment. "Leona," he whispered.

"B-bee." Her voice sounded hoarse. As the insect looped around and droned back toward the shutters, she screamed again. She kicked at the blanket about her feet and tried to press further against the cupboard.

Aldwin swallowed to clear the vile taste from his mouth. He'd thought some fresh air inside would benefit them both; he hadn't expected a bee would find its way in. He'd failed to consider all the consequences of his actions. As, all those years ago, caught up in the excitement of his game, he hadn't once thought Leona's life would be at risk.

Pent-up regret pummeled him. More compelling than his remorse, though, was the need to safeguard Leona. Offer comfort. Let her know that never, ever, had he meant to scare her or cause her harm.

"Oh, God," she moaned again.

"'Twill be all right," he soothed as he set down his knife and snatched a rolled blanket from his makeshift bed.

"B-bee."

"Do not worry."

Leona sniffled.

"I will send it outside. I promise."

The bee buzzed against the shutter. The insect was as much

a victim, he realized grimly, as Leona; it only wanted to find its way out. He batted the window ledge with the blanket. With a startled buzz, the bee flew up toward the roof trusses.

Again, Aldwin flicked the blanket, forcing the insect to veer toward the open doorway.

Leona whimpered.

"Go!" he cried.

The bee flew down toward the table. Then, as though sensing freedom, it went out the door.

Aldwin hurried to close the panel.

Throwing aside the blanket, he crossed to Leona and dropped down beside the pallet. The toes of his boots scraped on the dirt. The hard-packed ground bit into his knees, but he blocked out his discomfort. His needs were far less important than hers.

She was shivering. Her body still folded tight, she didn't look up. Judging by her posture, she was doing her best to shut him out. To confront the emotional sting all on her own.

How like her, to shoulder her pain alone. How true to the proud, independent spirit of hers that, of all unexpected happenings, he'd grown to cherish. But she didn't have to carry this torment all by herself. He could help. *Wanted* to help. If she'd let him.

The silence in the cottage grew. He sat back on his heels and waited for a small sign from her to show she recognized he was there for her. Fighting for patience, he curled his fingers against his thighs. If he had his way, he'd draw her into his arms whether she wished it or not. The temptation to do just that made his palms itch. But he must wait.

At last, he dropped his head in a sigh. "The bee is gone," he said, knowing, even as he spoke, 'twas a senseless statement. But, somehow, he must get past her emotional barricade.

She sniffed and blew out a shaky breath. He dried his sweaty palms on his hose. Now, could he hold her? Or must he wait until he knew for certain she'd accept his comfort?

He shifted his right foot, to find 'twas going numb. Turning his lower body so as not to strain his stitches, he sat on the end of the pallet. The straw filling rustled as he bent his legs up to brace his arms on his knees.

With a tiny smile, he realized he and Leona were closer together now. 'Twould be easier to draw her away from the cupboard and take her into his embrace. Tucking her head under his chin, he'd hold her until her sobs quieted. He'd whisper words of comfort—as he had long ago while she lay motionless in the river—until the tears dried on her face. He'd tell her, in gentle ways, that he was sorry.

If she let him.

A painful tightness locked in his chest. She might tell him to leave her alone. And he couldn't blame her.

"Leona." Daring to move even closer, he reached out, his hand hovering over her crossed arms. How he longed to touch her. To prove he could be as gallant as a *chanson* knight.

Holding his breath, he placed his hand on her forearm.

Warmth. Softness. A hot spark of physical connection.

She tensed. Her fingers twisted into her tresses, an unspoken response to his touch.

When she moved, the rope around her wrist shifted, revealing a red mark. His guilt bit deeper. Not only had she endured the bee, but she couldn't move to safety. She was helpless to escape her bonds, just as years ago.

Moisture stung his eyes. She must think him the most

wretched of men. How could he convince her he never meant for her to suffer in such a way? That he'd never intended to revive the pain of long ago? If only she understood how much he wished that day had never happened.

Frustration rushed out of him on a bitter oath. Closing the space between them, he reached up and grasped the rope. Her head whipped up. She stared at him, her eyes reddened and heavy with tears. The anguish in her gaze . . . His heart clenched.

"I will free you," he said, very gently. "I promise, I will never tie you again."

Her lips moved on a swallow. Then she nodded.

Untying her would take a while. Cutting the rope would take moments. Rising from the pallet, he strode to the table, picked up his knife, and returned to sit beside her. She watched through her tangled hair, her mouth a taut line, while he carefully sliced the knife across the rope. The binding fell away.

He threw aside the dagger. It slid across the dirt before coming to rest near the table.

Her shoulders lowered on a heavy exhalation and then she rolled her arms, the right first, and then the left. Reaching up, she rubbed the muscles between her neck and shoulders.

Stand up. Walk away, his conscience cried, *before you do something rash.*

He couldn't leave her. Walking away was the act of a coward. Staying, facing her anger, providing solace, was his duty. Especially when he was responsible for her being upset.

"Are you all right?" he asked.

She squinted at him through mussed strands of hair. Judging by her expression, she was wondering if he'd tripped and knocked his head while outside. She looked so endearing, he might have chuckled. However, that wouldn't be a good idea.

He held up one hand, his fingers splayed in surrender. "A foolish question, I know. But . . . I want to help. If I may."

Looking away, she pushed the strands from her face. Her lashes glistened with tears. A droplet slipped into the corner of her mouth. At least she wasn't sobbing. Her shaking had lessened, too.

Then her head turned, and the full force of her liquid gaze settled on him. Her eyes looked almost gold. Such beautiful eyes.

She didn't answer. Didn't give him permission to help her.

"I am sorry," he whispered. He tried to keep the anguish from his voice, but it bled through.

Still, silence.

"I am sorry, too, for what happened when we were young."

At last he'd given voice to the guilt that had eaten at him for long, long years. He waited, hoping for the hint of a smile from her and a nod of forgiveness. Gestures that would free him from his emotional hell.

Instead, her shoulders stiffened. The reminder of that afternoon, and his part in what happened to her, was obviously more painful than she could consider right now.

Her gaze began to cool, and he sensed her retreating from him. He couldn't let her block him out. He must fight for her forgiveness. Fight, as any worthy knight would, for . . . her.

Catching her hand, he wound his fingers through hers. "Please, Leona."

"Aldwin—"

"I know what you endured years ago. Agony no one should have to suffer—especially not because of someone else's foolish mistake." He forced words past the tightness in his throat. "Do you know how I felt, watching you suffer such pain? Seeing you lying in the river, your body swollen with bee stings? All because of a game I had convinced Ward to play?"

Her eyes dampened again. Her fingers twisted in his. "I cannot—"

"You remained with me every day since then. In dreams that tormented me in the night. In moments of despair. My God, Leona, the guilt . . ." He wished he didn't sound such a witless idiot. "I will never forget the shame I brought my parents. Or forgive myself for hurting you."

Leona's lips trembled. He thought she was going to tell him to go away.

"I want to know," she whispered.

"What?" Aldwin wondered if she meant to ask him about Ward. If, by chance, she did ask, he'd tell enough of her brother's last days to appease her, and no more. Ward would have wanted it that way.

"Why," she began, "did you tie me to the tree that afternoon? I did not want to be bound. We could have played the game pretending I was tied."

She hadn't asked what he dreaded. Aldwin smothered a sigh.

"I said so, several times. You would not listen."

He caressed her knuckles with his thumb. "I remember. That . . . haunted me, too. I tied you because I was determined to play the game my way. You see, I"—he blew out a breath—"I wanted to be the one to set you free."

She frowned through her tears. "Really? I thought you hated me."

Aldwin chuckled. "You were the only girl who wanted to slay me. All the others were flirtatious."

"How terrible for you." Was that a smile softening her mouth? He hoped so.

"With your eyes flashing and that stubborn jut of your chin," he went on, "you were . . . beautiful."

She tsked and dried her eyes on her sleeve. "I was but a child."

"And beautiful," he repeated. "Not nearly as beautiful, though, as you are now."

Her body stilled on a sharp, indrawn breath. "Aldwin."

She sounded breathless. Hopeful. Intrigued. Did she remember each stunning kiss they'd shared over the past few days? He did. He'd woken last night to feel her lips upon his and the downiness of her cheek against his fingers. He'd remember her taste until the day he died.

Leona stared at him, her eyes huge. What would she do if he kissed her now? From the trace of desire in her gaze, he sensed she wouldn't push him away.

Or hit him.

Neale or his children would arrive soon. But, surely, until then, a kiss—*one* tender, gallant kiss—would be all right.

Anticipation roared inside him with such ferocity, his hand holding hers began to shake. How he yearned to kiss her.

Don't be an impatient fool, Aldwin. Take care in this fragile moment, or you will ruin all.

Fighting his rising hunger, he leaned forward and kissed the top of her head. "Leona," he whispered, "my lioness."

"Lioness." The word quivered from her lips. Almost a kiss in itself.

"Aye," he said against her salty cheek.

A breath rushed from her. But she didn't tell him to quit

kissing her. Neither did she draw back.

"You must know how I"—*want you*—"care for you," he said against her creamy soft skin.

"Oh—"

He kissed the side of her mouth. Licked away the last, glistening tear.

Her lips parted, suggesting that intimate touch stunned her.

And then, very gently, he swept his lips over hers.

Her hand in his flew up, like a robin startled from the hedgerow. He hovered, his mouth before hers, their breath mingling in an exquisite moment of possibility.

Would she take the comfort he offered, or shove him away? The choice must be hers.

He blinked, and she closed the space between them. Clamped her arms around his neck with a whimpered moan. Slid her tongue against his lips.

"Leona—" His acknowledgment was crushed by her roving mouth. She sucked. Delved. Squirmed against him. A scorching shudder racked his body. Heat. Fire. Oh, God, he couldn't possibly hide his rising desire for her.

He gasped against her mouth, wrestling with the blinding urge to push her backward onto the pallet and slide between her legs. *One* kiss. Tenderness. 'Tis what he offered. All he meant to offer.

Aye, he wanted more—what man wouldn't?—but after her fright moments ago, he'd be taking advantage.

"Kiss me, as before," she panted against his mouth. Her voice blended into a growl.

His loins heated, even while a tiny part of him resisted. She wasn't thinking clearly; emotionally vulnerable, she didn't realize what she was saying. Still, as he scrambled to resurrect his chivalry, her right hand wandered down the front of his tunic.

"Lioness." He caught her sleeve, and then her wrist. Nibbling her cheek, he tried his best to distract her from what—Ah, God—seemed to be her intention.

"Kiss me." Her lips ground against his. And then, her left hand found his manhood.

With the lightest caress, her fingers brushed his swollen heat. He gasped.

Her delicate touch implied she'd touched him by accident. Yet she'd deliberately moved her hand down his belly. And, knowing her, unless he stopped her, she'd touch him again.

Shivering at that wondrous thought, he said, "W-wait." For what, he didn't know. His fuzzy mind refused to focus. If she caressed him like that again, he'd never withstand the agony.

Sighing against his mouth, she dropped her hands. For once, she'd obeyed him. Even as he expelled an astonished breath, her fingers twisted into his hair to grasp huge fistfuls and hold him fast. Her breasts squeezed to his torso, while her lips moved over his. Sensations so exquisite and arousing . . .

A groan ripped up inside him. And then, his restraint shattered like a cracked lance.

Matching her hunger, he kissed her back. He thrust his tongue into her mouth, and she met his parry. He sucked. She nibbled. He teased. She tormented.

His mind spun. Never had he experienced such gut-twisting bliss.

She gasped, licked, and matched the deepening exploration of his tongue. With another, impassioned groan, he rose up on his knees, sliding his body up hers to tower over her. Her hands fell from his hair. Linking her arms about his waist, she tilted her head back, keeping their mouths joined in a kiss, an instinctive acceptance of his lead.

Their bodies strained together, each movement marked by the whisper of their garments. Aldwin shuddered, his blood running fast and hot. His hands burned as they clenched into her gown, capturing silky strands of her hair as well as cloth.

Not enough. He wanted—*needed*—to be closer still.

Still kissing her, he leaned his full weight against her. Urged her backward.

A whimper broke from her. Doubt dimmed his desire for one, painful instant. Before he could coax her with his hands, her body yielded. She shifted back. He followed her down, kissing, urging, until she lay beneath him on the pallet.

Above her on his hands and knees, he whispered, "Lioness."

Her gaze sly, she reached up and pushed aside hair that had fallen over his face. Then she grabbed the front of his tunic and pulled his head down to her level. Their lips clashed in a fierce, slippery kiss. When he lowered his hips, easing the rest of his body down into her welcoming embrace, she moaned.

An answering moan rose within him. The incredible feel of her . . . He wanted to tear his mouth from hers, throw back his head, and roar.

Through the haze in his mind, he heard a dog barking.

Outside.

His lips pressed to hers, he stilled. The mongrel might not belong to Neale, but the bark sounded similar.

"Oy!" a man shouted. "Come back 'ere, ye silly 'ound."

Neale. If he came upon Aldwin lying atop Leona . . . Not a wise idea.

"I am sorry," Aldwin said, pressing a last kiss to Leona's lips. He rose up to his knees, and then stood, straightening his clothing.

Another bark, very near.

A knock sounded on the cottage door.

CHAPTER SEVENTEEN

The knock sifted into Leona's dreamy bliss. She pushed up on her elbows and blinked at Aldwin spearing his hand through his hair that she'd recently mussed—including the bit at the back that stuck out like a puppy's tail.

He looked down at her, shook his head, and grinned. For a moment, all seemed to fade away. All except him, that enticing smile, and his smoldering gaze that told her he wanted to kiss her again.

Turning on his heel, he strode to his knife lying on the floor, picked it up, and sheathed it. Then he came back to her, stretching out his hand. He clearly wanted her to rise. "Leona."

"Mmm?" Her mind felt sluggish, as though she tried to pull thoughts through a thick blanket.

"I must answer the door." His gaze dropped to her lips, still tingling from his attentions. "I sent one of the night guards to Neale's home. I asked him to bring us some fare and water for you to wash."

The lingering pleasure clouding her mind vanished. Ignoring his hand, she shoved up to standing and brushed a hand over her creased gown. "You set guards outside last night?" She knew he was determined to get her to de Lanceau, but God's teeth, he'd tied her to the cupboard!

The mirth faded from Aldwin's gaze.

Another knock rattled the door. "Milord?" She recognized Neale's voice, tinged with uncertainty.

"One moment," Aldwin called back.

His focus returned to her, and she braced herself against a flood of confusion and dismay. His resolve to prevent her from escaping shouldn't surprise her. He'd admitted his desire to achieve knighthood, and his commitment to de Lanceau took priority above all else. Yet, somehow, she couldn't quell the disappointment chilling her like icy water.

"Setting guards was a sound decision," Aldwin said.

She crossed her arms. "How so? You tied me to the cupboard and boarded the windows. Moreover, you slept between me and the wretched door."

A flush stained his cheekbones. "As I said before, I will not let you get away."

"How could I?" She thrust out her arm to display the redness on her wrist. "If set guards as well, why did I have to sleep with rope binding me? Do you think 'tis pleasant to sleep tethered like a mule?"

His gaze darkened, even as he glanced at the door. "Look—"

"I stitched your wound. We kissed!" she said. "We did so again, moments ago!"

His palm flew up. "Shh!"

"I will *not* hush!"

He leaned forward, his face set in a menacing scowl. She must be mad, for even while arguing with him, she craved his kiss.

Focus on Aldwin, the Warrior, she told herself, *not Aldwin, the Tender Lover. Keep a tight grip your foolish heart, and you will prevail.*

"Keeping you inside was not the only reason for posting guards," he said. "I wanted to be sure we were safe."

She snorted. "Of all the—"

"The poachers we fought yesterday may be searching for us. They will want to avenge their dead friends. I will not risk harm to you while you are in my care."

In his care. How dare he make his kidnapping of her sound so inoffensive?

"The poachers cannot know where we are," she growled.

"Aye, they—"

"We were not followed."

He raised his eyebrows. "Are you certain?"

"Even if they did come to this town," she said hotly, "who would tell them we are staying in this cottage?"

"Word can travel quickly in a small village, especially when all the folk know one another."

True. Her own experiences had taught her such. Months ago, the folk in the town skirting Pryerston Keep seemed to know of her mother's accident even before Leona.

She tried to think of another point to defend her argument. Before she could say one word, Aldwin crossed to the door.

He pulled open the panel, letting in brilliant sunlight. Neale stood a respectful distance from the threshold, no doubt trying to allow them some privacy. He was holding a small iron pot, an earthenware jug, and a cloth sack, and talking to Soot snuffling in the dirt.

When the door opened, Neale bowed. "Good morn, milord. Me wife made barley pottage with 'oney and milk ta break yer fast. Me daughter will soon bring 'ot water." As he approached the doorway, he held up the sack. "I also 'ave food fer yer day's journey."

"Wonderful." Aldwin smiled and took the offerings. "Let me give you the stew pot from last night."

Neale waved a hand. "Leave it. We will clear up the cottage once ye're gone."

"'Tis most kind of you."

Leona scowled. Aldwin looked relaxed and pleased with the morning's developments. How rotten, when, despite her annoyance, her body still yearned for him.

Neale's gaze slid from Aldwin to her, then darted away. "Is there aught else ye or the lady require, milord? I will do me best to find it, if ye ask."

"I think we have all we need," Aldwin said.

Leona sensed his questioning gaze upon her. What she needed—to immediately return to Pryerston—he wouldn't grant her, so why did he bother to seeking her opinion? She met his gaze and then turned her back on him.

Drawing up her sleeve, she inspected her reddened skin, glad to see the irritation wasn't too severe. She'd apply some of the ointment she'd used on Aldwin's stitches. That should help quicken the healing.

"I will leave the fare here," Aldwin said close by. She glanced over her shoulder to see him put the pot, jug, and sack on the table. "Eat what you like."

She nodded.

"I will be outside, discussing a few matters with Neale, if you need me."

For what? her mind answered. *To spoon-feed me my pottage?*

She forced away the not-so-unpleasant image of him winking at her and leaning across the table to tip a spoon into her open mouth.

His lips tightened, as though he'd hoped for a reply from her. His expression reminded her of a short while ago, when he'd rescued her from the bee. Thank God he'd been able to deal with the insect, or she'd still be huddled by the cupboard, crying like a little girl.

How she hated that she'd been vulnerable before him. He'd eased her fear, though, with such gentleness. He'd soothed her, shared his private anguish, and made her smile. And when he'd touched her and called her "Lioness," he'd made her shimmer inside. A beautiful, feminine feeling she wanted to know again.

Aldwin started to turn away. 'Twas gallant of him to offer to help her again, if she wished it. She mustn't let him leave without saying so.

"Thank you," she murmured.

Looking back at her, he nodded. Then he smiled. He looked so handsome, her stomach swooped.

"Be ready to leave soon," he said, before he crossed to Neale, stepped outside, and closed the door behind them.

Leona pressed her hand to her mouth, still tasting his kisses. Foolish, aye, but despite all Aldwin had done to her and all that loomed ahead, she wanted to lie back down on the pallet again.

With him.

‡ ‡ ‡

"De Lanceau is not coming," Sedgewick groused and slid his hand over his nose, shiny with perspiration. Standing in the shade of trees fringing a meadow, he looked a bit wan.

Leaning back against a tree, Veronique swallowed down a scathing retort. Did Sedgewick really believe Geoffrey wouldn't come to such a significant meeting? Judging from the sweat streaming down his brow, the baron was turning coward.

How disgusting.

Veronique shifted her focus to the flower-dotted meadow. All looked serene. Exactly as moments before.

A heady tingle shot through her. Soon, all would change in one, climactic moment—like a brimming bucket tipped over to reveal a secret kept from view.

Ah, but she couldn't wait!

"Veronique, why are we still here?" Sedgewick muttered.

She narrowed her gaze, then turned away from him. "We will wait."

So de Lanceau was late for their morning meeting. That didn't mean he wouldn't arrive. In the shriveled nook of her heart that had once loved him, she knew he'd come. He wouldn't be able to resist, if he thought she had his pendant.

He'd also be curious. Oh, aye. Very curious, as to why she'd wanted to see him.

When the baron grumbled once again, she barely resisted the urge to swing around and smack his face. Irritation prickled like a rash across her skin. He knew how important this meeting was to her, how she'd craved the moment de Lanceau saw, for the first time, the one destined to someday cut him down and take all that was denied her and her son.

Sitting beside her on the weed-sprinkled ground, Tye yanked out a stringy dandelion and tossed it into a growing pile of uprooted plants. Several of his little fingers were stained green. Keeping him clean was an impossible task.

A bird twittered and darted overhead, casting a quick shadow, and he glanced up. Sunlight edging through the overhead leaves touched the wavy mass of his hair curling to the shoulders of his brown woolen tunic. Mumbling in his odd little way, he resumed his weeding. How innocent he looked, his face flushed with concentration, his little mouth pursed . . .

No doubt sensing her gaze, he looked up. "Mama, I—"

A whistle. Or was it birdsong? There was a loud chorus coming from the trees several yards behind her.

"Hush, Tye."

"Hungry."

She pressed a finger to her lips. "Shh—"

"*Hungry!*" He threw a clump of dirt.

"*Hush!*" Her hands fisted as she looked again at the meadow, then at Sedgewick, scratching his chin. Movement—a tiny branch swaying back into place—drew her gaze to the mercenaries standing in wait. A score of warriors paid to obey her and the baron's every command. Armed with bows and arrows, crossbows, and swords, they'd protect them during the meeting and ensure she escaped unharmed.

Catching Sedgewick's gaze, she said, "Send men to check on the watchers."

"You heard the signal?" His voice caught on the last word.

"I am not certain. I do not want Geoffrey to surprise us."

The baron nodded, and then gestured to the three closest men. "Go check on the others. Whatever you do, do not give away our position."

"Aye, milord," the nearest man said. The three slipped into the undergrowth, moving as silently as shadows.

Sedgewick's hand slid to the sword belted to his hip. "If

'twas the signal, we must be ready."

Indeed, we must. She couldn't wait for what would happen.

Tye grumbled and threw another mound of dirt.

Ignoring him, Veronique smoothed a hand over her gown to check the knife strapped to her thigh. Then she touched her hair, left loose to fall to her waist; de Lanceau had preferred her to wear it that way while they made love, and she meant for him to remember their passionate, exhausting trysts. While her gaze traveled over the meadow again, she listened, hoping to hear a signal from the two lookouts posted in the brush alongside the road that ran past the meadow. One man looked to the north; the other, to the south. No one could approach without them noticing.

"Mama." Tye's face crumpled with frustration while he pushed to his feet. He ran to her side and tugged on her skirt.

"Tye—"

"Want to go home." He stamped his foot, kicking up dirt beneath his grubby leather shoe.

With him complaining, she'd never hear the lookouts. Batting away his hand, she glared down at him, pleased when his eyes widened with uncertainty.

"Tye, be quiet. I told you—"

His mouth trembled. "Go home."

A horse's neigh carried from across the meadow. Veronique's head snapped up. Her hands clenched and unclenched at her sides. Blood hammered with a thrilling urgency in her temple, and she strained to see what was unraveling.

He's here, he's here, her pulse pounded. Her shaking hands ran over her bodice.

"Stand at the ready," the baron muttered close by. Brush shifted behind her, indicating the mercenaries were preparing for the impending encounter.

Not a rider or warrior in sight.

Yet.

Sedgewick cursed. "Veronique, stop him."

Grasses crunched ahead of her. Tye was running into the meadow.

"Tye!"

Still at a run, he jumped at the sound of her voice, shrieked, and kept running, his hair bouncing with each step.

Spitting an oath, she rushed forward. She caught up with him and snatched him up. He struggled to get away, but she shoved him onto her left hip.

Tye screamed. His fisted hands beat upon her breast.

Wretched child! He was ruining her glorious moment. "Stop fussing," she snapped, "or I—"

A line of armed riders wearing helms and full chain-mail armor emerged from the opposite stand of trees. Stumbling ahead of them were the two sentries they'd posted. One lurched as he ran, an arrow jutting from his leg. Blood streamed down the other's face.

Tye stopped squirming to stare wide-eyed at the approaching warriors. She followed his gaze, glancing at each rider. Which one was de Lanceau? She hadn't seen him for several years. Yet she'd likely know him as soon as her gaze fell upon him.

The rustle of grasses grew louder as the running men reached her. Lurching to a halt, his hand pressed to his bloody leg, the first one dipped his head in an attempted bow. "Milady, we—"

"Out of my sight," she said between her teeth. Later, she'd settle these two idiots' failures.

"But, milady." The man's face contorted with pain. "De Lanceau's men surprised us. We did not—"

Veronique looked away in a cutting dismissal, while shutting out his pathetic pleas. She fixed her attention on the men riding toward her, their horses' bridles jingling. The broad-shouldered warrior in the middle, wearing an embroidered surcoat over his chain-mail armor, thrust up his hand. The horses halted. Impressive, how that small gesture commanded so much.

"Mama." Tye pulled on her gown.

Veronique jostled him on her hip. "Quiet."

He grumbled and tugged again at her clothing, but she stared at the warrior flanked on either side by men with their weapons poised for attack. *Geoffrey.* Even from this distance, she recognized the hard set of his jaw. And his mouth . . . As skilled at issuing orders as 'twas at giving kisses.

A quivering ache wove through her. Of all the many lovers she'd taken, he'd been the best. How humiliating that after all he'd done to her, she still desired him.

He would suffer for that most of all.

Clearly confident in his men's ability to protect him, he reached up and drew off his helm. Shiny brown locks slipped down to his shoulders. A strand of hair drifted across his cheek and he swiped it away with a mail-clad fist before setting the helm in his lap.

Veronique clenched her thighs against a potent flutter. *Handsome* was an inadequate word to describe his bold, masculine beauty. This day, he seemed more muscular than she remembered, his face more bronzed, his expression more calculating and commanding.

Misgiving slipped like cold fingers across her nape. He was certainly fitter than when she'd approached his bedside years ago, not long after Aldwin had shot him with the crossbow bolt during the battle for the keep at Wode. Holding a vial of poison, she'd stared down at Geoffrey's ashen face slackened by unconsciousness and silently cursed his will to live. The steel-tipped bolt Aldwin had fired had pierced a hole in Geoffrey's chest; Geoffrey should have perished then. But he'd stubbornly clung to life, and for that reason, she'd agreed to murder him herself—if not by poisoning, then by slamming her knife down into his heart.

How she'd craved that victorious moment when he died. No longer would Geoffrey stand in the way of the baron's prior arranged marriage to Lady Elizabeth Brackendale. The wedding would've gone ahead and the next part of Sedgewick's clever plot to seize control of all of Moydenshire would have fallen into place, bringing him and Veronique immeasurable power and wealth.

That is, if that bitch Elizabeth hadn't foiled Veronique's murder attempt. If Veronique and the baron hadn't been arrested and imprisoned, before they managed to escape. If Geoffrey hadn't recovered to marry Elizabeth and become lord of Moydenshire.

Tye squirmed against Veronique, and, forcing a smile, she glanced down at his tousled head. Her and the baron's plotting had failed years ago, but much had happened since then. Now, 'twasn't a matter of "if" they'd succeed in destroying Geoffrey, but "when." For she had a new weapon, now, to bring about his ruin.

The swath of grasses and wildflowers between them stirred in the breeze, emphasizing the volatile silence. She smoothed Tye's hair while holding Geoffrey's gaze. When his focus shifted a moment to her hand, her grin widened.

"Show me the pendant." Geoffrey's voice boomed in the meadow.

Veronique refused to let her smile waver, although surprise

rippled through her. His first words were about the wretched jewel. He hadn't made the slightest attempt at courtesy. He hadn't called her by her given name. Was she so unimportant to him that he didn't feel he *had* to respect her in such a way? Even though she'd shared his bed for two years?

Anger flared anew in her breast. Forcing a pleasant tone, she said, "Good day to you, my lord."

His head didn't dip in reply. Neither did his fierce expression change.

"Do you have my ruby pendant?" He sounded even more threatening. "Where is Aldwin? Was that earlier missive I received at Branton Keep a ruse to draw him into an ambush?"

Earlier letter? Ambush?

Veronique steeled herself against the lash of Geoffrey's words, while making note of what he'd revealed. If she guessed correctly, Leona had sent that first letter to him after taking the pendant from Pryerston, and Geoffrey ordered Aldwin to get the jewel. That Geoffrey asked after the ruby meant it wasn't in his possession—and never would be, if Clif accomplished what Veronique had asked of him.

She grinned at that thought and took a sultry step forward. Geoffrey might try to intimidate her and rule this meeting as he'd manage a matter of estate. But she'd waited a long time for this moment; she'd lead this day, as she had so many times in her dreams.

She tightened her arms around Tye, whose eyes shimmered with uncertainty. Then she laughed, a coarse chuckle borne from the desires in her soul.

De Lanceau cursed.

At last, a reaction.

"Not even a 'good day, Veronique'?" She didn't bother to

soften her bitterness. "For shame, milord."

His lips curled back from his teeth. "The pendant—"

"Do you not remember me? Have you forgotten how you sweated and groaned above me? How, in your bed, I wrested gasp after—"

"Silence!"

"—pleasured gasp from you?"

Several of Geoffrey's men snickered, before others shot them warning glares.

Geoffrey's face darkened with fury. His huge war horse shifted, tossed its mane, as though sensing his master's irritation.

Pleasure glowed inside her like fiery coals. 'Twas dangerous to goad him further, but she enjoyed hurting him. "Do you not recall—?"

"Still, you do not obey my order or answer my questions." He sounded angry enough to draw his sword and cut her down where she stood. "Did you and Sedgewick deceive Aldwin? Did you bring the pendant today? Or is this meeting another one of your attempts to trick me?"

"Milord, the baron and I do not know of Aldwin's whereabouts, an ambush, or the first missive you mentioned. I only ordered one letter sent to you." Veronique arched an eyebrow. "Do you not recall it?" She couldn't *wait* to reveal the truth to him. To witness that glorious moment when he realized his life was forever changed.

Tye whined and squirmed against her, but she held him tighter. Bending her head close to his in what would appear to be a tender maternal gesture, she hissed, "Stop."

"You are overbold, Veronique. What I recall is that you and Baron Sedgewick betrayed and tried to murder me. For your treachery, you were arrested. You were locked in the king's dungeons. Which gives me very good reason to arrest you now." Geoffrey looked to his men, as if to give a prearranged signal.

She laughed. Raising her free hand, she gestured to the trees. Vegetation rustled behind her, and she sensed the mercenaries edging out of the forest shadows, their weapons at the ready.

"Ah, I see Sedgewick now. He is sulking behind the hired ruffians." Geoffrey's mouth flattened. "Those thugs cannot protect you from me."

"Is that so?"

"I shall take great pleasure," he growled, "in chaining you and the baron to my dungeon wall. There, you will live, day after day, night after night, until the end of your wretched lives."

Barely able to contain the excitement burgeoning inside her, she laughed. "You would be so cruel? To the mother of your *son?*"

Murmurs rippled through the line of riders.

"Son?" Geoffrey didn't even blink.

"Aye, milord." She looked down at her boy. "His name is Tye. He is living proof of the pleasure we shared. How good 'twas, when we coupled."

Geoffrey's mouth whitened. How she'd love to know the thoughts reeling through his mind. Astonishment? Anguish? She hoped the revelation cut him so hard and deep, he'd never again sleep well at night.

"This boy is not my child."

She managed a shocked little cry. "Tye's eyes are the same silver color. And his face." She trailed her fingers down his grubby cheek. "The likeness is remarkable. You cannot see the resemblance?"

Doubt flickered in Geoffrey's gaze for the barest instant, before his expression again hardened. "You"—he bit out the word—"are a woman of endless lovers—"

"Including you, my lusty lord."

His eyes flashed with fury. "And how many others? You are more foolish than I thought, Veronique, to try to manipulate me in this way."

Wound him again, her mind screamed. *Make his soul bleed. Make him suffer for the way he cast you aside, like a common whore, for that bitch Elizabeth, who became his wife.* Pressing her hand to her bosom, softening her voice with indignation, Veronique said, "Do you mean to deny that we lay together?"

"Nay."

"So you do remember our affair, then?"

"Regrettably, I do."

Regrettably. She almost choked on her fury. If she asked, would he say he found no ecstasy in their coupling? That, certainly, would be a lie. However, before she taunted him further, she must make him see that Tye was his child. If he admitted to being the boy's father, before all these witnesses, all the better. That could serve her well.

"One of our last nights we made love at Branton Keep," she said, "I got with child. Mayhap even the eve before you rode off to demand vengeance for your father's killing." With a slow, sensual glide that mimicked the way she once caressed Geoffrey's naked skin, her fingers slid between her breasts, where Tye's innocent hand pressed against her. "Your passion was certainly fierce that night. 'Tis no surprise our union produced a strong, healthy son."

The disdain in Geoffrey's stare didn't waver. "Your next lover was as likely to be the father."

"There was no other," she said, "not for a while."

"A *while?*"

She forced down a shriek. Did he think she fornicated with every able-bodied man she met? Did he believe she had no discretion as to whom she took into her body? Rage seared through her in a brutal tremor, but she forced herself to concentrate on all she hoped to achieve this day. Screaming at Geoffrey now would achieve naught. And she'd lose sway over his men, some of whom looked unsettled, indicating her words were making an impact with them.

Far wiser to nurture those seedlings of doubt she'd strewn in this meadow and bind Geoffrey, emotionally, to Tye, who'd one day seize all from his sire. If she had her way, Tye would run a sword straight through Geoffrey.

Touching her little boy's shoulder, she said, "You are unkind, milord. I speak only the truth."

"Ah." The faintest smile touched Geoffrey's lips. "Then show me the pendant. Prove to me you meant to return it to me, as you wrote in your missive."

A scream burned in her throat. She trapped it, silenced it, before it betrayed her. "You care more for that pendant"—she forced a shocked tone—"than your own son?"

A low chuckle broke from Geoffrey, a sound that mocked every gloating thought she'd savored during this meeting. "As I expected. You never intended to relinquish the pendant." He looked to the man at his right and nodded.

The riders aimed their weapons. At her and the mercenaries.

Her arms tightened around Tye. He choked a sob, and fear whipped through her. If they dared to hurt her son . . . But the Geoffrey she knew wouldn't harm a child. Above all, one who might be of his own flesh and blood.

Tye quivered. "Mama," he whispered, pointing to the riders. "S-scared."

She hated the way his shaking voice made her ache inside. "Shh," she soothed. "I will protect you." Glancing up, she met Geoffrey's stare. Compassion flickered in his eyes.

"No one needs to come to harm," he said. "Put the boy down. Hold your arms out at your sides, Veronique, where I can see them. You and Sedgewick will surrender to my men, and there will be no bloodshed."

"And then what?"

"I will arrest you both for the crimes you committed years ago. Once you're securely imprisoned, I will investigate your whereabouts over the past years and discover if there are any more offenses."

A gritty laugh broke from her. "How easy for you, once I have surrendered, to simply kill me here. 'Tis the most convenient choice for you, aye?"

"Veronique—"

"Next, will you murder Tye, so your *respectable* lady wife and children will never know of him?"

"M-Mama," Tye whimpered. Tears welled in his eyes.

Geoffrey signaled again to his men. The riders didn't move, but she sensed the confrontation had accelerated to the next stage. Her grasp on the moment was slipping away.

She shifted Tye in her arms. His little arms and legs flailed, and he shrieked as she flipped him so he faced Geoffrey and his men. Her arm across his stomach, she pinned him against her body.

"*Mama!*"

"Look at him," she cried, dodging his fists and the backward thrust of his head. "Look upon your son. Your bastard. Look well, for he will destroy you!"

"Veronique!" Geoffrey snapped. "Put the boy down."

"Never!"

"Do as I ordered. I do not want to harm him or you."

Tye screamed. "*M-Mama!*"

Geoffrey kicked his horse forward. "God's blood! You will hurt him."

Triumph burst from her in a gleeful laugh. At last, she'd reached him. Grabbing fistfuls of her skirt, she yanked it aside to snatch the dagger from her thigh. She shoved the knife against Tye's neck.

Her little boy screeched.

"If you care what happens to him," she shouted, "do not come any closer. Tell your men to stay away." She stepped backward, toward the line of mercenaries.

Geoffrey halted his horse. Blowing hard, it jerked its head, the chime of the bridle sharp in the eerie silence.

"Veronique." Geoffrey's voice sounded taut. "Do you really care for your son?"

Still moving backward, she laughed. "*Our* son, milord. Of course I do."

"Yet you put him in jeopardy. You brought him here knowing there would be a confrontation and even bloodshed. You hold a knife to his throat. Why do such things?"

Why, indeed.

Tye bawled, his body shaking in gulping sobs. He sounded terrified. She fought the inconvenient, motherly need to turn him to face her, kiss his cheek, and hug him. "I know you are miserable, Tye. Look well upon your father," she said in a voice loud enough to carry. "Remember how he refused to acknowledge you. Remember all he has denied you. What happens from this day on is *his* fault."

"Enough!" Geoffrey roared. "For the boy's safety, put him down. Let one of my men take him away from here. 'Tis no place for a child."

Give up her means to Geoffrey's downfall? Give up her son, who provided the perfect shield against any attempts to kill her?

"'Tis the right decision, Veronique."

"I think not." Her next backward step brought her alongside a mercenary holding a broadsword. Several other men stood beside him.

"If you cooperate," Geoffrey said, "I will let Tye visit you in the dungeon."

She laughed, a ruthless, disparaging chuckle that echoed through the meadow. "You have lost, milord."

A muscle flexed in his jaw.

"Look upon your son, so very different from the boy your wife birthed you."

Geoffrey's face tautened. "How do you know—?"

"Tye will grow up to despise you." She edged toward the forest, and the horses tethered there earlier.

"I will not ask again," Geoffrey barked. "Surrender—"

"He will kill you!"

She spun and raced into the undergrowth, while lowering the knife. Tye bounced in her arms. He screamed. A low branch slapped her arm, and he screamed again.

Shouts, whinnies, and thudded hoofbeats erupted from the meadow.

"Do not harm the boy!" Geoffrey yelled.

Veronique smirked. How noble. From Geoffrey, however, she expected no less.

Arrows whistled through the air. With a *thud*, one embedded in a nearby tree. She raced on, ignoring the brush grabbing at her gown.

Footsteps crashed behind her. Raising her dagger, she whirled, to see Sedgewick approaching.

"Mercenaries," he wheezed while wiping his face. "Fighting de Lanceau."

Clanging swords carried from the meadow. Cries. Screams of pain.

Through the trees ahead, she spied their horses, and the four mercenaries left to guard them.

Turning Tye in her arms, she let his head settle into the crook between her neck and shoulder. As he cried against her, she grinned at the baron. "To Pryerston Keep. I cannot *wait* to celebrate our victory."

CHAPTER EIGHTEEN

With a firm tug, Aldwin tightened the strap of his destrier's saddle, the familiar smells of leather and horse a reminder of the ride ahead. And his duty, soon to be fulfilled.

Looking up at the sky, he found the sun behind the trees near Neale's barn. Midmorning already, but if he and Leona rode with only short stops, they should reach Branton Keep by nightfall.

Startled squawks erupted near Neale's cottage's front door. Soot had flopped into the dirt among a crowd of chickens, inviting Leona to scratch her belly. Dressed once again in her own clothes that Gillian had cleaned yestereve, Leona dropped to her knees and gave the dog's chest a hearty rubbing. Soot groaned, a sound of utter delight.

"Silly dog," she murmured.

Aldwin tried not to let his gaze linger—they must begin their journey—but he couldn't stop his gaze from traveling over Leona's profile. How vibrant she seemed, her face aglow while her tresses shone in the sunlight. He wished he could see her that way every day.

Concentrating again on the saddle, he forced himself to think of what needed to be done before their travels. Not an easy task, when memories of her lying beneath him, panting, wanting, made him want to drag her back inside the cottage and finish what they'd begun. To sit another whole day with her thighs brushing his . . . Argh!

Leona glanced at him. That one look shot heat straight to his loins.

He averted his gaze and ensured, for the third time, that his saddlebag was secured. *Keep focused, you besotted fool.* Until they were safely within Branton's walls, his beautiful captive still might try to flee. She'd already proven to be more resourceful than any woman he'd ever known.

Rom snuffled at Aldwin's shoulder, clearly eager to be on the move. Patting the horse's glossy side, he turned toward Leona. "We must be on our way."

Leona rose.

Good. She wasn't fighting him. He deliberately hadn't told her that only Neale's wife and babe were within earshot. Neale had left earlier to deliver eggs and finish other business in the town; his older children had gone to work the fields. If Leona knew so few were around, she might try to run. Neither did he want another confrontation this morn.

With his booted foot, he pushed over a wooden mounting block. Holding tight to Rom's reins, he waved to the horse's back. "After you, Lioness."

A hint of rebellion touched her gaze. Still, she stepped up onto the mounting block, reached up to the front of the saddle, and hauled herself up. Straightening out her gown and cloak, she stared down at him, her hair shot with gold.

Aldwin swung up behind her. Rom sidestepped, rocking Leona's body more snugly against Aldwin's. He didn't shift away—and neither did she.

Surprise spread through him, along with a sense that in some significant way, their relationship had changed.

Setting aside the thought to ponder later, he checked his weapons one final time, and then nudged Rom with his heels. The destrier wheeled toward the main road.

"Will we reach Branton Keep today?" Leona asked, her voice carrying over Rom's rhythmic hoofbeats.

"Aye." He'd make certain they did.

"What will . . . happen to me there?"

Aldwin longed to draw her close, kiss her hair, and assure her all would be well; he'd do all he could to spare her from the consequences of her sire's willingness to help Veronique and the baron. Yet Aldwin had heard only her account of the situation at Pryerston. There might be far more she hadn't told him, because she'd wanted to protect herself or her father. De Lanceau must undertake a full investigation, and Aldwin dared not guess what his lord might or might not decide.

No doubt unsettled by his silence, Leona twisted around to look at him.

"I cannot say," Aldwin answered. "'Tis a matter for de Lanceau to decide."

Leona's expression turned pensive. "Surely you have some say in the matter."

He resisted the lure of her tempting mouth. As much as he cared for her and hoped for a happy resolution, his vow bound him to his lord, not her. So close to achieving his lifelong ambition, he'd be a fool to let her stand between him and knighthood.

"I will report on what occurred over the past days," he said, looking across the lush green field on the road's right side. "I'll make my recommendations. I cannot promise, though, that my lord will accept my suggestions."

"Or mine."

Glancing back at her, Aldwin raised his brows.

"I am a loyal subject. Should I not have an opportunity to offer my thoughts?"

Aldwin glanced again at the field, where birds swooped to catch insects. De Lanceau was a just man; he'd let her speak. "I am sure you will have your say."

"Good."

Unease coursed through him at the determination in her voice. With tears brimming in her eyes, she might portray Aldwin to be a cruel knave who, although he knew she was a noblewoman, treated her with dishonor. The red mark on her wrist supported her claim. If she handed the pendant to de Lanceau, insisting she'd meant to return it to him all along, she'd have his gratitude.

Aldwin focused on the dust-blown road ahead. If that moment came, he'd defend his actions. So he hadn't treated Leona like a delicate flower. He'd done what he believed was necessary to succeed in his mission—and get his willful captive to cooperate. After Aldwin's years of diligent service, de Lanceau knew Aldwin's character. Moreover, de Lanceau knew how headstrong women could be; his own lady wife was as stubborn as Leona.

The saddle creaked as Leona faced forward. She said no more. Did she believe she had the last word? He'd let her believe such.

Ahead, a church steeple rose over the roofs of two-story townhomes, and Aldwin thought back to Neale's sketch in the dirt that morn. After collecting a fresh supply of crossbow bolts from the blacksmith—an associate of Neale's who knew a good armorer and owed Neale a favor—Aldwin would head for the road scoured out centuries ago by the Romans. Neale insisted this road ran straight and true toward Branton Keep's lands. This route would be safer than lesser known roads, too, since 'twas well-traveled.

The scent of baking bread, the *clang* of a hammer, and merchants' shouts guided Aldwin through the town to the cobbled square cornered by the stone church.

"The door," Leona said as they rode near. "Just as I remembered."

A semicircle of intertwined carvings above the doorway merged into two figures—a man and woman—wrapped around with leafy vines. The figures stood on either side of the wooden door banded with wrought iron.

"See the serpent?" With her finger in the air, she traced the carved snake slithering over the doorway. Then she pointed to the figures. "Adam. Eve."

"Impressive." How many men had seen these doors and pondered their own temptations?

He dragged his gaze from Leona's awed face and headed Rom into the square. Town houses rose toward the sky. Assorted shops, situated on the homes' ground levels, featured leather goods, pottery, clothes, and other wares set out on fold-down wooden shutters.

A tavern sprawled along the square's opposite side; its sign, held by worn rope, hung at an angle above the door. Horses stood by a water trough, while townsfolk, arriving by cart or on foot, chatted or made their way to make their purchases.

Shielding his eyes against the glare of sunlight, Aldwin

searched for the blacksmith's. There. By the baker's shop. He guided Rom through a gap in the crowd.

As he drew near, Aldwin caught sight of a broad-shouldered man with unkempt black hair standing by a forge, examining a yellow-hot horseshoe at the end of a pair of iron tongs. Shaking his head, the blacksmith set the horseshoe on an anvil and brought his hammer down with a sharp *clong*.

Sickles, tools, locks, and other metal objects covered the interior walls of his shop.

Aldwin drew Rom to a halt beside the premises. "I am looking for Stowe."

The man turned, his ruddy face streaked with grime and sweat. "Ye found 'im."

"Neale said you could help me."

The man's eyes brightened. "That I can, milord." His appreciative gaze skimmed over Leona before he set down the tongs, still holding the horseshoe. "Come in. I will fetch yer goods."

"Thank you. We are eager to be on our way."

Stowe nodded. With a muffled grunt, he hurried off to the back of his shop. Aldwin slid from Rom's back and then helped Leona down.

Keeping a hand on her arm, he escorted her inside the building. Blended voices drifted in through the open shop window and door, along with the rumble of more arriving carts.

After pulling her arm free, Leona wandered to a bench spread with different-sized iron rings. She glanced out the window.

A frown knit her brow. "Aldwin."

"Mmm?"

Her hands curled. What had she seen? Or was she going to ask him again about her fate once she reached Branton Keep?

Aldwin crossed to her, his focus shifting to the crowd outside.

"There," she said. "By the tavern."

Three men garbed in long, green cloaks confronted an apron-clad man, likely the tavern's proprietor. Two men stood with their backs to Aldwin. The third, his head bowed and his hands on his hips in a gesture that oozed impatience, looked at the ground.

Clif.

The tavern owner's mouth moved before he gave a fierce shake of his head.

"The man who attacked me in the cavern," Leona said, so quietly Aldwin almost didn't hear. "He wore a similar cloak."

"'Ere ye are," the blacksmith said, his boots rapping on the earthen floor as he strode toward them with a quiver of bolts. "Fine quality, they are, as Neale asked." He tapped his nose. "Got a friend who makes the best bolts."

"Aldwin," Leona said, more urgently.

He nodded to her, trying to ignore the sweat beading on his forehead. They must leave *now*. If the poachers saw Rom, he and Leona would be in danger.

"Thank you, good man." Reaching into the coin pouch at his belt, Aldwin withdrew some silver and shoved it into Stowe's hand.

A cry.

A muffled *thud*.

Leona gasped. "The poor man—"

"What is goin' on out there?" Stowe peered out the window.

"Come on," Aldwin snapped. He grabbed Leona's hand and pulled her toward the doorway.

Light shifted in the shop window. A customer? Or a poacher searching for them?

"Oy!" Stowe groused. "Move, ye bastard. Yer blockin' me view."

"I ask again"—Clif bellowed in the sudden silence—"and I ask all who 'ear me! I am looking fer a man. 'E's travelin' with a woman."

"Oh, God," Leona whispered.

Drawing his sword, Aldwin edged toward the doorway. Hellfire. He'd left his crossbow tied to Rom's saddle. He never imagined he'd need it in the brief moments they'd be inside the shop. What a stupid, stupid mistake.

Through the open doorway, he saw frightened villagers jostling in the square. Somewhere in the crowd, a child began to bawl. He hauled Leona over the threshold.

Two men rushed at him—one of them, the oaf from the cavern. Aldwin swung his sword, slicing the first thug's arm. The man howled.

At the same time, Leona kicked the cavern thug.

"Come on!" Aldwin yelled, racing toward Rom but a few steps away.

A sharp tug on his arm made him stumble. Then an eerie gurgle reached him.

"Leona?"

He spun. Sucked in a painful breath.

Her hands clawing at her throat, Leona stood against the wall. Beside her, his fingers twisted into the pendant's chain, stood the poacher from the cavern.

"I knew I would find ye," the man leered, his knife glinting against her breast. "I will 'ave that gold. And all else ye denied me."

✠ ✠ ✠

Leona choked for breath, her vision blurring as the chain tightened around her neck. The links bit deeper. With a shaking arm, she swatted at Peyton.

He laughed. "Not this time, love."

Anger seethed inside her while the chain tightened even more. Her face scorched as if she'd leaned into a bonfire. Stretching up on her toes, squeezing back against the wall, she tried to ease the unbearable pressure. She wouldn't die at Peyton's hand. She wouldn't!

"Let her go," Aldwin said from somewhere close by.

"Try ta save 'er, and she dies."

A moan came from across the square. The tavern owner, she realized, through the pressure threatening to burst inside her head.

Just as blackness swirled into her vision, Peyton's hand at her neck shifted.

A grisly *thwack*. A pained cry.

The pressure at her throat eased.

Leona gasped for breath. As her head fell forward, the chain whipped up over her face and hair. Peyton had taken the necklace!

Her body sagged. She must stop him, but, Oh, God, she was sliding to the ground.

A strong arm looped around her. "I have you."

Aldwin.

"Pen . . . dant," she croaked, trying to point.

Metal chimed. While she blinked and raised her head, she heard a *clink*. The jewel landed in the other poacher's hand.

"Ald—"

"I know. I will get it back. I wanted to be sure you were

safe. Now sit," he said, pushing her forward onto a bench outside the blacksmith's.

Swords clanged. Squealed. As her surroundings came into focus, she saw Aldwin fighting the other poacher. Peyton stood bent over at the wall, his hand pressed to a bleeding stomach wound. He looked up at her, spittle dripping from his mouth.

He still held his knife.

As he staggered toward her, fury whipped through her veins. She stood on weak legs, looking about for a weapon, and saw the iron tongs still holding the hot horseshoe.

Peyton smirked. "Give up now, love."

She snatched up the tongs. "Never." A feral cry burst from her as she lunged and slammed the tongs into his head.

He fell.

"A good arm ye 'ave there." Stowe came up behind her, catching her elbow to steady her. "What do these thugs want with ye and Lord Treynarde? What did ye do ta them?"

"Yesterday, Aldwin defended us from attack by these poachers. He killed two of them."

"And now they want yer 'eads."

She nodded, then gestured to Rom. "Please help me up."

After setting aside the tongs, Stowe dragged over the bench and helped her onto it. She pulled herself onto Rom's back.

From her vantage point, she saw many of the townsfolk were huddled on the church steps; others crowded behind wagons and peered from shop windows, unable to leave the square, because the ways out were blocked by armed poachers. Clif had grabbed the proprietor around the neck and pulled him away from the tavern door. A knife gleamed at the tavern owner's throat. Sweat glistened on his face. Watching Aldwin and the other poacher fight with obvious fascination, Clif and his two grinning cohorts seemed to be waiting on the outcome.

Clif's gaze slid to her. He smiled, the look of a man convinced he'd already won the battle—a stark contrast to the petrified expression of the tavern owner.

Resentment boiled inside Leona. None of the townsfolk deserved bullying, especially because of her and Aldwin. "Stowe," she called down. "Please hand me that poacher's knife."

As the blacksmith handed her the weapon, a sharp cry broke behind her. She glanced back to see Aldwin's opponent stumble. Blood stained the front of the man's cloak. He groaned and limped toward Clif, his sword listing downward.

Rom's saddle shifted. A heavy weight landed behind her.

"Down," Aldwin said by Leona's ear, before shoving her forward against Rom's neck. The crossbow appeared in her side vision.

Still holding the tavern owner hostage, Clif spoke to the shorter, blond-haired poacher beside him, who hurried toward their injured colleague.

Leona held very still, acutely aware of Aldwin's body pressed against hers. A ghastly quiet stretched across the square, amplifying the injured poacher's uneven footfalls.

Nearing his blond friend, he held out the jewel.

The crossbow trigger clicked. The bolt shot free and plowed into his back.

Blood spattered. He teetered sideways.

As he fell, the blond man snatched the jewel from his dead fingers.

"Hellfire," Aldwin growled.

"We 'ave the jewel," Cliff called, taking it from the blond man. "Now we want both of ye."

Clif yanked the proprietor's head back to expose more of his neck to the knife blade. The man whimpered. "Surrender and we will spare 'is life. Refuse"—Clif tipped his head toward the shops—"and we will kill townsfolk until ye do."

Shrieks erupted in the crowd.

"The pendant is not enough?" Aldwin bellowed. Leona sensed him reloading the crossbow.

Clif laughed. "There is a reward out for ye."

Leona's hand tightened on the knife.

"For ye and that jewel, there'll be riches enough"—he looked at his men—"for us ta live like lords."

His men roared their approval.

"What does he mean? What reward?" Leona muttered.

"Veronique's doing, I vow."

"But how—?"

"Stay down."

Aldwin shift his weight behind her. She sensed his intense concentration.

Clif frowned. "Will ye surrender? Or—?"

The bolt whistled free. Pierced one of the ropes of the tavern sign above Clif. Embedded in the building wall.

Stowe whistled. "A shot worthy of legend."

Clif looked up. "What—?"

The board dangled. Swayed.

Cursing, Clif lunged sideways. Taking advantage of the distraction, the tavern owner dropped to the ground.

"Oy!" the blond poacher cried, as the proprietor dashed for the tavern.

At the same instant, the sign plummeted. With a weighty *thud*, it hit Clif's left shoulder.

His body jerked like a puppet yanked by an angry master. Roaring, Clif twisted toward Aldwin, and then collapsed on his knees on the cobblestones. He clutched at his arm slanting at a grisly angle.

Now safe in the tavern doorway, the proprietor waved to Aldwin in thanks.

"Get them," Clif roared. "Now!"

Drawing their swords, the blond poacher and his friend started toward Rom.

"We will get ye, Treynarde," the blond man sneered.

"Ye will suffer fer killin' our friends," the other poacher growled.

Rom tossed his head and back stepped, his bridle clinking. Leona grabbed hold of his mane to steady her balance, while Aldwin thrust the crossbow into her lap. "Keep it safe. Hold on."

Before she could say another word, he kicked Rom's sides. The destrier surged forward. His hooves clattered on the cobblestones as Aldwin swung his sword down in a swift arc; it met the blond man's weapon, whipping toward Rom, with a shrill *clang*. The man stumbled from the blow's force.

The second poacher lunged, his sword aimed at Aldwin's leg, but Aldwin deflected the blow. A second strike, and the man's sword hit the ground, light flashing down the blade.

Cheers rose from the townsfolk.

Aldwin glanced about the square. "Clif?"

"There." Leona pointed. His face contorted with pain, Clif was speaking to several men, while pulling himself up with his good arm onto a horse.

Fury poured from Aldwin. She sensed it as keenly as she heard the blond poacher running in another strike. "Look out!" she shrieked. Aldwin spun Rom around, but the man was approaching too fast.

She forced herself to focus. *Remember what Ward taught you years ago*, a little voice inside her said. *You can defeat this thug.*

She swung back her arm and hurled the knife. It plowed into the man's chest. He gaped, first at the dagger hilt jutting from his body, then at her. His eyes shifted out of focus before he collapsed, lifeless.

"I . . ." she whispered. "I did it."

"Nay!" the other poacher screamed, dropping to his friend's side.

"Hellfire!" Aldwin wheeled Rom around again.

Leona frowned back at him. "What do you mean? I saved us from attack."

His arm at her waist squeezed her tight. "You did. Well done. But Clif is riding out of the square. He cannot get away with that pendant."

‡ ‡ ‡

His sword raised, Aldwin urged Rom into the crowd. The townsfolk moved away, providing an opening to the main road leading out of the square.

Even as he nodded his thanks, Aldwin clamped his jaw. Clif was already a good distance ahead.

"Do not let them get away!" shouted an angry voice behind them. "We'll lose the reward."

"To the 'orses," another man yelled.

A scruffy-haired poacher standing watch near the church raised his sword; he raced toward Rom. Aldwin tightened his grip on his blade, trying to ignore the pain stabbing down his side and the trickling warmth against his skin. Baring his teeth, he brought the sword swinging down.

He met the poacher's strike and grunted as the clash shuddered through his torso. The man cursed. Stumbled. Before the poacher could raise his weapon to attack again, Aldwin spurred the destrier into the dirt street.

The clatter of hooves echoed off the stone buildings rising skyward. Ahead, peasants turned, wide-eyed, as Clif neared them without caring to slow his mount. They dashed aside to let him through. They gaped when, moments later, Rom raced past.

More hoofbeats—horses at a pounding gallop—came from the direction of the square.

Leona's head whipped around. "The poachers are following."

Aldwin swept strands of her hair from his eyes and tried not to growl. "Aye."

As they raced on, he dared not part his cloak to look at where his tunic stuck to his skin. Without doubt, he'd ripped open his wound. Later, he must see how many stitches he'd torn.

God's blood, he had to recover the pendant. He couldn't fail his lord. He wouldn't return to Branton Keep without the jewel.

Aldwin squinted against the dust hazing the street. Some yards away, Clif galloped by an old man leading a donkey cart piled with firewood. The man ambled into the middle of the street, clearly deaf to Rom's approach. Past him, children were shrieking and running in a game, while their fathers stood by an alley, talking. When Clif raced near, the youngsters screamed and scrambled to get out of harm's way.

The fathers shook their fists and shouted.

"He is mad," Leona muttered, her gaze on Clif, before she gasped. "Oh! He almost ran down that little boy!"

Forcing down a surge of frustration, Aldwin slowed Rom

to a trot. De Lanceau forbade harming innocent folk, especially children. He rode past the cart and peasants, and then, seeing the route was clear, kicked the destrier into a canter.

Clif was no longer in sight.

Blinking against the dust, Aldwin glanced along the street. Where was the bastard?

"Oh, nay," Leona whispered.

Aldwin reined Rom in while he scanned their surroundings. The hoofbeats behind them grew louder, masking any sounds from the nearby alleys. Soon—too soon—the other poachers would be upon them.

Neale had given only a rough idea of the town's layout in his sketch that morn, and hadn't mentioned any of the alleys leading off the street. Clif must have gone into one of the closest. The right one, or the left?

Both alleys looked much the same: grimy and well-traveled. But the thunder of pursuit forced Aldwin into the one on the right.

Rotting vegetables tumbled from several broken crates. The stench! Strong enough to make a man retch. Leona covered her face with her cloak sleeve. Flies buzzed up in a swirling mass and she shrieked before pressing against him. Her body shook, as it had earlier in the cottage.

"Just flies," he said against her ear.

"N-no bees?"

"None." He waved insects from his face.

A triumphant shout came from behind them. One of the poachers had spotted them. From the resounding cacophony, several riders had entered the alley in pursuit.

Leona glanced over her shoulder. "Aldwin."

"I know."

He spurred Rom onward, past piles of splintered wood, broken pottery, and food scraps, his gaze on the end of the alley ahead. They raced into a street.

Hooves pounded in the near distance. A man came into view down the street. When he saw them, he smirked and raised his sword.

The poachers intended to trap them. And still, no sign of Clif.

Aldwin fought bitter dismay, for escape, not getting back the pendant, must be his priority now. He and Leona mustn't be captured, for if they were, what they knew about the treachery at Pryerston Keep would die with them.

He urged Rom into another alley, shorter than the first. Cats feasting on scraps scattered as they barreled past.

When they emerged into yet another street, a woman carrying a basket of clothes gasped and dropped the garments in the dirt. Shaking her head, she bent to gather them up.

"Please. The main road to Branton Keep," Aldwin shouted. "Which way?"

Thrusting a work-worn finger, she said, "Take the right fork."

Reaching into his coin bag, he tossed her some silver. She beamed.

Dirt flew beneath Rom's hooves as they raced down the street lined with town houses. And then, the route broadened, splitting a short distance ahead into two roads.

Shouts carried from close behind.

The scruffy-haired poacher—followed by several others—galloped toward them from a street ahead, clearly trying to cut off their escape. His drawn sword gleamed.

Leona tensed in Aldwin's grasp.

Aldwin wielded his own weapon, clenching his teeth against

the pain in his side. He mentally judged the distance to the right fork. They'd outpace the thugs, if they were lucky.

If not . . .

Muttering a silent prayer, he kicked his heels into Rom's sides.

The huge horse soared forward and streaked past the scruffy-haired poacher. The man cursed, while Rom galloped onto the road's right fork.

"Get them!" another poacher screamed.

The sun-drenched road swam before Aldwin's eyes. He shook his head, fighting to stay focused; he wouldn't yield to his agony.

He must have made a sound of discomfort, because Leona frowned back at him. "What is wrong? Are you—?"

"I am all right." He had to be, until she was safe.

Wheat fields spread on either side of the road. Farther ahead, he saw the fringes of a forest. If they couldn't outrun the poachers, he'd try to outwit them in the woods. He had enough bolts left to put up a good fight, if need be.

The poachers' horses sounded perilously close behind.

On they raced, until the trees' shadows fell across the road. Long grasses and shrubs grew along the verge, some tall enough to screen a man hiding behind them. As the forest's coolness swept over him, Aldwin searched for a way into the woods.

Hopefully, they were far enough ahead of the poachers for—

Leona cried out.

A man ran out onto the road ahead of them, his sword raised.

And another man.

"Hold!"

CHAPTER NINETEEN

A scream welled up within Leona as the two men neared. How unfair that she and Aldwin had escaped the poachers in the town, only to be captured by their cohorts in the forest.

She wouldn't submit to these cutthroats. Neither would she and Aldwin be sold to Veronique for a reward. She'd rather die fighting than—

"Dominic?" Surprise lightened Aldwin's voice.

With the gritty scrape of hooves, Rom's strides slowed.

Leona swallowed. Aldwin knew the brown-haired warrior coming to their side?

"Aldwin." Dominic grinned before his gaze slid to Leona, then down the road. "You are expecting friends?"

The *clop-clop-clop* of hoofbeats intensified.

"We are being chased by poachers. They have information on the baron and Veronique."

"Just the two we are looking for." Dominic's gaze sharpened with interest. "We must chat with these poachers." He signaled into the woods. Riders in full chain-mail armor began to emerge from the undergrowth. "Be sure our approaching guests are greeted properly," he called to them. "Once they are disarmed, bring them to Lord de Lanceau."

The riders galloped off toward the poachers.

Dominic waved Aldwin toward the deer path leading into the forest. "Geoffrey will want to speak with you. Oh"—he raised his brows—"I warn you, he is in a foul mood, due to a meeting with Veronique."

"Meeting?" Aldwin frowned. "When?"

"Earlier this morn. 'Tis one reason why we are in this part of Moydenshire. I will explain all later. Then"—he nodded to Leona—"we will also make the proper introductions."

Before she could reply, Dominic loped toward the other warriors who'd taken up position along the roadside.

Rom's bridle jangled as Aldwin urged Rom into the forest.

"How do you know these men?" Suspicion gnawed at her. "Can you trust them?"

"With my life. Dominic is a good friend of mine and de Lanceau's best friend; they met while on crusade. The other men are from Branton Keep's garrison."

A low-hanging tree branch brushed against Leona's leg. She hardly felt it, quelled by the awful realization she was headed toward a new kind of captivity. Sooner than she'd thought, she'd be facing Lord de Lanceau.

How did she explain all that had occurred at Pryerston Keep without implicating her father? She must. Would de Lanceau believe her, even if every word she spoke was true?

She forced down a rush of dread, while Aldwin steered the horse through the forest. The trees soon opened into a small meadow bordering the river. Armed men watered their horses, while others, bloodied from an earlier battle, sat on the grass while fellow knights stitched their wounds.

She glanced at Aldwin, wondering if the sight of the needles unsettled him.

He wasn't focused on the injured, but a tall man with shoulder-length brown hair standing apart from the others. His back faced them, but an aura of authority seemed to linger around him, snaring their attention without him turning their way or saying a word. He stood with his hands on his hips, his hair spilling around his surcoat's shoulders; he looked down the river as though watching it wend its way into the distant fields.

This man must be de Lanceau.

"Aldwin," one of the wounded warriors cried. "We were wondering what had become of you." His gaze shifted to Leona and he loosed a low whistle. Other men noticed her, too. Several snickered.

Leona's face heated. She stared straight ahead and tried to ignore the blatant ogling.

"I do not recognize that wench," another of the men-at-arms muttered. "Do you?"

"She does not look like one of his lady types," another said.

Wench? One of his lady types? The ordeals of the past few days suddenly pressed up inside Leona, making her painfully aware of her worn garments, untidy hair, and tattered emotions. How she'd love to swing around in the saddle and screech at those men for talking about her. 'Twould not be a good start, though, to what might be a difficult meeting with de Lanceau.

Smothering the words burning in her mouth, she curled her fingers into her palms.

De Lanceau turned.

"Milord." Aldwin dipped his head.

"Aldwin."

De Lanceau's attention settled upon Leona. Her startled mind registered handsome features, a commanding stare, and the narrowing of his gray eyes before she bowed her head. "Milord."

"We spoke with Dominic a moment ago," Aldwin said, his voice rumbling behind her. "He mentioned you met with Veronique."

De Lanceau's head dipped in a terse nod. "Not long after you left Branton Keep to retrieve the pendant, I received a missive from her, claiming she had it. Of course, I had my doubts, but I decided to meet with her, for I hoped to finally arrest her and the baron. She also promised important . . . information."

A chill rippled through Leona. The way he emphasized *information* and then swept his hand across his face indicated 'twas vital news indeed.

What had Veronique told de Lanceau? Had she portrayed Leona's father as a traitor who planned to keep the jewel to defy de Lanceau, because of the tragedy that had befallen Leona's mother? Leona knew little about Veronique, but wouldn't dare underestimate the woman's manipulative nature.

"Milord," Leona began, determined to tell the truth about her sire, "the necklace—"

"—is not in Veronique's possession," Aldwin cut in, heedless of Leona's frown. "At least, she did not have it before your meeting."

"Where is the jewel?"

"I fear we do not know, milord." The saddle creaked as Aldwin's weight shifted. "We were attacked by poachers a short while ago in Anwenbury, and—"

"You were injured." De Lanceau gestured to Aldwin's side;

his parted cloak revealed a crimson stain on his tunic.

"I was wounded yesterday, milord, in another skirmish with the poachers. However, in today's fight, one of them took the pendant from around Leona's neck."

De Lanceau's brows shot up, and Leona fought the renewed heat creeping into her face.

"You were wearing it?" he said.

Nodding, she struggled not to blush all the more.

"For safekeeping," Aldwin quickly added. "She wore it while we traveled to Branton Keep to hand it to you."

Leona pushed back her shoulders as de Lanceau gave her an assessing glance over. He must think her a brazen woman to presume to wear such a costly jewel that he intended for a lady other than her. Would that reflect badly upon her, and her father, in the coming days?

"Did you send me the letter arranging the meeting at the Raging Bull Tavern?" de Lanceau asked, his tone thoughtful.

"Aye, milord."

"And who, exactly, are you?"

She cleared her throat. "Lady Leona . . . Ransley."

"Ransley," he murmured. "A name I know well."

Her stomach squeezed into a knot.

"What relation are you to Lord Ransley of Pryerston Keep?"

"His daughter."

"I see. Then you must know some of what is being reported to me by my local spy. Above all, that armed mercenaries are being recruited in the nearby town and sent to Pryerston."

Trying not to let her shoulders slump, she nodded. "I heard such. My father did not hire them. That, I promise you."

"Indeed?"

"He despises mercenaries. Veronique and the baron are the ones responsible."

De Lanceau's gaze shadowed. "A telling development in itself."

Leona forced down a dismayed cry. From de Lanceau's expression, she guessed what he was thinking: that Veronique and the baron had convinced her sire to turn traitor and Leona didn't want to accept such.

"I assure you"—she refused to let her voice waver—"my sire is loyal to you."

"The wax on the missive I received from Veronique bore your father's seal."

Shock tore through her. "They must have forced him to add it."

"Knowing them, 'tis a possibility." De Lanceau's keen gaze slid past her to settle on Aldwin. "What I gather, then, from all you have told me, is that we are not much further along than when you began your quest days ago. The jewel is still missing and may still fall into the baron and Veronique's possession to be used against me."

Aldwin's harsh sigh stirred Leona's hair. She sensed his intense disappointment and how difficult 'twas for him to admit he'd failed his lordship. "What you say is true, milord. With all due respect, though, I do not consider my mission finished. We learned a reward was offered to the poachers for the pendant, as well as Leona's and my capture."

"A reward, you say?"

"Aye. I have no doubt Veronique offered it. The jewel is likely on its way to Pryerston Keep now. I would like to investigate my suspicions, milord."

A wry grin tilted de Lanceau's mouth. "I am certain you would." When he set his hands on his hips again, his smile faded. "I, too, want to know what is taking place at Pryerston. We will ride on to the keep, whereupon I shall demand to speak with Lord Ransley."

Oh, God. If her father was drunk and in one of his rages, he might refuse to let de Lanceau in—especially if the baron and Veronique were encouraging a show of defiance.

"If he will not let me enter, we will besiege the keep."

Besiege Pryerston? Leona pressed a hand to her mouth. She'd never experienced such an attack, but had heard accounts of them. Good folk died, livestock perished, and to rebuild afterward could take months. To think of Pryerston devastated in that way . . . Nay. She couldn't let that happen.

"Milord," she said, drawing the full force of de Lanceau's gaze. "A siege is not necessary. I can get you and your men-at-arms inside Pryerston."

"Will I not be admitted if I announce myself at the gates?" De Lanceau's bold stare demanded an explanation why her sire wouldn't welcome a visit from his liege.

"Of course you would be let in, milord," she said, hoping 'twas not a lie. "With all we have heard about Pryerston, though, I thought you might want to enter the keep as quickly—and inconspicuously—as possible."

"Leona." Aldwin didn't sound pleased by her recommendation. Why not? Did he believe 'twas not a lady's place to speak of such matters with her lord? Yet if she could save lives of people she cared about, and spare Pryerston a battering, she must forge on.

"I know the location of the postern gate," she said. "There is also another way into the main keep, built long before my father took possession of it."

"Go on," de Lanceau said.

"A hidden passage in the keep's wall leads from the bailey up to the lord's solar. The outside door is close to the kitchens. I was told this way in was built many years ago to allow a previous lord's lover to visit him in secret, because his lady wife despised her."

De Lanceau's lips twitched with a faint smile. "You have traveled this passageway?"

"My brother and I loved to play in it when we were children." Fighting a sudden pang of loneliness, she said, "'Tis very cramped and the steps are uneven, and my father soon forbade it, because he believed 'twas dangerous. He ordered the doors locked and the key destroyed." She shrugged. "He kept one key. I know where 'tis." Pausing a moment, she added, "I hid in this passageway days ago when Veronique and the baron asked to speak in private with my father and he took them to his solar. I listened through the door that opens into his solar, and heard every word of their conversation."

For a long, agonizing moment, de Lanceau studied her. "I am not a man to skulk around in secret passageways."

Her hopes plummeted. "But—"

"However, your suggestion has merit, since we do not know how many mercenaries are inside the keep."

She couldn't hold back a relieved sigh. "Thank you, milord."

"'Tis settled, then." De Lanceau looked toward his men, as though to stride over to them and relay orders.

"Not quite, milord." Leona trembled inside, even while she forced herself to speak the words that might well be viewed as a direct challenge.

"Leona!" Aldwin muttered, this time in clear warning.

When de Lanceau's astonished gaze settled on her again, she rushed on. "Milord, along with the rumors about Pryerston, you must have heard of my father's drinking."

"I have."

"All I ask is that you consider what he has endured over the past months. My older brother's death. My mother's tragic accident earlier this year. He loved her very much."

"As I gathered from his letter."

She cringed inside at the thought of what de Lanceau must have thought of that missive. Keeping her voice strong, she said, "Very soon, I am sure, my father will overcome his despair and once again be serving you as he should. Please, milord. I hope that you remember . . . even the best men make mistakes."

"Leona," Aldwin snapped.

A curious glint brightened de Lanceau's eyes, as if her words meant more to him than a heartfelt plea for her sire.

Glancing at Aldwin, his lordship looked about to speak, but shouts and tramped footfalls emanated from the forest. Rom sidestepped, no doubt unsettled, and she grabbed his mane to hold herself steady before glancing at the woods.

Dominic headed toward them, surrounded by his armed colleagues. The poachers stumbled along in their midst.

De Lanceau's expression hardened. "Tend to your wound, Aldwin," he said, turning away. "I will see what these ruffians can tell us."

‡ ‡ ‡

Crouched by the side of a large rock, her skirts bunched up in her lap, Leona leaned toward Aldwin, a threaded needle in her fingers. He'd removed his cloak and bloodstained tunic and sat naked from the waist up on the rock partly buried in the riverbank.

As the needle neared his flesh, his already strained expression seemed to tauten further. Was he going to faint? She hoped not. While she prided herself on her strength, she doubted she could haul him upright on her own.

When de Lanceau had ordered him to have his wound tended, she'd quickly offered to help. Knowing Aldwin's fear of needles, she hoped to save him any possible teasing from his friends. Above all, she wanted to know why he'd seemed so annoyed with her when she spoke to de Lanceau. She couldn't explain why understanding Aldwin's thoughts was so important to her, only that 'twas.

"Tsk-tsk," she said while she gently touched the wound she'd cleansed moments ago.

Aldwin hissed. The tension surrounding him seemed to escalate.

"Sorry, but—"

"Do it quickly," he growled.

Aye, my grumpy lord. Pressing her lips together, she told herself he spoke in that surly manner because he was anxious and in pain, because of a wound he'd got while protecting them from murderers. He'd been very brave and fought well, despite his injury. He'd saved her life. For that, at the very least, she owed him these stitches.

She worked in silence for several moments, aware of the

ducks squawking farther down the river, the breeze stirring her hair, and the voices of de Lanceau and his men questioning the captives. And, God help her, mercilessly aware of Aldwin: the purely male smell rising from his warm skin; the whisper of his breathing; his beautiful physique that coaxed her to touch and feel. Part of her ached to rejoice that they'd escaped the poachers and, for now, were safe.

When she snipped the thread and sat back on her heels to examine her handiwork, he exhaled a sharp breath. "You should not speak to de Lanceau so."

Leona resisted the urge to glance up. "What do you mean?"

"You must realize how precarious your situation is. You are in no position to tell him what to do in regard to your father's keep."

Trying not to give in to anger, she said, "I see no wrong in speaking my thoughts or suggesting a plan he had not envisioned. My way into the castle will save lives."

"Your manner was overly bold, for the daughter of a man under suspicion from her lord."

Aldwin's temper sounded very close to erupting—which made her even more annoyed. Why couldn't he respect her views on the matter? Was he angry because she'd offered a good suggestion, when he didn't have positive news for de Lanceau? She looked up into Aldwin's blue eyes and steeled herself against the unwelcome anguish inside her. "I was not discourteous to Lord de Lanceau."

"Look,—"

"The good people of Pryerston Keep are my family. I feel responsible for them. If you were in my position, would you not want to save lives by preventing a siege?"

Aldwin looked downriver. Avoidance.

"Well?" she pressed.

"I just . . ." He shook his head. "I do not want you to be rash. To speak or do something foolish you will regret days or years from today."

"Well," she muttered, "I would not be the first to be rash or foolish, would I?"

As soon as the words left her lips, she wished she could take them back and crush them into nothingness.

Before she could utter another sound, his hand plowed into her hair. His fingers seized the back of her skull so she couldn't turn away. Eyes blazing, he bent his head to hers.

"Careful. Stitches," she managed to croak, before he paused.

The heat of him, so angry and impassioned, stirred a bittersweet fire within her.

"You deserve better," he said against her skin, "than to have your life tarnished by dishonor."

His words—so unexpected—shocked the air from her lungs.

"Some mistakes are difficult, if not impossible, to rectify. They will haunt you for the rest of your living days." His voice became a rasp on the last words, and she knew he was speaking not only of the bee stinging incident years ago, but his near murder of de Lanceau.

Her attention slid to Aldwin's mouth, so near and beautiful. How she wanted him to look upon her not with anger or concern, but desire.

"I will do my best to watch over you, but—"

"I can look after myself." She tried to slip out of his grasp, but he wouldn't let her go.

"Not in this matter," he said firmly.

"Why not?"

"Because, Lioness, your rash nature is akin to my own. In many ways, we are hewn from the same stone." His fingers tightened in her hair. "Our impulsiveness is both empowering and a curse."

True. As impetuous as she might be, though, she'd never abandon her loyalty to her sire.

"Your father's mistakes are not yours. Do not make them so."

Aldwin spoke as though he still had a right to command her, even though she wasn't his captive any longer. With a swift tug, she pulled from his grasp. Shoving against the rock, she stood.

"Promise me, Lioness, you will not do anything foolish."

"Are you concerned for me? Or are you more worried that my actions might somehow reflect badly upon you?"

He pushed to his feet. "Leona—"

"You do not want any impediments to succeeding in your quest. To being hailed as a hero and knighted." How she hated sounding bitter. But she could barely contain the confusing and painful emotions burgeoning inside her.

Aldwin drew a rough breath. His body seemed to loom taller. Broader.

"Be honest. Knighthood is all you wanted." Hurt and anger thinned her voice. "You told me so yourself. And 'tis what you mean to have."

"In part," he said, "yet—"

She blinked away the damning sting of tears. "'Tis of little consequence what happens to my sire or—"

"You?" The word ground between his teeth. Before she could move away, his arm snaked around her to yank her against his body's muscled heat. "There you are wrong." His breath rasped over her cheek, sparking a rush of fiery tingles inside her. "That is why I will not let you ruin the rest of your life."

"And how will you do that?"

Aldwin's arm tightened, impressing the scent and feel of him upon her. Then he stepped away and snatched up his cloak and tunic. Without a backward glance, he strode toward the other men-at-arms.

‡ ‡ ‡

Aldwin stood with his friends and listened to de Lanceau interrogate the poachers. Or, rather, ask questions that the cutthroats refused to answer with more than sullen glares.

Aldwin shrugged against his tunic chafing his back, his stitched side, and his ribs. Every part of him chafed, while fine, emotional grit seemed to scratch his heart.

He massaged his shoulder and tried to ease the tension that had gathered there while he spoke with Leona. Stubborn woman. Had she listened to one word he said—advice intended to help her—or ignored them all, because they'd come from him?

He'd been sorely tempted to—

"Here." Dominic slapped a rolled garment against Aldwin's stomach. "My spare tunic. Far cleaner than the one you are wearing now, and"—he wrinkled his nose—"sweeter smelling."

Aldwin scowled. "Why, thank you."

Dominic grinned.

Bending at the waist, Aldwin shed his dirty tunic and pulled on the clean one. As he straightened with a groan, Dominic's smile faded.

"'Tis quite a gash on your side."

"A gift from the poachers," Aldwin said.

Dominic's gaze slid to the riverbank, where Leona no doubt still stood. "Protecting your fair damsel?"

"Leona is not *mine*."

"Leona," Dominic repeated while tapping his jaw. "A fierce name for such a beautiful woman. Who is she?"

Dominic found her beautiful? Aldwin fought an irrational surge of jealousy. Dominic was happily married with a wife and son; he had no interest in wooing Leona. "She's the daughter of Lord Ransley, from Pryerston Keep."

"Ah. Does she know what is happening at her father's castle, then?"

"She does, although she refuses to accept her father may be a traitor."

Aldwin risked a glance at the water. Leona stood with her back to him, her hands on the fetching curve of her hips, peering down the river. Was she determining the quickest way to flee?

His scowl deepened before he swiveled in her direction.

Dominic's hand on his arm halted him. "Leave her. She cannot slip away."

"You do not know Leona."

"Nay, but Geoffrey posted men down the river. They will stop her if she wanders too far. In the meantime, you should speak with Geoffrey. There are, shall we say, developments."

"Do they concern the pendant?"

Dominic blew a sigh. "Not exactly. Geoffrey must tell you the rest. Ah, here he is now."

Footfalls sounded behind Aldwin before his lord came alongside him. Anger and strain lined de Lanceau's face.

"Well?" Dominic asked.

"We will get naught from those bastards. Not unless we

torture them, and I have no wish to do such." Glancing at Aldwin, he said, "Your wound is stitched?"

"Aye, milord."

"Good. Then walk with me. Dominic, you too. Both of you are to listen well."

"Of course, milord." Dominic chuckled. "I always listen well, although my lovely wife might say otherwise."

De Lanceau groaned and rubbed his forehead.

When they'd walked a fair distance away from the other men, Aldwin said, "Dominic mentioned there are new developments."

His lord's stride slowed. "A diplomatic way of putting the matter."

Diplomatic? Aldwin frowned. "Milord?"

Halting near the bank, where long grasses blended into a wind-stirred patch of reeds, de Lanceau turned, his expression grave. "I learned today that Veronique has a son. He is close in age to my Edouard."

"Aye?" Was the boy somehow connected to Veronique's plans for the pendant?

"She claims I fathered her child."

Shock slammed through Aldwin. "*You?*" He blinked and then mentally reviewed the necessary timeline. "Milord, you did . . . ah . . . lie with her, before you fell in love with Lady Elizabeth." Aldwin, too, had resorted to diplomacy. He tried to keep his thoughts from wandering back to de Lanceau's quest for vengeance years ago—that unsettled time when Aldwin had been persuaded to shoot him.

Standing here with his lord, thinking of that terrible mistake, made Aldwin's skin chafe all the more.

"We all know Veronique is a cruel, manipulative bitch,"

de Lanceau went on. "I do not want to believe her claim. Still, I must admit, 'tis possible."

"More than possible," Dominic said. "Tye looks like you."

De Lanceau exhaled through his teeth and closed his eyes, as though he didn't dare accept the truth. "How am I going to tell Elizabeth? What will she think of this news?"

Aldwin's gut twisted, for he hated to think of the turmoil this would cause de Lanceau's loved ones, especially Lady Elizabeth. "What will you have us do, milord? However we can help—"

"Veronique is not beyond harming the boy to wound me, as she proved today when she threatened him with a dagger," de Lanceau said quietly. "Whatever happens at Pryerston, he must be taken away from her and protected. I will not have that innocent child suffer because of me."

‡ ‡ ‡

Swallowing a mouthful of red wine, Veronique turned from the table where Ransley snored, spittle sliding from his mouth onto the soiled cloth. He'd fought the drink being poured from the jug into his mouth—quite valiantly for an old man—but, bound to his chair, he couldn't fend off his stronger opponents. One of them, the mercenary bowing before her now.

"Clif is 'ere ta see ye, milady."

With good news, she hoped. She welcomed a hot shiver of anticipation.

With a wave of her hand, she dismissed the mercenary, while half-listening to the footsteps growing louder in the stairwell.

Clif emerged, and she fought a startled gasp. His face looked ashen, and his scar even more stark. Moreover, his broad, handsome body appeared distorted, for he leaned with his left shoulder and arm drooping toward the floor.

Veronique frowned. "What is wrong with you?"

"Aldwin," Clif muttered. "Broke me shoulder."

Petulance clung to each word. Was he expecting sympathy? Loving coos and a tender hand on his brow?

Veronique bit back her tart reply; she still needed him. "Where are Aldwin and Leona? Did you capture them?"

"Me men are chasing 'em. They've likely got 'em by now."

She hoped so, for his sake. Forcing a concerned smile, Veronique said, "I am sorry you are hurt." She set aside her wine goblet and crossed to him.

A crooked smile tilted Clif's mouth. "Ye can ease me discomfort later."

Ease his pain later? An arrogant assumption—

"First"—he flinched while reaching into his cloak—"ye will 'ave this."

A delicate gold chain with a gleaming ruby dangled from his fist.

De Lanceau's necklace.

Veronique sucked in an elated breath. "Clif!" Her hand shook as she reached for the gem.

He snatched it back, grimacing when his shoulder shifted. "I want me reward, as ye promised. Then ye may 'ave the pendant."

Reward? Oh, he would receive it, all right.

A brazen laugh swelled within her while she pressed closer, the scents of sweat and leather clinging to his garments. His smoldering gaze focused on her mouth she'd repainted crimson not long ago.

"Your reward." She smiled up at him. "I am glad you reminded me."

He nodded while his tongue slicked over his bottom lip. "I will be as wealthy as a nobleman. Ye"—he grinned—"will be me lady. We will never leave our bed."

Her eyelid dropped in a saucy wink while she slid her arms around his waist and crushed her breasts against him. He groaned at the nearness of her enticing cleavage.

"How clever you are, to have got the pendant," she murmured, while carefully reaching into the hem of her gown's sleeve. The hilt of a small knife brushed her palm.

"I *am* clever." Clif grinned. "And—"

She rammed the knife into his lower back.

His eyes flew wide.

She wrenched out the dagger. Stabbed again. When he roared and grabbed for her arm, she darted back.

Clif staggered. "You bitch!"

"Aye." Veronique laughed. Spinning on her heel, she strolled away to pick up her wine goblet.

With a pained whine, Clif slumped to the floor.

As quiet settled throughout the hall, deserted except for Ransley and the dogs, she walked back to Clif, nudged his limp hand open with her foot, and picked up the pendant. As she held it up to the fading light, she giggled like a naughty child.

A scraping sound came from behind her.

She whirled.

His head half-lifted from the table, Ransley squinted at her through bloodshot eyes. His focus slid to Clif's corpse before he shook his head and moaned.

"Aye, Lord Ransley," she said with a cruel laugh. "Soon, you will be dead, too."

CHAPTER TWENTY

Standing by the partly concealed wooden door in Pryerston Keep's curtain wall, Leona drew her cloak tighter to her body and glanced at de Lanceau, less than three strides away. In the darkness, she could barely make out his features; only when the moon escaped the overhead clouds did his expression become clear. But he, Aldwin, and the rest of the men had followed close behind her ever since they'd left the horses tethered in the aspen grove a short distance from the keep.

Before the moonlit castle had come into full view alongside the road, de Lanceau had motioned his men to guide their mounts into the trees. "We do not want the sentries on the wall walk to hear our horses," he'd said. His men had dismounted, tethered their animals, and taken up their weapons with astonishing speed.

Then de Lanceau had turned to her. Moonlight had touched his eyes as he gestured to the keep. "Lead the way, milady."

Leona had sensed Aldwin's piercing gaze upon her. He'd said little to her since they spoke near the river, but she'd caught him watching her, his eyes shadowed with torment. Each time she caught his gaze, he'd looked away.

Again, she'd steeled herself against the pain gnawing inside her and nodded to de Lanceau, then headed through the undergrowth. With the whispered snap of ferns and crackle of twigs, the men had followed her to the castle's high outer wall. The scent of damp stone carried on the breeze while the warriors flattened back against the wall, their weapons at the ready.

Even before the last man fell into place, de Lanceau nodded to her. She nodded back, stooped, counted over five rows of stone, then carefully wiggled out the loose chunk of mortar. She slid her finger into the opening and took out the key. After pushing the mortar back into place, she eased aside branches of the bush growing in front of the door and slid the key into the lock.

Leona sensed Aldwin's gaze upon her once more. She felt it so keenly, as if by looking at her he saw through her defenses to her heart. It ached for him, even if he seemed determined to avoid her.

Shoving aside her anguish, she turned the key in the lock. At first, the mechanism, rarely used and as old as the curtain wall, refused to budge. Then, with a muffled *click*, it gave.

Leona pushed the gate open. The panel creaked inward to reveal a swath of weed-choked grass. She stepped through, took the key from the lock, and set it under a rock near the wall.

The whisper of garments and muted *clank* of weaponry alerted her the warriors had followed her through.

Using the looming keep as her guide, she led the men along the wall toward the low-roofed buildings in the inner bailey.

The kitchen's rear door, which opened close to the henhouse, stood open. Light filtered out into the night, as did hushed voices.

"Ye must not talk like such," a woman—little Adeline's mother—said, her softened voice growing louder as she walked closer inside the kitchens. "Ye'll end up locked in the dungeon like Twig and Sir Reginald. Or killed, like those poor men in the 'all."

Leona smothered a gasp. Men killed? Twig and Sir Reginald in the dungeon? What else had happened whilst Aldwin held her captive?

"We cannot let matters go on like they are," Adeline's father, Pryerston's cook, replied. "Why, if Lord Ransley—" He moved away, across the kitchen, and his words became blurred by the clatter of crockery. Leaning against the kitchen wall, Leona strained to hear.

Holding up a cautioning hand, de Lanceau stepped past her, pressed his back to the door frame, and glanced inside. Turning back, he pointed at Leona, then at the open doorway.

She nodded.

"Milord." Aldwin stepped forward, his crossbow at the ready and his quiver slung over his shoulder. "I wish to go first."

Leona stepped past him into the light.

He grabbed her elbow, jerking her back into the shadows. She muttered a curse, but still, he didn't look at her, despite the almost visible spark their bodies had made when they touched. Her throat hurt as she looked at his taut, determined profile. Didn't he feel that tension buzzing between them?

She tried to brush past him, but he forced her back. "Milord," he bit out, "if the baron or Veronique are in there—"

"Not likely," she whispered. "'Tis best if I lead the way. The castle folk know me. If they see you first—an armed stranger—they might sound the alarm."

A peculiar gleam lit de Lanceau's eyes. He looked about to grin. Instead, he waved his hand toward the kitchens. "Go."

His breath rasping between his teeth, Aldwin released her. A saucy retort warmed her tongue, but she stifled it and hurried through the doorway.

Her shoes tapped on the stone floor as she headed toward the nearby worktable, covered with an array of breads and fresh pastries. The sweet scent of honey hung in the air, and, when she rounded the corner toward the main work area and cooking fires, her gaze fell upon a blond-haired little girl, sitting on a wooden stool, licking honey from a spoon. Adeline. Some distance across the kitchens, her parents were having a quiet but heated discussion.

"—and just 'ow would ye do that?" the mother said. "Are ye—?"

Adeline looked up. "Lady Leona!" The spoon dropped to the floor.

Leona smiled and pressed her finger to her lips. "Shh."

The girl lurched from the stool and hobbled forward on her bent legs. Leona ran forward, and the child threw her arms around her. "Milady!"

His face breaking into a grin, the cook hurried toward her, drying his hands on a cloth. "Milady! We 'ave worried about ye."

Leona scooped Adeline into her arms, relishing the little girl's hug. "I have missed all of you," she said, keeping her voice low, "but I am back now."

"Lady Leona." Adeline's mother wiped her teary eyes. "If only ye knew what 'as 'appened—" Her face drained of color. "Oh!"

Leona followed her gaze to where de Lanceau and his men were striding through the back doorway. Aldwin stood by the nearest cooking fires, scanning the room, his crossbow poised in case of attack.

The cook's mouth trembled. "Who are these men? Mercenaries, like all the others?"

Wiping honey from Adeline's chin, Leona said, "These warriors are loyal to Moydenshire's liege." She gestured. "Lord Geoffrey de Lanceau."

"*The* Lord de Lanceau? Of Branton Keep?"

She nodded.

"Oh!" The cook dropped into a bow, while his wife flushed and curtsied. "I did not expect ta ever meet ye, milord. 'Tis an honor."

"I thank you for your welcome," de Lanceau said quietly. "Tell me, are there mercenaries in the bailey?" He pointed to the closed door at the building's opposite end.

The cook nodded. "Some of 'em sleep around fires out there. They keep watch on us folk. They do not want us plottin' against 'em." He frowned before he gestured to the pastries. "They've 'ad us bakin' all sorts o' sweets and 'ave eaten through most of the storeroom's supplies. And the drink . . ." He shook his head. "I am sorry, milady."

He looked so devastated, she touched his arm. "I know you had no choice but to do as they demanded." After kissing Adeline's plump cheek, Leona set her down. "You said Twig and Sir Reginald are in the dungeon?"

The cook's wife nodded. "They 'aven't 'ad food or water since they returned 'ere. Veronique said they'd starve unless they told 'er where ye were."

Leona clenched her hands on a wave of anger. "We must rescue them."

"And yer father," the cook said, his expression sobering.

Oh, God. "Where is he? Is he all right?"

"'E's in the great 'all," the cook murmured. "A prisoner. Veronique 'as kept 'im drunk and threatened ta kill anyone who 'elped 'im."

A choked gasp broke from Leona. "How could she?"

Dominic stepped forward, drawing his sword. "With your permission, milord, I will free the men in the dungeon."

De Lanceau nodded. "Take five others with you. We will meet you inside the keep."

"Thank you," Leona whispered.

With a gallant nod, Dominic signaled to several warriors and stepped away.

"What can we do?" the cook asked, while his wife's head bobbed like an apple in a water trough. "There must be a way we can 'elp."

"With your permission, milord," Leona murmured, "there is." When de Lanceau motioned for her to continue, she said, "You can start telling the other servants his lordship and his men are inside the keep. Ask the others to find a weapon—even a broom or a candlestick—and keep it in secret close by. We may need them to fight. You must be careful, though, that the mercenaries do not learn of this plan."

De Lanceau nodded his approval.

The cook grinned. "Ye can trust us. We'll start right away."

"Lady Leona," Adeline piped up, "I want ta 'elp, too."

"You can stay right here in the kitchens and keep watch on the food," Leona said with a wink. "All right?"

As the cook, his wife, and Adeline turned away, Leona looked at de Lanceau. "I will fetch the key to get us inside the keep."

"Hurry."

She dashed into the storeroom. Empty bean, vegetable, and flour sacks lay stacked on the shelves. The barrels of salted meat and fish? The spices she'd hoarded for the most important events? She dared not look. Luckily, though, the casks of expensive wine on the top shelf hadn't been touched. Stretching to reach past them, she found the iron key, tied with a loop of string.

Returning to the kitchen, she said, "Milord, please follow me."

She led the men outside again through the back door, then across the bailey to the keep's wall. With the moon hidden by clouds, they moved in inky darkness. Yet the men behind her made little sound, clearly aware of the mercenaries patrolling the wall walk above and the voices drifting from farther down the bailey.

After a moment of feeling her way along the wall, she found the wooden door. She inserted the key and, holding her breath, turned it. The door clicked open. After removing the key, she curled her fingers around it.

When she drew the panel wide, a breath of stale air wafted out to greet her. The musty scent whisked her thoughts back to when she'd listened in on her father's meeting days ago, and she shuddered. Dreading what she'd find, but knowing she must go on, she stepped into the passage wide enough for only one person to travel at a time. A sticky cobweb floated down from the stones overhead, and she swiped it away, almost hitting Aldwin, behind her, in the face.

If only she had a torch to guide their way. But a burning reed would be noticed by the guards. They'd have to proceed in the dark.

She reached out for the stone wall and her hand touched another. Startled, she yanked her fingers back.

Behind her, Aldwin sucked in his breath.

Heat rippled through her, kindled by the raggedness of his inhalation. He stood so near, his breath stirred her hair. The anguish inside her sharpened.

She stretched out her hand again and found only cold, damp stone. Lifting her gown up a fraction, she set her foot on the next step.

Upward she traveled, with Aldwin, de Lanceau, and his men close behind. The tap and scrape of their footfalls seemed to surround her like a discordant battle chant. They *were* going to war, for Pryerston. What would they discover when they stepped out into her father's solar? What of the rest of the keep?

The passage turned, and the dankness in the air began to clear. Faint light washed in through cracks in the wooden door ahead.

Reaching the panel, she pressed her ear to it and listened, but heard no sound from beyond. Was the chamber empty? Or were the room's inhabitants asleep?

When the footfalls behind her quieted, she listened again. Not even the faintest snore. Still, to be safe, she'd keep her voice down.

"I may need help with the door," she whispered over her shoulder.

"Remind me. Where in the keep are we?" de Lanceau whispered back.

"The solar. The door is concealed behind a tapestry. No one has used it for a very long time."

"Are you certain the door will open?" Aldwin asked.

Nay, but we will get through this barrier, even if we have to smash it down. She pushed the key into the lock and tried to turn it. The lock wouldn't budge.

Leona wiggled the key. Withdrew it. Shoved it into the lock again. Still, it didn't yield.

Sweat coated her palms. She dried her hands on her cloak,

determined to try again.

"Let me." Aldwin reached around her.

Before she could whisper a reply, he knocked her fingers from the key. His hand closed on it. Turned.

No engaging click.

"If I could get closer..." he said.

She frowned back at his shadowed profile. "How?"

"Turn sideways."

"So we are belly to belly?" She hadn't meant for her hushed words to end in a squeak.

A muffled snort echoed from one of the other men.

"'Tis the only way." Aldwin didn't sound happy about the matter, either. A faint rattle sounded, and she realized he'd slipped his quiver from his shoulder.

Step by small, awkward step, she turned her body sideways, her garments rasping when they brushed the wall behind her. Aldwin edged in front of her, his boots bumping her shoes.

"Sorry," he muttered, his breath upon her brow. Their arms touched, and he grunted. As his lower body squeezed against her, she stifled a groan. If her father saw the two of them like this, he'd draw his sword and skewer Aldwin. And the way her innards shivered at their closeness was utterly... shameful.

Aldwin shifted against her while he turned the key and shoved the door at the same time. Once. Twice.

The lock released.

"Well done," de Lanceau murmured.

The panel creaked open. With a muffled *thump*, it hit the tapestry beyond. Thrusting his hand forward, Aldwin eased the wall hanging over the other side of the door on a swirl of dust. His crossbow at the ready, he entered the solar.

Leona stepped out. Sneezed.

Gasped.

The solar might be empty, but her father's bed—the one he'd shared with her mother for many years—was a rumpled mess. An array of items, including clothes, wine goblets, and cosmetic pots, littered the trestle table, as well as the bedside one. The scent of rosewater clung to the air.

Heaped in a shimmering pool before the bed was a red silk gown. It lay as though the wearer had let it slide down her body before crawling onto the bed—and not to sleep, judging by the tangled bedding.

"Veronique is sharing my father's bed?" Leona said in horror.

Bile scorched the back of her mouth. Her father had loved her mother; he'd always love her. Had Veronique preyed upon Leona's father's loneliness to seduce him? Had Veronique decided that by coupling with him and pretending she cared for him, she'd make him more agreeable to her loathsome plans? Leona fought the urge to retch.

The rasp of metal alerted her that de Lanceau now stood beside her, his sword drawn. As his lordship handed Aldwin his quiver, the other warriors gathered in the solar. De Lanceau didn't glance at the bed, although he must have noticed. "The great hall," he said.

"Down the stairwell," she choked out, waving to the chamber door.

De Lanceau nodded, strode to the door, and threw it wide.

She blinked hard. She should go with him and his men, if only to support her sire. Yet her feet seemed rooted to the floorboards. Her gaze riveted to the bed.

Her father was fornicating with Veronique? "Nay," she

muttered. "Nay!"

A hand touched her arm. Aldwin. He'd stayed behind with her.

"The bed," she said hoarsely. "My father . . ."

"We do not know what happened here. Do not try to guess."

Aldwin's firm voice and rational words eased her dismay. "You are right."

"Of course I am."

Her gaze flew to him, to catch his wry grin.

"Arrogant turd," she muttered, smiling back.

He winked. "That is the Leona I know."

She balled her hands into fists. "I will find out exactly what has gone on here." She spun toward the doorway.

"Wait."

Faster than she thought possible, Aldwin cut between her and the embrasure.

"You cannot confront Veronique," he said.

"Really?" Leona thrust her chin up, bringing her mouth closer to his.

"Really. If she believes you are a threat to her, she will kill you. Challenging her is foolish."

"She will not murder me in my father's keep. Not with de Lanceau's men searching for her." Barely holding down her temper, Leona tapped her foot. "Aldwin, if you do not move—"

"I would rather tie you to the bed and fetch you once the fighting is over."

A flush skittered over her skin, intensifying with the darkening glint of his eyes.

"You promised not to tie me again," she said, rather breathlessly.

"Regrettably, I did." With obvious reluctance, he stepped aside.

She rushed past him and out into the passage, where a draft swept over her. Half-listening to his brisk pursuit, she hurried past the chambers reserved for her father's guests, now empty—

A door immediately ahead swung open, spilling light into the corridor. Caution shrieked through her, and she lurched to a stop, a moment before Aldwin plowed into her from behind.

"Oh!" Leona pitched forward, tripping on her gown's hem.

Aldwin staggered beside her, bracing his hand on the stone floor to break his fall. At the same moment, an object clattered by his feet.

"Tye!" a woman called from within the chamber.

A little boy raced into the corridor. Straight into Leona.

He smacked into her legs. Wobbling, he grabbed at her cloak to steady himself, before he blinked up at her.

Straightening, Leona caught her breath. She'd seen this face before. While his features were softened by childish pudginess, the boy looked just like his lordship.

She glanced at Aldwin. "Why, he resembles—"

"De Lanceau," Aldwin confirmed, before rising to his full height and glancing at the floor.

His lordship was this boy's sire? Before she could consider that thought, a young woman stomped through the doorway. "Tye! Come back—Oh, Lady Leona!"

Leona smiled at the daughter of one of the stable hands. The young woman's gaze slid to Aldwin, and she flushed. "I am sorry, milady," she said. "'E is a 'andful, this 'un."

Still clinging to Leona's skirt, Tye sniffled. His mouth parted on a wail.

"Shush, now," the woman grumbled. "Come back to yer bed."

"Want Mama."

His forlorn cry touched Leona. She smoothed her hand through his tangled hair. "There, now. Your mother will be back soon."

"When?" Tears spiked his lashes.

"Well, I—" A round object gleamed near her right boot. Did it belong to the little boy?

Before she could bend and pick it up, Tye pulled away from her, clapped his hand around it, and raised it to his face. "Look."

A piece of amber, surrounding a . . . *bee!*

She choked down a shrill cry. She stumbled back, her hand at her throat, and looked at Aldwin. The bee, held forever inside the resin, must be his.

His mouth flattened and he nodded.

"Bee!" Tye's gaze brightened with awe. He pushed his finger over the amber's buckled surface, his misery forgotten.

"'Tis not yours," the young woman said.

Tye frowned. "Mine!"

"How long have you had that?" Leona whispered to Aldwin.

"Years." His voice sounded heavy with the weight of responsibility.

How many years? Had he found it the day she was stung, or acquired it later? She wanted to ask more, but he motioned toward the stairwell. "Come on."

"Your amber," she said.

Aldwin was already striding away.

‡ ‡ ‡

At a brisk pace, Aldwin approached the stairwell ahead. His face still burned. Thankfully the shadows hid his weakness, above all from her.

He'd never meant for the amber to fall from his pocket, or for Leona to find it. He'd never wanted to frighten her, or reveal how much that incident had shaped his life, most of all his desire to break from his past dishonor. His determination had hardened like resin, while he'd fought to reach the highest honor within his grasp: knighthood.

When Leona saw the amber, he'd felt, for a moment, as if he stood before her naked, his very soul exposed for her judgment.

Aware of her hurrying along behind him, he forced his difficult thoughts aside. If she resented him for keeping the amber, so be it. The resin belonged to Tye now. And, as much as Aldwin cared for Leona, and as much as he longed for her respect, he'd never abandon the duty that had made him who he was.

The pendant was somewhere here at Pryerston. He'd find it and see it delivered safely to de Lanceau.

The stairwell's shadows fell upon him, and he slowed, keeping a tight hold on his crossbow. The stairs were well lit, a point in his favor. If anyone tried to attack, he'd see their shadow.

Faint footfalls sounded from lower down the stairwell. Then Aldwin heard a man's gruff voice. His words sounded slurred.

"Father!" Leona brushed past Aldwin into the stairwell, her cloak wafting at her ankles.

"Wait!" Aldwin muttered, knowing, even as he ran after her, she wouldn't listen.

Down he followed her, until the passage led into a soaring great hall illuminated by blazing torches along the walls. Smoke rose from the huge fire burning in the hearth along the far wall. Dogs peered out from under a table, near the raised dais where a gray-haired man sat in a high-backed oak chair. Several wine jugs rested beside him on the table covered with a grimy tablecloth.

"Oh, God!. Father!" Leona rushed toward the man.

As Aldwin glanced about the rest of the hall, two of de Lanceau's men-at-arms rose from the bodies of three mercenaries sprawled near a table, where a game of sticks lay in disarray. Judging by the fresh blood on the rushes, the mercenaries had died only moments before.

"The hall is clear," one of the men-at-arms called to Aldwin.

"De Lanceau is on his way down to the bailey," the other added.

Aldwin nodded and headed to the dais, trying to tamp down the unease scuttling through him. After all the years since Leona's bee stings, the unanswered letters, and Ward's passing, Aldwin would finally meet Leona's sire. How senseless to worry what the old man thought of him, especially when Ransley could well be a traitor. Yet the past had finally caught up with all of them in this one moment, a realization that brought a fresh sweat to Aldwin's brow.

As he drew near, he realized Lord Ransley was bound at his hands and feet to the chair. Aldwin blinked against the overpowering stench of wine, sweat, and heaven knew what else.

"Who did this to you, Father?" With a strangled sob, Leona stepped onto the dais.

Ransley looked up. His bleary eyes seemed to struggle to focus. "Leona?"

"Aye." She threw herself against him and buried her face in his hair.

His eyes closed, and his grizzled features softened with gut-wrenching relief and joy. Unwelcome envy tugged at Aldwin; he forced himself to look away.

"Thank God you are sshafe," Ransley said hoarsely.

She sniffled and eased back. "Why are you tied to this chair? Who dared to do this to you?"

"Veronique." Ransley's lips twisted. "Dangerous." His gaze filled with concern. "Leona, sshe is looking for you—"

"We must untie you."

Ransley frowned. "Sshe will know you are here. Leona—"

She caught his face in her hands. "There are two men-at-arms keeping watch by the stairwell," she said. "'Twill be all right. We will explain once you are free."

Stepping forward to the edge of the dais, Aldwin handed over his knife.

With a grateful smile, Leona took the dagger and began to cut the ropes. A moment later, the bindings tumbled to the floor.

Ransley groaned as his arms fell back into their natural positions. "Thank you." He rubbed at his wrists gouged by the bindings.

"Can you stand?" Leona asked.

With an unsteady nod, Ransley lurched to his feet. He flattened his hands on the table, while his body swayed from side to side. As he gathered his balance, his gaze settled again on her. "Where have you been?"

Aldwin sensed her disappointment in the stiffening of her spine.

"When Twig and Sir Reginald came russhing into this hall, sshaying you had been kidnapped from sshome tavern by one of de Lanceau's men—"

"'Tis true."

Leona's gaze slid down to Aldwin, and, without looking away, he repositioned the quiver on his shoulder. Whatever she told her sire about her abduction, Aldwin would answer to it.

"You took the pendant, assh well."

She nodded. "After overhearing your meeting with the baron and Veronique—"

"You lisshtened? Why, you—"

"I decided since the jewel rightfully belonged to de Lanceau, it should be given to him. I arranged the tavern meeting."

"And put yoursshelf in danger, assh well assh Twig and Sshir Reginald. What a foolissh, rassh thing to do!" He wavered while he thrust an unsteady finger. "Did you know Veronique hassh a reward out for you, Daughter?"

Aldwin almost laughed as her gaze sharpened and her chin raised; he'd seen that reaction often in the past days. "I am sorry to have worried you, but 'twas the best decision for all at Pryerston. Father, you must listen—"

"Lisshen?" he roared. "I want the bastard who abducted you."

"Father—"

"Where issh he?"

Aldwin fought a crushing sense of inevitability. "I am here, milord."

Ransley's head swung and he glared at Aldwin. "You?" He slammed his hand down on the table, knocking the earthenware jugs together. "You dare to sshtep within my keep? You will sshtand before me with that sshmirk on your lips? Why did you come? To demand a ransshom for my daughter'ssh return? Well, you will not get one."

"Father, if you will listen—"

"To what?" He threw up his hand. "Next, you will be sshaying he lay with you and that 'tissh perfectly acceptable!"

Aldwin bit back a curse.

Leona's face clouded with an expression of such anguish, Aldwin wanted to slip his arm around her. He should have guessed Ransley would believe Leona had been violated; any father would think such. Because of Ransley's assumption, Aldwin stayed as he was—although inside, he yearned to draw her close and comfort her.

"Lay with me, Father?" Leona said in a whisper-thin voice. "As you did with Veronique?"

Ransley's mouth dropped open. "What mean you?"

"I saw the solar." Her body trembled through a shudder. "Her gown by the bed."

"Do you really believe I would . . . ?" Ransley shook his head. "I would never betray your mother that way. I sshwear to you, I have not been to the sscholar in dayssh. Veronique and the baron must have sshlept there, while I"—he flinched—"was tied to my chair."

"While she kept you drunk," Leona said, "and threatened to kill anyone who helped you."

Remorse tightened his features. He glanced at the nearby jugs and swallowed, as though he craved a drink.

"Father, nay."

Ransley scowled.

"No more drink," Leona said.

The hurt in Leona's voice roused fierce protectiveness within Aldwin. Did her sire not see how his drunkenness had hurt Leona? Did he not realize how much ruin he'd caused, when, as lord, he was responsible for the welfare of all within his jurisdiction—especially that of his daughter?

When Ransley didn't draw his gaze from the jugs, Aldwin leveled his crossbow. "Listen to her."

Ransley lifted his brows, for the weapon pointed at his chest. "You bold knave. You dare to threaten me?" He raised his hand.

"N—" Leona cried.

A *click*, and the bolt leapt from the crossbow. Ransley gasped. The bolt slammed into the jugs, sending them smashing together. Wine sprayed. Bits of pottery scattered across the table and onto the rushes.

The men-at-arms whistled.

Wine running down his hair, face, and tunic, Ransley blinked at Aldwin. "Who in hellfire *are* you?"

"Aldwin Treynarde, milord."

Wiping his face with his sleeve, Ransley froze. "Treynarde, you say?"

"Aye."

"His skill with the crossbow is hailed in a *chanson*," Leona said, glancing at Aldwin. A smile touched her mouth, a sign she approved of his dramatics.

Grinning in return, Aldwin looked back at her sire. Instead of the awe or anger Aldwin expected, sadness shadowed Ransley's face. He stared down at the filthy tablecloth as though his thoughts had slipped back into the past. "I know the name well, and not because of the *chanson*."

A frown creased Leona's brow. "How—? Wait. You met Aldwin after I was stung. You saw him when you carried me away from the river."

Ransley nodded. Still, Aldwin sensed he wasn't thinking of that tragedy, but one more recent: Ward's death.

He didn't want to discuss Ward; later, when Pryerston was in de Lanceau's control, Aldwin might venture down that painful path. "Since you know who I am," Aldwin said, "you also realize I fight for Moydenshire's lord, Geoffrey de Lanceau. He is here—"

Ransley's eyes flared. "At Pryersshton?"

Leona nodded. "He has come to save the keep."

With a low cry, Ransley swept his hand over his soiled tunic.

Before Aldwin could ask Ransley about Veronique and the baron's whereabouts, Leona caught her sire's hands. "Please, help us get the pendant for de Lanceau. Help us take Pryerston back from the baron and Veronique. 'Tis what Mother would have wanted. So would Ward."

Ransley's mouth pinched. "Of all the moments to speak of your brother."

"If he were here now, he would pick up a sword, join de Lanceau's men, and fight."

Aldwin shifted his attention to the men-at-arms, who were clearly listening to the exchange while keeping watch on the entry to the hall. Looking at them was far easier than seeing in Ransley's gaze an acknowledgment of Ward's demise.

"Why do you look so?" Leona demanded.

Aldwin glanced back. Moisture glistened in Ransley's eyes as, wavering, he straightened away from the table.

"What have you not told me about Ward?"

"Leona," Aldwin said, determined to stay focused on his duty, "we cannot discuss such now. We need to get the pendant. Lord Ransley, where should we start—?"

A *crash* echoed in the stairwell: a door slamming against a wall.

Leona jumped and her fingers tightened on the knife she still held.

The men-at-arms raised their swords.

Ransley bent and snatched up a section of his cut bonds.

Footsteps sounded in the stairwell leading up from the bailey. Over shouts, clashing swords, and other battle noises floating up from outside, Aldwin determined several people approached.

Friends? Or enemies?

"Stay behind the table," Aldwin snapped to Leona, as he cocked his crossbow.

The whistle of a crossbow bolt came from the stairwell. One of de Lanceau's men cried out as the bolt pierced his chest and jutted from his back. He staggered backward before collapsing on the floor.

The other man-at-arms raised his sword. Five men wearing boiled leather hauberks—mercenaries—rushed into the hall. Aldwin raised his crossbow, aimed, and shot one of them. But the man-at-arms was quickly overpowered, and fell to the rushes, dead.

"God's blood," Aldwin muttered, reloading his weapon.

"Aldwin," Leona cried.

As he raised the crossbow, he became aware of the unnatural silence. The mercenaries had quit fighting? Why?

He caught the cloying essence of rosewater.

Her crimson-painted lips easing into a smile, Veronique stood in the great hall, surrounded by more mercenaries. She'd raised one slender hand in clear command to hold fire. Her other hand gripped a bloody dagger. More blood spattered across her snug-fitting gown.

Close behind her stood Baron Sedgewick. His sword glistened with blood, and, as his gaze settled on Aldwin, he grinned.

"Aldwin. Leona," Veronique murmured. "How perfect to find you here."

Chapter Twenty-One

Sweat dampened Aldwin's hands, but he refused to look away from Veronique's cold stare. In the instant before their gazes met, he'd noticed her face had aged a bit since he saw her years ago, but her chestnut brown hair was still long and lustrous, her body as supple as a young woman's.

Many men would find her desirable. Beautiful, even. Those fools couldn't sense the malevolence surrounding her like a dark veil. The sensual way her fingers curled around the knife handle—a kind of perverse caress—made goose bumps ripple across his skin.

She wouldn't hesitate to use that dagger again. On him, Leona, or Lord Ransley. Or anyone else she deemed a threat to her ambitions.

Aldwin's fingertip touched the crossbow's trigger. A quick shift to the right, fire, and he'd kill her. A clean shot. One so easy, he'd not get it twice. A swift death, however, was too merciful for all the evil she'd wreaked upon others over the past years, especially de Lanceau; moreover, his lordship wanted her and the baron alive to face punishment for their crimes.

Hellfire!

His gaze shifted to the baron. Triumph glittered in the bastard's piggish eyes.

"You cannot win a fight against us," Veronique said, her narrowed gaze sliding to Leona and Lord Ransley. "Put down your weapons."

"If we refuse?" Aldwin demanded.

The baron tugged on Veronique's sleeve. "De Lanceau will be upon us soon."

She shoved him away. "He will not dare to harm us, for you see"—she smiled—"we now have three hostages." Signaling to the mercenaries, she said, "Injure them if you like, but do not kill them. I want them on their knees."

"Nay," Ransley yelled. "Sshtop this—"

"Shut up, fool."

Ransley's face reddened with fury.

Out of the corner of his eye, Aldwin saw Leona raise her dagger. Fear for her lanced through him. He had to protect her, keep her from the bloodshed . . .

"Go back through the solar," he called over his shoulder. "Warn de Lanceau."

"Aye, Leona." Ransley flicked his hand. "Go!"

Aldwin half-expected her to protest. But she must have realized the urgency of her task, for she nodded, turned, and ran for the wooden stairs leading to the keep's upper level.

Straw crunched as the mercenaries advanced. Aldwin spun and squeezed the crossbow's trigger. The bolt plowed into the closest man's chest, spraying blood. He fell backward with a grisly *thump*.

But two more mercenaries were already upon Aldwin.

"On their knees," Veronique shrieked, her words becoming

a wicked laugh.

He would *not* be helpless before her and the baron. Never again would he be prey to their manipulations. When the mercenaries thwarted his attempt to reload his crossbow, he swung it like a club, while trying to draw his sword. With a stunning slash of his broadsword, one of the mercenaries knocked the crossbow from Aldwin's grasp. Splinters of wood flew from the bow as it skidded across the floor. The other mercenary grabbed hold of Aldwin's sword arm, preventing him from drawing his blade.

Heedless of the pain in his side, Aldwin kicked. Shoved.

Behind him, Leona screamed in pain.

He recoiled, fear crashing through him. *God's blood, nay!*

He risked a glance. A mercenary had caught her before she reached the stairs. She struggled to free her wrist crushed in his scarred hand, her face white with agony.

"Leona!" Ransley lurched off the dais toward her. "Stop! You are hurting her."

A solid weight slammed into Aldwin's gut. He groaned and lashed out with his fists, unable to stop one of the mercenaries from hauling the quiver from his shoulder and tossing it aside.

"Stop!" Ransley roared.

"Shut up," Veronique screeched. "Get back on the dais."

"I will not!"

"You will," she bellowed, "or your daughter dies."

Aldwin tried to shake away the fog clouding his mind, just as a boot slammed into his back. Pain raced through his body. Still, he fought as the mercenary shoved him down to his knees. But the blow, combined with his throbbing side, sapped Aldwin's strength.

He sagged to the floor, panting, with sweat running down his brow. The mercenary stood behind him, his sword at Aldwin's neck.

"There." Veronique's gown whispered as she crossed to him. "Much better."

Only for you, bitch.

With a huffed breath, Leona landed on her knees beside him. He stole a quick glance. No blood or visible wounds. He hoped she wasn't badly hurt.

"Leona," Ransley moaned from the dais. An admission of defeat.

The scent of rosewater mingled with the musty stench rising from the rushes, as, hips swaying, Veronique drew near. She tapped the flat of the dagger blade against her palm, smearing blood across her skin.

Swish. Tap. Swish. Tap.

Pushing his shoulders back, Aldwin stared straight ahead, refusing to look up at her, even when she stopped close enough to gently brush aside hair that had fallen over his right eye. He jerked away from her touch.

"Still stubborn, I see." Her voice sounded akin to a purr.

He clamped his jaw.

"Tsk-tsk." Her fingers skimmed down his hair. Despite the sword at his neck, Aldwin tried to turn his head away, but her clever hand followed. Her throaty laugh taunted him, ignoring his cursed protest, while her fingers slid under his chin. Tightening her grip to a painful pressure, she forced him to look up at her.

Muscles at the back of his neck cramped and pain knotted his shoulders. But his breath hissing through his nostrils, he glared back at her.

She smiled. "De Lanceau values your life."

Aldwin dared to defy the pain of her fingertips. "Only as his servant."

A mocking glint lit her eyes. "More than that, I vow."

The baron hurried to her side. "Let me kill him now." His lips slid into a ruthless grin. "He must suffer for betraying me to de Lanceau years ago."

"Patience," Veronique murmured.

Aldwin tamped down a shudder. What was she planning? Even as he registered the thought, she flipped the knife in her hand and dragged the leather-wrapped hilt along his jawline. A deliberate taunt. The scents of blood and leather filled his nostrils. As the dagger moved with a whisper, the sharp tip skimmed perilously close to his shoulder blade. She could slice his flesh whenever she desired.

Leona swore under her breath.

"I want to kill him!" the baron groused. "Then throw his head into the bailey. De Lanceau will know we shall win this battle for Pryerston."

"His head? Not something more"—Veronique's gaze slid down Aldwin's body to his groin—"interesting?"

Like what, bitch? My ballocks? She would enjoy maiming him so. The thought of her hands on his privates made his blood run cold.

The baron also seemed shaken by the idea, for he cringed.

"A shame," Veronique drawled, "to damage such a handsome example of manhood." Her hand dropped away and lingered in the air. "Of course, we do not have to hurt *him*." Her gown rustled as she faced Leona.

"Let her be," Aldwin growled, attempting to rise. The mercenary kicked him back onto his knees.

Veronique tittered. "Do you care for her?"

More than you can possibly know.

The knife rose and fell once again. *Tap. Tap.* The sound, akin to rainwater dripping onto an iron pot, resonated in his brain. He sensed Leona's sharpening fear, although she kept her head high.

Ransley moaned again. "Leona."

Tap. Tap.

Veronique looked down at the knife, as though deciding how to make her first cut. "Did you know, Aldwin, you can spare Leona from harm?"

"Really?"

The disbelief in his voice clearly amused Veronique, for she winked as she glanced at him. "I know you are not yet a knight. You do not have your spurs. But you *crave* the honor of knighthood." Her eyes gleamed with her impassioned words. "'Tis what you truly desire. Aye?"

Aldwin tried to steel the dismay from his expression. How did she know that about him? Had his ambitions been so obvious?

"Three long, devoted years you have served de Lanceau," Veronique went on. "Still he has not made you a knight."

"He does not have to. I pledged lifelong servitude to him—"

"*Why* does he not award you that honor? *Why* does he deny you what you rightly deserve? He has knighted lesser-deserving men than you, has he not?"

Aldwin tried to ignore the discontent stirred up by her words.

"Nay," Leona snapped. "Do not listen—"

"I can give you knighthood," Veronique cut in, as the mercenary holding Leona slapped her. Aldwin struggled, but Veronique turned his face away. "All you must do"—her breath swept his cheek in a pretend kiss—"is agree."

Revulsion coiled inside him at her closeness. Yet each moment she spent talking to him, he kept Leona from serious harm. He silently prayed he could keep Veronique distracted until de Lanceau rushed in from the bailey. "Agree?" he bit out. "To what?"

"To join us. To fight for us, as one of our knights."

He blew a sharp breath. Was she mad? She couldn't honestly believe he'd comply.

"Veronique," the baron grumbled. "'Tis not as we planned."

"I know," Veronique said. "This scheme is better. With Aldwin's cooperation, we can learn all of de Lanceau's secrets far sooner than we expected. We will destroy his lordship and his devoted family. We will take his empire and make it our own."

Doubt, but also interest, flickered in Sedgewick's gaze. "When will I have my revenge for what Aldwin did to me?"

"Revenge?" She cackled. "We can finally have the riches and power denied to us when de Lanceau wed Lady Elizabeth. Surely 'tis more important than Aldwin's death?" Her tone softened with petulance. "Surely you love me enough to want that for us, Sedgewick?"

The baron frowned and wiped his flushed face. "He must agree. He will not yield his loyalty to de Lanceau."

Aldwin stifled a snort. Exactly. If they thought he'd nod and say "aye"—

Veronique turned away. "He will."

The certainty in those two words brought an awful tightness to Aldwin's chest—especially when she gestured to the hearth.

The baron's face lit with glee. "Indeed, he will." Rushes crackled as he scuttled away.

Sweat ran down between Aldwin's shoulder blades as he glanced at Leona. Her gaze revealed her anxiety, but she bravely held his stare. His heart squeezed in his chest. How proud he was of her. How he . . . loved her.

Logs in the hearth settled with a *clunk*, and then the baron returned, brandishing a piece of kindling. The end burned red-white. Hot enough to sear flesh, eyes, or . . .

Ransley made a choking sound. "W-what are you going to do?"

The baron grinned. "Aldwin is going to say 'aye.'" He thrust the burning stick toward Leona's face.

Her body, held by the mercenary, quivered.

"Stop," Ransley cried. "Please."

Veronique laughed, grabbed a handful of Leona's hair, and yanked her head back to expose the smooth column of her neck. "We will burn her and cut her, until you agree."

With her neck at that angle, Leona must be in agony. Her chest rose and fell on urgent breaths, but she didn't make the slightest sound of pain.

"Leona," Aldwin whispered, claiming her gaze.

"Do not agree," Leona croaked.

Aldwin swallowed hard. How much he wanted to say to her, above all, that he loved her.

He couldn't bear to see her tortured because of him. Yet how could he betray de Lanceau? To become one of Veronique's knights was to live by dishonor—to embrace all he loathed about himself.

"Hurry up, Aldwin," the baron goaded. He turned the stick in his fat fingers.

"Do not harm her," Ransley said, his voice weak with horror. "I beg you."

The mercenary behind Aldwin chuckled.

"Aldwin will not agree," Veronique muttered. "Proud fool."

The baron chortled. "Then so be it."

The stick moved.

"Nay!" Ransley cried.

"Hold!" Aldwin said at the same moment.

The baron paused, the kindling dangerously close to Leona's cheekbone. She shuddered, as though she felt the heat singeing her skin.

Veronique raised the knife to Leona's throat. "Say you will be one of our knights, Aldwin."

A sudden draft swept over the floor, chilling his legs. The nearby wall torches flickered. Close by, a door banged against stone.

Someone had thrown open the lower door.

Gruff voices carried up from the bailey.

"Quickly!" the baron yelled, his gaze darting to the stairwell. "Agree!"

Footfalls pounded in the passageway.

His mouth twisting on a roar, the baron rammed the stick against Leona's cheek.

That very instant, she wrenched sideways. The stick hissed through air. With a sneered growl, Veronique yanked her upright again by her hair. Blood ran down Leona's neck.

Aldwin cursed. "Leona!"

"Join us!" the baron roared.

"Join you?" de Lanceau said from the stairwell. "I think not."

Chapter Twenty-Two

Turning her head a fraction, Leona glanced toward the stairwell, defying the brutal pressure of Veronique's fingers twisted into her hair. Leona's neck ached with the unnatural posture, but her hopes soared at the sight of de Lanceau standing just inside the great hall.

"Lord de Lanceau," her father murmured, and she heard the scrape of his boots as he dropped into a bow.

Blood stained de Lanceau's surcoat and chain-mail armor, but his grip on his sword looked strong and sure. Dominic stood beside him, and more of de Lanceau's men-at-arms filed in behind them. Still more fighters came into view, among them servants from Pryerston wielding brooms, axes, and candlesticks.

The cook and his wife had done well. Leona fought a grateful sob.

De Lanceau's gaze slid from Veronique to the baron. "Your hired thugs are defeated. Surrender."

The baron exhaled a nervous sigh, while Veronique rolled her eyes. "All those mercenaries, outwitted by your men?"

"And the good folk of Pryerston."

"I do not believe you."

De Lanceau's flinty gaze didn't waver. "Come with me to the bailey. I will show you."

An ugly silence fell, an unspoken battle for dominance, as all awaited Veronique's reply.

A disparaging laugh broke from her; it rose to a taunt. "You insult me. Do you really think I will walk into your trap, Geoffrey?"

De Lanceau glowered. "Do *not* call me by my given name."

"Neither will I surrender," she continued as though he hadn't spoken. "You will yield. If you do not . . ." Veronique yanked Leona's tresses hard enough to pull out strands of hair: a command to rise. A muffled chime accompanied the movement—a sound like the pendant's chain. Veronique didn't seem to be wearing the ruby, though.

Again, Veronique tugged. Leona's scalp burned, and she longed to spit curses. But if Leona wanted to get away, Veronique and the baron must believe her to be frightened and obedient.

Lowering her lashes to hide her rage, Leona struggled to her feet, the mercenary's hand on her elbow. The baron edged the hot stick aside enough to let her stand, but kept it close to her face. While Veronique no longer gripped Leona's hair, the tip of the dagger pressed against Leona's neck; it slid into the blood running down under her chemise to her breasts. As Leona looked up, de Lanceau's gaze riveted to her, and shock lanced through her at the fury emanating from him.

"Release Leona and Aldwin," he growled.

"They will remain as they are, Geoffrey, until you and your men lay down your weapons." Veronique's bawdy laugh echoed. "I cannot wait to have you on your knees."

Leona's attention slid to Aldwin. His gaze slammed into her. In his eyes, she saw anger, worry, and . . . tenderness.

His poignant stare drove like a bolt through her heart. She blinked as tears pricked her eyes. A terrible anguish spread through her, for she'd been so determined to be annoyed with him, she hadn't once thought they might die in the fight for Pryerston. How did she tell him she'd give anything—*anything*—to lie in his arms again?

The crunch of straw drew her gaze to de Lanceau. "You will surrender, Veronique." As he took several steps forward, he signaled to his men. They moved into a semicircle, blocking the escape to the stairwell.

Veronique whispered an oath.

"Yield," de Lanceau commanded. "Accept you are my prisoners. Your lives are forfeit for the crimes you committed against me and countless others. If you do not obey, I will kill you in this hall. The choice is yours."

The oniony scent of sweat filled Leona's nostrils. The baron's face dripped moisture. "You will kill us despite what you say, de Lanceau," he muttered.

De Lanceau frowned. "Baron—"

Sedgewick's fingers shifted on the stick. The hot end edged closer to Leona and she stiffened.

"Burn in hellfire, de Lanceau," Sedgewick sneered.

"That pleasure is all yours, Baron. You are damned for betraying my sire and mortally wounding him when I was a boy. You will answer for every treacherous deed you committed against me, as well as my kin."

Sedgewick snickered. "Not if I kill you first."

De Lanceau smiled, a dismissive slant of his mouth, before

his gaze shifted to Veronique. "Where is my pendant?"

"Why would I know?"

"She has it, milord." Leona's father pointed at Veronique. "A man brought it to her."

"I think 'tis hidden in her gown," Leona said, ignoring the pinch of Veronique's knife. "I heard the chain chiming."

"Is that so?" De Lanceau glared at Veronique.

"Mmm?" she said with a coy sigh. Then a gloating laugh broke from her. Her gown whispered as the knife moved away from Leona's neck.

While Leona sucked in a relieved breath, her gaze met her father's. He winked and then began edging toward the end of the dais. His steps looked steadier than before, but he couldn't be free of the drink's muddling effects yet.

What was he going to do? Why didn't he just stay where he was, out of danger?

Metal chimed close by. Leona glanced at Veronique, to see the ruby pendant slide from an opening in her sleeve's hem.

Light from the torches glinted off the gold and the magnificent ruby. "'Tis very beautiful," Veronique said, dangling the jewel between her fingers. "A treasure worth killing for."

The baron chortled. "True, my love."

De Lanceau glared at her. "Bring it to me."

"'Tis mine now." Veronique grinned.

Leona almost choked. *Hers?*

"Yours?" Sedgewick said. "*Ours*, you mean."

Veronique bluntly ignored the baron and slipped the pendant around her neck. "'Tis a small portion of the riches I would have enjoyed as your courtesan when you became Moydenshire's lord. Riches, enough," she went on, "to care for me and Tye for years. Riches I deserve, for all you denied me, Geoffrey, when you told me you no longer desired me."

Bitterness tightened in each word. She sounded consumed by her misguided love for de Lanceau—a distraction Leona mustn't waste. She steeled herself for escape, even as she saw her father creep away from the dais.

"Veronique," the baron snapped, stepping away to better look at her. "'Tis not as we planned, either. What do you mean—?"

Veronique cackled and started to raise her knife to Leona's neck. "Accept, Geoffrey, that you have lost—"

Leona hurled herself sideways, slamming into Veronique. With a deafening screech, Veronique stumbled. At the same moment, Leona's father ran forward and whipped Veronique across the shoulder with his cut ropes.

She screamed. "You—!"

Leona bolted, ducking the baron's roar and the swing of his stick.

A scuffle erupted behind Leona. She whirled to see Aldwin fighting with the mercenary who'd subdued him earlier. Her sire was grappling with Veronique.

"Nay!" Veronique screamed. "*Nay!*" Her face tautened with rage.

Armor rattled as de Lanceau's men edged nearer.

His hand clenched around the pendant's chain, Leona's father tried to pull the jewel from Veronique's neck. The knife in her hand flashed downward.

"Father!" Leona shrilled. If he was wounded—

A child's cry carried from upstairs. Tye. He must have heard his mother's distress.

"Stay back!" the baron shouted, wielding the stick as though to ward off the advancing warriors.

Veronique gasped. "*Nay!*"

With a victorious shout, Leona's sire held up the pendant. "Milord!" He drew his arm back, clearly planning to toss the jewel to de Lanceau.

Sedgewick threw his stick to the floor. He drew his sword. And lunged.

For Leona.

‡ ‡ ‡

Aldwin held his breath as Leona threw herself against Veronique. *Well done, Lioness!* Pride rushed through him, filling him with anticipation of battle, while he concentrated on the mercenary holding the sword to his neck. The instant Aldwin sensed the thug's attention had shifted to the fight, Aldwin surged to his feet.

At the same time, he slammed his fist into the mercenary's leg. The man howled and went down on one knee, while slashing with his blade. A brutal kick, and the man's sword arm went limp, his forearm broken. The sword clanged on the floor and skidded toward one of de Lanceau's men-at-arms, who snatched it up.

"Surrender," de Lanceau's man said, thrusting the weapon in the mercenary's face, but whatever the thug said was drowned by Aldwin's expelled breath. The baron was attacking Leona. The lethally sharp sword glinted as it whistled through the air. A near miss. Far too near for Aldwin's liking.

He spied his quiver of bolts and glanced about the floor for his crossbow, but it must have been kicked aside. Frowning, he snatched up the stick Sedgewick had discarded, skirted the warriors battling the rest of Veronique's mercenaries, and edged toward the baron.

"Sedgewick!" de Lanceau roared.

"Leona!" Ransley cried, continuing to struggle with Veronique. Metal glinted as he knocked the dagger from her grasp.

Her face taut with concentration, Leona darted backward, but knocked into a bench drawn up to the trestle table. She shot her arm back, fighting for balance.

The baron laughed. Before she could scoot away, he shoved the tip of his sword against her breastbone, shielded by her cloak.

She froze. Her chest rose and fell, while the blade sliced through to her bloodstained bodice.

Aldwin's heart pounded against his ribs, each beat more agonizing than the last. One shove forward, and the baron would pierce her flesh.

She would *not* suffer that pain.

"Now," Sedgewick roared, turning sideways to meet the gaze of de Lanceau and his men. "I will have that pendant."

Veronique swore and grabbed for it, but Ransley held it above her reach.

"Throw it to me, Ransley," the baron said, "or I will kill your daughter. While you watch."

Still holding the jewel aloft, Lord Ransley moaned. He glanced at de Lanceau.

"Sedgewick, your grievance is with me," de Lanceau murmured. "Not Leona."

"Not entirely true. She stole the pendant from us days ago. Planned to betray us to you. For that, she should *die*." His gaze darkened with murderous intent. "The pendant!"

The baron's hand shook, and Leona winced.

"In truth, Baron"—Aldwin stepped closer—"your grievance is more with me than the others. Have you forgotten how my testimony of the crossbow shooting years ago helped to send you to the king's dungeon? I took Leona captive days ago to force her to reveal your and Veronique's latest conspiracy; I planned to tell my lord."

Sedgewick's lips formed an evil grin. "'Twould hurt you, aye, to see Leona killed?"

God, aye. Part of me would die with her. If he lied and said "nay," he'd shame his feelings for Leona. If he nodded, would the baron kill her out of spite? "Let her go," he said, unable to keep the plea from his voice. "I will willingly take her place."

"Aldwin," Leona whispered.

"'Twould be the perfect revenge, would it not, to murder me here before my lord and my friends?" Aldwin added, hoping his words appealed to the baron's depravity. *Let her go*, his mind pleaded. *Let me protect the lady I love, even if I must give my own life.*

He sensed Leona's stare, her unspoken request for him to meet her gaze. With great effort, he refused. He meant what he said about taking her place; he wouldn't change his mind.

"'Tis an enticing offer," the baron said.

"Aldwin," Leona rasped.

The necklace's chain clinked. Struggling as de Lanceau's men-at-arms tried to subdue her, Veronique swiped at Ransley. He shifted the jewel in his fingers and looked from de Lanceau to the baron.

Geoffrey thrust up a hand. "Hold. No one gets that pendant but me."

The baron's lip curled. He looked at Leona. Smiled. His fingers shifted on the sword's hilt, as though he readied to thrust.

Aldwin lunged. Before the baron started to glance up, Aldwin whacked him across the small of his back with the stick.

Sedgewick tensed. Aldwin caught the scent of burning cloth before the baron lashed out at him with his sword.

"Run!" Aldwin yelled to Leona.

She dashed away from the table, toward Dominic and the other warriors. At the same moment, Aldwin heard de Lanceau shout, "Now!"

The pendant flew through the air.

The baron roared and ran for the jewel.

Aldwin hurled his weight against Sedgewick. With a furious squeal, the baron pitched sideways and stumbled, the tip of his sword scraping the floor.

The pendant landed on the rushes, close to de Lanceau.

With a feral cry, the baron shoved Aldwin aside, raised his sword, and ran toward his lordship.

Footfalls pounded on the wooden staircase.

"Milord!" Ransley cried, pointing.

Gripping her skirts in both hands, Veronique hurried toward the keep's upper level. Either she'd realized she was defeated and intended to escape, or she had another scheme she intended to get underway.

"God's blood," Aldwin snarled and looked again for his crossbow. There, in the shadows under a table. Weaving through the fighting men-at-arms and mercenaries, he bent, grabbed the damaged bow, and retrieved his quiver.

As he rose, he looked for Leona and her father. To his relief, they stood some distance from the fighting, embracing. Safe.

Close by, swords met with a loud *clang*. Their weapons touching, the baron and de Lanceau glared at each other. Then, with a triumphant growl, his lordship forced the baron back two steps from where the pendant lay.

"Aldwin," de Lanceau yelled. "Get the jewel."

"Aye, milord."

"Dominic, take the rest of the men. Secure the upper chambers. Whatever happens"—*Clang*—"Veronique is not to take the boy from here."

Beckoning to several others, Dominic led them up the stairs after her. Glancing over her shoulder, Veronique ran along the wooden landing that led to a passageway's entrance.

Swords shrieked. Men shouted and grunted. Yet the battle sounds seemed to fade for one moment as Aldwin stooped, drew the pendant from among the dirty rushes, and closed his fingers around it.

"You have lost, Sedgewick," de Lanceau said. "Yield."

Sweat streamed from the baron face. "Lost? Because you have the pendant? Never." He bared his stained teeth. "I have waited years to fight you. I will *crush* you for taking Moydenshire and Elizabeth from me."

Geoffrey laughed. "I rescued her. She never wanted to wed you; she loathed you."

"'Tis true," Aldwin said. She had, indeed. She'd told him just how much.

"She would have learned to love me. Veronique did."

"God's blood!" de Lanceau shouted. "You meant naught to Veronique. Have you not realized that by now?"

"Shut up!" the baron screeched.

Stepping back, de Lanceau gestured to the landing, just as Veronique disappeared into the passage. "Look. She has abandoned you."

"Shut up!" Sedgewick swung his sword in a wild strike. "You will die like your wretched father."

Clang. De Lanceau's jaw hardened. "Not this day."

"You will *beg* me to die, just like the great Edouard de Lanceau did. You will plead for me to deliver that one"—*clang*—"last"—*clang*—"blow to end your misery, while your blood runs—"

A snarl twisted de Lanceau's mouth. He lunged forward. Thrust. His blade sank into the baron's belly. "My father never begged."

Sedgewick gasped. "Ahhh—"

"I was there. I was only a boy, but I saw you wound him."

The baron blinked down at the blade embedded in his gut. A crimson stain spread across the lower part of his tunic. His eyes dampened with dismay.

"Never will I forget the moment you cut him down," de Lanceau said. "Never will I forget how you betrayed my father, who had once called you his friend. Neither will I forgive how you sullied my family's honor with false accusations of treachery."

A shrill gurgle bubbled from the baron's slackening mouth. His fingers tightened on his sword, tilted downward. Was he going to dare one last attack?

Devious bastard. Aldwin aimed his crossbow.

"Today," de Lanceau said softly, "my father is finally avenged." He yanked his sword from the baron's flesh.

"Bas"—blood peppered Sedgewick's lips—"tard." His body swayed. His eyelids drooped, and he looked on the verge of collapse.

"At last, you are punished for what you did to my father, me, and my lady wife." De Lanceau looked to his men-at-arms. "Be certain—"

The baron's slitted eyes opened. His lips curled in a bloody sneer. His whole body quaked as he hefted his sword.

Click. The bolt flew from Aldwin's crossbow. It plowed

straight through the baron's forehead, splitting flesh and skull.

His body fell back onto the straw.

Glancing at Aldwin, Geoffrey grinned. "Thank you."

Aldwin smiled and nodded. Then he stepped forward and handed the pendant to de Lanceau.

"Your mission is complete," his lordship murmured.

"Not quite, milord." A sharp pain pinched Aldwin's heart. Returning the pendant to de Lanceau seemed the easiest part of his mission. Far simpler than resolving his relationship with Leona.

A feminine-sounding grunt snapped his gaze to the dwindling fight between de Lanceau's men and the mercenaries. When he spied Leona, clutching a tall silver candlestick with both hands, his eyes widened. Near her, Lord Ransley was helping two other men-at-arms bind an unconscious thug.

Before Aldwin could march toward Leona, she brought the weapon swinging around to crash into the head of the mercenary who'd restrained her, who'd been brought to his knees by two men he recognized: Twig and Sir Reginald.

With a groan, the mercenary crumpled to the rushes.

Sir Reginald beamed. "Excellent work, milady!"

Thrusting his skinny fist in the air, Twig cheered. "Only a few thugs left." His eyes twinkled. "Did I tell you what we did to the ones in the bailey?"

Sweeping hair from her face, she shook her head.

"We followed your advice from the tavern, milady." Twig grinned. "We fetched them all a drink!"

God's blood. Trying very hard not to scowl, Aldwin started toward them, still unnoticed by the three.

Leona frowned. "What do you mean, 'a drink?'"

"We served them that wine from the storeroom."

"Oh, Twig—"

"A special reward from Veronique, we said. Got a quick drink into them before his lordship and Dominic attacked." Twig tapped his head. "We could not have come up with such a brilliant plan without you."

At the crunch of Aldwin's boots, Leona looked his way. She smiled warmly, before Twig roared and rushed forward, brandishing his sword. "You! You are that knave who—"

"Twig!" Leona shouted. "He is our friend."

Stomping to a halt, Twig frowned. "Did he not insult you at the tavern? Kidnap you?"

"Aye," she murmured. "But 'tis all over now."

All over now. How three words could imply so much.

Aldwin passed by Twig and halted before Leona. Her beautiful eyes glistened.

"Are you all right?" he murmured, relieved to see the blood at her neck was dried and not still flowing.

"Aye. You?"

He nodded. How he wished they could be alone, to confirm to each other they really were unharmed. He'd examine her body bit by tantalizing bit, with his lips, tongue, hands—

"Milords," Twig said, hauling Aldwin from his lustful thoughts.

Leona's father strode to them. So did de Lanceau.

Ransley dropped into a respectful bow. "Lord de Lanceau."

"Lord Ransley."

His grizzled head still bent, Ransley said, "I owe you the greatest apology, milord. I failed in my duties to you, as I failed my daughter."

"Lord Ransley—"

"I vow before you and these witnesses"—he straightened,

trembling—"that I will never again taste a drop of drink."

De Lanceau's eyes narrowed before he glanced over at the warriors guarding the defeated mercenaries, and then the castle folk gathered nearby. "Later, we will discuss this matter. Lord Ransley, you will remain in this hall with my men. Until Veronique is found—"

Footfalls echoed from the upper level, along with a child's plaintive cry. As Aldwin glanced up, and the others around him turned to look, Veronique strolled out onto the landing with Tye in her arms. Dominic and four other men with drawn swords surrounded her.

Tye clung to Veronique, his arms wrapped around her neck. Tears shone on his face. "Mamaaaa."

"Quiet." Her gaze shifted to Sedgewick's corpse, but her expression remained indifferent.

"Did you search her for knives?" de Lanceau called to his men.

Dominic nodded. "We found only some jewelry. Since the pieces were likely stolen from this keep, I confiscated them."

When Veronique's attention settled on de Lanceau, she cupped the back of Tye's head with one hand and kissed his brow. A tender gesture. Her features didn't soften, though, and her stare remained icy. Misgiving hummed in Aldwin's mind.

"A wise decision, to yield," de Lanceau called to her.

Veronique smirked. Her expression raised the fine hairs on the back of Aldwin's neck. She was plotting something. But, what?

Her hips swayed as she moved closer to the landing's railing. The men-at-arms followed, staying a short distance away.

"Yield to you?" She laughed.

The sense of unease inside Aldwin rose to a clamor.

Beside him, de Lanceau frowned. "You still defy me? You

cannot escape my men."

She chuckled, before her mouth contorted into a smile of pure malice. "You have lost, Geoffrey."

"The railing," Aldwin choked.

That same instant, she grabbed Tye around the waist.

Geoffrey roared. "Get her away from—"

Before the guards could stop her, Veronique threw herself to the railing and held Tye at arm's length.

Over the steep drop to the hall floor.

Tye's body went rigid. He screamed.

"Oh, God," Leona moaned.

A gasp rippled through the others in the hall.

As the shrill echo of Tye's scream faded, Veronique grinned. *"Lost."*

CHAPTER TWENTY-THREE

Leona pressed her free hand to her throat, unable to tear her gaze from the sight of Tye dangling like an oversized doll in Veronique's hands. Tears welled in Leona's eyes, for he still held the amber. His fingers looked as white as bone clenching it.

"Mama!" he whimpered.

If Veronique let go, he'd be severely injured in the fall.

Or killed.

His shuddered breaths—sounds of sheer terror—carried in the tense stillness pervading the hall. Leona's arms ached to embrace him and hold him tight, and promise he'd never be that frightened ever again.

As she looked up at Veronique's triumphant face, anger flared. Did Veronique have no care for her son? How could she use her own child in her grievances against de Lanceau?

Dominic tipped his head to the men-at-arms behind her. At the same moment, she said, "Order your men to step away."

"Stop this cruelty." Geoffrey growled. "Put. The boy. Down."

"S-scared," Tye whispered.

"Tell your men. Now," Veronique went on, "or I will drop Tye. 'Twill be your fault if he is crippled or dies. *Yours*, to regret for the rest of your living days."

"Nay!" Throwing the candlestick on the rushes, Leona hurried across the hall to stand beneath Tye. His head tilted, and, his eyes stark with fear, he looked down at her. The anguish in his expression . . . She couldn't bear it.

"Do not be afraid, Tye," she said gently. "'Twill be all right."

The same words Aldwin had spoken to her, years ago, when all hope seemed lost. Yet they were the right words, for she wouldn't let Tye come to harm.

"Stay away, Leona," Veronique snapped.

"This is my father's keep," Leona answered. "*My* keep. No child will come to harm here because of you." Holding Tye's gaze again, Leona stretched up her arms. "If you should fall, I will catch you," she murmured. "I am good at catching. My brother taught me, so you need not be afraid."

Tye shivered a breath.

Rustling straw alerted her someone else approached. Aldwin reached her side and set down his crossbow. Raising his arms, he said, "I am here, too."

"So am I," Lord Ransley said, striding over to join them.

"I, too," Twig and Sir Reginald said together. Other castle folk hurried forward to raise their arms in support.

Tossing back her hair, Veronique laughed.

She let go with her left hand.

Tye screamed anew as he hung at an angle, with Veronique's right hand clenched into his tunic and hose. Tears streamed from his eyes.

"*M-Mama!*" He flailed his hands and legs.

Seams ripped.

"Oh, God," Leona cried.

"Did you hear that tearing sound, Geoffrey?" Veronique gloated. "My arm is shaking, for it grows weary of holding Tye. Do you want him to fall?"

"Do you want the boy to be harmed?" de Lanceau shot back.

"The boy," Veronique taunted. "Your bastard son."

"*Enough!* Pull him up, Veronique."

Her eyes glinted, but she didn't obey. She drew a small knife from Tye's hose and held it at his chest. Astonished cries rippled through the throng waiting to catch him.

"You will let me leave Pryerston unharmed, or I will kill Tye."

The boy screeched.

Over his cries, Veronique shouted, "Do you understand?"

"Aye," de Lanceau grated. "Pull. Him. Up."

"Your word, as Moydenshire's lord."

"You have it," Geoffrey roared.

She yanked Tye up over the edge of the railing and slipped her arm around his waist. Holding him tight to her, she poised the dagger at his neck. He sobbed, his face pressed to her bosom, his little fists clenched together against her cleavage.

"Dominic, take your men and escort Veronique to the bailey."

"Aye, milord." Dominic's dark scowl left no doubt how he felt about her.

"Give her a horse. Open the keep's gates, and see that she leaves," de Lanceau said.

Her head at a saucy tilt, Veronique sauntered down the stairs. Her smug gaze lashed Leona, and she was tempted to elbow her way out of the crowd, walk over, and slap the merciless bitch. Yet Leona would never forgive herself if Tye got cut by the knife.

Dominic, Veronique, and the guards disappeared into the stairwell. Squeezing the bridge of his nose, de Lanceau sighed. He stood, motionless, his eyes shut, until the forebuilding door boomed closed.

"Milord—" Aldwin said.

"'Tis not as I wished, either. But I will not see that boy hurt in my eagerness to punish his mother."

"With respect"—Aldwin shook his head—"she now knows your weakness."

De Lanceau's mouth tightened. "Weakness, or what is right for a boy too young to speak for himself? No child should witness a parent being injured or killed. 'Tis . . . enough to haunt the boy for life."

Leona sensed he wasn't just referring to Tye, but to the loss of his own father long ago.

As de Lanceau shoved hair from his brow, resolve glinted in his eyes. "The fight this day is not over, that I promise you. Veronique may have got her way, but she knows I am not a man to yield."

"True." Aldwin grinned.

"Sedgewick, who helped pay for and carry out her treachery, is dead. She will find it far more difficult to work her evil without an ally to manipulate. She is alone, without money, with a child to care for. Moreover, every man, woman, and child in this county owes loyalty to me. One day, she will make a careless mistake and we will snatch the boy. Then she will have no choice but to surrender to me. Or die."

Leona couldn't resist a smile. That would be a great day,

indeed, and one worthy of its own *chanson*.

Approaching de Lanceau, her father bowed. "However I can help you, milord, I shall. I am in your debt for rescuing my castle."

"You are." De Lanceau motioned to the rest of his men-at-arms, standing nearby. "Help the folk clear the bodies from the hall and bailey. Treat the wounded prisoners, but hold them to be taken to Branton Keep. Ransley"—his forceful stare settled on Leona's sire—"you and I will talk."

Dread trailed through Leona. Her father had a great deal to explain to de Lanceau; as much as she yearned to speak for her sire, 'twas a discussion he must manage on his own. Pryerston was secured, the pendant safely in de Lanceau's possession, and her father had vowed to quit drinking, but de Lanceau might well take Pryerston away from her sire and award it to another lord.

A painful thought.

And Aldwin . . .

Her gaze strayed to where he stood talking to several of his warrior friends, his quiver on his shoulder and his crossbow in his hand. Torchlight washed over his muscled back as he gestured, then laughed. The sound wove through her, rousing a sweet shimmer of joy, anticipation, and relief that they were alive.

As though sensing her stare, his head swiveled. He met her gaze, and a powerful, invisible thunderclap seemed to shatter the space between them.

His stare darkened with sensual hunger.

A slow tremor rippled through her.

"Lioness, you and I must talk."

‡ ‡ ‡

Aldwin waited, a few steps behind, while Leona opened the door to a chamber on the keep's upper level. "We can talk in here." She glanced over her shoulder, her face lit by the candle she carried, and a hint of shyness softened her features as she motioned him inside.

He crossed the threshold, his boots creaking on the chamber's plank floor. His gaze swept the shadowed room, while Leona set down the candle and removed her cloak, then moved about to light more candles. Soon, a flickering glow played across the bed's plain blue coverlet. A chair and sheepskin waited before the hearth laden with unlit logs. A small, leather-bound book with warped pages lay on the chair's seat: Ward's sketchbook.

Bittersweet nostalgia swept over Aldwin, at the same moment that pale light washed across the floorboards. He glanced toward the window, to see Leona standing with her hands on the shutters' edges, looking out. Moonshine swept over her, giving her skin the hue of fresh cream, while accentuating her high cheekbones and lush mouth. His gaze slid, like a wayward finger of light, down her bodice to her breasts.

Enrobed in moonlight, she looked beautiful, serene . . . A warrior queen resplendent after a victorious battle.

His hands longed to touch her. *Feel* her. *Know* her, in all ways.

A ravenous ache spread through his groin as his attention returned to the bed. "Whose chamber is this?" he asked, although he knew the answer.

Her hair glimmered as she faced him. "Mine."

He'd known. Still, an astounding blend of emotions walloped him: surprise, excitement, and desire. Bringing him to her chamber wasn't at all appropriate for an unmarried lady.

But she wasn't like any lady he'd ever met.

The hunger in his loins intensified. If she'd brought him here to couple with him . . . His pulse leapt. Nay, he mustn't dare assume. His lustful imaginings could well be wrong. And, lying with her in this chamber, without being betrothed, would be dishonorable.

He struggled against his disappointment. Instead of dwelling on how much he wanted to seduce her, he must use this moment to divulge the truth about Ward. She deserved to know what had happened to her brother, and how highly he'd thought of her—

Leona's gown rustled as she walked past Aldwin and shut the door.

Clasping her hands behind her, she leaned back against the rough-hewn panel and studied him, her gaze bright with determination. Aldwin's sweaty fingers tightened on his crossbow. What thoughts were going through her mind? Did she know how much he desired her, that to see her standing there, so close and lovely, nearly drove him mad with yearning?

"No one will disturb us." Her husky voice sent a shudder of promise racing through him.

"Good," he said, while he acknowledged she was right. All the other warriors and castle folk were clearing up after the battle. Still, 'twould not be long before he and Leona were missed.

"There is much I"—*want to do to you*—"need to discuss with you," he said, switching his crossbow to his other hand to dry his palm on his tunic.

"And I, you."

He nodded. How he hated this awkwardness—as if he were alone with a woman for the first time.

Trying to decide how to begin, he headed to the trestle table near the window. His gaze fell to the objects lying there: burning candles in iron holders; a wooden comb; a pot holding three wilted roses; and a piece of yellow silk adorned with clumsy needlework.

She laughed from beside him. "I do not think I will ever master embroidery. My aunt was so patient with her teaching, too."

He smiled. "'Tis a charming flower."

"Butterfly, you mean."

He winced. "Of course. I see now."

Leona frowned, but humor glinted in her eyes. "You need not be kind. I know 'tis awful."

"Mayhap you simply need more practice. And"—he added with a grin—"patience."

"You sound just like Ward." Sadness filled her gaze.

"Leona." Aldwin set down his crossbow and caught her hands. "I am sorry I did not tell you before about your brother. During the past days, I wanted to tell you all, but I thought . . ." He tried to find words that didn't make him sound judgmental or heartless.

"I want to know the truth. Please."

He nodded and inhaled a steadying breath. "As you know, Ward went to the East to help defend the lands King Richard had claimed for the Christians. From what Ward told me, he found the journey to Acre and the Eastern sights fascinating."

"I guessed that, from his sketchbook," Leona said softly.

"About four months after he reached that port city, he was beaten in a skirmish with Turks. In the fight, his sword arm was slashed to the bone, and the wound became corrupted."

"Oh, God," she whispered.

"The Knights Hospitallers cut off his lower arm to try to save his life. Unable to wield a sword, not able to serve the king, Ward had no choice but to return to England."

"*What?*" Leona blinked hard. "Father told me Ward died in foreign lands."

Squeezing her fingers, Aldwin said, "Ward feared he couldn't return to Pryerston. He wasn't a battle hero. Neither had he been knighted, as your sire had fervently wished. Moreover, with only one arm, Ward felt he wasn't able to defend and maintain Pryerston as a lord's son should."

Tears swam in Leona's eyes.

"Entirely by chance, while fulfilling a task for de Lanceau, I came upon Ward in a small inn in northern Moydenshire. The corruption had spread through his body. Feverish, weak, and having run out of money, he could no longer travel. I sent a missive to my lord, telling him I would be delayed in my return to Branton Keep, and I stayed and cared for Ward as best I could." Aldwin tamped down rising anguish. "I was at his bedside when he died. In a letter, which I sent to your father along with the sketchbook, I detailed all Ward told me in his last days."

"I never saw that letter," Leona said. "My father told me Ward had died in battle."

"I know."

A sigh parted her lips. "I realize why you did not tell me about Ward before now. You thought I would be disappointed."

"Aye. Especially when you viewed him as a hero."

Aldwin yearned to embrace her and shoulder some of her pain. When she met his gaze, however, she smiled through the tears clinging to her lashes. "Whatever befell him, he will always be the Ward of my memories: brave, strong, and invincible."

Aldwin smiled back. "That is how I shall remember him, too."

Her focus dropped to their joined hands. "'Twas honorable of you to spare my feelings. You protected me . . . as a noble knight would protect his lady."

"I guess I did."

"Likewise, you protected me from your true opinion of my embroidery."

Her lashes remained lowered, keeping him from reading the expression in her eyes. Yet there was warmth in her voice he hadn't noticed before.

"Needlework is far from the most telling quality of a lady. Far more important, you are strong of will, loyal to those you love,"—his voice softened—"and . . ."

"And?" Raising her lashes, she snared him with the golden fire of her stare.

He released one of her hands, unable to stop himself from catching a honey-brown wisp of hair curling down by her cheekbone. "Irresistible."

A blush stained her face. "Stop." She swatted at his hand, but not forcefully enough to deter him.

"The most beautiful, irresistible lady," he went on, "I have ever encountered." His fingers slid down her hair to linger over her breast. "Which is why—"

Her hand rose to cup his. Longing shone in her eyes. "Kiss me."

Lust shuddered through him. *Aye, Lioness. With such fire, you'll never crave another man.* Yet, on his honor as an aspiring knight, he mustn't abandon all reason and lie with her; then he truly would be the disreputable knave Lord Ransley had claimed him to be.

With great effort, Aldwin fought the desire to sweep her into his arms and carry her to the bed. "Leona, we—"

"Kiss"—she pressed his palm to her breast—"me."

His thoughts scattered as he registered delicious warmth, plump flesh, and her hardened nipple beneath her gown.

"Lioness." He growled and covered her mouth with his.

Her lips opened as though she starved for him. Her tongue clashed with his in a fierce, wet rhythm. Thrust. Glide. Suckle. God's blood, how he craved her!

A shivered groan broke from her, and then her hands rammed into his hair, grasping fistfuls. Her nails scratched his scalp in a mindless frenzy that set his whole body aflame with desire.

His hand instinctively squeezed her breast tighter. A gasp wrenched from her, sucking his breath into her mouth. Rising up on tiptoes, she brushed her body against him. With the sinewy arch of her back, her breast pressed more firmly into his palm.

He growled again, a rough, carnal sound.

When he claimed her mouth once more, she eased away. She lured him, he realized through the arousal dominating his thoughts, toward her bed.

The voice of reason nagged like a prim chaperone. Leona wasn't a courtesan, although she had the hungry little moans and gasps just right. She was a lord's daughter. A woman who by her esteemed birthright deserved to be courted and—

"Aldwin," she whispered against his mouth. She pressed kisses against his flushed skin.

He shuddered, even as her hands slid under his cloak, and then his tunic. The hot bliss of her hands . . . "H-hold," he choked out.

She hesitated, only long enough to meet his gaze. Her cheeks flushed with anticipation, she was more beautiful than he'd ever seen her.

"'Tis what you want," she murmured, "to join with me."

"More than you can imagine." He tried to think clearly. "However—"

Her eyelids fluttered on a coy smile. "'Tis what I want, also." Again, she squirmed against him. "Ever since the cottage, I cannot stop thinking about . . . us."

Aldwin swallowed down a hoarse cry. He, too, had thought about them coupling. Over and over and over again, until his need for her was sated. If that were possible.

Her gaze suddenly turned solemn. "When the baron and Veronique held us prisoner in the hall, and I realized we might never have the chance to be together—"

He kissed her. "That is over now."

"Aye, but soon, you will be returning to Branton Keep with Lord de Lanceau."

"Leona—"

"Please. Give me this moment with you. Let us finish what we began in the cottage." Her eyes sparked. "If for no other reason than what you forced me to endure as your captive."

Aldwin laughed. "And what you forced *me* to endure."

He expected her to be indignant. Instead, she winked before withdrawing her fingers from his tunic. "Then we owe it to each other."

How neatly she'd turned their discussion around to suit her desires. If only he could give her what they both wished. But he couldn't. Not without a betrothal between them, for as fiercely as he was tempted, he mustn't ignore his knightly morals.

"Why do you not touch me?" she whispered.

He groaned, sensing his willpower wavering. "Lioness—"

"Am I not enough of a lady for you?"

Argh! "Of course you are. Ah, God, Leona—"

Cloth whispered. He suddenly realized she'd taken a step backward, untied her gown, and was drawing it and her chemise over her head.

He could only stare, helpless to look away, as, with a muffled whisper, her garments fell to the floorboards. She stood naked before him.

Her breasts were as perfect as he thought. So was her smooth belly, leading down to her curved hips and thighs. He'd never seen a more lovely woman.

She tipped her chin up. "Well?" Her voice held a glimmer of uncertainty.

He swallowed hard. "Well," he echoed, wondering if he'd ever be able to speak a full sentence again. Fisting his hands, he fought the urge to reach out and trail his fingers over her flawless skin, to explore her curves, shadows . . .

She closed the distance between them. His embattled senses tried to resist her scent, her warmth, her smoldering stare . . .

No man could deny her. Not even a knight.

Sliding his arm around her waist, he yanked her flush against him, causing the bolts in his quiver to jostle together. "Lioness," he said against her lips, "how you tempt me."

He pushed his quiver from his shoulder and dropped it to the floor, followed by his cloak. Then he reached down, slid his other arm under her knees, and, being careful of his stitches, scooped her into his arms.

His conscience shrilled a reminder about chivalry. Yet while he recognized the voice of reason, she twined her fingers in his hair and smiled at him in a way that shot renewed heat through his body. He kissed her brow, then drew back the coverlet and laid her upon the bed. Her limbs fell easily, her pose welcoming. Eager.

His. As he'd dreamed.

Oh, God, aye.

He knelt above her, pushing aside the hair fallen over the side of her face. She turned her cheek into his palm, nuzzling, the soft brush of her skin painfully arousing.

And then her hands were under the hem of his tunic, reaching for the fastenings of his hose. His manhood pulsed, and he shuddered.

Obviously puzzled by his reaction, she frowned. "Do I hurt you?"

He blinked. "What? Nay."

"Then why—?"

His fingers skimmed over her bare breast, and her eyelids fluttered on a moan. "Because you give me pleasure."

"O-oh."

He circled her beaded nipple with his fingertip. "Understand?"

"Mmm."

Her determined hands moved again. The fastenings of his hose yielded, and then her fingers touched him.

G-G-God above.

He clenched his teeth, her exploration close to torture. His groin hurt. His body shook, yearning for that glorious moment when he plunged into her. But, despite her show of wantonness, he guessed she was a virgin. He'd do all within his control not to cause her pain. "Leona," he ground out, "I cannot—"

She whimpered. "Show me. I do not know—"

"Aye, Lioness, I will." But he was still clothed. An impatient oath bubbled inside him, for this first time, as they came to know each other's bodies, they should both be naked.

He kissed her, catching another whimper, while he grabbed his tunic. Breaking the kiss for a moment, and taking care not to strain his wound, he pulled the garment over his head. Tilting his body sideways, he nudged aside her curious fingers and slid his hose down his legs, letting the cloth fall to the floor along with his boots.

Glancing back at her, he caught her looking over his nakedness. He grinned and then swept his hand up her thigh to the shadow between her legs.

She gasped.

He slid his fingers through her curls, coaxing her legs wider apart. Her face flushed. Her back arched against the white linen sheets. He sensed her body reaching. Opening. *Wanting.*

Urgency shivered through him.

His.

Now.

He moved over her, sliding his legs between hers to rest his body upon her. Her half-lowered lashes flickered. Anticipation tightened her features, and her breath puffed against his jaw.

"Leona," he whispered, shaking with need. "I—"

"Please!"

Love you.

His manhood brushed the damp entry to her body. He eased into her, a sensation so magnificent, he moaned.

"Aldwin!"

Poised above her, he steeled himself for her acknowledgment

of pain. Instead, she bit her kiss-reddened bottom lip and tilted her hips to take him in farther.

"C-careful!" He didn't want to hurt her. But before he'd voiced the whole word, her legs clamped about his lower back. With a little growl, she pushed their joined bodies tighter together.

Her maidenhood yielded, and he slid deep.

A sigh broke from her.

"Are you hurt?"

Her moist eyes flickered open, before her fingers touched his cheek. "Only a little."

"Good."

"Mmm, *'tis* good."

He nibbled her mouth. "'Twill soon be *very* good."

As her gaze turned questioning, he slowly drew back his hips and pushed forward once more. She shivered and then squirmed beneath him.

"Leona," he breathed as he rocked against her. She moaned. Her hips flexed, coaxing him to repeat his thrust.

He bent his head, inhaled the honey-sweet scent of her sweaty skin, while he kissed her. "Pleasure?"

"Mmm," she purred.

Her throaty answer mirrored the growl rising inside him. His body tautened, preparing to run wild with need, to race toward that release still tantalizingly out of reach.

He sank into her again. Tasted her astonished gasp. Felt her inner muscles begin to clench.

His eyes squeezed shut as he thrust. The pleasure!

He drove harder. Faster. Racing toward . . .

"Aldwin!" Her voice shattered on a shrill cry.

Helpless to hold himself back, he thrust again. Again.

Until, with one last push, he leapt over the edge of conscious thought into bliss.

‡ ‡ ‡

Indulging in a lazy sigh, Leona snuggled back against Aldwin and drew the bedding closer about her shoulders. His body cocooned her with his warmth and masculine scent. Until now, she'd never considered lying naked alongside a man, her body cradled by his, but this embrace was heavenly.

Lifting her right hand, she trailed it along his arm stretched upon the moonlit coverlet, while marveling at the bold definition of muscle and sinew. A warrior's physique. But he'd been so tender.

What they'd shared moments ago was impulsive, raw, and beautiful, in a way she'd never forget. Not months from now, when the days she'd spent with him became less clear in her memory. Or even years.

Despair pinched her, and she closed her eyes to force it away. As much as she loved Aldwin, she knew their relationship could never be more than 'twas now. He wanted to be revered as one of de Lanceau's knights, an honorable man who championed duty wherever his lord sent him. Aldwin wouldn't want to be bound to a woman whose father once helped wanted conspirators and failed in his responsibilities to his liege.

Moreover, as Aldwin's colleagues had pointed out earlier, she wasn't like other noblewomen. She couldn't be meek, elegant, or coiffed even if she tried, and didn't have a large dowry to compensate for her shortcomings.

His arm beneath her shifted. "Leona."

She sighed. "Aye?"

He kissed her hair. "I hate to even speak of this—"

"Then do not."

His laughter rumbled. "As much as I would like to stay here with you, we should return to the great hall."

She blinked away the sting of tears. "Must we?"

His breath gusted over her cheek. Then he shifted, gently pressing upon her bare shoulder in an unspoken request for her to turn onto her back.

She obeyed, her body falling to the warmed sheets. She couldn't meet his gaze, though. Her heart hurt too much. If only they didn't have to part ways, but he had the soul of a noble warrior. She mustn't hinder his destiny.

"Look at me," he murmured.

Oh, God. Did he realize she yearned for him, more now than before?

"Lioness."

He caught her chin and made her look up at him. "Are you all right?"

Forcing a smile, she nodded.

Warmth glistened in his eyes that traveled over her in blatant appreciation before he kissed her. "Get dressed and come with me. Before your father starts searching for you."

A good point. While she wasn't ashamed of lying with Aldwin, she'd rather not have her sire discover her naked with him in her chamber.

When Aldwin pushed up to sitting, the rope bed shifted. He moved to the edge, stood, and then reached down to pick up his garments. She tried not to stare at his well-muscled arse dusted with fine hairs, but 'twas so perfectly formed she couldn't resist.

As he straightened, her gown landed on her lap.

"Enough ogling." Aldwin sounded annoyed, but when he glanced at her, he grinned.

Hmm. So he could touch and stare at her at will, but she couldn't do the same? That didn't seem fair.

He shook out his tunic and pulled it over his head, not seeming to notice her hesitation. Of course not. He was thinking about claiming his knighthood and resuming his duties for de Lanceau.

Leona snatched up her gown to find her chemise snarled up inside. When she rose from the bed to straighten her garments, a stain on the sheets caught her attention. Her virgin blood.

Aldwin met her gaze, and she knew he'd noticed the mark, too. When the servants came to change the linens, they'd see, and then the whole castle would know she was no longer a maiden and ruined for a future husband who'd expect his bride to be unsullied.

She didn't care. Whatever the consequences, she'd face them.

Aldwin touched her arm. "'Twill be all right, Leona."

She steeled herself against the softness of his voice. "I know." Not looking at him, she drew her chemise over her head and stood to shake out the creases.

Fully dressed, Aldwin held out her gown. A gesture of intimacy. As she took the garment, their fingers brushed, and she smothered a fresh bloom of despondency.

"Shall I help you?"

"Thank you, but I can manage." She fastened the garment and smoothed it into place, then quickly tidied her hair.

After donning his cloak and picking up his crossbow and quiver, Aldwin opened her chamber door and they stepped out into the passageway. When he drew the door shut with a firm *click*, Leona blew out a shaky breath. Had de Lanceau finished speaking with her father? The fate of this keep and its good folk remained unknown to her.

She would find out, though, once they reached the great hall.

A man was striding toward them in the torch-lit passage.

Dominic.

"There you are. Aldwin, Geoffrey is asking for you. Where were you?" After glancing from Aldwin to Leona to the chamber door, Dominic arched his eyebrows.

Aldwin brushed past his fellow warrior. "We are headed to the great hall now."

"I see." Dominic matched Aldwin's strides, while glancing back at Leona, following close behind. To her annoyance, her face warmed. "All is well, Lady Ransley?"

"Aye."

"Why would it not be?" Aldwin grumbled.

Dominic's chuckle carried in the passage. "You hope to be knighted at the end of this mission. You would not wish any misunderstandings to muddy that honor."

"No misunderstandings," Aldwin said, sounding tense. Moments later, they reached the stairwell and hurried down to the hall.

The baron's body was gone, and servants were replacing the bloodied rushes with fresh ones and dried herbs. Leona glanced through the chattering crowd of men-at-arms and castle folk until she spotted her father, standing near the dais, speaking with de Lanceau.

Aldwin strode toward them. As she followed, both men looked their way.

De Lanceau smiled. "Aldwin."

"Milord." He dropped to one knee on the rushes and bowed

his head.

Leona frowned. 'Twas rather dramatic of Aldwin.

De Lanceau waved his hand. "That is not necessary, Aldwin. Rise. I have spoken at length with Lord Ransley and—"

"Milords." His head still lowered, Aldwin said, "I ask your forgiveness and consideration."

A knot formed in Leona's throat as she studied his blond head. What was he doing? Why must he delay the announcement of what was to become of Pryerston?

"Explain," de Lanceau said.

"In private, please, milord."

De Lanceau paused before motioning to the crowd in the hall. "Leave us."

The throng filed out, until only Leona, her father, de Lanceau, Dominic, and Aldwin remained. The fire crackling in the hearth seemed unsually loud, and she clasped her hands together to ward off unwelcome nervousness.

"What do you wish to tell us?" de Lanceau demanded.

"I ask forgiveness for my failures in my mission to bring you the pendant. Failures I realize may cost me my dream of knighthood."

"I see," de Lanceau murmured, frowning.

"I also ask forgiveness for lying with Lady Ransley."

Leona gasped. "*Aldwin!*" How dare he speak of their intimacy before these men? How could he be so insensitive? Her face flamed.

"You did *what?*" her father bellowed. "I knew you were a knave! I knew it. Leona, my poor daughter . . ."

She cringed at the anguish in her sire's voice, while rage and hurt welled up inside her. Plowing her hands into her hair, she looked at the trusses overhead and tried to think of a way out of the quandary.

"You took Lady Ransley to your bed," de Lanceau said, his tone severe.

"Aye." Aldwin blew out a breath. "Actually, her bed."

Leona groaned an oath. "Aldwin, please." Next, would he say she seduced him like a lusty tavern courtesan? How humiliating!

"You lay with her in this keep?" her sire raged. "You, who almost killed her with your senseless game when she was a girl?"

Aldwin visibly tensed, but he didn't move from where he knelt. "Aye. 'Twas rash and irresponsible, I know, but . . . Aye."

"My daughter, ruined! 'Tis unacceptable! Lord de Lanceau—"

As his lordship held up his hand and looked about to speak, Aldwin added, "I am a man of honor, milords. I take no action lightly. I accept full responsibility for my weakness and want to make this situation right. Therefore, I ask to be granted Leona's hand in marriage."

Leona choked. Lowering her hands to her sides, she glared at Aldwin's back, sorely tempted to march over and wallop him. He'd turned their wondrous lovemaking into some kind of honorable duty? He felt he had no choice but to wed her, since he yielded to the serpent of desire and disgraced her?

Through a blinding haze of fury, she heard de Lanceau call her name.

"Lady Ransley," de Lanceau said again, his gray gaze studying her. "Did Aldwin force you to your bed? If so—"

Unable to look at her sire, she shook her head. "'Twas what I wanted, too."

Her father moaned. "Leona."

Aldwin pushed to standing and smiled at her.

Tears blurred her vision. As she blinked them away, his

smile vanished.

He hurried to her.

"How could you do this to me?" She stepped back, painfully aware of the other men witnessing her anxiety. "I will *not* marry you. Not this way!"

Before she could move out of reach, Aldwin caught her hands. The gentle press of his fingers sent anguish slashing through her.

"I realize how my words must have sounded."

"Do you?" She smacked his shoulder. "You arrogant . . . *turd!*"

Dominic snorted a laugh, and a grin softened Aldwin's mouth. "I deserved that. Yet I spoke true, Leona. I wish you to be my wife."

Earlier in her chamber, lying in his arms, she might have longed for such. But now? "Why do you wish it?" she bit out. "Because you regret being impulsive? You feel guilty for what took place between us?"

"Never." Lifting her right hand to his lips, he kissed each of her fingers. "What we shared was beautiful. Passionate. Unique. Just like you."

Leona sniffled. "Aldwin—"

"I said such because . . ." *I am trying to salvage my wretched honor before my lord, so I can finally be knighted—*

"I love you."

She squinted at him. "What?"

He smiled with such tenderness, her stomach swooped. "I love you, Lioness. I vow I loved you since we met many years ago. I want you to be mine."

"God's blood," her father muttered. "I need a drin—I mean,

to sit down." A bench scraped somewhere near the dais.

Leona's breath rushed out on a shaky gasp. What should she believe? She was so afraid to give in to the giddy joy surging inside her. "You are not asking me out of a sense of duty?"

Still holding her hand, Aldwin dropped to one knee on the rushes. "If I never attain knighthood, I will accept such," he said gravely. "As long as I can spend my life with you."

"I cannot believe what I am hearing," Dominic muttered.

"Indeed." De Lanceau sounded equally astonished. "You would give up knighthood to wed this lady?"

"Aye."

She trembled inside as Aldwin gazed up at her, his handsome face most solemn. "Leona, my Warrior Lioness, will you be my wife?"

Her lips quivered into a smile. "The wife of an 'arrogant turd'?"

He chuckled. "I hope one day, you might bestow upon me a more affectionate name."

She smiled, tears flooding her eyes. "One day . . . I shall."

"You . . . ?" His eyes widened. "Then . . . ?"

"Aye, I will marry you."

"Leona!" He lunged to his feet, drew her into his arms, and crushed his lips to hers. With a happy cry, she melted against him. Was it wrong to want to grab his hand and race with him back to her chamber? Oh, but how she wanted to—

De Lanceau cleared his throat. "You realize, Aldwin, that you are not the first man to have his heart conquered by a strong woman?"

Aldwin frowned. "Conquered, milord?"

De Lanceau grinned before looking at her sire. "Lord

Ransley, of course, must give his blessing to this arrangement. Do you, milord?"

With Aldwin's arms firmly about her waist, Leona glanced at her father. *Please, say "aye."*

"Well,—" he grumbled.

"Within the next few days," de Lanceau added, "I will send a letter of commendation to Aldwin's parents, to advise them of his exceptional work on this difficult mission. Among his accomplishments, I will be sure to note how he rescued Leona from cutthroats, helped liberate Pryerston from murderous conspirators, and saved my life in the midst of a bloody battle. He is, in my opinion, a hero worthy of his own glorious *chanson*."

Aldwin had flushed scarlet. "Thank you, milord."

"I vow your parents will be very proud of you." De Lanceau waved a hand. "Of course, I cannot forget to mention you will be knighted as soon as possible."

Aldwin swayed against Leona. "Milord, did you say 'knighted'?"

"I did." De Lanceau smiled, and Leona couldn't help smiling, too. "You have well earned your golden spurs. Also, I have told Lord Ransley he has one last chance to prove he can rule his estates as I expect; otherwise, I will give his holdings to another lord. I will return in two months. Meanwhile, I am appointing men here to help with whatever is needed." De Lanceau pointed. "Including you."

Aldwin grinned. "I am honored, milord."

"Tell me, is there much of the reward money left? If not, I will issue the full amount to go into Pryerston's coffers—"

"Oh, milord," Leona gasped.

"—in thanks for Lady Ransley's efforts to get the pendant to me." De Lanceau looked at Leona, and then her father. "I vow there is much need here for that coin."

Indeed, there was. At last, Adeline would have her special shoes.

Smiling through her joyful tears, Leona glanced at her sire. Dragging a hand over his face, he met her gaze, and then pushed from the bench. He came to her and Aldwin's side.

"Do you love this man, Leona?" he asked, at last.

"I do, Father. I always wondered why I survived the bee stings years ago. I thought, in the past days, I was destined to save Pryerston from the baron and Veronique." She blinked back tears. "I realize, now, I lived to love Aldwin."

"Lioness," Aldwin whispered before kissing her.

Her father shook his head. Then, with a grudging smile, he extended his hand to Aldwin. "If you have tamed Leona's spirited heart, you may have my blessing."

Aldwin shook hands. "Thank you, milord."

As de Lanceau and Dominic congratulated her sire, Aldwin drew her aside. Against her mouth, he murmured, "I love you, Leona. I promise I will be an excellent husband."

"I hope so, for I intend to be an excellent wife." She brushed her hips against his in wanton invitation, relishing his startled gasp. "I must warn you, though, that if you are tempted to neglect me for other duties—"

Aldwin laughed. "Never. On my honor, as a knight, you are more than enough temptation."

Don't miss the next exciting historical romance by
CATHERINE KEAN

A Knight's Persuasion

ISBN# 9781605420967
US $7.95 / CDN $8.95
Historical Fiction
MAY 2010
www.catherinekean.com

CATHERINE KEAN

My Lady's Treasure

The Treasure of Love . . .

Facing the tall, brooding rider by the stormy lakeshore, Lady Faye Rivellaux clings to her goal — to rescue the kidnapped child she vowed to protect. At all costs, she must win back the little girl she loves as her own. When the stranger demands a ransom she can never pay, Faye offers him instead her one last hope — a gold cup.

Brant Meslarches is stunned to see the chalice. Worth a fortune, it's proof a lost cache of wealth from the legendary Celtic King Arthur does exist, as Brant's murdered brother believed. Brant can't return the little girl to the lady whose desperate beauty captivates him. Yet, now that he's seen Lady Faye, he can't let her escape his grasp; she is the key to his only means of redemption.

The last thing Faye wants is an alliance with a scarred knight tormented by secrets. But, she has no other way to rescue the child. Risking all, she joins Brant's quest. And finds some things are more valuable than gold.

ISBN# 9781932815788
US $6.99 / CDN $8.99
Historical Romance
Available Now
www.catherinekean.com

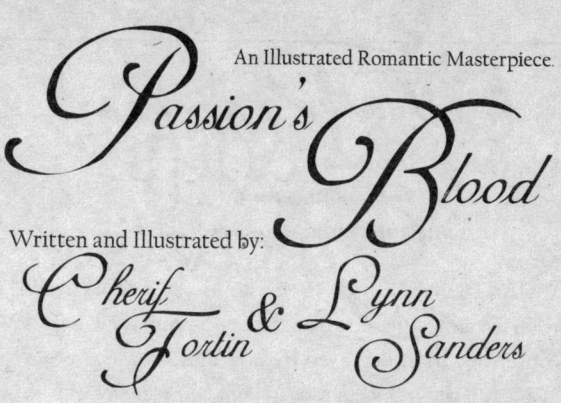

An Illustrated Romantic Masterpiece.

Passion's Blood

Written and Illustrated by: Cherif Fortin & Lynn Sanders

Lady Leanna is a flame-haired beauty loved by her betrothed, Prince Emric, desired by his loathsome brother, Prince Bran. Although in love with Emric, Leanna has still not made her peace with the knowledge that this arrangement was forced upon her.

Prince Emric, noble and courageous, rides to war, ignorant of his brother's dark treachery.

In a net of betrayal and violence, the young lovers must preserve their faith, and Leanna must keep Emric alive with her love and the magical powers she herself does not fully understand . . .

ISBN# 9781605420622
US $25.95 / CDN $28.95
Illustrated Romantic Masterpiece
Available Now
www.fortinandsanders.com

The Promise

*In a dangerous world,
sometimes the greatest risk is love...*

In 1525, Günter Behaim is a Landsknecht (a professional soldier in the service of Emperor Charles V). Günter has been betrayed by love and promises not kept. As a result, he has sworn to make few promises of his own and keep those unto death. However, when his friend is mortally wounded while saving Günter's life, he gives a pledge to marry his betrothed. To keep his promise, Günter must use every weapon in his romantic arsenal to convince the reluctant woman to marry him. As his passion for her grows, he realizes he is falling in love. Is he prepared to risk his worst fear: having his heart rejected once more?

The Spanish beauty Alonsa García de Aranjuéz is determined to withstand Günter's relentless pursuit. Haunted by a gypsy's curse on any man who loves her, Alonsa yearns for Günter, but fear for his safety forces her to rebuff him. As she struggles to deny the growing attraction between them, she begins to realize that fate may have other plans. With danger surrounding them, will Alonsa bite from the forbidden fruit? Or will Günter be bitten instead by the mysterious misfortune that seems to plague any with the courage to become... Alonsa's love?

ISBN# 9781933836966
US $7.95 / CDN $8.95
Historical Romance
MAY 2009
www.tjbennett.com

From the author of *First, there is a River*

Jasper Mountain

Kathy Steffen

Two lost souls struggle to find their way in the unforgiving West of 1873 . . .

Jack Buchanan, a worker at the Jasper Mining Company, is sure of his place in the outside world, but has lost his faith, hope, and heart to the tragedy of a fire.

Foreign born and raised, Milena Shabanov flees from a home she loves to the strange and barbaric America. A Romani blessed with "the sight," she is content in the company of visions and spirit oracles, but finds herself lost and alone in a brutal mining town with little use for women.

Surrounded by inhumane working conditions at the mine, senseless death, and overwhelming greed, miners begin disappearing and the officers of the mine don't care.

Tempers flare and Jack must decide where he stands: with the officers and mining president—Victor Creely—to whom Jack owes his life, or with the miners, whose lives are worth less to the company than pack animals. Milena, sensing deep despair and death in a mining town infested with restless spirits, searches for answers to the workers' disappearances. But she can't trust anyone, especially not Jack Buchanan, a man haunted by his own past.

ISBN# 9781933836584
Trade Paperback / Historical Fiction
US $15.95 / CDN $17.95
Available Now
www.kathysteffen.com

The Senator's Daughter
Christine Carroll

Sylvia Chatsworth, flamboyant daughter of a U.S. Senator, and Lyle Thomas, rising star in the San Francisco D.A.'s office, are the city's latest item. Until the tabloid news paints Sylvia as a party girl too naughty for Lyle, and her parents suggest they'd be happier if she disappeared. So she does just that.

For a hefty fee, the Senator sends Lyle off to find his daughter. When Lyle locates Sylvia in the Napa Valley and finds she's changed her image, he's intrigued enough to delay turning her in. Attraction growing, they hide out at a romantic Victorian Inn.

Lyle isn't idle, however. He's hot on the trail of some questionable real estate trades—schemes that connect a missing developer and his vintner brother, the D.A., and the Senator's "blind" trust. When a local spring in wine country turns up with mercury pollution, Lyle and Sylvia wonder how far someone would go to crash land prices and pull off a real estate coup. And is her father hip deep in Mafia activity?

With their growing love threatened by arson and attempted murder, there's also the question of trusting Lyle...when Sylvia discovers he's on her father's payroll...

ISBN# 9781933836300
US $7.95 / CDN $9.95
Contemporary Romance
Available Now
www.readchristinecarroll.com

Be in the know on the latest
Medallion Press news by becoming a
Medallion Press Insider!

<u>As an Insider you'll receive:</u>
• Our FREE expanded monthly newsletter, giving you more insight into Medallion Press
• Advanced press releases <u>and breaking news</u>
• Greater access to all of your favorite Medallion authors

Joining is easy, just visit our Web site at <u>www.medallionpress.com</u> and click on the Medallion Press Insider tab.

medallionpress.com

Sign up now at www.twitter.com/MedallionPress
to stay on top of all the happenings in and
around Medallion Press.

For more information
about other great titles from
Medallion Press, visit

medallionpress.com